How to FACE ETERNITY

ISBN: 979-8-9904595-0-2 (Paperback)
ISBN: 979-8-9904595-1-9, 979-8-9904595-3-3 (Hardcover)
ISBN: 979-8-9904595-2-6 (EBook)

Any references to historical events, real people, or real places are used fictitiously. Names, characters, and places are products of the author's imagination.

Cover Art by Trif Designs
Internal Design by SH Clasen
Edited By Sage Santiago

Printed by Best Day Ever Publishing in the United States of America.

FIRST EDITION 2024.

BDE Publishing
Oregon City, OR 97045-0821
www.SHClasen.com   www.BDEPublishing.org

Trigger Warnings & Author's Note

This is an adult romance novel. With that being said, the sexual themes are mild for the genre (let's call it cozy), but they are still present, along with violence, language, and alluded assault.

Remember, this is a story about vampires and tends to lean on the horror side of immortality. Thus, this is not for those squeamish of blood and gore.

When beginning this story, keep in mind that this is part one of a two-part series. If you wish to see the story through, you will have to read Part II, which does have stronger sexual themes as well as other possible triggers. Keep that in mind when beginning the ride.

Also, this series is *awful* for those who are afraid of love, affection, and HEA.

Reader discretion is advised.

Table Of Contents

THIS'LL HURT YOU A LITTLE BIT, HOW'S THAT SOUND 1

WHY DO YOU INSIST I'M TURNING INTO SOMETHING...14

YOU LOOK LIKE YOU COULD BE A BOATLOAD OF TROUBLE FOR HIM........28

SOMETIMES MURDER IS THE GREATEST MERCY...34

IN THE FACE OF ETERNITY, THAT'S THE BLINK OF AN EYE............................45

BOUND BY BLOOD..62

HE'S NOT HURTING ANYONE—UNLESS YOU ASK HIM TO 80

THERE ARE BETTER WAYS OF ENGAGING YOUR SENSE OF TOUCH 91

THERE'S SOMETHING IMPORTANT I WANT TO TEACH YOU................................100

BE A GOOD LITTLE MEAL, WON'T YOU...110

LOVE IS AN EMOTION MEANT TO LAST NO MORE THAN A HUMAN LIFETIME
....128

HOMEWRECKER COULD DEFINITELY HIT THE SPOT..139

HOW DID YOU TAME MY GRUMPY LONE WOLF..155

HOW DID I GET STUCK WITH A CHEEKY LITTLE MINX LIKE YOU 174

MUCH LIKE MY MORTAL LIFE, I'LL KEEP THIS BRIEF..187

WHY ARE YOU IN MY BED..195

YOU KNOW THAT I ONLY HAVE EYES FOR YOU...209

EVERYTHING GETS BETTER FOR THOSE WHO CAN WAIT...............................227

IN IMMORTAL RELATIONSHIPS, THERE IS ALWAYS SUFFERING 245

CALL IT YOUR FINAL LESSON IN IMMORTALITY 251

A LITTLE WAGER IN LOVE AND WAR..257

IS THAT...KINKY..269

I WANT TO BE CLOSE TO YOU...278

ONCE YOU MAY HAVE BEEN A HERO, BUT NOW YOU'RE JUST A COWARD
....285

I WAS NOTHING BUT A GLIMMER IN HIS BRIGHT ETERNITY.............................295

WHAT KIND OF STUPID, LOVE STRUCK FOOL HAVE YOU TURNED INTO
....306

FEED, PREY, FUCK...318

I WILL ALWAYS LOVE YOU, NO MATTER WHAT YOU CHOOSE IN LIFE..........328

YOU SEEM MORE CONFIDENT THIS WAY..339

I KNOW HOW YOU TOIL IN THE SHADOWS...348

YOU ARE USELESS AND REPLACEABLE, JUST LIKE THE REST...................356

Acknowledgments..367

Playlist

(All Covers)

"Head Like a Hole" – Sam Tinnesz
"Hand That Feeds" – tribes.
"No Rain" – Sleeping With Sirens
"Burning Down The House" – Ki:Theory, FYOHNA
"Cry Little Sister" – CHVRCHES
"Eyes on Fire" – Gold Souls
"Enter Sandman" – SHEL
"People are Strange" – Tribe Society
"Tainted Love" – Milky Chance
"Shout" – Losers
"Stripped" – Shiny Toy Guns

Explore more at SHClasen.com/Playlists

My story begins where some might end:

the night I died.

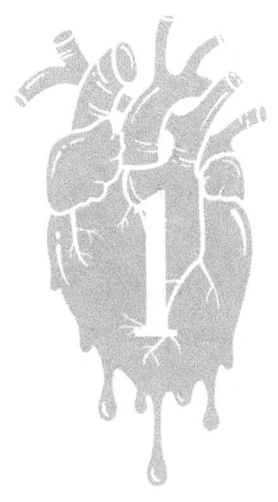

THIS'LL HURT YOU A LITTLE BIT,
HOW'S THAT SOUND

MY LUNGS BURNED. A long, ceaseless scream reverberated against the walls of my wheel-based prison. Within a bent arm's reach was every corner of the trunk's interior—a space so confined I would have *killed* for the chance to stretch out my legs for a second. The claustrophobia summoned from breathing the same uncirculated air had become suffocating, inducing a kind of panic that tied my stomach in knots.

Every corner the vehicle took sent me rolling into a new wall of its trunk's interior, making it seem like the space was encroaching on me with each curve in the road. I felt as though I'd been bound and locked in that mobile prison for hours, my limbs cramped and throat raw. But surely it hadn't been anywhere near as long as it'd felt. In fact, not so long ago, I was having a perfectly boring Tuesday.

The spring sun had risen and set along the skyline without a hitch. All the while, I'd avoided any undue attention from my dear old Johnny. I'd left the Roufe mansion for a little time alone, hoping it would be the icing on the cake that was a refreshingly peaceful day.

Venturing downtown, I was positive that nobody in the city of Creswell would mess with Leanne Cowitz, the future wife of Creswell's most notorious crime lord. For that reason, it didn't feel necessary to call for an entourage, and I'd strolled the streets with no more than my cell and a smile.

Little did I know that trusting my reputation would be the catalyst for my downfall.

The Roufes were renowned in Creswell for being at the top of its organized crime ring. That made them like gods among men in a city ruled by crime, but it also meant they had plenty of rivals. Everyone wanted a piece of what they had, and it wasn't limited to Creswell—the outlying tri-cities had rings of their own clamoring for Creswell's treasures.

Being Johnny Roufe's number one bitch came with plenty of those treasures, but it was also exactly what put a target on my back and got me stuffed into the trunk of a rival Mafioso's Cadillac.

Now, we were speeding down a progressively windy road and I was merely a passenger for the ride. With each twisting turn and jarring pothole, it became increasingly obvious where we were headed. There's only one place near Creswell with such chaotic terrain where a criminal would take a hostage like me—the forest on the outskirts of town, a location where teenagers ventured to get away with delinquency and criminals went to get away with homicide. Out there, nobody would hear me scream.

The man who'd kidnapped me definitely planned to murder and bury me in the woods. Even my overly optimistic convictions could admit to that obvious truth.

Others had warned me time and time again that ill fate befell any girl of Johnny Roufe's, yet I still hadn't listened to Jayleen when she'd told me to write up my last will and testament. She'd jokingly suggested it after I'd become steady with the infamous crime lord. In her words, "You've obviously got a death wish if you're dating Johnny. In that case, I want your will to give all the grand mafia wife clothes you own to me when you inevitably die in a horrible 'accident' after your first couple's spat." While she's my best friend, I'm not so fond of her stating such a morbid—albeit accurate—proposition.

Johnny and I had dated long enough I knew how to stay on his good side—or at least the side that kept me alive—but I'd always known I could get wrapped up in his family's business. That meant I could, inevitably, end up in the trunk of a Caddy on my way to some unforeseen fatality. So, while I *should* have expected something like this, the bells hadn't officially tolled for me.

My sweating palms and racing heart reminded me I still lived. As long as the heart in me continued to beat, there were ways to make it out of this situation with my vitality intact. I just needed to think of one.

Think, Leanne, think.

I took a break from my futile screaming and surveyed my surroundings. The interior of the tiny trunk was pitch black, but I'd long since adjusted to it. The inside handle to open the trunk lid had been removed. Any tools to jam into the handle's void were also long gone. I'd already kicked on the door with all my strength, but to no avail.

With no solutions coming to mind in the small and dismal cavity of my mobile prison, the aching feeling of defeat threatened to rot in my stomach. I may have succumbed to it, if not for that inkling of bullishness burning hope into the back of my mind. It contested the bitter nausea and reminded me to *breathe*.

Life in Creswell wasn't easy for anybody, but we all had our own ways to get through each day. If I gave up my fight every time life looked bleak, I wouldn't have made it twenty-three years in this town.

Living a risky lifestyle meant I would duly accept my death once it became unescapable. However, my situation hadn't escalated that far yet. I still had my fight in me, and I wouldn't give it up until my feet were already in my grave.

Swallowing any lingering self-doubt, I planned to wait until the stout, bald man who'd nabbed me stopped to retrieve me. Once he lifted up the trunk lid, I'd be ready to start kicking and clawing, even biting, if that's what it took. If that plan didn't work, at least I'd be on the offensive. The idea of standing up to that man and failing stood the hairs on the back of my neck on end, but laying down and accepting my expiration left a much fouler sensation in my throat.

If this is my last night, at least I'll end it kicking and screa—my body crashed into the roof of the trunk and crumpled into the wall above my head.

Accompanying the squalling of brakes and the gnashing of gravel under the wheels, the vehicle entrapping me shuddered to a stop.

There was a momentary silence before the contrasting sound of footsteps gave way to panic-stricken murmurs inside the car. The voice of the stout man was fraught but inaudible as it bickered with another. Close behind, a hoarse, ear-splitting shriek echoed within the confines of the vehicle. As quickly as it began, the scream halted, turning into a thunderous thud as a considerable mass rattled against a loose stone surface. Then, a dubious, wet *crunch*. The sound could have been anything: scattering rock, heavy branches snapping, the shattering of bone. But I didn't want to imagine it as the latter. The image of bones splintering and squelching through flesh in harmony with that unnerving *squish* made my stomach churn. Even picturing the recipient as my kidnapper was a grotesque sight, certainly uglier in my mind than it could have been in person.

The ensuing silence was as deafening as the first and just as short-lived. Those heavy footsteps headed back in my direction. Not a single breath passed between my lips, fear of who might be on the other side of my prison keeping me as sedentary as the dead.

The footsteps didn't stop. They continued past me and

steadily faded into the potentially endless darkness of what could have been my last night among the living.

If we were on one of the forest roads, as I'd suspected, then I'd remain stuck inside the trunk of that car until somebody found me. It could be days—weeks, even. I'd have to gnaw through the damn floorboards to get out before I starved to death or got eaten by the rodents that could more efficiently gnaw their way in with me.

Wouldn't a quick death be better than that? What if whoever is outside the car is on my side? What if they are working with Johnny? What if they are looking for me? In a sudden breach of rationality, I pummeled my fists against the metal trunk lid and screamed. "Help! Please!"

I never heard the approaching footsteps, but without warning, light flooded my vision; even the vast darkness outside was brighter than what I'd become accustomed to.

Highlighted only by the glow of taillights against its shadow, a figure hovered over my open prison. His skin was light like ivory, emphasizing his sharp, thin features and prominent jawline. Although cast in shadows, the man was clean—not a speck of stubble in sight. A dark tousle of hair fell over his forehead and framed his jaw, completely untamed and polar from the vividness of his face in the night.

He was gorgeous—most certainly not related to Johnny or the other poorly endowed Roufes. The dignified nature radiating from his stature shook me to my core, and he hadn't moved; most certainly not comparable to any of the exhibitionist mobsters I'd become acquainted with.

So, who was he, and why was he there?

More importantly, was he an enemy? Should I fear him?

He narrowed dark eyes in my direction, his jacketed arm still holding up the lid to the trunk. He didn't say a word, instead he stared at me. I, however, had my mouth agape and eyes wide, gripped with an inability to move, much less get a word out.

First to break the silence, the man finally asked through gritted teeth, "Who are you?"

Something about the malice that seeped from his glare took the air from my lungs and doused my body in trembles. "Uhm." My voice cracked, my own name eluding me.

Abruptly filled with a raw biological need to flee, I surveyed the dark, wooded scenery behind the man. Tightly knit evergreen trees loomed overhead, only adding to the darkness of an already black night. The smoldering red of the Caddy's taillights did very little to illuminate the scenery, though I had a feeling there wasn't much to see. Trees, and more trees, filled with a silence so loud it echoed of nothingness. On the gravel, close enough to be seen in the shadows, a ruddy liquid flooded the ground like a pond had surfaced in the road. At the center of the pool laid the crumpled body of the man who'd kidnapped me and thrown me in his trunk. An incomprehensible heap on the ground; a form mangled beyond recognition as a human corpse.

My throat tightened, making me suddenly grateful for the darkness that shrouded most of the gruesome scene.

Other than the man standing in front of me, there was no one else around. The woods were deathly silent, and there wasn't a lick of motion within eyesight. Could this man have possibly done such a thing so quickly on his own?

He still stood over me, a heavy scowl painting his facade where slow, steady breaths almost concealed the way his nostrils flared in my direction. He was rigid, all the way up to the hand that clenched tight against the metal in his palm. Though his size was not wide in relation to his height, he probably still weighed two of me. That size difference was apparent when he leaned in, making me cower, although I had nowhere to physically retreat.

His steady eyes flicked over me, but their sockets were taut and nothing about the way they narrowed revealed a hint of prospective mercy.

With an adrenaline spike akin to a baseball bat to the chest, I did what felt most natural in such a presence: I bolted.

Triggering a little bit of fight and a hell of a lot of flight, I kicked the lean man blocking my exit and sprung out of the trunk. Without a moment's pause, I scrambled into motion over the loose gravel.

Unfortunately, I didn't get more than a foot outside my prior prison before I was halted by his grip, tight around my arm. I tugged, but the man hardly shifted an inch. His strength was uncanny on such a lean build. It was like being restrained by a linebacker, and he only held me by the wrist.

One heavy sigh later, he demanded, "I asked you a question. Who are you?"

"M-My name is Le-Leanne? Leanne Cowitz."

"That's great," he drawled, his tone completely blasé. His

once narrowed gaze had softened, hardly hinting at his prior hostility. "But I don't care for your name. Who are you? Why were you in Paulo's trunk? Why are you relevant to me?"

If I answer truthfully, will it incriminate me? "Uhm." I shook violently.

"I'm growing exceedingly tired of this. Answer the damn question." His voice, though robust and baritone, was also clipped and rolled, as if he spoke with an accent, but not one I recognized.

I had no attention or time to dwell on it as he cinched my wrist tighter in his already firm grip. "I don't know why he kidnapped me! I'm Johnny's girl. That's all!"

He looked me over, his nose hovering like a search dog sniffing for contraband. This man's now apparent accent only exaggerated his apathetic drawl. "One of Johnny's consorts, huh?"

Consort? What century is this? And who is he calling a consort? I'm Johnny's one and only—thank you very much!

He continued, "I don't have any beef with Johnny right now, so I don't know exactly what to do with you. But I suppose if all you are is one of Johnny's whores, nobody would miss you very much."

How dare he.

Like the optimistic idiot I am, I did what I could to escape the grueling maniac. I whacked his restraining arm, spun my wrist upward, and head butted him with as much strength as I could muster. Darkness filled my vision, blacking out the world for a split second, but before I knew it, I was running. My feet were doing their job without me asking them to.

I sprinted until my legs burned, the sudden burst of exertion unnatural to them. That, and any other aches, had to be suppressed or they might hinder my escape. As branches snagged my hair and blood from my open wound blurred my vision, I ignored it all. Sight didn't matter, there was nothing to see but the endless void of grey trees as I flew by.

In a single moment, that void stopped rushing past, the air stalled, and my dashing legs were subdued, completely severed from the forest floor.

With a slam, my body was wracked with pain as it impacted against the nearest tree. Rough, callous bark snagged my clothes and tore at my shoulder's showing flesh. A force constricted around my neck, hindering the air in my lungs. Grasping for the source of my suffocation, my hands landed on warm flesh—a single fist wrapped around my throat, holding me off the ground. Materializing in front of me was the glowing pale skin and sharp eyes of a predator.

Completely concealed in a black button up jacket, I couldn't tell if this man strained at the weight of me, but his lax expression suggested no. While I gasped for breath, he stayed completely composed.

Who is this man? What is this man?

He looked me over once again, a low brow brooding as I struggled in his grip.

Pulling me in by the neck, he let my feet tap the ground, relieving the pressure of gravity on my spine. In the oddest gesture, he leaned into me—like a lover might to their beloved—but instead of bringing his lips to mine, he slithered them up and over my brow before dragging his tongue across my forehead.

"Egh." A single disconcerted noise escaped my lips as my entire body tensed.

When he retracted, crimson blood stained the recesses of his mouth.

The man smiled wickedly, revealing elongated incisors that came to a point which disappeared below his bottom lip. The long, vicious fangs glowed in the moonlight, reminiscent to those of a cat or a snake or maybe, most accurately, a fictional creature of the night—a vampire.

This can't be real.

"Are you scared?" he asked, his tone picking up with his giddy grin. Curiosity in me renewed; he looked... playful?

"I-I..." Couldn't speak. The shakes were coming back and crippling my voice.

In front of me stared the face of death—calculating eyes too obscured by darkness to tell their color, but not too much to prevent sensing their nature. My heart weighed heavy with the truth that I wouldn't escape this. Not with my life. Not from something that was too strong to break and too fast to outrun.

I wasn't entirely naïve, only chiefly optimistic. So, while I would fight for every opportunity to avoid meeting my maker, I'd also had my whole life to come to terms with the fact that things very well could end like this. Well, maybe not exactly like this—as this was an unforeseeably strange event in the presence of an equally strange foe—but I knew I would ultimately succumb to the hands of a powerful man who would see me as nothing more than an objectifiable pawn. I was beneath the kind of men I catered to. That was the world I'd chosen to live in. I knew my place on their chessboard, and like that little plastic figurine, I had no control over when they captured me. I'd only ever been living on borrowed time, not even worthy of a checkmate.

Finally, that euphemism was catching up with me in the most literal way, and this strange man's face would be the last that I'd see before I died.

The tremors wracking my body abruptly stopped.

At least I'd die at the hands of this bizarre, inhuman stranger, and not at the hands of someone I knew—someone I was supposed to look to for safety, someone I loved, someone who would, in time, betray me.

If this man killed me, it wouldn't be betrayal, it'd be some awful coincidence, and that was a superior way to go. If I needed to find the positive in this situation, that would be it. I was positive that this was the hand I wanted to die by. Not the others whom fate had waiting for me up the road or back at home.

Accepting this death was not pessimism. It was merely seeing an opportunity to escape and taking it.

Every muscle in my body relaxed, and I fell limp in the man's grip. "I'm not scared," I finally responded.

His impish smile dropped. "Why not?"

"Because you should kill me. Get it over with so I don't have to go back to a life of true fear."

"Well, that's no fun," he murmured, pulling me close as if we were going to embrace in a familiar hug.

Wilted, I let him drag me in and wrap his arm around my waist, one hand still clasped at my neck. Whatever he had in store, surely it would be over soon, and I'd receive my glorious escape from this dreadful situation—this dreadful life I'd chosen. That was my encouraging outlook—my encouraging outlook for the end.

Locking his eyes with mine, the man whispered, "This won't hurt you." He leaned in, paused, then pulled away to look me in the eyes one last time. "Actually, that's no fun. This'll hurt you a little bit, how's that sound?"

The words tumbling from his lips fogged my mind, but I didn't have much time to ponder the feeling before he leaned in and sank his teeth into my neck.

Fire spread through my veins from the puncture of his teeth, and I could do nothing but scream. Even reserved to let this man take my life, it was only natural how I fought against his grip, my body's innate response to flee from the sensation of his dagger-like fangs buried in my skin. It was useless, however, as he held me in his powerful arms. Although unable to move, my cries continued to escape me until the world began to fade.

As I slipped into unconsciousness, the torture also slipped into nonexistence.

This was it, the moment I'd both feared and awaited.

Finally, I would die.

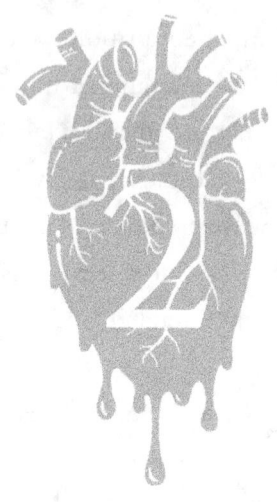

*WHY DO YOU INSIST I'M TURNING
INTO SOMETHING*

SUNLIGHT STREAKED across the sky, pounding against my draped eyelids, while the distant echoes of bustling city streets filled the air.

With a start, I pushed myself up onto one arm.

Beneath me, a rigid wooden bench pressed into my weary bones, its unyielding surface digging into every point of contact. Wind rustled the trees above and brushed against my skin, sending goosebumps over my scraped-up arms. The scent of fresh-cut grass wafted through the air, harmonizing with the rhythmic blend of children's laughter and the metallic creaking of swings in motion. Over the horizon of tall trees, I could barely make out the tops of skyscrapers peeking through.

How'd I end up in a park on the outskirts of town?

Reality still circled the drain as it struggled to funnel its way back into my head.

A kidnapping, a metal prison, and a bald man who threw me in his trunk?

Unstable thoughts left me with an empty sense of panic.

Scrambling off the bench, I fell to the ground, acutely aware of the aching that resonated through every inch of my body. "Ow," I groaned, the discomfort surpassing the memory of flipping my Jeep down a drainage ditch in high school.

The cheerful screams coming from the play structure nearby made my head ring with each piercing sound. The ringing itself turned sour in my head like bile in my throat and manifested into an actual need to vomit in the bushes. After pulling myself to my feet, I did so shamelessly, regardless of the passersby. I probably looked like a drunk, though that wasn't the case. *What is the case? What happened to me?*

An image of the man who'd "rescued" me from the back of that Caddy flashed in my mind. *Was all that real? How'd I end up here?*

Memories of the previous night began piecing themselves together, but that still didn't seem to answer any of the questions I had—or make any real sense of their own.

Accepting that this confusion wouldn't easily dissipate, I gathered myself and ran to find my way out of the park. Once I'd gotten to Fifth Street, which I recognized as close to my apartment, I steadied my bearings and headed home.

I stumbled through my apartment door and nearly fell into the coffee table as the world spun so viciously I couldn't tell up from down. The next thing I knew, I was in the bathroom, puking my guts out again. Through a repulsive mixture of tears and snot, I peered into the toilet, horrified to discover that this time I'd *literally* puked my guts out. In the porcelain bowl, blood and viscera was mixed with the contents of anything I'd had to eat in the last twenty-four hours.

What is wrong with me?

Climbing to my feet, I dared to look in the mirror. Not only was there dried blood caked over the spot where I'd practically cracked my skull open head butting that man the night before, but I was covered in dirt and dried up leaves. Bloody residue stained my lips from my vomit, and on my neck was the strangest red mark. It was in the same spot where the man had bitten into me the night before, but instead of leaving me with teeth marks, there were two red holes that stung like hell to the touch. Around them, the skin was red and swollen, pulsating with a dull pain. The veins themselves were a strange dark color, as if infected. It resembled a snake bite... or a vampire bite as described in fairy tales. Oh god. How crazy did I have to be to think I'd seriously been bitten by a vampire?

This was too much for me to handle on my own. I needed help. Physically, psychologically—well I wasn't sure which yet.

After splashing some water over my face, I changed my clothes, covered my neck with a scarf, and threw on a pair of sunglasses to conceal my increasingly sallow eyes. Grabbing one of my many burner phones, I called Jayleen and demanded that she meet me at the café below my apartment. Not minutes later, the two of us were sharing a table in a quiet corner where nobody would overhear us.

Jayleen scoffed at my appearance. "What'd you get into last night? You look like the disheveled mistress from hell."

Skipping the formalities, I took off my glasses and pulled down my scarf. "There's something wrong with me, Jayleen. I don't understand what's going on."

Her eyes widened in genuine bewilderment as she looked me over. "What happened?"

With that, I told her everything. From the kidnapping to the possibly imaginary vampire attack.

"I told you being involved with Johnny would only bring you trouble." She snarled at her words, looking as if she was envisioning herself strangling Johnny Roufe with her own two hands.

I clasped my hand over my mouth as another wave of nausea threatened to unleash itself. Once the feeling ebbed, I continued, "The kidnapping aside, what's wrong with me, Jayleen? What is this fucking mark on my neck?" I slammed my fist down onto the counter.

She jumped at my sudden intensity. "You're right." She nodded, sobering quickly. "It's very strange—what's happening to you. The nausea could be from your head injury, but it doesn't explain the neck wound or the blood in your vomit. And, okay, let's play devil's advocate for a moment. Say you were bitten by a vampire and that could have something to do with your symptoms. Maybe you're changing into a vampire?" A little chuckle escaped on the tail of her words.

I, however, wasn't laughing. Everything hurt too much to

think about laughing. "And maybe I'm *dying,* Jayleen," I spat.

"Well, how are we supposed to know that? I'm not the person to ask. All I know is what I've seen from Hollywood movies, and they've certainly never depicted anything so horrifying as," she motioned to my entire being, "this."

With that gesture, I took out my phone to observe what she was referring to. Opening the front-facing camera, I was devastated to see my worsening state. My eyes had sunken into their sockets and the bags under them were now a dark purple. My skin was yellow, my once shimmering green eyes a glazed-over shell, and my glowing golden hair that I'd worked so hard on was now as dull and lifeless as straw. The mark on my neck was spreading in the shape of my veins and looked nothing like anything I'd ever seen in my short stint at nursing school years ago. I didn't look like that man who'd attacked me the night before. He was handsome; his skin and eyes glowed with health and vitality, nothing like the way I looked now. I wasn't turning into anything—I was dying.

"I-I don't want to die," I murmured, practically to myself.

Though I'd been so willing and ready the previous night while under duress. Now, I couldn't help but think it wasn't my time to die. Call it a second lease on life, but if it had been my time, then I would have died while in the very capable hands of that fair skinned grim reaper who'd bit into me.

If that wasn't how I was meant to die, then this couldn't be it either. I wouldn't give in twice.

Thin breaths left me in near hyper-ventilative pants. "What do I do? What do I do?"

Jayleen splayed her hand over my shallow cheekbones. "Okay, okay. *Maybe* you are turning into a vampire and you simply need to drink some blood to bring some life back into you!" She smiled with renewed hope shimmering in her brown eyes.

"Why do you insist I'm turning into something?"

"Oh, come on! That's what would happen in all the movies and stuff! So, here!" Jayleen took a breadknife off the table and attempted to slit the palm of her hand. She did it so impulsively that when the blood started to trickle out, she closed her fist and looked at me with wide eyes. "Wow. That hurt so much more than I'd expected." Shaking off her shock, she held her hand up to me and opened her bloody palm in front of my face.

It smelt like iron and made my stomach turn on end. I snarled in disgust. "I'm not going to drink your blood, Jayleen."

"Just do it. Hurry up before people start to stare." Jayleen's eyes darted toward the waitress milling a few tables away.

"Shit," I murmured, pulling her warm palm up to my lips. Upon raking my tongue over her open wound, I gagged at the horrifying bitter taste of blood. Without warning, vomit flooded up my throat and I aimed for the nearest planter vase by our table.

Jayleen's own face went white as she watched. "Gross. Maybe that wasn't the best idea."

"Oh god. What am I going to do?" I begged again, coming full circle.

Jayleen lit back up, always the one with some kind of crazy idea. "Remember how you said that Johnny's Granny was super interested in all that weird mystical culty shit?"

I nodded.

"Well then, your best bet is to go ask her about it. Even if it isn't something strange like 'vampires,' maybe Granny has some advice to help you out. She seems like a really wise old lady, right? And the man seemed to know Johnny, right? Maybe she knows something about this mystery man specifically. And if all else fails, you'll be in the mansion and you can go to the Roufe's doctor. After all, there could very well be a diagnoseable explanation to all of this."

She was right. Though I didn't want to see Johnny—or any Roufe—in my condition, I *could* sneak into the house to look for Nonna. I trusted Nonna to keep a secret for me, since she was rarely swayed by Johnny's requests or demands. I would certainly have to be careful of who else I came across in my current condition, however, and sneaking around without prompting a scene might prove difficult after last night's debacle.

"Here, I'll drive you over there." Jayleen wrapped a napkin around her still-trickling palm and then clasped her clean hand around mine, pulling me to my feet. The two of us made a quick jaunt to her car before she sped us onto the freeway and toward the other end of town, where the Roufe Estate sprawled across the countryside.

Jayleen dropped me at the front gates and from there probably went to get stitches in her hand. If I lived through the day, we'd have to have a talk about the rampant impulsivity that led to her thinking—or not thinking—that'd been a good idea.

For the time being, I had my own shit to worry about.

Past the gates, I had to get inside without alerting any of the guards or happening by anyone who'd tell Johnny I was there. Once inside, I could hear Johnny's little boys playing up the hallway.

I had a lot of qualms about being in a serious relationship with Johnny. Being with him was more of a risk than a reward, but I stayed because the rewards were always so damn alluring. One being getting to care for his boys. Their mom was a bitch, and they were surrounded by mafia, yet they were still somehow sweet little kids. The eldest was a pain in the ass, but I suppose that's what happened when your dad was a piece of shit and your replacement mommy (me) wasn't old enough to biologically be your mother.

I wouldn't say I loved the Roufe boys, but I cared for them as much as I could any of Johnny's kin. They were still innocent and untainted by their family's corruption. Unfortunately, I knew that wouldn't last, and there was nothing I could do about it.

Nonetheless, I wasn't there for them. In fact, they were the least of my concerns and they would have all sorts of worried questions based on my appearance; avoiding them would be best, so I hid when they came running by. After successfully sneaking past them unseen, I landed at Nonna's room and slinked inside.

"Nonna," I whispered, looking around the large, vaulted room that was bigger than most people's homes. It was practically a library and homed almost as many spiderwebs as it did books.

"Hello, my dearest Leanne. What brings you here?" Her gentle old voice was meek, even when echoing through the cavernous room.

"I came for some advice…"

Nonna hobbled up to me from where she rose from a table in the center of the room. When she looked me over, her wrinkled eyes grew increasingly wary. "Does Johnny know you're here, dear?"

"Um, no, I'm only stopping by. I have some questions…" I didn't want her to tell Johnny about this yet. "For a friend… not for myself."

"Mhmm." Her wrinkled lips pursed with doubt. "And what is it?"

"You study the occult and stuff like that, right, Nonna?"

"Mm, yes." She narrowed her eyes in my general direction but offered me a seat at her table, nonetheless.

Taking it, I decided to begin with the most ridiculous of theories, to get them out of the way. "Well, my friend is interested in learning about vampires in the modern day. Do you have any information about them?"

"Hmm." She thought for a moment. "That is such a broad question. Are you asking for real information, or simply pondering hypothetical mythologies?"

"Do you have *real* information?"

"Of course. What specifically would you like to know?"

"My friend is most specifically interested in vampire bites. She actually thinks she might have been bitten by one. Haha, how crazy is that?" I laughed aloud, weak and nervous.

"Hmm." She didn't laugh at all, and I shut my trap. "She'd surely want to seek help in that case. Unfortunately, there's not much anyone could do for her. She'd have to seek out the vampire who'd bitten her in order to save her life. Otherwise, she'll die once the venom has spread. It usually takes about twenty-four hours. Not a pleasant process either." Her eyes pinned me like little needles that knew my secret.

"So, you think that vampires are real and that she most certainly *could* have been bitten?" *How absurd.*

"I'll let you in on a little secret, my girl." She leaned in close, reminiscent of a teen ready to spill some good tea. "I *know* vampires are real, and I can prove it to you however you'd like me to. Vampires are very much all around us, specifically here in Creswell. They often stay hidden in their own communities, but the Roufes are well-versed in working alongside them. There are just some things we cannot do on our own, and that's when Johnny is left to call in the help of immortals. It's why we've thrived above all other families in this city for so long." Her brow wrinkled further in my direction, and she went on, "That's why I assure you, if she believes she's been bitten, she should seek help *immediately.*"

So, it was true, and like I'd guessed: I was dying a slow and painful death. But by the sounds of it, I wasn't dying slow enough. I'd be the hypothetical dead girl in twenty-four hours or less. One whole day? How much time did that give me? Until after dark, at least, but probably not much more. That wasn't nearly long enough. "So how would she find him—the vampire that bit her?"

"She wouldn't. There are over a hundred vampires in our Tri-City area; finding the exact one would be impossible. A vampire always erases the victim's memory of their encounter, so I'm surprised she'd recognize what was happening to her. Most would simply think they've caught a terrible flu and pass without ever being the wiser. Without any recollection of the vampire in question, there's no way to know who it was or how to find them."

But I still had all of my memories from the night before, didn't I? I remembered the vampire in question's terrifying features perfectly. I remembered his chiseled jaw, his slim nose, and his hard brow. I remembered him down to the cold look in his eyes, even in such darkness. The memory of him had haunted me since the moment he sunk his teeth into my neck.

"But I do remember," I blurted out. "I mean—what if my friend did remember perfectly what he looked like?"

"Impossible."

Finally, I gave up my futile charade and spoke truthfully. "Nonna, please help me. It happened last night. I remember him perfectly, though. I can explain every detail of the man who bit me."

Nonna's grey hair bounced atop her head as she nodded knowingly. "Do you realize the predicament you've gotten yourself in, dearest? There's no good way out of this."

"Please, Nonna, *please* don't tell Johnny. I'm begging you."

"How do I explain it to him when you are dead or worse?"

Worse? What is worse than death? "It's your choice when that time comes, but at least give me a chance to right this first! I'm not ready to die yet!"

"Fine." Nonna rubbed her temples. "What did he look like?"

"Well... he had really dark hair. He was tall and lean. His skin was super light, and he had strong cheekbones... and sharp fangs?"

"Anything helpful? Facial hair? Tattoos?"

"No facial hair, and I don't know about tattoos. He was fully covered, I didn't exactly have time to ask him to undress for me."

"How did it happen then? Where were you?" It was obvious from her tone that Nonna was doing her best to work with what little I'd given her.

"Well, long story short, I was kidnapped by a man last night and thrown in his trunk—I think he was related to the Grioris. By the time he'd driven us what seemed like ten-plus miles down one of the forestry roads, this supposed vampire guy showed up, killed him, and was going to leave after that. But then I screamed, and he noticed me. I told him who I was, and he said he knew Johnny but that he didn't think he'd miss me because he thought I was a 'consort.' Then he bit me."

"You say he just showed up to kill the man who kidnapped you and then he was going to leave? And he said he'd worked with Johnny before?"

"Yeah, and yeah."

"Did he have an early English accent?"

"A what?"

"An old English accent? Hurry up, dear, you don't have all day."

Thinking back, he did have a unique sound, but I was dealing with too much panic to worry about the strange man's accent at the time. It could have been European. Maybe it was old English—whatever that meant. "I suppose, yes."

"God damn it, girl. I was hoping this wouldn't be the case. It is both good and bad news."

"What? Do you know who it is?"

"The good news is that I believe I know who it was. It's most likely a vampire by the name of Riftan. He has come around here and there. He's done favors for Johnny and Johnny has done favors for him. I believe that's exactly how he came across you last night. He was surely doing a favor for Johnny, and you were an unacquainted casualty. The bad news is that after feeding from a human, any smart vampire will hypnotize their victim and erase their memories simply by looking them in the eyes. He's plenty smart enough to have done so, and I have not a clue why he'd have chosen to leave you with your memories intact. All I know is that the reasoning can't be good."

"But you know who he is! So, doesn't that mean I could find him? Doesn't that mean I have a chance?"

"I don't know where you would find him. He finds you, never the other way around. Even then, he's fickle, and the likelihood that he'd help you is next to none. I can assure you, with Riftan, you might as well forget about this whole thing and enjoy your last few hours, dear."

26

"But… but he left me with my memories. Why would he do that if he didn't want to help me? Or at least give me a chance?"

"I told you, I have no explanation for that, girl. Maybe he wanted to torture you a little more. Otherwise, if it is because he wants you to find him… Well, that's going to be a problem in and of itself. You may be better off dead. So, we can only hope it was the former."

I really wish she'd stop with the 'better off dead' hints—they're not helping! "Where can I start looking? I won't stop until I've successfully keeled over and died."

"You could check the internet for clubs—vampires often frequent establishments filled with an array of mortal flesh to choose from. Also, I suppose there *are* a few bars around town that are known to cater especially to vampires. When someone is looking for a favor that only a vampire can help with, they would go there—even at the risk of never leaving."

"Okay, fine, which ones? I'll write them down."

YOU LOOK LIKE YOU COULD BE A
BOATLOAD OF TROUBLE FOR HIM

FOUR ESTABLISHMENTS later, and I'd caught nothing but dirty glares from daytime bargoers.

The sun had already begun its angular descent toward the city skyline. Soon, it would get dark, and I didn't know if that'd be better or worse for finding a vampire. If daytime is like their nighttime, isn't that when they'd go to clubs? Like how humans go at night?

I didn't know, but I also didn't think I'd been anywhere that looked like a "vampire club." All I'd found was some human alcoholics.

One club tucked away in the corner of an alley looked like it could have vampiric regulars, but the bouncer wouldn't let me through the door due to how terrible I looked. He probably thought I had some sort of serious drug addiction. I didn't blame him after I'd blatantly puked in the dumpster at the end of that same alleyway.

That wasn't the first or last puke stop along my route either. By the fifth bar I was so weak my legs were wavering in their ability to continue. My search needed to be more efficient. I needed a little more strategy and a lot less hollow optimism.

Finally, off the recommendation of the bartender at establishment number five, whom I'd asked some choice questions to, I came to the Equiluxe Night Club on Harrison Avenue. It had been harder to find than the others, tucked away on the backside of a lesser-known building. Not to mention it had zero social media presence, which gave me a good feeling. It had an enigmatic vampiric aura slathered all over it, all the way down to the wrought iron door with a sliding eye slit. With the light outside waning, the neon sign above the door glowed a bright purple against the grimy alleyway brick. It illuminated the name Equiluxe in swooping letters and the iron slit on the door slammed open when I approached.

Steadying myself under the neon light, I listened to a gruff voice as it asked, "Who do you know here?" That wasn't something I was used to hearing at club entrances. Not when cash spoke louder than words.

"Uh—" I stuttered, my voice hoarse. "Um, Riftan. Riftan told me to come here." I lied confidently through my feeble lips.

A harsh gaze looked me over through the slit in the door.

"Fine, come in."

This was it. I'd found the place. The bouncer knew Riftan. Would that mean he was inside? The metal creaked as it opened for me, and the humongous man behind it ushered me inside. The prospect of finding my savior had me nearly jumping out of my shoes, but I held in any relieved verbal sentiments.

I followed the man down a dimly lit hallway until it opened into an expansive room where lights flashed and swayed like in any normal club. There were a few individuals dotted around the interior, but the dance floor lacked debauchery, the music too low to encourage such a thing. Maybe it was still early for a vampire club.

The hair on my neck stood with the sensation of being watched. It was the first time all night I'd had that feeling. Everyone on the street had avoided me, likely for fear that I might ask them for some change.

Ignoring the newly acquired feeling, I made my way to the bar and asked the bartender if she'd seen Riftan around. I tried my best to make it sound like we were old acquaintances, as if that were remotely believable.

"He's not here." She looked me over with roving eyes that picked apart every detail of my being, down to the threads on my tightly wound scarf.

"Does he come here often?"

"Why do you need to know?"

"Because I want to talk to him. Do you know where to find him?" I pushed, leaning over the counter to assert myself.

"I don't share customer's personal information," the

woman drawled. "That'd be unethical."

"I don't care about ethics! Tell me where Riftan is!" I snapped, unable to control my tone though I knew my attitude would get me nowhere.

The girl was unphased, her gaze lingering past me only to fixate on an unfamiliar arm that slid around my shoulder.

Jolting away from the sudden touch, I gasped. The strong arm let go, but only enough to let me spin around to face the man it was attached to. He reached out with a deadly fast hand and steadied me close to him. The first thing I noticed was the tidy blue suit he donned. The second was the blond locks combed back into a short, styled hairdo that screamed CEO.

He smiled wide, undaunted to show the fangs that slipped past his thin lips. "So, you're looking for Riftan, dear?" His voice was soft—tranquil even—as he sat me down on a chair at the bar and took the seat next to me. His eyes crinkled with warmth, his shoulders tipping toward me, signaling as if we were about to have a friendly chat.

With that, the bartender shook her head and walked away.

"Y-yes. I need to talk to him."

"Hmm." The man looked me over with analyzing eyes like many had since I'd begun my bar hop for Riftan. Without another word, he yanked off my scarf, exposing my neck to the world.

"Hey!" I complained, grabbing at my garment which was already dangling a full arm's reach from me. There hadn't been any point in trying to contest him—he possessed the same stupid strength this Riftan guy had the night before—but that didn't stop me from snagging my scarf back the second he let go of it, which was before I'd had time to comprehend the full event. The fucker was too quick.

The moment he saw my neck, the man threw his defined chin up into the air, bellowing like I'd said the funniest joke in the world and we were laughing together. But I definitely *wasn't* laughing. "Oh dear"—He stopped to pat his cheeks that must have hurt from laughing at my expense—"I'm sorry, this is so comical to me."

You don't say.

He continued, still grinning up a storm. "Oh please, don't look so angry. It's not attractive on a girl as cute as you."

He can fuck right off for all—

"May I ask how you know his name? Did he tell you? How did this happen?" He pointed toward the mark on my neck.

"No… I got his name from someone I know. And how the hell do you think this happened? He fucking bit me!" I would have stood to assert myself, but my legs felt more like noodles than when I'd first sat.

The man raised a curious brow. "And you remember it?"

"Yes. Perfectly."

"Oh wow." His chest heaved with another bout of outrageous laughter. "This is going to be such a hassle for him." The man centered himself, looking me sternly in the eyes. His voice suddenly turned to ice. "I'll tell you where he is, but only because you look like you could be a boatload of trouble for him. I'd love to see where this goes."

His words were hopeful to my ears, but they slipped off his

tongue like daggers meant to harm. I didn't think I could trust a man whose playful demeanor so easily ran cold. If only I had the luxury of deciding who to trust and when. Unfortunately, my health was waning, and I wasn't going to be lucky enough to make those choices much longer.

"Please," I practically begged, "just tell me where to find him."

The man with the smoothed back hair and pointed chin looked away from me and flagged down the bartender, easily asking her, "Get me a pen and paper, will you, sweetheart?" Looking back at me, he winked. "Make sure you tell him that Darrin says hello, okay, dear?"

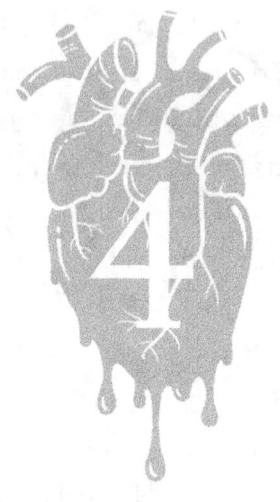

S O M E T I M E S   M U R D E R   I S   T H E
G R E A T E S T   M E R C Y

"MEADOW LAKE apartment complex, floor six, 68B." I read the paper in my hands aloud before admiring the pristinely painted black door in front of me with the gold-crested "68B" nailed in. The waning light from the city outside cascaded through the tall window at the end of the hallway, highlighting the expensive glass vases in each corner with a golden hour glow.

With one last deep breath, I steeled my waning strength for this *last* chance at living to see tomorrow. Then, swiftly and surely, I knocked on the door. When the only responding sound was the elevator ding down the hall, I knocked again, and then again once more.

A shuffle from within 68B had my heart leaping into my throat. "Riftan!" I slammed my knuckles against the wood in a fury. If that damn vampire didn't open this door, I was going to knock it down. I may have fallen weaker than I'd been five minutes prior, but it didn't matter, I'd find a way to break the damn door down.

"Riftan!" I screamed again, attracting the attention of several of the neighbors who peeked their heads through ajar apartment doors.

Just when I was certain somebody was going to call security on me, the locks clicked on the door I'd been pounding on. When it opened only wide enough for a dark-haired man to stick his head out, I was eye to eye with the familiar face that'd been haunting my waking nightmares. There was no mistaking the fair skin and strong features that announced I'd found the man I'd been looking for. I'd only seen him once, but I'd remember every square inch of that face until the day I died. And I hoped this wouldn't be that day.

Seeing him didn't scare me like it should have; it merely ignited deep-rooted rage for what he'd put me through. He was responsible for this, and I didn't care who or what he was, I'd find a way to make him pay.

He scrunched his nose at me. Before I could berate the man, he said, "Oh god. It's you."

Although his cold, narrowed eyes terrified me the night before, I no longer bothered to cower from his intimidating presence. An entire day of being nearly one with the dead would do that to a person, I suppose.

Having absolutely nothing new to fear, I pushed through the door, past the man, and into his apartment. He surely let me do it, or else I wouldn't have succeeded.

"What the hell are *you* doing here?" he asked. His deep voice had a melodic cadence hinting at an accent that would have normally been unfamiliar—old English, as Nonna put it.

"You know fully well why I'm here. Nobody else can help me but you. You did this to me. Now undo it."

"How did you find me?" He closed the door behind himself and locked it shut. That action alone should have raised red flags, but instead, it ignited my skin with excited tingles.

Unfortunately, I had no valiant answer as to how I'd found him. The best way to describe what had gotten me standing face-to-face with the only person who could save me was damned luck. So, instead of admitting that, I stood my ground and answered, "It doesn't matter. I'm here now, and you have to help me."

He examined me with eyes that were now decipherably a deep shade of blue that rivaled the ocean's depths. After a moment, he gave a light shrug of his shoulders and walked away, his reply, "I can't help you. You're going to die and there's nothing I can do about it."

"No way!" I squealed, my voice becoming nearly incomprehensible from the shock of his rudeness. "I know you can help me! I remembered your face. Nonna told me that you would have hypnotized me to forget it if you didn't want me to find you."

He bellowed a laugh and strolled into the spacious

contemporary kitchen situated in the center of the studio apartment. "I was giving you a *chance* at survival. That doesn't mean I *wanted* you to find me. I never actually thought you would. It simply made me feel better about killing you if I gave you that chance. That way, at the very least, you had those few extra hours to make peace with things."

"Well, I'm here now. I've used my last few hours simply trying to survive! And in that very comment, you admitted to having the capability to save me, or else there would be no reason to leave me those memories that would inevitably lead me back to you as my 'chance at survival.'" I made myself obdurate in his presence, standing tall and trying to toe off with Riftan. Despite my lack of fear for my own death, there was still something natural within me that reacted when he stepped closer.

"I can't save you. Now that you've been bitten, the only thing I can do is make you like me, and that's not something you want or something I'm willing to do."

"Like you? So, a vampire? Okay, fine. Do it. Anything for just one more day."

"Unfortunately, I can't give you just one more day. Turning you would mean infinite more days, and my conscience wouldn't be clean if I gave you that curse." He spoke as if he was really helping me, and not literally condemning me to death.

Planting my feet, I used every bit of my waning strength to shout at him, "This isn't about you! It's my life; you don't have the right to take it from me because you are afraid of your morally corrupt conscience!"

Without a moment's notice, his expression morphed and Riftan's alarmingly powerful hands wrapped around my throat, pushing me against his countertop. The air left my lungs, but it wasn't at the mercy of his grasp. In fact, his hands were gentle— not choking me, but steadying me in front of him. The only forceful contact was the bodyweight he used to pin me between him and the counter.

I caught a glimpse of his snarl and intense blue stare before clamping my eyes closed. Nonna had warned me how vampires got their way, and I refused to let him subdue my pleas with only a look.

There was a moment of stillness before Riftan realized I wouldn't be willfully opening my eyes for him. In response, he spoke in a harsh, accented tone, the warmth of his breath only inches from my own lips. "Do you have any idea why I did what I did to you?"

When he didn't continue without provocation, I shook my head.

"I was going to thrall you to forget what had happened and go on your merry way, but when I looked in your eyes to do so, all you wanted was death. You told me to kill you. I showed you mercy by doing what you requested; sometimes murder is the greatest mercy."

Keeping my eyes clamped shut, I whispered, the sound coming out feebler than I wanted it to. "That's not mercy. You could have killed me quickly like you did the driver, but instead, you cursed me to die this slow, hopeless death."

"As I said", his tone leveled once again, but he didn't let

up on the weight he had against me, "I was simply doing what my conscience thought was right. You had nearly twenty-four more hours to make peace with death. That seems merciful enough to me."

Does he plan to banter until he can trick me into opening my eyes? Fine, all the more time to convince him. "Well, your conscience was wrong—*you* are wrong. How could you let me die now that I've come all this way? There would have been no point in doing what you did in the first place. You'd have been better off killing me right off the bat. Now your conscience will have to live with *that*. It will have to live with the twenty-four hours I *suffered* fighting for the chance that *you* waved before me and then denied to me once I'd reached the finish line!"

"Maybe you are right." The weight of him left me and I nearly tumbled to the ground without his support. Lacking the warmth of his presence, I felt compelled to take a peek, only to find that he was still close and pinning those deadly eyes right on me. Still not sure if he was going to try and hypnotize me into walking right back out his door completely voluntarily, I decided to remain in the dark.

Riftan continued, "But how old are you now? Twenty-three, twenty-four? You already wanted to be done with this life—already wanted to die. How do you expect to enjoy an eternity? It would be irresponsible of me to give you immortality, and you'd be irresponsible to accept it."

This argument was leaving me weaker by the minute. Any hope I'd come in with was slowly slipping away. Despite any repercussions it might have, I opened my eyes to hold fast with his. My final pitiful statement on the matter being, "I *don't* want to die. I want to live to experience things I never have. I've never been out of Creswell and there's an entire world full of things I wanted to do—people I wanted to meet. Whether it was one day or an eternity of days, I'd take *any* opportunity to live my life differently than I have. I don't want to die like this. I don't want to die with *this* as my legacy." Tears beckoned at my eyelids and I found myself blinking them closed to hold back any pitiful waterworks.

Riftan's voice was shallow, but closer than seemed appropriate. "If I turned you, you'd have to leave everything you love behind. Your family, your friends, your entire life would be in the past."

I nodded. I'd never had a family, I only had one friend, and my life was most certainly a wreck to boot.

His tone lightened, turning his argument into a delicate warning. "Any heaven that you believed in won't accept you, and any hell you feared will be a vacation compared to what comes if you die." Silence followed as though he was awaiting my response—awaiting my agreement to a no longer hypothetical option.

I couldn't help but smile at the thought of him giving me a chance to decide. "Would any heaven have really accepted me anyway?"

"You will be damned to a fate worse than death."

"Nothing you say can change my mind." A stream of tears left my eyes, no longer confined behind drawn lashes when I peered up at him.

Riftan's sapphire gaze fixed on a single tear as it streaked its way down my cheek until ultimately dropping off my chin. When he returned to said tear's origin, he shook his head for reasons untold. I didn't understand the sentiment that lingered behind his softened eyes, but I perceived it to be more kindred than it should have been coming from this murderous stranger.

"You're lucky," he stated finally, his tone taking an upbeat turn. "You caught me during my down decade, and I was getting quite bored. I'll turn you, I suppose, but you'll have to stay with me until I can teach you how to face an eternity. Training someone like *you* may be exactly the fun I need to get out of this slump." He snarled, his raised brow revealing the wondering gaze that raked over me, giving a deviant perception of perverse intention to his statement. In a strangely contrasting way, his knuckles grazed my cheek, removing the tears that seeped from me.

"You will really do it?" My entire body went limp, flooding with relief.

"If you promise you understand what you are getting yourself into. Immortality is not a fantasy, it's a nightmare. I'll give you one last chance to resolve."

I didn't need another chance. I knew what I wanted. "Please do it. I don't care what I lose or what I gain or if it's a mistake. I want the opportunity to figure all that out for myself. I want the opportunity to learn my lesson, even if it's the hard way."

"So be it." Riftan wrapped his fingers through my arm and led me in the direction of his apartment's living space. I let him pull me along until we stopped in front of the angled couch overlooking an impeccable night line view of Creswell. Each of the little skyscrapers twinkled like diamonds in the dirt. "Sit," he demanded.

Without question, I did as he suggested, wiping the remaining tears from my eyes. My mind buzzed with everything it could mean for me, if he was truly turning me. I hoped that he *was* really turning me like he'd claimed.

Kneeling until we were at the same level, Riftan's breathtaking eyes searched my face one last time, reflecting only a glimpse of guarded apprehension.

My heart pounded in the silence—or so it felt. Though, surely my pulse didn't beat quite like it was supposed to. Each melodic thump was a little slower than the last, and I quivered at the thought that Riftan might be stalling until my life slowly gave out.

Before I could noticeably lose hope, Riftan let loose a finalized sigh and lifted his wrist to his mouth. A moment later, he offered it to me, dripping fresh crimson blood. "You'll have to drink my blood. That's what will turn you."

"Really?" The memory of Jayleen's sour blood stained my mind and left my expression pinched.

"Now is not the time to be squeamish," Riftan scoffed, rolling his eyes at me. "If you have really thought his through, then you have to know that there is plenty of blood drinking in your future."

"No, I know that." I hadn't meant to sound so disgusted. If I indeed needed to get used to that taste to survive, then I would. It just might take me some time. Putting any averse thoughts behind me, I took his dripping wrist in my hand. I didn't exactly know how to go about drinking it, and it seemed so incredibly odd to put my lips on him—a bleeding stranger. In a way, I wished he would do it for me. However, it was obvious from his patient position kneeling by my side, and the casual look on his face, that he wasn't going to force this on me. I had to do it myself—no matter how bizarre it seemed.

Shaking away all reservations about the oddity, I closed my mouth around the bloody puddle on his wrist. I did everything in my power not to taste the warm liquid that came from his veins, but it was impossible to ignore. Every bit that contacted my tongue as it grazed over what was once an open wound was as sour and bitter as I'd expected. It was revolting, but I had to tell myself that it was a little milder than Jayleen's, if only to keep it down.

I wasn't sure if what I'd taken of his blood was enough, but it seemed as though Riftan's inflicted wound had already stopped bleeding and there wasn't any way to pull more of it into my mouth. I couldn't have forced myself to draw any more regardless, the one slurp having been enough to make me gag. Luckily, that little bit must have been sufficient, because Riftan pulled his arm away, wiping the remaining blood and saliva onto his dark jeans.

Though the taste still stained my tongue, I was too weak to care. If I'd wanted to vomit it up, I no longer had the ability. When gravity pulled down on me violently, Riftan caught my shoulders and laid me on the plush couch.

He spoke gentle words, matching that of the tenderness in his fingers as he wiped his blood from my lips. "You're going to feel really tired. Just let yourself sleep. You will wake up in a couple of hours and everything will feel different, but you'll be alive—depending on your definition of it."

His features were going blurry before I had the presence of mind to understand his words. I tried to fight consciousness as things started to fade, as was my instinct. It was only once Riftan's words had set in that it dawned on me I needed to make peace with the actuality of what was to come. Despite the feeling that I should do the opposite, I let myself lose the battle with sleep as it beckoned me toward darkness.

Riftan's careful fingers were the last thing I felt as they left my lips in exchange for the delicate skin at my neck where they rested until everything—even his touch—was merely a memory of my consciousness.

IN THE FACE OF ETERNITY,
THAT'S THE BLINK OF AN EYE

I WAS FUCKED.

I didn't know *shit* about vampires, and yet I'd happily agreed to jump right into living as one.

Growing up, I hadn't read fantasy stories or pondered ancient mythologies where one might learn a thing or two about vampire lore. Hell, I hadn't even read *Twilight* like the other middle school girls. Reading was for nerds—fantasy was for nerds. I was too cool to be one of those girls. Too popular, too mature, too busy trying to make it in a shit hole like Creswell. I didn't have any family or skills and I thought I could make up for it by having the most friends. I was *the* "it" girl, not some fiction nerd.

Look how far that popularity got me. My crown certainly *was* shiny atop my pile of shit.

So, as far as being turned into a vampire went, I didn't have an inkling of a clue what I was getting myself into. I wasn't afraid to start a new life—mine was the kind of mess I'd willingly forget in a heartbeat—but would this truly be the terrible curse this Riftan guy swore it was? Would I have to become an emotionless murderer? Would I be able to do it if it meant survival, or would I choose my own death over taking another's life?

Was this a mistake?

I didn't have time to ponder any of it because, like I'd been struck by lightning, my entire body jolted with more than consciousness. My lungs struggled for air, my heart beat faster than I'd ever remembered it pumping, and each nerve on my body lit with overwhelming stimulation akin to feeling every sensory input imaginable.

I sprung upright. Though short-lived, the scream projected from my lips was brutally loud, echoing against the walls and piercing my eardrums until they burned from the agonizing intensity. It mingled with the cacophony of cars honking too loud, engines whirring and buzzing, phones ringing—vibration, scrape, beating thump—it was all too much. My hands covered my ears as a cry beckoned at my throat.

Fortunately, I was immediately plucked from my absorption in the stimuli. Riftan's face appeared in front of mine, his hands firmly gripping my chin where my every follicle protested being handled. He was more stunning than I had ever thought, even in the darkness that surrounded us. With that, I realized that every light had been turned off, yet things still glowed magnificently. His face was as bright as it had been in the fullness of light, and it was sublime. His hair was darker than I recalled, the endless void of space mingling in each strand, only highlighted by the healthy shine of it. It contrasted, so bizarrely alluring, against his poreless white skin that framed the strength of his prominent bone structure and radiant eyes. How hadn't I noticed how stunning he was? How had I never recognized how beautiful anything in this world could appear?

He was a murderer. He'd tried hard to kill me, as he'd probably done to many others before. Yet, that wasn't enough to deter me from acknowledging how captivating he was.

While the emergence of his attentive look helped to ease a bit of my tension and distract me marginally from the chaos, it didn't stop the noise, and it didn't stop the prickle of his touch.

I'd never been one to habitually weep, but tears like the ones I'd cried earlier streamed down my face from the agonizing experience of it all. I couldn't escape the sounds, the touch, the senses. I couldn't get away, and it shook me with terror.

What had happened to the world in the time that I'd been asleep?

Riftan's voice was loud in my ears, though as I watched his supple, tender lips move only slightly with each word, it was obvious that he was whispering. "Everything is going to be really oppressive at first. I can turn out the lights, but I can't turn off any of the sounds. I'm sorry, but the best thing you can do is suffer through them for now. I promise you, it will get better soon. Don't fight it, just realize that it will get better."

That wasn't what I wanted to hear. I wanted it to stop. I wanted to be done with the torture. I wanted to feel *nothing*. "Please get your hands off me." I choked out the request, aching for a bit of relief.

Riftan did as I asked, pulling his hands from my chin and sitting back on his heels. As he got farther from me in the darkness, I could still see him plain as day. The spot where he'd once touched my vulnerable skin now caught the brisk cold of emptiness and found no alleviation from the pain. My heart sank and my skin ached. His warmth had been overwhelming. The blood rushing through his veins and the beating of his heart against my chin, all felt through the palms of his hands, had been panic-inducing. But it wasn't until it was gone and all that remained was the barrage of noise that I realized it wasn't a bad kind of overwhelming; it was good. It overpowered the others—if only a little.

Craving that reprieve, I dropped off the edge of the couch and tucked my head into Riftan's chest. He didn't stop me, only hesitated a moment before wrapping his arms around my back and holding me tight. The thumping I'd heard before was undoubtedly the sound of his heart, because it was louder now—deafening, actually—with my head in his chest. But it smothered many of the other sounds, his body buffering some of the traffic on the streets below.

Everywhere his skin touched mine was both painful and appeasing at the same time. His tantalizing contact was enough to wane the dread-inciting noises from all around, but it was all still deafening, as though my senses were splitting hairs on whether to focus on Riftan's touch or the blaring car horns and millions of voices. When he drew a gentle line down my bare arm with the palm of his hand, the scales tipped, and the sounds weren't so overbearing anymore. My skin ached from his touch, but it was enviable in comparison to the alternative.

When he stopped, and the sounds came piling back in, a whimper escaped my lips along with the tears that seeped from behind my eyelids and stained his white t-shirt. Taking the hint, he touched me again, this time tracing up until he was rounding my chin where it sat pressed against his beating chest.

A sigh left my lips as his caress soothed my ache like ice on a wound. This time he didn't stop, and the world mollified around me. The longer we sat like that, the more I thought the universe might equalize.

The thought of sleeping and forgetting about the painful overstimulation was tempting enough to take it as soon as I could get it. After what felt like hours of torture, I finally became comfortable enough to fall asleep in Riftan's arms.

A knock on the door startled me awake, and the arms wrapped around me held tighter. I found the strength to lift my head and look around. The sounds were oppressive but not severely painful, manifesting into a persistent headache rather than a piercing assault on my ear canal.

Riftan sat, watching as I separated myself from him. He didn't move for the door, or make any contrary movements at all.

"Aren't you going to get the door?" I asked, feeble words

scraping together despite the pain they left in my throat and against my ears.

His voice was somehow quieter than mine. "That was a knock three floors away."

"No... it was—" The knock had most certainly been right at his door.

His lips parted into a genuine smile, the first I'd seen from him. Fangs that I'd only ever felt on my skin hinted visibly at the corners of his mouth. "You'll get used to it," he whispered, giving me a soft pat on the cheek before standing from where I sat huddled on the floor.

My breath caught in my chest at the thought of his departure, but the horde of senses no longer attacked me, and I realized I didn't need his touch to handle them. They were all still present, but they were becoming nearly bearable.

Riftan dropped a blanket around my shoulders before walking toward the kitchen. His bare feet on the hardwood floor were like thunder in my eardrums, and I wrapped my head up in the blanket that tickled my skin with its velvety embrace. I'd never felt anything so soft, and it was a proper replacement for Riftan's warmth.

That was when I realized I was exceptionally temperate. While feeling the warmth of the blanket over my shoulders or the heat from Riftan's embrace, I didn't become sweaty or clammy. I wasn't too warm, even when I could feel heat encompassing me. Contrarily, the cold hardwood under my butt was noticeably cool, but it didn't give me chills, and my normally freezing feet were neutral to the touch. I could feel warmth and I could feel cold, but it didn't cling to me, as if my body adapted to them before I could feel anything but comfortable.

A loud tapping sound echoed from the kitchen. "Come in here." Riftan spoke in his peculiar accent from the other room.

Slowly, I did as he said. The air that moved across my skin when I made any motion prickled my flesh and whirred in my ears. There simply was no way to walk slowly enough to stop the sensation from bothering me or to stop the thunderous creaking of the floor under my feet. Just the blanket dragging behind me was a low and abrasive itch to my senses. Once I'd finally made it to the stools that rested at the granite counter, I warily sat, attempting to ignore the pain from every little sound my chair created.

"Drink this." Riftan carefully placed a glass full of red liquid on the counter in front of me. No matter how careful he was, the clink of glass on stone ground against my eardrums.

In agony, I huddled farther into my blanket.

"It will make you feel better," he taunted with a light tap of his finger on the counter.

"Will it make the noises stop?" It was wishful thinking.

"No, only time will do that, but it *will* cease the pain that the noises cause."

I nodded and stared into the glass. It was a dark and ruddy liquid, the smell wafting into my nostrils like bitter rust. "Is this blood?"

"Yes." He waited patiently.

"Whose blood?" I hated to think of the poor soul.

"Someone who is still out there somewhere alive and none the wiser. Okay? Is that what you wanted to hear?"

"Yes, I suppose." I dropped my lips to the edge of the glass but struggled to make myself tip it back. If all my senses were so much stronger now, could I keep it down? The memory of the viscous feel and acidic taste of metallic, cerise blood made me visibly gag.

Riftan glanced toward the ceiling like I was testing his patience. "Will you just drink it? It won't be as bad as the last time, I promise."

Taking his word for it, despite not really knowing its worth, I tipped the glass back. I expected to choke on the taste, but I was prepared to swallow it anyway. I could discern every little drop and the exact spot that it slithered over the flesh on my lips, but that was where my heightened senses stopped. The moment it passed my teeth and entered my mouth, what I'd remembered as harsh and unpalatable was instead completely muted. There was still that hint of a bitter, bloody taste, but it was tolerable—if anything, it was sweet. The taste wasn't terrific, but I was able to knock it back regardless.

When I lowered the glass, a hint of a smug little smile tugged at Riftan's lips. The traffic down below still buzzed in my ears, but the blaring ache that it caused began to fade. Without meaning to, I sighed a powerful, relief-stricken breath from my lungs. I couldn't imagine going back to how I'd felt moments earlier. And just like that, I could sense myself being dependent on the way I felt basking in that moment.

I'd once been addicted to cigarettes for eight months when

I was eighteen, and this was... so much more than that. I already knew if I went back to the way I'd felt prior to that drink, I'd panic. This was like the strangest nicotine high I'd ever felt, and I only hoped this would last longer than those had. "You were right," I confirmed. "That wasn't quite as bad as before."

"Obviously, I was right. All of your senses are going to be heightened, save for your taste buds, which will be dull and slightly off. You'll be glad for it—it's the only thing that makes drinking blood bearable. Soon you'll learn to crave it and then you'll have to learn to stave off those cravings. But don't fret, I'll be here to help you through it. There's a lot more I'm going to have to teach you before you can go out on your own, too. So, why don't you save us the argument and trust me next time I ask you to do something, okay?"

Slouching into my seat, I promptly felt ashamed for questioning the worth of his word. Maybe I didn't need to worry about that. Maybe he earnestly wanted to help me. Just to be sure, I asked him, "Why are you *really* helping me? You were so adamantly against it when I first came here."

"I told you, I was bored. You offered me something to do." His tone was as casual as ever. Then he shrugged and added, "And you *did* kind of catch me in a tricky situation. I'd be a hypocrite if I left you with your memories but didn't help you when you found me. I'm a man of my word, and it would be rather poor form to commit to something so significant and then fail to see it through. You're here now, so I suppose you earned it. I locked myself into that obligation when I chose not to thrall you."

I nodded. Whether that was exactly what I wanted to hear, I wasn't sure, but it'd have to do.

"So," Riftan continued with an upturned grin, "you just died. How do you feel?"

"Horrible," I grumbled. "But the opposite of dead. I've never felt so much before. And I can hear my heart beating. I'm certainly not dead."

"You both are, and you aren't. You were dead for six hours, now you are somewhere in between. Your heart will beat faster than before, but weaker. That will be the easiest way to tell apart other vampires without tasting their blood or seeing their teeth. They'll possess a heartbeat faster than any human could survive with."

I'd like to say that the information was collected like a sponge, but my head was so wracked and inundated that his words were going in one ear and out the other. "Ugh. What do I do now?" was all I could muster.

"You need to call anyone who might wonder where you've gone and tell them you're going on a trip out of the country. You don't know when you'll be back, *if* you'll be back. It's a real *Eat, Pray, Love* scenario."

"Ah, shit." I'd accepted the idea of never seeing anyone I knew ever again when Riftan proposed it the first time, but now that it came to following through, I was getting figuratively cold feet. Not because I'd miss anyone, but because I was scared to take charge of my life—scared of what Johnny might do if I hinted at my ability to exist without him. Evermore terrifying was the thought of what Johnny would do if I told him blatantly that I was leaving him indefinitely. "Johnny will actually kill me if I tell him that."

"You're going to have to get used to the idea that nobody can kill you, Leanne. You're already dead." He was matter-of-fact in his statement, but then his head perked to the side. "Are you Johnny's girlfriend?"

"Yes, who did you think I was when you pulled me out of that mafiosos trunk and I said, 'I'm Johnny's girl'?"

"I thought you meant you were one of Johnny's hookers."

I scoffed. "I'm not a *hooker*! I don't even look like a hooker!"

Arching a brow, he slithered his gaze over me. "Are you sure? You're a little young for Johnny. Do you not have sex with him for money?"

"No! I'm not a *hooker*!"

He looked around the room, searching for a better answer. "So, what do you kids call it nowadays? A sugar baby?"

With no better response, I growled under my breath.

Riftan let out a hearty laugh that stung my ears. He stopped when I ducked back under the blanket draped securely around my shoulders. "I'm sorry." His voice still tickled with humor. "This is too good. I had no idea you were Johnny's steady. This is really going to piss him off. I love it."

With a shudder, I peeked out of my blanket to glare at the dark-haired man who continued to giggle on the other side of the counter.

"Don't look so narky," he insisted, his sharp incisors

glowing at me. "You'll be free to do whatever you want when I'm done with you, and you'll never have to go back to Johnny for anything. Be it fear or money that are the reasons you were with him, I'll teach you how to get plenty of each of those things for yourself. You can have all the money you'd like and be feared by anyone who opposes you. I promise."

The idea of having those things was tantalizing, but Creswell was all I'd ever known. "And after you're done with me, am I allowed to come back here?"

"I advise that you don't, but who will I be to stop you? At that point, it will be none of my business what you do."

At least I'd get to see Jayleen again if I wanted. "Okay," I agreed. Reaching into my pocket, I took out my phone, careful not to bump any of my surroundings. The sound of my clothing and skin rubbing together had waned and no longer caused me agony, but I knew the sounds my phone made would. For that reason, the first thing I did was turn off any possible tone it could emit—including vibration—without looking at the screen. Forgoing the deadly pitch that would come from a phone call, or the blinding light that would come from the dimmest setting on my screen, I slid the phone over to Riftan. He took it knowingly; I had to curate a message for him to send to both Jayleen and Johnny—the only two people who would care or cause a ruckus when I didn't show up tomorrow... or possibly ever again.

I took my time thinking up something that would sound as sincere as possible to its intended audience. Jayleen's message was more to assure her that I was okay, just had a fever, nothing vampire related, and that I was getting out of town due to the whole kidnapping incident. Johnny's was briefer, as I knew he'd have a cow regardless of what I said. He didn't know of my vampire problems, and I didn't expect Nonna to nark on me. However, Johnny would have found out that I'd been kidnapped the night before. Certainly, he would know that I'd survived, and he would know that I was going to be *pissed* about the whole ordeal. I decided to use that in my message to him.

I may have always been guarded about what I said and did around Johnny, but he still knew I had a temper—and being thrown into a trunk was exactly the type of thing that would send me overboard. For that reason, my deciding to up and leave after all this wouldn't be so hard to believe. Unfortunately, that didn't make the idea of telling him any less distressing.

When my nerves got the better of me, and conceptualizing my message to Johnny ended with a lot of "umm," and stutters, Riftan was there assuring me with grand words about how there wasn't a single thing Johnny could do to hurt us. We were untouchable, or as he put it: "completely on a different plane of existence than Johnny's pitiful mortal operation."

Sending that message gave me chills even when my skin was otherwise temperate. But the moment Riftan said it was done, the sensation morphed into something warm and tingly. I never had to go back to Johnny. That could be a chapter in my life that I forget about completely with no repercussions—well, if I didn't consider being turned into a vampire and tossing my life upside down a repercussion. This truly was a rebirth. I'd attained a new life I could make it into whatever I wanted it to be.

In the blink of an eye, Riftan was gone, only a puff of black fog remaining where he'd stood. Reappearing over my shoulder, he slipped my phone down on the counter in front of me without making a single sound.

His presence bristled at my back, the compression of air moving between our bodies enough to prickle my sensitive skin. With that moving air, I could sense exactly how much space there was between our flesh without seeing him, all while the sound of his beating heart pulsed loud enough to triangulate exactly where he stood.

His breath draped heat over my ear. "Is there anyone you told about me? Anyone that knew you were looking for me? Even just my name?"

"I don't know. Several strangers in the bars, some vampire in a club..." I couldn't for the life of me remember his name. "Oh... And Nonna is who told me your name. She knew I was bitten by you, but I don't think she'd tell anyone."

"I'm not worried about strangers, or other vampires. Nonna, however, I'll *take care of* later."

"Wait." I cut him off before he could possibly say any more. "*Take care* of her? You aren't going to hurt Nonna, are you?" I must have worn some horrified expression when I looked up at him.

"Of course not," he scoffed, settling down in the painfully creaky chair next to me. "I'd never hurt the innocent old hag. I simply meant that I'd thrall her to forget about your conversation, that's all."

58

"If you are going there anyway, can you just thrall Johnny to forget about me, too?" It was wishful thinking.

"How long were the two of you an item?"

"Three years."

"Nope. Not a chance. That's way too long a period to thrall away. While I'm not entirely opposed to turning Johnny's brain to mush, I don't want to have to deal with the repercussions of that coming back on us right now. My duty is to teach you, for the time being, not to start a war with the Roufes. If you'd like, we can do that *after* you're trained."

I wasn't interested in that, or anything involving the Roufes, but I asked, "And how long *will* that be, before I'm trained?"

"I don't know. A year, maybe a couple, give or take, depending on how much I like you or if I simply want to get you out of my hair as quickly as possible." He followed up with a wink.

"Years?" I scoffed, nearly choking on the pain from my own escalated voice.

"Yes, dear. In the face of eternity, I assure you, that's the blink of an eye."

Years may have been no time at all for him, but not me. Having only ever lived twenty-three years, spending a *couple* with him seemed excessive. I wasn't prepared to spend a couple of years with Riftan. After all, he was the sole reason my life had been upheaved. Technically, he *had* killed me—or so he described my state as "dead."

While he'd been relatively kind to me since I'd awoken on

his couch, I still didn't think we were *buddies*. But, If I *had* to spend the next couple of years with him, then my starting question would tell me exactly how inconsequential those years would be to him. I asked, "So, how old are you really?"

"I was born in 1243. I have no idea how old that makes me. You do the math." He eyed me with a smirky look, slighted that I ask him to add it up for me.

My brain was much too muddled to do any math, and I couldn't use my phone, but I'd gotten enough to base my consensus: very inconsequential.

Riftan continued regardless, "Seven hundred and… eighty-something."

That amount of time was nothing my tiny human brain could comprehend living through, so I simply nodded in response.

"Well, since you're still fresh, I'm not going to push anything on you today. Why don't we just talk?" He suggested it in a friendly tone, placing his elbows up on the counter with a vibrative *thunk* that I wouldn't have heard before he'd turned me into whatever I was now.

"Okay."

"I know your name, you know mine, obviously. That's about the extent of what we know about each other. Why don't you tell me about you, then I'll tell you about me—and I promise I'll do my best to keep the seven hundred- and eighty-plus-year summary brief." The white of his teeth glimmered in the darkness once more and I couldn't shake the feeling that I was talking to a completely different person than the one who'd taunted and tortured me the night before. From the moment I'd reawakened, all Riftan did was smile. Although his words were glum, his cheeks were pinching upwards in a way that lit his face with character. His threatening little fangs showed unashamedly—the same fangs that I'd once felt tear through my flesh. Even with those dangerous incisors showing uncouthly, his authentic, supple-lipped grin still made my heart flutter in my chest. It was sincere and… cute. A full-grown, seven hundred- and eighty-year-old man, as intimidating as could be, still somehow possessed a smile that could be described as *cute*.

There were stories behind that smile, and I didn't want to hear only the abbreviated summary. "And if I ask for the unabridged version?"

"Well then, I'd say you better get comfortable. But regardless, you're still up first."

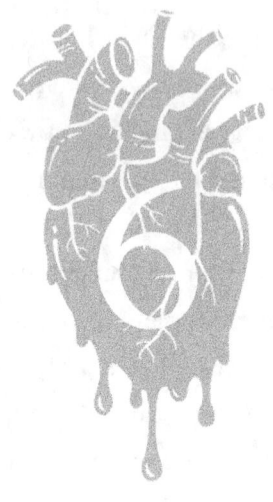

BOUND BY BLOOD

IT SEEMED TRIVIAL to tell Riftan about my twenty-three years of life when I knew he would soon tell me about his seven-hundred-plus, but he pretended to be interested in everything I had to say, despite how insignificant it may have been to him. We needed to know more about each other, even if simply to make our obligatory time together more bearable. But I was still feeling a curious but pleasurable warmth from feigning friendship with him. He was much more than bearable like this, and he treated me like maybe he thought the same of me. It was almost like he'd never tried to kill me.

If we truly did have to spend years together, then this could be considered a good start. Good enough to indeed pretend like *this* was the start, and not the night before.

When I was done sharing with Riftan everything that I could possibly think of, he shared with me his story—starting from the present and going backward in time.

He described his "off decade"—as he liked to put it—was much like taking a vacation from work. He apparently enjoyed taking vacations every several decades, where he'd do anything but get involved with human dilemmas. He'd broken that ideal when he got involved with Johnny's mess of a mafia business a couple of years back, which in turn had led him to me. Supposedly, he'd always had a problem staying out of organized crime-type circles since getting embroiled during the 1920s. Now, he felt inclined to keep crime families in line when things started to get out of hand—like when the Grioris decided to kidnap Johnny's girlfriend for ransom. But that obviously wasn't their only offence, since Riftan had no idea I was in that Griori's trunk until I started screaming. "Happy accident," he'd called it.

He then outlined a rough depiction of his whereabouts in the centuries prior to the twentieth. In the nineteenth century, he was an underground slave liberator after being "personally responsible" for legislature passed in the late eighteenth century to allow and propagate slavery in the United States—a mistake he believed he'd never be able to make up for. Though, he went on to say it wasn't the worst mistake he'd ever made, all the while ominously leaving out what those superior mistakes might have been.

During the seventeenth century, he'd toured Asia in an attempt to stay out of European conflicts, as he'd spent much of his previous centuries enthralled in battles over land and treaties that didn't have anything to do with him. That being said, he'd fought lots of wars prior to that before finally realizing human conquests would never end and in no way profited him. He lamented spending so many centuries on something so frivolous, but that he didn't have to regret it, since he had many more to make up for it. He did say he was grateful for his "little decade vacations" because it let him enjoy the best of each century's arts, even before he'd learned to let humans be humans and fight their own wars.

Unfortunately, his story ended when he turned into a vampire in 1269. He showed no interest in sharing anything before then, so I decided to ask, "Well, what about when you were a human? Who turned you? Who were you before?"

He bared a little grin that showed only his left fang. "That's very mortal of you to want to know about my human life after everything I just told you."

A shrug hinted at my shoulders. "How else am I supposed to relate to you?"

"Darling, I lived in the 1200s. You aren't going to relate to me regardless."

He had a point. "Okay, will you humor me?"

"Fine." He breathed a sigh. "I was born in a small English town called Normereg. Like many of the time, my mother died giving birth to me and my father had died at war, so the church took me in. The priest trained me to be a knight and treated me as his son. So, when I was injured at war, he turned me into a vampire to save my life. There wasn't much else. I was only twenty-six, very close to your age now, and I only ever knew combat and conflict. I didn't have any relationships, aspirations, or friends, so the story is short."

"The *priest* turned you?" I snorted, the idea of a vampire priest striking me as comical.

"Yes, and then he trained me much like I will you."

"Do you still talk to him?"

"He was killed and burned at the stake many centuries ago," Riftan stated.

My smile dropped. "Oh, god, I'm sorry. That's terrible."

"It happens. Just because you are immortal doesn't mean you can be careless. Attracting the wrong attention can summon a heavy downfall—as his was. The only people you have to fear are other vampires and vampire hunters. If you are an adept vampire, even they aren't much of a threat. But the moral of the story is: watch where you stand out, because a vampire hunter's radar is not one you want to be on."

I certainly didn't want to think about being burned alive, so I nodded profusely, my eyes going wide.

"Don't you worry your pretty little head." Riftan's dark hair fell to the side when he cocked an observant look at me. "I won't let anything happen to *you*. We are bound by blood now. There's not anyone out there who's going to lay a finger on you—not over my dead body."

His words, spoken in such a sincere tone, spread an unfamiliar warmth through my bones. But I didn't let it distract me. Unsure of how deep his obligation for my safety might run, I requested clarification, "Bound by blood? What does that mean? Does it hold significance?"

"To some, it doesn't. To me, it does. It means that my blood turned you, and in that way, we will always share something in common. Not only that, but it was me who chose to give you this curse, and for that, I'm responsible for you. I will always feel accountable for you. It's kind of like having a child, I suppose."

Ick. The last thing I wanted was to think of Riftan as a father figure. Not that I'd ever had one of those, but still, he was far from what I wanted to imagine. The hot and muddled feeling that sparked deep in my belly whenever he flashed that devilish little grin he'd been giving me was certainly not the kind of sensation one should get from a blood relative. The growing urge to have his warmth against my fickle skin again surpassed what was appropriate in the presence of any sort of paternal figure. "I definitely won't be thinking of you like a parent," I assured him, doing my best to swallow around the unsolicited lump of desire forming in my throat.

Luckily, he waved the notion away with the flick of his wrist. "I would hope not. It's not the same type of thing anyhow. I merely thought it would be the best way to explain it to you."

"So how many more are like me? How many have you turned?"

"Honestly, not as many as you'd think. Only five others. It's not an action I tend to take lightly. It's cruel, as it *is* a curse."

"Who were they? Will you tell me about them and why you turned them?"

Riftan pursed his rosy lips before assenting. "The last one I blame on getting soft in my old age. He was a middle-aged man named Calvin. He was deathly ill, but he still didn't want to die. He'd sought out all sorts of enigmatic and supernatural remedies, but nothing worked. He had severe lung cancer that had spread all over his body. He'd sought out witches, but they couldn't help him. He came to me, and of course, I turned him down much like I did you at first. Unfortunately, also like you, he was incredibly persistent and for some peculiar reason, I ended up being quite fond of his spirit. He also didn't have any family to get in the way of his decision. I tested his will and devotion much more vigorously than I did yours before turning him. But that was because even in his ill state, he had a lot more time to mull over the pros and cons of immortality than you did."

Riftan sighed, leaning back in his chair. "Before that was a friend of mine named Jameson. He was one whom I'd freed from the slave trade and then worked with in freeing others. I never planned on turning him. We worked perfectly well side by side when he was human. We'd become like partners in crime over the years, and when he was shot in the back with a pistol, he asked me to save him. I knew full well that he understood what he was asking for after years of being around me, so I turned him before his death. I trained him for longer after that than I did anyone else. He's probably the only person I know who I might not be able to beat in a fight—I'm glad for that. Not only does he know everything I've taught him, but an abundance of other things he learned far before and after meeting me. He's the best marksman I know, and he certainly didn't learn that from me. I use guns as rarely as I possibly can. I suppose that's because for the majority of my life wars were predominantly fought with swords and not handheld projectile weapons like they are now."

He paused for a moment to reminisce, and I took the opportunity to ask a question. "Do you still speak to either of them?"

"Jameson, yes, absolutely. Calvin, however, not since I let him go off on his own. He's the adventurous type—never was much of a fan of company. More of a lone wolf, and he liked the opportunity for solitude that being immortal gave him. I tend to prefer the same, so I've let him be."

I nodded, hoping to coerce him into continuing.

"It goes a little downhill from there. After stepping away from warlike conflicts around the 1680's, I was more desensitized than I am now. That's what happens when you're a soldier for a few hundred years. I ended up turning and training a woman named Meridith who had a vendetta against a group of thieves who'd murdered her family and ended up being a part of a larger illegal trading organization. She was vindictive and murderous, and I'd turned her anyway. As desensitized as I was, I didn't care then for her wellbeing and how changing her would affect her mentally. I just wanted to see her murder a national gang of thieves with her bare hands. There was no other motive, and I didn't consider what would happen after it was done. She'd be immortal and never die to be with her family in the afterlife—as she believed. So, after she inevitably got her revenge, all that was left was her shallow, hopeless immortality. Without purpose, she no longer had any control and let herself fall into primordial instincts. I'd created a monster with insatiable blood lust. And because of that... I had to kill her."

He gave me an inhibited smile and kept going. "Before that was someone I'd been to war with many times. He was the first one I'd purposely changed, and the first I trained. His name is Darrin. And before you ask; no, we don't talk." His firm tone hinted that maybe they weren't on good terms. He then continued, hastily trying to bypass the previous statements. "The first person was the most complicated. It was entirely an accident; I didn't understand what I was doing. It was kind of like you. I bit her and regretted dooming her, so I turned her. I didn't stick around to train her though because I simply didn't know any better. When she awoke, completely scared and confused, she took out an entire town in her own misunderstanding. Without knowing what she was or why she'd done what she did, her confusion turned to infuriation, and she took it out on humans. She attracted a lot of attention and was quickly thwarted by vampire hunters." He ended his story with a shaky sigh.

Running a hand through his thick head of ear-length hair, Riftan said no more. His eyes failed to meet mine, unlike how confidently they'd captured my gaze during his long-winded story telling.

"So, that first girl, she woke up to *this*"—I motioned to my entire existence that still thrummed with the overstimulation of senses—"all by herself? I can't imagine surviving this if you weren't here to help me from the start."

"Yes, well, there are plenty of people out there who turn without anyone sticking around to spoon-feed them. They usually end up fine. In fact, right now I could turn on all the lights, blast the radio, and you'd be in agony, but in a couple of hours, you'd adjust and be fine, too. For that matter, you'd end up adapting much quicker than you will with the gentler way we are going to go about it."

Regardless of what I meant to do, I felt my face contort at the thought of him actually turning on all the lights and blasting the radio. It seemed hard to believe that I'd survive something like that, but I had to trust Riftan's assurance that I would. Nonetheless, I was thankful he was going to go easy on me.

"Thank you," I told him sincerely. "I mean, it was shitty of you to try and kill me in the first place, but I appreciate that you are being patient with me now."

"Glad I could make up for my transgressions," he joked, returning that clever smile to his sultry lips. "Besides, we have all the time in the world. I don't need to push you and make you hate me right from the start. Just tell me if we are going too fast, and I will adjust for you. It's been a long time since I was turned, and I won't be able to help make you comfortable if you don't communicate with me, okay?"

"Okay." If I was going to be doomed to an eternity of vampirism, at least the person who'd turned me didn't seem all bad. He was obviously only showing me his good side, but it was hard to see past his chipper fangy smile and shining blue eyes.

The two of us may have started on the wrong foot—with the killing and all—but I thought we would get along fine. For the first time that day, my muscles unraveled.

Riftan stood and patted me on the head. "You seem to be feeling better. Will you be alright for an hour or so here by yourself if I leave to take care of some things?"

Since he'd mentioned it, I noticed I did feel worlds better. He'd distracted me enough with fanciful tales and eye candy that I hadn't noticed my ears no longer buzzed and things had started to equalize. I felt far from perfect, but it was slowly becoming bearable. "Yeah, I'll be fine. I'm actually feeling okay."

"Great." Riftan strolled away from me, stopping by the fridge across his kitchen. Pulling open the door, the entire room illuminated from the intense white light inside.

With a yelp, I pinched my burning eyes closed and tucked my head under the blanket still tight around my shoulders.

Riftan laughed as if that was in any way comical, but then quickly apologized. "Sorry, I didn't think about it. Here." From under my blanket, I saw the butt of an amber bottle as it slid in front of me. "Drink all of this before I get back. As a newborn vampire, you need to feed more than most, and it'll do you good to get used to the taste."

I examined the amber bottle and sniffed the liquid inside of it. It was blood, smelling identical to the drink he'd offered me before. "Why is it bottled?" I raised my eyebrow at the seemingly senseless formality.

"Because it's less off-putting than drinking it out of a bag." He shrugged. "I know someone who bottles, so I buy some from him whenever I can. It's preferable to what you'd find at a hospital. And whether by placebo or by truth, it seems to taste better."

Swirling the ruddy liquid around in the bottle, I did my best to pretend it was beer and took a swig. Going down, it wasn't much worse than the taste of a cheap beer—or even an expensive IPA. The alkaline tang stained the back of my tastebuds, but it wasn't completely adverse. While I hadn't had anything but top-shelf liquor and the fanciest merlot since meeting Johnny, I had once been a college freshman. Thanks to that, I was no stranger to choking down a beer or two—or four or eight. The almost sweet aftertaste blood had taken on since waking up on Riftan's couch was maybe even preferable to any beer I could imagine it as.

"Atta girl," Riftan cooed as he grabbed his coat off the rack and made for the door. Before leaving, he added, "If you have an emergency worth blinding yourself over, I put my cell phone number in your phone as an emergency contact."

I didn't plan on having such an emergency, but I appreciated the precaution.

At the door, I eyed Riftan snagging a pair of sunglasses off the key hook. With the darkness in the room, and the time of day I'd arrived, I hadn't thought for a moment that it could be daytime. The thick drapes over the windows gave no hint of light bleeding through.

"Wait," I called after Riftan before he could turn the

doorknob. "Is it daylight outside? What time is it?"

He stopped and looked at his watch with a marginally exasperated sigh. "Yes, it's three-thirty in the afternoon."

Well, shit. I'd slept a fraction of the day without a clue how much time had passed. The sun outside was already up and preparing to make its descent again. The thought of that big white ball of light made me cringe, chills traveling up my spine. Thinking about looking at the day-lit sky with my sensitive eyes settled angst into my bones. Which begged the question, would I ever see that burning star in the sky ever again? Vampires technically couldn't go out in the sun, right? "Wait, you're going out mid-day?" I asked Riftan. "Can vampires do that? Won't you, like, burn alive or something? Or is that a myth?"

"It's not a myth." He played along, though his brows raised impatiently. "But there are lots of ways to get around it." Riftan proceeded to roll up his sleeve and point out a black tattoo resembling a pentagram surrounding the sun. "I have a witch's sun spell, but that's not the only way to walk around in the daylight."

"Will I ever get one of those?" I asked, watching as he rolled his sleeve back over an otherwise unassumingly muscle-weaved forearm.

"That's a conversation for a later date. Why don't you focus on not being blinded when I open this door?"

When he reached for the handle, I tucked my head into my hands, where I could cover my eyes and wait for him to leave.

After the door *whooshed* closed and clicked shut behind him, I listened to Riftan's footsteps as he made his way to the elevator. They paused for a moment, then continued to what I thought I remembered as the stairwell. That was confirmed when I heard his feet patter down each consecutive step. I was amazed when I could hear him pass each level, and only started to lose him when his steps mingled with the chaos of other footfalls on the busy street below. I shook my head to get the sound of shoes on pavement out of it. Unfortunately, now that I'd been listening for them, I couldn't stop hearing the shuffling movements, along with the constant murmuring of a hundred voices and an avalanche of dings, rings, and—I covered my ears with the blanket. It helped to muffle the sounds, but what I really needed was a distraction.

Lifting the bottle of blood that I was to finish by the time Riftan returned, I decided to explore the small studio apartment. I'd be trapped there until I disciplined the disarray that were my heightened senses, so I might as well get familiar with it.

Never letting go of my literal safety blanket, I trudged through the living room and inspected the little office nook in the far corner. The apartment was nice—lavish even—like the outside had projected. The kitchen boasted modern features adorned with sleek grey cabinetry and stainless-steel appliances, while the living room featured a plush grey throw rug beneath an elaborate stone coffee table. For an old man, Riftan possessed top-notch electronics, including a large TV mounted on the wall and an expensive laptop adorning the desk.

Above, the loft was wide open, the only path up being the wrought iron stairs on the far wall. Intrigued, I ascended the clanky steps, pausing only when the foot of a large bed with tousled grey sheets and a black comforter crested my view of the room. Momentarily, I questioned how discourteous it would be to snoop in Riftan's bedroom, but quickly decided I didn't care and continued my exploration.

The bed sat pushed against the black far wall, opposite the banister but otherwise centered across the room. Along the other two walls were long grey dressers without much décor on top, only a couple of dusty books and an unburnt candle on each. Under my heels was the same dark oak as downstairs, and my only escape from the thunderous sound of my heels on its surface was the thick rug that extended from under the foot of the bed. Wiggling my toes between the rug's fibers, I followed it to the edge of the banister. Three green plants sat on top of the iron railing that overlooked the apartment. Two of which were leafy and green, flourishing like they'd been perfectly nurtured. I imagined that they got plenty of sun when the floor-to-ceiling blinds at the front of the apartment weren't drawn over the massive windows. But even that didn't seem to be enough for Riftan to keep the third plant alive. It was a suffering succulent which looked brown and dry despite the wet soil at its base. I knew from experience that succulents were fussy, and it was likely that Riftan had over watered it. The thought of him over-caring for anything prompted a quiet chuckle.

Leaving my drink by the banister, I meandered back to the bed and flopped down on the foot of it, sinking into the rumpled down comforter. The ceiling was unfinished with exposed ducting, but painted black as though that was the industrial look the designer had been going for. I stared at it, pondering what little entertainment I had without my cell phone or other technology in a stranger's apartment. I couldn't even stare out the window for fear of burning my retinas out.

In what should have been silence, my ears rang with chaos that breached the limits of my accustomed hearing. Tucking my blanket back around my head, I muffled the sound as much as I could before giving in and focusing on the most beckoning parts of the clutter.

I eavesdropped on a couple quietly bickering next door. Fixating on one thing was easier than trying to shut everything out altogether. I could get lost in the argument and the other sounds dulled into a low hum on the peripherals. Until their voices grew louder and angrier—more painful. Seeking refuge from the spat, I attempted to shift to the woman singing in the shower a few floors up—three floors, I believed.

The sound of the water droplets hitting her skin harmonized with her soft voice. When she reached the chorus, the volume building, her sound also became too much for me to take and I moved on to something else.

Someone played a gentle tune on that same level. It was soft and slow, with a gentle arrangement of instruments that gave it an air of Middle Eastern origin. It held my attention indefinitely, reminding me of something they'd play in a yoga studio, which probably explained the rhythmic breathing and elevated heart rate I could hear coming from that same room. That was the sound I didn't stray from. It was enough to lull me to the brink of rest before Riftan's gruff voice summoned me back.

"I see you made yourself at home," he said in a tone that aired somewhere between displeasure and humor in its own odd way. "The least you could have done is make the bed."

I uncovered my face to see him standing over his bed with a smirk that matched the aforementioned tone.

Realization struck that he was standing over *his* bed and I had fallen asleep there without his permission—which was probably rather disrespectful.

"Oh, shit, I'm sorry. I was looking around and then I fell asleep... on accident."

"That's fine. You'll need your rest." He turned his back to me and dropped a pile of folded clothes on the grey dresser closest to the stairs. "I brought you some clothes from your apartment. Enough to get you by until you can handle going outside."

"Thanks," I mumbled, watching Riftan wander over to the loft railing.

He grabbed the bottle that I'd left there when I'd admired his attempt at a green thumb. Squinting at it, he sloshed the half-full bottle of liquid around. "I told you to finish this."

"I'm sorry, I meant to. I just fell asleep."

"While you do need your rest, you need strength more, especially for what comes next." He gave a boding nod. "The best way to gain strength is by drinking as much as you can, especially for the first few weeks."

I raised an eyebrow at him. "And what exactly is it that comes next?"

"Well, you have to overcome these senses sooner than later, and quite frankly, I've been rather easy on you since I do feel responsible for putting you in this situation. That means I don't plan on doing anything that may be overly torturous to you in the process of helping you overcome the basic sensory overload that all new vampires start with, but I'm also not going to let you sleep in my bed with a blanket tucked around your head forever. Fragile treatment is not generally my style, and it's going to get old much too quickly—especially when I want to move onto the fun stuff in a few days." His tone had hardened, making me tuck my blanky under my legs as if he was going to try and steal it from me.

"What exactly is the 'fun stuff?'" I asked meekly, attempting to think of anything that wasn't confronting the challenges of sight and sound.

"You'll see in time," he teased with a coquettish grin. "But first you must finish this"—he handed over the bottle of half drunken bitter liquid—"and then you have to conquer your senses enough to function in public without a blanket turban."

I sighed, taking the bottle from Riftan as he sat down next to me at the foot of his bed. Swirling the liquid in the glass, I stared at it with the apprehension of what it meant once I finished it.

I glanced at Riftan's patient face, waiting for me to do as he'd said.

He was completely on board with this whole thing, and I supposed I could understand why. I was his pet project—the excitement that he'd been waiting on to break up the monotony of whatever his *normal* was. But this was my life too now, and it wasn't something I'd been waiting for or even hoping for. He'd successfully thrown everything I knew upside down and the only thing I could do about it was nod and follow blindly.

I had no option but to trust in him as someone who knew much more than I. That meant I was practically a slave to whatever he wanted of me. All I could do was hope that he'd want the best for me, and not abuse the inequity of our positions. No matter how optimistic that hope was, I had to grasp at *anything* that could make the situation feel safer.

Taking one last look at the promising eyes set under Riftan's dark brows, I told myself those eyes held only the best intentions for me and knocked back the bottle of bitter—now room temperature—liquid. The taste was getting better, more bearable with every drink, but I still had to bite my tongue to stave off a shiver as it crossed my taste buds.

In the end, I kept it down, ready for the next.

With any luck, the onslaught of senses that was my every waking moment would be as easy to get used to as that bottle of heinous acrid blood.

IT TOOK FOUR DAYS before I could so much as open the blinds during the dead of night and gaze at the city lights below. Even then, the havoc of downtown was too much for my sensitive eyes and could only be tolerated in small doses.

I'd learned that distraction was the key to overcoming any single one of my senses. So, much like I'd used Riftan's touch as my distraction in the first few moments of this new, tumultuous experience, I was finding other ways to distract from the more demanding of my senses.

Listening to music was one of the most suitable distractions I'd found. Though some genres were still too raucous, there were many kinds of music that, when played at a low level, could offer me some tranquility. A pair of noise-canceling headphones and a Loreena McKennitt album were enough to get me through any kind of sensorial meltdown— even when it felt like everything was caving in on me.

Aside from those more reasonable tactics to soothe the dishevelment, I'd found other methods to use when music wasn't an option. Touch, as I'd learned early on, was a sense that was just as strengthened as the others. The difference was that it wasn't as overwhelming as sight and sound could be. For this reason, pain—such as a pinch—was helpful in pulling from those other senses when short-lived relief was necessary.

Luckily, Riftan was gentle with me, like he had insisted he would be. He let me cling to my safety net of headphones and the soft blanket that was never far away—though I could tell he was bored of how slowly I was adjusting. He insisted my senses would equalize once I started to reincorporate myself with them. But I still loathed the idea of venturing into any crowded place.

He'd often raise his brows and stare at the ceiling when forced to make concessions to my sensitivities, but he'd always assent. His patience never ceased, and he was generous in sharing a comforting embrace when that was the only thing that could soothe my aching nerves.

I depended on Riftan, looked up to him as I might a mentor, and while he referred to me as a "worthy companion" I didn't think that quite did justice to how I felt about him. Riftan had rescued me from a life of dreadful monotony, and for that, he was more like my savior. If anything, he was closer to my knight in shining armor than a companion—despite how ironic and cliché it may have been that he once actually *was* a knight. And though being stuck in a studio apartment, only the two of us, had its own level of monotony, I now had a whole eternity to look forward to. An eternity that would be free of Roufes and completely mine and mine alone. I would be free to live a life in the shadows as society raced by. I could watch empires rise and fall as many times as this earth would sustain. That, in itself, was a beauty I'd only just begun to consider— and every time I doubted its appeal, Riftan was there to assure me how wonderful it'd be. I was thankful for that, thankful to him for giving me this new life.

However, granting him that kind of blind admiration wasn't something I took lightly. I was wary of my feelings for him—or maybe wary wasn't the right word. Riftan was unafraid of moments when I needed his touch and tender when I needed his care. That left an apprehensive sense of hope settling in the part of my heart that was softening toward him.

So, in the end, curiosity may have been the best word to describe how I felt about our future—a tense but curious interest in how things could unfold in this first new chapter of my life.

Car engines were an absolute assault to the eardrums, and it was nearly two whole weeks later before I could ride in one.

I had a sneaking suspicion that was the final test before I had to fully reincorporate myself into society. However, I still went into panic mode at the thought of going into public. As if it wasn't bad enough as a human, now there were so many more reasons to fear a mass of bodies.

It would be so loud and hectic, not to mention I had no idea if I'd crave human blood—which I'd already come to appreciate the taste of. Though Riftan assured me that wouldn't be the case, I could hear an element of doubt in his voice indicating maybe he wasn't sharing the whole truth.

By the third week, I entirely expected Riftan to drag me onto the streets of Creswell, but just when I thought I was ready to handle such a task, he threw me a curveball. "We are leaving tonight. I've arranged for us to stop by your apartment so you can pack up anything you want to bring. Everything else will be staying here."

"What? What happens to everything that I leave behind?" My lease couldn't be renewed if I wasn't living there, so where would all my things go?

"I'll have everything else packed into storage under your name, but I don't have any idea when or if we'll be coming back. That's why you need to only leave the things you don't care about."

My chest ached at leaving my stuff behind but, quite frankly, I knew I shouldn't need those belongings anymore. Some clothes, a toothbrush, and a cell phone were all I needed to start a new life, and a new life *was* what I wanted... right? "Where are we going?" I'd known we would be leaving as soon as I had a handle of my senses, but the time being upon us sent anxious jitters through my spine.

"I haven't completely decided yet, but it's time for you to get out and experience some new things. I don't want you doing that here in a town full of people you know and who know you. We will be starting fresh someplace else. Luckily, the world is our oyster. I was initially thinking of Prague, only because I know several contacts there, but we can go wherever you would like. Do you have any other suggestions?"

"Prague? You mean, like, Europe, Prague? As in the most beautiful city in the world?" I nearly choked on the excitement of such a proposition.

"Well, the '*most* beautiful' is debatable. But yes, Prague is a city in Europe, Czech specifically." He answered as if such a vacation weren't nearly as tantalizing to him as it was for me. "The nightlife there can be good for those like us, and I suppose it'd be a good place to cultivate a newborn vampire. We can go there if that sounds like something you'd want to do?"

"Would I ever!" I was already jumping up to grab what few belongings I'd acquired in Riftan's apartment. Such an adventure couldn't wait—so it was good I didn't have much to pack.

Riftan's smug grin signified that he, too, was eager to get going—or at least as eager as I'd seen him get. "We'll leave tonight after sunset, okay?"

"Okay! I'm so excited! You know, I've never—"

He interrupted, "Left Creswell. Yes, so you've mentioned a few times." The tight little smirk over his lips grew into something more genuine that showed his glossy white fangs.

I still didn't have any of those, but when I questioned it, Riftan told me that they'd come with time. I guessed that meant they'd grow in? They definitely hadn't yet. I also asked how he hid them since they were abundantly obvious every time he smiled, and his response was, "You don't. We are mystical creatures brought into this world by magic. We aren't exactly designed for *blending in*. Regardless, the world is strange enough these days that it doesn't matter. People walk around with fangs all the time; nobody would think to believe those with fangs are a real vampire unless the person observing them knew what else to look for."

That was information I took in stride, as was everything he shared with me. I was constantly learning something new, all of which would become an aspect of my everyday life as a vampire. That was another reason I was grateful to have Riftan by my side. Most specifically when it came to the dreadful new things—which reminded me: "Wait, Europe… So, we will have to take a plane? Isn't a jet engine, like, the loudest thing in existence?"

"Ah, yes, but I got you a present." Riftan held up a box that had previously been none of my concern.

My curiosity heightened, though I was already full of excited jitters. "A present?" Taking the box, I quickly deciphered that the contents were a pair of noise-cancelling headphones—high-quality ones, at that.

"You'd probably be fine without them since you've come so far, but this way you don't have to stress about it, and they'll be more effective than the lousy old ones you've been using."

"Thank you!" I admired the box, and my worries about flying faded away.

Now waiting would be the hardest part, since sunset was still three hours away. It was, however, a necessary wait, since I couldn't safely go out into the daylight. I wasn't sure that I'd ever get used to the whole inability to go in the sun thing, but that was another one of those things Riftan assured me I'd adjust to. It also wouldn't be forever, as he promised me an eventual tryst into the sunlight with the help of witch's magic— whatever the hell that meant—and I was sure that it didn't mean getting the spell thing like he had. I was supposed to *really* earn that—as he'd told me—but supposedly there were lots of other magical options for safely venturing into the sunlight as a vampire. Any of those were more likely the method he'd offer me when the time came. That is, if he truly did plan on keeping his promise. I couldn't imagine *never* seeing the sun again—the idea was melancholy.

That evening, we stopped by my apartment to pick up some stuff before we were off to the airport. I felt a little forlorn to be leaving everything I knew behind—both my belongings and life as I knew it. I was certain, though, the adventure ahead would be greater than any life I could have had in Creswell. For that reason, I didn't have to look back, and that liberated me from all the weight on my shoulders.

When we got to the airport, I was surprised to pull into the far left terminal, where they departed private planes. Instead of asking a million questions like I usually would, I simply gave

Riftan a curious look.

"What? Did you think we were going to be flying in a cramped municipal plane with a hundred wretched humans?" His tone was more humorous than the anger his words might have denoted.

"Well, yes, to be honest. What else would I have thought?"

We pulled through a large metal gate and were all the way on the tarmac before Riftan parked the car. Mere feet ahead waited a sleek private jet, its lights illuminating a set of steps poised for boarding at the entrance door. On the top step, several men in dark suits filed out and down the stairs. They then stood idle, limbs straight and attentive like large, mysterious bodyguards in waiting. Riftan exited the car and one of the men advanced to open my door. He remained motionless until I stepped out into the night, only then closing the door behind me. Silent but gesturing, he directed me toward the boarding stairs.

Riftan was at my side in that instant, stating, "Well, consider this your first formal lesson then: you have the power to get whatever you want now. Be it a private jet, new car, or anything you desire—there is always a way to get your hands on it if you know what you're doing." He snapped his fingers at the large man who stood by the car door. The man rushed over to Riftan. When they locked eyes, Riftan spoke slowly and clearly, "See to it that Ms. Cowitz gets anything she wants for the duration of our flight."

Without a nod or any other acknowledgment of Riftan's order, the man turned to me, his eyes void of any significant thought or emotion, and asked, "Is there anything I can do for you?"

I may have thought that this man was taught obedience for his line of work, but there was a look in his eyes that made me think twice. It was the same dead look that each of the suited stewardesses and bodyguard-looking patrons shared.

"No, I'm fine—" I tried to assure the man, but Riftan interrupted.

"Tell him to bark like a dog."

"Why would I do that?"

"To see that he will do it."

Riftan was only confirming what I'd come to believe. "You thralled him, didn't you? Are they all thralled?"

"Yes, of course they are. That's how you get what you want—by tricking the minds of daft mortals." He spoke with the same prideful tone he often used when discussing humans.

"Great," I said with some degree of sarcasm.

Riftan paid no mind to my response and added, "You have to tell him something though, or he's going to be absolutely beside himself the entire trip."

Sure enough, the man hadn't moved from his spot, eyes pinned on me like he was awaiting my every move. "Go make sure my bags get safely onto the plane," I directed, quickly adding, "Please?" Though he'd already scurried away to do what I'd asked.

Seeing that Riftan had already made it up the long metal stairs and was entering the plane, I jogged my way up behind him. "When do I get to learn how to thrall people like that?"

Ducking inside the private jet, I was struck with a jaw dropping sight. The interior was spacious, as big as I'd ever imagined a passenger plane, yet instead of endless rows of seats, there were two couches lining the walls and a table on the left. Fluffy armchairs were positioned across from the couches, and two more were neatly arranged side by side at the table. The entire space was adorned in a clean and sleek grey tone, making the plane seem more extravagant than any apartment I had ever owned.

"Don't get ahead of yourself." Riftan sat by the table and motioned for me to take the seat next to him. The private jet had left me so stunned, I could barely recall what Riftan was telling me not to get ahead on. Raising my eyebrows, I waited for him to continue. "There are a lot of things you'll have to learn before you can effectively undertake the art of thralling. Be patient with the progression of things, will you?"

"Fine." I took my seat next to Riftan and watched as several servants boarded the plane. One of them being the large man who'd been thralled to obey my every whim.

While three of our entranced companions took their seats in a separate cabin by the entrance, the large man sat only feet from us and trained his eyes right on me. I smiled, his stare making my muscles tense. There was no response from his blank expression, not even a blink crossing his eyes.

"Why is he so fixated on me?" I whispered to Riftan, avoiding the unyielding gaze.

Riftan shrugged, his errant shoulder nearly bopping me in the chin. "It happens sometimes. Everyone responds a little differently to hypnosis. Given the type of demand, who you're demanding, and the thoughts and emotions of the one giving the demand, the outcome can be different each time. Some become hyper-focused on the task given, as this gentleman obviously has. He'd also previously been thralled to have little emotion whilst accompanying our flight, as have the others, which aids in altering the memories they have of our interactions, so that could influence his attentiveness as well."

"Well, can you make him stop?"

"And why would I do that? He's not hurting anyone—unless you ask him to. Take advantage of this. You've got someone who will accommodate your *every* desire. Besides, I gave his thralling a deadline. He'll be over it after we land."

"Ugh." I wasn't ready for a nearly twenty-something-hour flight with some stranger never taking his eyes off me.

Doing my best to zone out everything, including him, as we readied for departure, I slipped my new headphones over my ears. Above the unyielding gaze of the thralled gentleman, Riftan was the hardest thing to ignore as he slipped his hand over my jean-clad thigh. He knew I was nervous about this venture, but he had a strange way of showing his vigilance. I much favored his cordial touch over him basically thralling me a slave.

Without sparing him a glance, I dropped my hand over his. I *could* probably afford to relax a little. With Riftan by my side, I had a feeling there wasn't anything I couldn't handle.

THERE ARE BETTER WAYS OF
ENGAGING YOUR SENSE OF
TOUCH

I'D NEVER BEEN in an airplane before—not even with Johnny. While the spacious private jet Riftan had procured for us could hardly be considered typical air travel, I still had first-time jitters.

Though the noise canceling headphones over my ears did numb out the engines' roar, I still knew it was there, and that made me a little twitchy under my blanket cocoon. Maybe Riftan saw that, and maybe that's why he decided to slip me a short, clear glass in combination with a convincing nod toward it. Pulling my headphones down, I sat up and took it from him. "What's this?"

"Gin." He smiled. "It's the best liquor I could find in the

cabin."

My nose scrunched at the thought. I'd had one too many bad experiences with gin—you could say I was getting too old for that kind of liquor. "I prefer the frilly mixed kind of drinks."

"You haven't tasted any liquors since you turned. Your opinion might have changed as your tastebuds have. I can assure you that gin is one of the better."

My face hardly relaxed from its appalled state as I brought the glass up to my nose to have a smell. While my taste buds were dulled, my sense of smell was so much stronger, and smelling something before I tasted it was always my first and worst mistake. The pungent sting of alcohol burned my nostrils, instantly springing water to my eyes.

That was stupid.

Riftan wore a melodramatic look but said nothing, which was generous of him.

Shaking off my revulsion, I took a drink; curiosity got the better of me, wondering how the taste would compare to what I expected. While I'd anticipated the strong bitter and somewhat piny bite I remembered gin to have, that wasn't at all what I tasted. This had the burn of alcohol but dimmed to a hardly notable degree; it was smooth—almost sweet.

"Weird. It's actually good," I agreed, shock highlighting my tone.

"Told you," Riftan gloated. "Bitters are sweeter, and sweets are more bitter. That includes alcoholic beverages, so you probably won't prefer the sugary ones anymore."

That was a bummer to hear. I'd always loved a good

mixer—maybe a mimosa.

Though I'd started to get used to the changes in my taste buds and how that affected what I wanted to eat, I still longed for the taste of sweets again. I didn't need to eat to sustain myself, and I only really needed to drink blood to stave off hunger, but sometimes I thought cake would really hit the spot better than a gallon of blood ever could. Unfortunately, I would no longer enjoy cake the way I used to; but the sweet, serendipitous taste of my next sip of gin was nearly enough to stave off a cake craving, which was odd given my former familiarity with both cake and gin.

Loosening up, I sunk into the plush couch around me. The normal buzz of a straight beverage like gin would usually affect me quickly, especially at the rate in which I was suckling on the tasty treat. When it didn't, I queried, "Wait, is this going to affect me the same as it would have before?" Everything about my body had changed so much that I wasn't sure I could get drunk anymore.

Riftan let out a rich, warm chuckle. "If you're asking if you can get drunk, then yes, you could if you had enough, but inversely, you won't stay that way for long. Alcohol is, in itself, a poison, and you'll heal from its effects exponentially faster now."

"I suppose that's good because otherwise this"—I raised the glass of gin—"could be dangerous."

"Enjoy it." He raised his glass until it clinked against mine. "You don't have to be so high-strung all the time."

I'd always thought of myself as the opposite, so it was

ironic Riftan would label me as high-strung. Though, I supposed the only side of me he'd ever seen was the one that hid underneath a blanket 24/7.

Multiple glasses of gin later and my anxiety was a thing of the past, and the tension over my senses was long gone. Unfortunately, I did sober rather quickly, and the drinking process would have to be restarted once I could feel my muscles winding tight again. A few cycles of that and nearly eighteen hours in a skyborne metal tube—no matter how extravagant—had proven to make even me stir crazy.

By the time we were landing, I was raring to get out of that plane and hit the town, still riding my most recent drunken cycle. As though he were taking advantage of my newfound enthusiasm, Riftan didn't spare a moment to take me directly into the center of the city. Our belongings were left to the thralled attendants and Riftan insisted they'd make it to our place before we got there—wherever "there" was. The only information I'd gotten was that we were staying in a condo in the city somewhere, but I supposed that's all I'd understand anyway. It's not like I knew anything about where we were. We were in a whole new country—hell, a whole new continent. And it was so much different from my little Creswell.

At least, different is what I'd expected it to be, but as we drove through Prague's city streets under the shroud of night, it resembled nothing more than what I was used to back home.

The buildings were all constructed in a similar fashion, some smaller and concrete and some skyscrapers of glass and metal. The sidewalks hugged buildings and were dotted. with decorative trees. I'd never been anywhere else, so I didn't know what I was expecting, but I'd expected it to be *different*. Instead, the only difference I'd noticed was that I couldn't read any of the street signs.

As if the universe sensed my disappointment, it began morphing the horizon before my very eyes. Slowly at first, one or two old, gothic buildings popped up on the hillside out my passenger window. Each one was set apart from the rest by a bright light that cast the stone in yellow, separating it from the darkness of a moonless night. Sharp crenelations poked the sky, so totally polar from the chopped, flat roof of a Creswell skyscraper. A wide river ran adjacent, multiple bridges crossing its span, one of which we were driving over, giving me a fantastic view of the rest.

Pressing my nose against the window, I took in every bit of the spectacle. It was everything I'd anticipated… it was more.

I could only imagine the way the city might look in the daylight, illuminated by more than some measly colored bulbs. I wished I could conquer the sun for one day to see the true beauty of the sprawling man-made creation.

For fear of burning alive, I wouldn't get that, but I would get to see it like this, lit up in its own gothic, glorious way. Be it artificial, there was still something magnificent about how each perfectly aimed spotlight highlighted the archways and peaks characterizing those thousand-year-old buildings.

Soon we were among them, and they were not a distant vision but a looming reality that crowded the skinny cobbled streets.

As Riftan parked the car along the street, I swung open my door and hopped onto the sidewalk. The city before me beckoned, and I felt the impulse to dance my way through its cobbled streets. I wanted to marvel at the arched windows of each storefront, memorize the many statues that lined the medieval architecture, and smell every culturally unique pastry curated in the bakeries—even if I knew I'd hate the way they tasted. However, Riftan was quick to catch me by the arm, warning me once again "not to get ahead of myself."

Telling a drunk girl who'd never left her little town *to not get ahead of herself* in the center of downtown Prague was the most irritating concept he could have come up with.

"I took you here to explore," Riftan agreed with a stern brow. "But you must calm down. There are going to be a lot of people out, even at night, so I need you collected. Understand?"

I nodded, my loose hair bouncing against my face as I exaggerated the movement. I'd survived a plane ride without a care in the world. Not to mention there'd been several other humans with us then, too. Never once had I considered eating them, so that was one less problem to be concerned with.

As if to prove that wasn't the problem Riftan was hinting at, a trolly car zoomed by, ringing a bell before driving over the crosswalk ahead. That chime alone was enough to make my ears feel like bleeding. What was worse was that I could hear every single voice from within the bus-like vehicle. The volume of them wasn't the painful part, but the clutter of overlapping speech was. Without meaning to, I shrunk into my secondary security blanket—Riftan.

Still cowering, I fought my own convictions to not give up. I wanted to stretch my limits, no matter how scared my body was of it. Riftan's hands gripped my shoulders, gently pushing me out of his bubble of safety. With that little gesture, he'd also deemed it time for me to face what I'd been avoiding.

Summoning all the courage I could muster, I squared my shoulders and released a steady breath, displaying the composure Riftan had requested of me. He nodded and guided me down the sidewalk.

Still early evening, the streets were lit by artificial lamps and still held a substantial gathering of people. Passing by them, I could hear every soul's breath in cadence with their heartbeats. I'd gotten used to the sound of my own heart beating in my chest, and Riftan's, too, but these were different. They were slow and intense, a different tempo from what I'd become accustomed to.

In the open square where bodies gathered in masses to admire the looming gothic architecture, I maintained the poise I'd hoped to have in a public setting. The sights, sounds, and smells weren't consuming me. They were merely background sounds, only slightly more hectic and loud than your typical white noise. I'd even been able to appreciate the little tour Riftan was taking me on, showing off the most iconic buildings in the main square with an in-depth and personal history of each of them.

When the street narrowed, we were forced to push past a group of people so thick that there wasn't a substantial pathway between them. My heart raced before ever getting near them, but my fear of losing Riftan in the throng kept my feet in pace with his. When the women were cackling loud and the men's baritone voices boomed close to my ears, I pinched my arm to distract from the muss.

"You're doing quite well," Riftan offered after we'd cleared the large gathering of people unscathed.

I looked up to see his sincere eyes searching for any inclination of discomposure. "Yes, I'm fine." I squeezed the flesh on my arm once more to thoroughly disregard any growing anxiety that made the smells ripen and the floodlights burn against my fragile eyes.

"Are you pinching yourself?" His eyes fell to my hands, and he narrowed his gaze.

"Yes." I dropped my hands away from each other. "It helps lessen everything else."

"I suppose that's one way to distract yourself. I'm impressed with your ingenuity, but I do believe there are better ways of engaging your sense of touch. It doesn't have to be *pain*." His statement thickened with lascivious intent, heightening the tingle that followed his fingers as they slipped into mine and gave them a squeeze.

Although I didn't believe he had meant what he said with any carnal denotations, it was hard not to take it that way when his tone was always laced with some sultry drawl. That with his exotic accent was enough to make me weak in the knees a million times over. He was right though: there were better ways to distract than pinching myself. All I needed was for him to speak to me that way, and I didn't need his touch to add to it— though I *would* be interested in more of it.

And now *distracted* was an understatement.

FROM THE LARGE open windows in our spendy-looking condo on the outskirts of town, you could see the gothic city in all its majesty. There was even an ornate balcony to overlook it—if the sun wasn't out.

Inside, it was similar to Riftan's old apartment—small but luxurious. There was still a loft, but instead of harboring a bedroom, it held an extra room that Riftan suggested using as a study. Below it, there were the two bedrooms, each similar in size and both with their own attached bathroom. Our bags had been dropped off, and there was no one around to be seen, which led me to wonder if those who had been thralled were now off and on their merry way.

Before the sun rose, the automatic blinds had drawn

themselves over the tall windows, shielding the room from natural light. If it weren't for the prominent silver clock on the wall, determining the time of day within would have been impossible.

I poked around the condo until that clock indicated that it was around eight in the morning. Riftan was less curious, forgoing a look around for a spot on the couch, where he thumbed through a journal. He gave me space to explore, but by the time I was admiring the soil of the potted plants by the TV, Riftan was watching me over his pages instead of reading them.

"What?" A smile crept onto my lips as I straightened up.

"This little condo can't be so interesting."

I shrugged. Anything new was interesting to me.

"Go to your room and get some rest, will you?" Riftan prompted.

"Why? It's only eight in the morning?"

"Because we are going out tonight and I want you to be rested." He dropped the journal onto the large oak coffee table in front of the couch. "Besides, you need to adapt to sleeping during the day. You're a night dweller now, after all."

"Fine." Though I found it unlikely that I could sleep under the cryptic pretenses of our pre-planned night out, I went to my room. Even if I couldn't sleep, I could unpack and settle into my new home. By the sounds of it, we'd live there for a while, so there was no sense in feeling like a stranger in that room.

As night fell over the sky once again, the automated blinds rose, and my room was illuminated with the moon's gentle glow tickling every darkened surface. The subtle white light spreading from the tall windows provided a strangely serene awakening, unlike the sun's piercing rays, which I was accustomed to waking up to for the last twenty-three years. Back in Riftan's Creswell apartment, I mostly slept at random times—whenever I was too tired to face anymore of my senses for the day. Riftan kept the blinds drawn whenever I slept, so I hadn't adjusted to this rising with the moon thing yet. Thankfully, Prague's alluring nightlife assisted that passive alarm. It whispered through my thick-paned windows, beckoning with the gentle songs of humanity laughing, shuffling, clinking, and singing from the streets, nearby bars, and local apartments, where people were settling down for dinner.

Out in the kitchen, leaning against a dark marble countertop, I found Riftan pouring a glass of red wine. Intricate hanging pendants cast him in a radiant glow, spotlighting his dapper attire. He'd swapped out his dark jeans for dress pants and a grey button-up shirt rolled up to his elbows. Though his dark, ear length hair was typically tossed and parted somewhere off to the side, this time it looked to have been combed back loosely—some sort of product holding it there—and in the back, his waves were brushed out and laid flatter than usual.

With a glance, he questioned me, "Why aren't you dressed?

Didn't I say we're going out?"

I examined the casual shorts and tank top that I'd gone to bed in. While in the presence of someone like Riftan, who I had admittedly adopted a *minor* crush on, I should have been a bit more mindful about how I dressed. But, given the confidence I'd adopted from my transition, clothing very rarely crossed my mind. Ever since being turned into a vampire, I felt nothing but *stunning* in my looks. My entire being had been upgraded—appearance and all.

Whenever I looked in the mirror, I had to stop and stare at the way my skin shone like a porcelain doll lit from the inside—void of the smallest blemish or pore. My hair also glowed like golden fibers of silk and my eyes were brighter than when I'd been human—like literal emeralds shoved into my eye sockets. Standing there in my lousy shorts, my legs gleamed like they'd been layered in body oil. I looked like a freaking celebrity—so yeah, maybe I'd been a little lazy about the way I dressed, but I could do that now because my vampiric resplendency made up for it.

When Riftan slid the glass of wine across the counter, I took a seat and his beverage offering.

Looking over him, I finally answered his question. "Well, per usual, you didn't give me any detail as to what, when, or where, so how was I supposed to know that I needed to fancy up?" Taking a small swig of the wine—without sniffing it—I was pleased by the taste that once in my life may have been described as astringent.

"It's Sagrantino," Riftan noted without question.

I'd tasted Sagrantino before and detested the bite of it. In fact, I'd never been much of a wine drinker in general, even when I had to fake it in front of Johnny's family.

"But," he continued, "In terms of 'what, when, and where:' out, as soon as you're dressed, and wherever you want."

"So, I suppose since you're all dressed up, then I should be too?" He'd made me pack for this occasion, so I shouldn't have been too surprised—as I wasn't.

"Yes. But hurry up, I'm getting bored of waiting for you."

"Okay, fine, I'll need a minute to choose what to—"

"Wear that black dress I saw you pack."

I could feel my cheeks redden at his request. He'd been right over my shoulder when I was packing my things, but I didn't think he'd paid such close attention. "Which one?" A lot of my dresses were black because once upon a time I'd been a natural red head, and black was by far the easiest color to style with the hue of my hair.

Since dating Johnny, I'd dyed my hair blonde, as that was what he preferred. I never did let go of my affinity for a little black dress though, even if I never planned on going back to my natural color.

Riftan answered with a little smile. "The one with the shoulder things."

"The off-the-shoulder dress?" I corrected.

He beamed from ear to ear. "Yeah, that's the one!"

"If you say so," I mumbled, turning away to hide the scarlet on my face. With that, I took my glass of wine to the bedroom, where I changed into the dress he'd suggested. It was slim and short with a slit on the thigh. The off-the-shoulder sleeves draped tautly against my arms with a regal sweetheart neckline. It was by far one of my fancier dresses and I'd planned on saving it for future outings—not necessarily our first night in town. But if that's what Riftan wanted, I would oblige. Especially since I'd never had a man take an interest in what I wore except to say, "That dress makes your ass look like a rare cut of meat," which was regrettably one of Johnny's favorite lines—whatever that meant.

Since I was already so dressed up, I decided to wear my posh matching black heels and some minimal but sparkly gold jewelry.

When I came back out into the main room, Riftan took me by the hand and spun me in a circle, bearing me his cheeky fang-filled smile. His voice draped a soft tone from parted lips, "You look breathtaking, love."

The only breath taken was mine when he'd said that so casually. The way the endearment "love" rolled off his lips so skillfully would probably have put any ordinary girl in a coma. My stronger, more resilient, vampire body was still weakened to near oblivion. Whether the word was meant for me specifically or simply a figure of speech, I couldn't help but feel gooey inside. With my mind a useless pile of mush, I merely grinned in response.

Riftan paid no mind to my sudden stupor and led us out into the night hand in hand.

Instead of taking the car like when we'd arrived at our condo, we walked out the front exit and onto the cobblestone sidewalk. Glowing streetlamps were the only source of light overhead, since the sun had set almost an hour earlier. Under the shroud of night, the streets still hummed with activity as night owls walked alongside us and taxis zoomed through the narrow street.

Leading the way, Riftan never strayed from his express route through the city. Seeing that he seemed confident in the direction we were headed, I stayed quiet and content with my hand wrapped in his.

When we stopped outside of a lively-looking social club with glass windows and an array of go-lucky patrons, Riftan turned his attention to me. "How do you feel? Nervous?" he asked.

I shrugged. The number of voices from inside hummed at a low volume, all conversing at different speeds about diverse topics. Fiddling with my skirt in my free hand, I gave him a small fib. "No, I'm fine."

Raising his brows and giving a satisfied nod, Riftan held open the door and motioned me inside. Sound funneled out the open door to meet me before I'd ever taken a step. The glass-fronted building had done wonders for killing the level of noise between there and the streets. My immediate urge was to turn tail and run, but I bit back on it and stepped into the madness.

That little social club's volume was nothing compared to what I'd experience in a dance club, or even a karaoke bar. The music was relatively low—for nightlife—and everyone inside had their wits about them. Those who spoke in groups did so at an appropriate volume, and to any mortal, it may have been considered an Arcadian establishment. Patrons all dressed in their best and fit in impeccably among the chic silver aesthetic that sprawled from the backlit glass bar to the glimmering crystal chandelier over the dance floor—which was really the center seating area sans a couple of tables. It resembled the kind of place you'd find trust fund kids and corporation owners out on trysts with their mistresses. That being said, I was glad this was our first stop. It was the right amount of mildly hectic to ease me into my sensitive senses.

"Come, get a drink with me," Riftan offered, making his way to the bar and adding, "It'll help you relax a little."

Am I really wearing my emotions right out on my sleeve? "Thanks." I took a seat, and he ordered me a drink I'd never heard of. He'd been correct thus far about what tasted good to my new tastebuds, so I didn't question it. "Have you been here before?" I asked, wondering how we'd meandered right to the place.

"No. I haven't been in Prague since 1943. I came here off a recommendation from a friend."

"You seemed to know exactly where it was."

"Yeah, this is the same building as a bar I've been to many times. So, you could say I *have* been here, but 'here' was slightly different back then."

"Got it."

The bartender returned with two small glasses full of dark liquor, plus four shot glasses of something clear.

"Why'd you get shots?" I complained.

"I told you. It's so that you can relax a little." He took one of the glasses and passed it over before passing two of the shot glasses as well.

"Riftan, you don't know me that well. I most certainly am not a 'relaxed' drunk."

"Oh please, you were drunk three separate times on the flight over here; I know exactly what kind of drunk you are."

"This establishment doesn't seem like the kind that would tolerate my kind of drunk," I insisted.

"Good. That will be all the more fun." He beamed, resembling a boy asking to go play with his friends. More so when he added, "Come on, Leanne. Won't you have some fun with me?"

There was not a single cell in my body that had the strength to say no to that. "Ugh fine." I kicked back both shots, and he did the same, as if finally getting permission to do so.

Not minutes later, he was beckoning me toward the small dance floor in the center of the social club. Had it not been for the pleading look in his eyes, welcoming me to oblige, Riftan may not have convinced me so easily. But, as it was, he was hard to deny.

More people had flooded onto the floor than when we'd first arrived. Merely swaying in the heap had us bumping into multiple bodies. That may have been torturous without a distraction as significant as Riftan pulling me close, buffering the clump of humans around us. He didn't show any hesitation in dancing a little dirty with me, putting his hips on mine and swaying slowly until I could feel every curve of him pressed against me.

Lightning whipped up my spine, kickstarting my heart,

making it thrum like it did for no one but Riftan. It threatened to pound out of my chest—luckily, loud enough to cover the sounds of other human forms in the mass. Conforming to him, I welcomed the panic that stirred in my abdomen every time he drove his hips into me. Eventually, I was *giddy* for it, completely disregarding the other people in the room and using every ounce of my brainpower to feel the way he molded against me.

After multiple songs, when the shots had already set in and ebbed, we took a break and made our way back to the bar. I was giggling like a bubbly schoolgirl and Riftan, likewise, wasn't shy to show his fangs even in a crowded room full of mortals.

At the bar, Riftan took a seat and dragged my stool closer to his. "Okay, now that you're comfortable, and coming down from your drunkenness a little bit"—Riftan grabbed me by the chin, pulling my gaze to focus on his—"there's something important I want to teach you tonight."

"Okay," I breathed, still flighty from moments before.

"It's by far the most important thing you're going to learn, and it's the first real thing I'm going to teach you." His tone was low, furrowed brows denoting a new seriousness.

Stifling my enthusiasm, I buried my smile to the best of my ability and nodded, attempting to match his tone. "Okay, Riftan, tell me what it is already!"

"I'm going to teach you how to feed from a living person."

BE A GOOD LITTLE MEAL, WON'T YOU

"LIKE... BITE THEM and drink their blood? But won't that kill them?" *Like it killed me.*

"Yes, theoretically, biting them is indeed a death sentence since you can't control the venom you inject when you bite, but it's not like you'll be killing them on the spot with your bare hands."

"I don't want to kill anyone. That'd weigh too heavy on my conscience. It'd be unbearable." Killing seemed like something I could put my foot down on, even if Riftan wanted me to do it.

"Look"—Riftan's hand slid across my cheek, leaving goosebumps in its wake—"I have a conscience too, but given what you are now, there are some things you're going to have to get over. Without blood, you will lose control, and it's not enough to simply survive off what you can get in a bottle or a bag. One day, you'll find yourself needing to know how to feed from humans, whether you like it or not."

"I'm serious. I can't do it, Riftan."

"It's not as bad as it sounds, I promise. Hear me out, okay?" His eyes were gentle and kind in as they prodded me to obey, and so I did—listening for the moment. "The world is filled with more bad people than you'll ever truly know. I can promise you that from my seven hundred-and-something years here. I'm talking about the kind who rape, murder, and take advantage of anyone who they deem less than them: people who wouldn't be missed by a single soul on this planet if they disappeared tonight. If you could find one of those people, wouldn't you think it justice for this world if you could rid it of them? And in turn, you get a meal—you get to let them contribute to the circle of life and maybe make their worthless existence mean something. So, I'm not asking you to kill some saint who volunteers their every waking moment to charity. But what if you kill *one* very, *very* bad person instead?"

"And what if I don't find anyone who fits that description?"

He patted my cheek. "My sweet, naïve girl. I promise we will have no shortage of scumbags for you to choose from. I'm sure there are at least five that fit the bill in this very bar."

"Fine. If I can find the absolute worst person I've ever met—"

Riftan started to snicker like he'd won, and I lifted my

finger to his lips to cut him off.

"—And I mean, the absolute worst! As in the kind whose children will praise his death: Then! Maybe, *only* then, I will agree to take his life."

"Yes, ma'am. That's good enough for me." We sat in silence for a moment, eyes flitting between each other. "Well," Riftan started, "are you going to go look for him, or what?"

"Oh. By myself?"

"Of course. You won't find him with me in tow. Go use those feminine wiles of yours."

Wandering eyes raked over my tightly fitted dress, hinting at the scheme he had in mind.

Some sick part of me thrummed at the idea of freely participating in this little hunt. In the past, I'd thrived on scouting out men at the bars, relishing in the response I could get from a simple bat of my lashes. Since dating Johnny, I hadn't gotten to partake in the activity for fear of getting either myself or the person I was flirting with murdered. I rose from my seat and surveyed the crowded bar. If I didn't find someone who could be deemed a complete scourge to the universe, I wouldn't kill *anyone* that night.

As I made to pass him, Riftan's hand clasped my arm, pulling me close until our noses nearly brushed. "If you find someone who fits the bill, take them through the kitchen and out the back entrance. I'll meet you out there."

"Okay." I watched his lips as they settled close in front of mine—close enough to kiss. It would have been so easy to close the limited distance between us... inches—if that. Maybe then we could forget about this whole killing a human thing and go back to our condo, just the two of us.

Oh, how I'd love to be doing that instead. My stomach started doing flips, butterflies turning to birds until I was swallowing the emotion down like a knot in my throat.

Riftan's lips tipped up into a sultry grin. "Don't look so glum. You can have fun with this. Okay?"

I nodded, took my drink in hand, and wandered out toward the dance floor. That would be the best spot for finding men looking for some ass. If I didn't spot one, I knew some scumbag would come along if I danced alone for long enough, and a scumbag *was* what I was looking for, after all.

The first two guys who came up to dance with me were, for the most part, harmless—annoying, but harmless. After that, I jaunted over to talk to a guy who ended up being an asshole, but not murder worthy. There were more like that, some of which I decided weren't worth my time based on eavesdropped conversations or short interactions.

No matter how long I'd been at it, every time I looked back at the bar, Riftan had his eyes pinned on me, which didn't help take any of the edge off. If only he'd concern himself with someone else for a few minutes, I might have been able to have some fun like he'd suggested, but instead, I felt scrutinized under his watchful gaze.

Taking another look at Riftan, my eyes wandered past his stoic form to settle on a man tucked away in the shadows. He sat in one of the plush booths in the back, a small woman folded so deep under his arm that she almost wasn't visible. Dark brunette ringlets draped her shoulders, an errant few falling over her face. Blinking slow, as if the act was laborious, the girl was continually sinking farther against this man, her head falling cockeyed in an unnatural position.

I used my enhanced senses to hone in on their voices from across the crowded bar. It was difficult to pinpoint them with so much going on, but all I had to do was match the voices to their lips moving. Then, I was able to isolate their conversation from those of the masses.

"I can take you back to my place, baby. Don't even worry about it," the man whispered to the girl, gripping her head so she couldn't look away.

"No. I want to go home. Please," she breathed, hardly able to keep her words together.

"It's okay. I'll call a couple of friends and we will take care of you."

"No…"

I was in front of their table in a heartbeat, a millisecond, less than the blink of an eye. My sudden appearance startled the man, but he was quick to regain his composure and share his sleazy smile with me.

"Hello there, beautiful. What can I do for you?" He laid on the cheese, acting as though he was some hit movie star. In truth, he was hardly cute enough to pass as an extra.

Matching that energy, I leaned over his table, showing off the ladies in my low-cut dress. "I noticed you a little bit ago, and I was wondering if you would buy me a drink?"

It'd been a while since I'd flirted with anyone. Luckily, I

didn't think it mattered much how rusty I was, given my newfound vampiric glory. All I really had to do was smile and flash some of my ethereal, smooth skin.

The man looked torn, glancing down at the girl under his arm. He hesitantly answered, "Well, I've already got someone sitting with me here. Can we take—"

"So, tell her to get lost. I'd prefer your company all to myself." I added a wink.

"Okay," he abided obediently, practically wagging his nonexistent tail in excitement. Without any care for the brunette's condition, he pushed her out of the booth. She wobbled, hardly able to stand on her own.

Pretending not to care how she looked, I slid into her spot next to the man. I quickly looked back at Riftan and tipped my head at the girl, who was now leaning against the wall and trying to make her way toward the door. "Already on it," he said under his breath, leaving the bar in a rush to help the girl.

"Thank you," I whispered, aware that if I'd heard him at such a low volume, he would probably hear me as well.

He turned back and winked before taking the girl under his arm and pushing out the door. I sincerely hoped his version of helping was the same as mine. I was confident that he wouldn't take advantage of her, but he *was* the one encouraging me to kill someone, so it was hard to decipher his true intentions.

"What was that, baby?" the sleaze ball next to me asked, slipping his arm around my shoulder.

"Oh, nothing. Drinks?"

"Yeah, sure thing. I've got some right here." He pushed

over a drink already on the table, forgoing ordering any new ones. That alone was suspicious. Bringing it to my nose, I did my best to ignore the sting in my eyes, instead smelling for any sign of tampering. What I found was a subtle hint of salt in a drink that shouldn't have been salty—something nobody would notice unless they had super-powerful senses like I did. That girl wasn't drunk; she was drugged.

"Thanks." I took a small sip, trusting that most poisons and drugs wouldn't have as much of an effect on me. "So," I began a conversation with the man, hoping to ensure that he was indeed the ultimate pig I'd been looking for, "what do you do for work?"

Puffing out his chest, the man began his spiel like it was rehearsed in the mirror. "I'm an entrepreneur. Last year I had to expand into an offshore account to hold all my money. That and I've been investing in some real estate. It pays the bills and buys my yachts." The way he exaggerated his expression, showing all thirty-two of his teeth at the mention of money, reminded me tragically of Johnny. That could mean his means of collecting said wealth was not as licit as he was trying to make it seem—either that or he was lying altogether about having it.

"What about family? You got any kids?"

"Probably. I don't know." He sipped his drink, rolling his eyes like he was already losing interest in our conversation. Apparently, all he wanted was a quiet piece of arm candy.

Deciding to move things along at his speed, I leaned in and kissed him. He definitely *wasn't* cute, so it was preferable that way—I didn't have to look at him with our lips locked. Luckily, he did smell nice enough, like expensive cologne. And holy shit was he a good kisser, his lips leading mine only a beat ahead, making me hurry to keep up. I suppose that was probably because the piece of shit had some practice on poor defenseless girls before me.

I decided to solidify my choice in killing him. Feigning utter innocence, I pulled away and hunched over, really playing at my act. "I'm feeling tired all of a sudden. Maybe I should go home."

"If you're feeling tired, I can take you somewhere more private so you can rest. How's that sound?" His voice was so cocky and sure. He knew exactly what he was doing. He'd clearly done it a thousand times.

"Thank you. I'm okay to stay here, though." I continued my performance, keeping my voice low and weak.

Closing the distance between us, the man kissed me again. This time harder and with more intent, his tongue coaxing at my teeth. It was almost enjoyable—kissing that dirtbag. Making out with someone I had the intent to kill had jitters creeping over my flesh and soaking into my bones. It was enthralling. *I am going to kill this piece of shit.*

When his smarmy hands started getting friendly with the edge of my skirt, I did my best not to simply kill him right then and there. Instead, I told him, "Maybe we *should* leave. I need some air."

"Okay," he agreed, following me eagerly as I got up and led him to the kitchen like Riftan had told me to. Past sizzling pans and pungent ovens, I tugged my prey through the kitchen and to a door in the back illuminated by a red exit sign. We burst into the alley, a crisp late-night chill embracing me with release from the club's muggy atmosphere.

Before I'd fully taken in a breath of fresh air, the man I had by the hand was stifling me, pulling me into him and shoving my back against the brick wall. His lips were all over mine, his hands not hesitating a moment before they were on an explorative journey of everywhere he'd left unventured on my body.

It nearly made me laugh—how desperate he was. "Do you like taking advantage of defenseless girls?" My tone was meek as I looked up at him from under my lashes.

"Shut up. It was you who wanted this." He smothered me with a sloppy kiss.

Retreating from his lips, I played a little more. "And what if I begged you to stop?"

"Don't act like such a teasing slut." He practically spit the words out before grabbing for my chest.

Straightening my spine, I beamed. "Okay, that's all I needed to hear!" Catching his grabby hand in mine, I pushed him away with more than a little force. He went sailing through the air, only stopping when he hit the far wall of the alley with a soft *plunk*. I didn't have a ton of experience with my new and improved vampire strength, and I honestly hadn't expected him to fly so far—but I didn't regret it. I giggled to myself. "Oops."

The scumbag scrambled to find footing in a pile of loose trash bags that he'd landed in. "You fucking bitch," he muttered.

I crossed the alley to meet the spot where he still fumbled

in garbage on the ground. He didn't cower or recede, which I took as insolence in the presence of me, who so obviously outmatched him. "That's no way to talk to a lady," I complained, reaching down to claw my fist around the man's neck and lift him back to his feet since he was too insufferable to get up on his own.

In a puff of grey smoke, Riftan materialized down the alley. Hands in his pockets, he sauntered up. "Well, it looks like you have this under control on your own."

The man in my hands squirmed, making a fuss. "Who the hell are you?"

We both ignored him as he fought to pull my hand from his throat.

"Yeah," I agreed with Riftan, "but I don't have any idea what to do with him now. I was waiting for you."

Riftan nodded. "Well, sorry to keep you waiting then. You can put him down now."

Doing as Riftan said, I tossed the man to the cobbled ground, away from the cushion of trash bags that he'd been lucky enough to fall on the last time I flung him. He crumpled to the street in a heap and gulped for air, not even attempting to regain his footing this time.

"You're sure this is the one?" Riftan confirmed.

"Yeah, I'm sure." I poked the heel of my shoe into his ribs and the guy groaned. "He's a real piece of shit."

Taking that as confirmation, Riftan turned to the man, who was slowly hobbling back to his feet. Riftan only took one step to put the two of them eye to eye, though he was looking down on the vile predator who was nearly a foot shorter. "This is her first time. Be a good little meal, won't you?"

The man got on his knees and stared directly through me, completely blank to the world, not a single thought or idea behind his eyes, entirely thralled.

"So, do I just... bite him?" I asked.

"Yeah, find a vein first." Riftan reached down with two fingers on the human's neck and then pointed to a spot. "It shouldn't be hard with your senses the way they are now. That part comes naturally."

I touched the place where Riftan's fingers sat and sensed the blood flow he'd been referring to. It rushed through this man's veins like a raging river. I could feel and hear exactly all the places where that river crested near his skin—all the places I needed to bite him.

Thankfully, Riftan had him kneel, so I only needed to bend over a little to put my lips to his neck.

He was soft under my teeth, but his flesh took more effort to break than I'd expected. I had all the strength in the world, but it felt like I was tearing into him, masticating the flesh under my teeth. Pulling back, I examined the very human-looking bite mark I'd given him. "This doesn't seem right." I looked up at Riftan, whose eyes were intent on where I'd bitten this man.

"Hmm." Leaning in, Riftan hooked his thumb under my lip and pulled it upward. Tilting his head, he admired my teeth. "I forgot that you don't have fangs yet. Well, you do—they are just too small to do anything with. I'll bite him. Then he's all yours. Is that okay with you?"

"Yeah."

Moving past me, Riftan took the man by his shirt collar and hauled him to his feet, only stopping to purse his lips and roll his eyes in the most exasperated way.

"What?" I asked, curiosity staining my tone.

"Ugh. It's nothing… I don't really like biting other men."

The notion seemed foolish, so I scoffed. "Why?"

"What do you want me to say? Because I'm an insecure straight male?" He let out a laden sigh before taking the man's hair and pulling his neck taut to expose the spot where my teeth had marked him. Riftan continued. "No… in all honesty, you shouldn't sexualize your meals. It's improper and yes, some vampires take it much too far, making it something it isn't. It's sustenance, and that's all. Unfortunately, I'm obviously a little guilty of it myself. I merely prefer a comfortable meal to be that of a female. I can't seem to help it."

I hadn't thought of it that way—though I'd never been picky about my sexuality much, either.

Putting his grievance aside, Riftan tucked his head into the man's exposed neck, a trail of blood pouring from the spot where his lips met flesh. The red liquid puddled over the human man's shoulder, fragrant and alarmingly alluring to my sensitive nose. My body naturally itched for a taste of him. Retracting from the river of blood, Riftan shoved the bleeding man back down onto his knees. Blood poured from the two deep punctures on his neck, which dipped into his veins much more effectively than my bite did.

Salivating at the rusty smell in the air, I pounced on the

man the instant Riftan was free of him. While I lapped at the blood excreting from his veins, the man didn't make a peep, only sat there silent and motionless. The thin muscles in his neck didn't tense as they should have under my lips. Instead, they were completely relaxed as I suckled on the wound Riftan had given him. Sucking from the incisions on his flesh, I pulled until I was effectively dragging the lifeblood from him.

The taste was both familiar and not. It was what I knew— what had sustained me for weeks now—but different: fresher, sweeter, more delectable. It was like that one meal you couldn't make at home, but your favorite restaurant does it perfectly. A culinary mystery you can't recreate. I was hooked on it.

I'd never been especially drawn to the blood of humans, but the moment this man's blood touched my tongue, my desire changed. I craved to bleed him. I never wanted to taste anything but him again. I'd rather drink his blood for eternity than ever breathe oxygen again.

While the taste pulled me in, the tingle shackled my bonds to this desire. The sensation was physical, it enraptured me, until it was mental, then it was euphoria in its purest form. The perfect thrum of satisfaction radiating through my limbs from drinking this horrible man's delicious blood was like nothing I'd ever experienced. I felt *everything* and nothing; numb, yet wholly responsive. I was nearly transported to a different plane of existence—my mind ready to fly off so it could stay like this forever.

"Slow down." Riftan's warmth kept me grounded, his breath hot against my ear as he whispered to me, "If you go too fast, it's only going to limit how much you can get out of him. Slow down, and when his heartbeat starts to weaken, you need to stop."

There was no way I was going to be able to stop. I didn't want to. Even with something as enticing as Riftan's lips on my ear, I couldn't stop. No matter how badly I wanted to follow Riftan's every demand flawlessly, I wouldn't pull my lips away from this man until there was nothing left to drink.

Much too soon, Riftan was in my ear again. "I can hear his heartbeat slowing. Stop now."

I groaned, blood gurgling in my throat, but I didn't stop. The idea of pulling my lips away from this source of magical euphoria caused my body to panic, tensing up as I bit into him with an urge to consume everything this man had to offer me. If I couldn't drain him dry, I'd take his flesh from his bones. Anything to have more.

Riftan's fingers wrapped around my shoulders, bearing down until the pain broke through my animalistic trance. Prying me back with more strength than I could fight, Riftan hauled me off the man. "I said stop now."

Gasping for breath, I did my best to lick my lips around each heavy intake so as to not lose any of that mortal's ambrosian blood.

"Are you in control?" Riftan asked, lacing his fingers under my chin and yanking my gaze to focus on only him.

"Ah," I attempted, still out of breath. "Yeah. I'm okay. That was crazy."

"Yeah. You actually did quite well. I've seen others tear

mortals to shreds during their first live feed. It gets exponentially more controllable from here on out, I promise."

Tearing that man to shreds would have been unavoidable if Riftan wasn't there. But my need to please Riftan outweighed my need to devour that human, and the reality of his presence was quick to replace whatever loss of composure I'd just experienced. Still in a blissful kind of daze, I pressed for more of his praise. "Really? I did good?"

"You did." He showed his fangs in a smile that made my whole face flush with warmth. "I'm going to thrall him so that he forgets about this, and then we can head back home, okay?"

"Okay," I agreed, still breathless.

Moments later, Riftan sent the human man on his way after thralling him to get himself cleaned up and out of dodge. I'd made a mess of him: blood stained his collar and seeped from the spots where I'd seemingly clawed into his shoulders during my stupor.

As Riftan had told me, the man would go back home, get sick the next day, and die in twenty-four hours of what a doctor would diagnose as heart failure. I *killed* that man, and I didn't regret it.

I had no emotions for the man I'd sentenced, but something inside of me still panged with guilt—guilt for *not* feeling guilty.

Wrapping his arm through mine as we made our way down the sidewalk, Riftan asked, "How do you feel? Are you doing okay?"

He must have thought I was bothered by what I'd done.

Killing is wrong; I'd said it should be the one thing I didn't have to compromise on. *Killing should bother me.* But the image of slaughtering that man, who was so ready to take advantage of the first low hanging fruit he found, involuntarily brought a smile to my face. "Is it bad that I'm totally fine?"

"No. I'm glad… I was a little worried about you at first. But from what I've seen, I think you're going to be just fine as a vampire."

"Thanks. I think I'm going to be fine as well. This way of life probably suits me—maybe that makes me a terrible person."

"You're not a terrible person. I think you're a great person. You're the type who can overcome any obstacle, big or small. That's why I think you're going to be adept with this new change. That's all I meant."

"Thanks…"

I admired the cobbled city streets as we walked back to our condo. It'd gotten late—or early, depending on how you looked at it. The sun would begin to rise in less than an hour, which meant I needed to be inside *soon*. Looking at the dark sky, I could only see a few stars dotted between the clouds. A cathedral, tall and spired, blocked a portion of my view. I wondered how those beautiful gothic cathedrals looked in the daytime, and something in my heart stirred with the hope of seeing that someday—no matter how trivial it may have been.

I sighed and looked back at Riftan. "Hey, what happened with that girl? Did you get her home?" I asked casually.

"Yeah, I called her a cab and thralled the cabby to make

sure she safely made it home. Why?"

"I wanted to make sure you helped her."

His eyes narrowed on me. "What else would I have done with her?"

"Maybe you chose to drink her blood. How was I supposed to know?"

He scoffed. "*Psh*. She seemed like an innocent enough girl. I wouldn't kill someone like her."

"So, you live off that rule, too? That you only kill bad people?"

"I try to, nowadays. I can't say I've always done it like this, but I'm doing my best."

I cleared my throat, holding back some form of anger that was sinking hot claws into my chest. "Um, excuse me? You bit *me*, remember? Did you deem me a lost cause to society like all the other bad people you kill?"

Riftan dropped my arm and put up his hands in a dramatic show of defenselessness. "I'm sorry! Your situation was a little bit different. Like I said before, I thought you were a hooker."

"Even if I *was* a hooker—though I most certainly am not— sex workers are people, too. And while 'innocent' might not be the best word to describe them, they most certainly don't deserve to be murdered!" I chided.

"Right." Riftan nodded but refused to look me in the eye despite my death stare. "And I'll apologize relentlessly for doing something so rash, but you looked so miserable back then. Call it insensitive to kill someone out of 'mercy,' but I've lived long enough to know that if someone is desperate enough to ask for their death instead of plead for their life, they're probably better off dead anyway."

I had asked him to kill me. So, could I really blame him for doing just that?

He continued, flashing a smile. "And I hardly regret it either. You were very tempting, you tasted good, and you looked so scared it was delightful. And hey, now we are here, and everything worked out for the better. I wouldn't call it a mistake, just a happy accident." It wasn't the first time he'd said that.

I smacked him on the arm for poking fun at my fear. "You're lucky that I'm happy with this outcome, otherwise I'd be very upset with you for saying something like that." And I *was* happy. I was so much happier than I'd ever been before.

It was crazy to think that I'd come by that happiness from my own death.

I'd died, but I'd gained a new life with infinite possibilities. I'd found freedom like I could have never imagined, happiness in my own abilities to overcome, and a companion in Riftan.

This new life with him wasn't the hell he'd warned me it would be. Instead, it was like my own *really* fucked up version of heaven.

LOVE IS AN EMOTION MEANT TO LAST NO MORE THAN A HUMAN LIFETIME

DIAMONDS GLITTERED in a celestial dance with Prague's night lights, all seen from my quiet corner leaning against the windows of our condo. Only the shadows of crenelations pierced through the artwork of the inky canvas created by the dim moonlight. I envisioned how brilliant that scene would be during the day, since I couldn't see it for myself.

"What are you thinking about?" Riftan asked, handing me a small glass of wine.

"About the sun." I released the tiniest laugh under my breath, as though it'd been a joke to myself.

"Do you miss it?"

"Something like that."

He brightened, changing his tone as if he'd moved on to a new subject. "Will you meet me out on the balcony in three minutes?"

Startled by his suddenness, I gave him a look.

Not waiting for my response, he turned tail and scampered off into his room.

Left in the silence of our living room, I figured that meant I was expected on the balcony in three. I couldn't be out there for long, since the sun would snake its fiery tendrils into the sky very soon, but I trusted Riftan to know that.

As I stepped out onto the balcony, the night embraced me with a serene chill. The weaving tapestry of the city and sky was more alive without the separation of glass between me and it. Finding the railing, I leaned into it, reaching my nose toward the unique mineral scents of ancient building stones and the meandering Vltava River.

Only a moment later, Riftan came dashing through the open door like an eager kid on Christmas morning. His hair, though styled earlier that night, flopped over his forehead when he screeched to a halt by my side. It was so far from his usual stoicism that it made me laugh outright. "What's gotten into you?"

He beamed, sharing a smile that lit up his entire face. "It's a surprise. Close your eyes."

I did as he'd said, all the while holding back a stupid, giddy grin of my own. I'd always had an impractical love for surprises.

My senses kindled at the touch of Riftan's fingers on my hair as he gathered it over one of my shoulders. A moment later, something cold draped over my chest. "Okay, you can look now."

Opening my eyes, I looked down at the golden chain wrapped around my neck. Hanging at the end and inlaid in golden prongs was a smooth oval stone about the size of my fingernail. Despite the dim light, the stone still glowed a brilliant amber with swirls of deep orange and flecks of white that flickered like tiny, imprisoned sunbeams. It was beautiful. Maybe not as glamorous as the many shiny things Johnny had once given me, but somehow more amazing than any of those less unique pieces. "What is this?" I asked.

"It's an enchanted sunstone pendant. With it, you can go out in the sun."

I squeaked. "Seriously?"

"Yeah. I was going to wait to give it to you, but I figured there is no harm in giving it to you now."

Tears welled in my eyes; my breath caught in my throat at the prospect of seeing Prague's lively streets in the daylight. "Thank you so much!" I crashed into Riftan with a suffocating hug.

Unphased by my fervor, Riftan patted my hair and held me until my heart beat so rapidly I knew he'd notice my discomposure. Setting his nose against my head, Riftan whispered into my hair. "Now you can finally watch the sunrise with me."

His statement sent me overboard, the butterflies in my stomach going feral for him. I should have pulled away, but I didn't want to be any farther from him. Not to mention, I couldn't look him in his stunning eyes. Not without this exchange ending in some sort of dirty shenanigan.

Gently snaking his hand between us, Riftan pulled my chin from his chest and motioned toward the sky. I tried to ignore the lightness in my head when he smirked, sparking a raw heat in my bone marrow that burned to be closer to him.

When he nudged me further, I responded obediently by shifting my gaze toward the changing sky. What was once a dark indigo, dotted with glimmering stars, now faded to aqua. In the distance, the sleepy city streets reawakened ever so slowly, one trolly honk at a time. Gold and pink hues spilled over the nearest buildings, painting the city line's horizon. For the first time all night, there was one thing that could captivate me more than the man who held me close.

As the first rays of sunlight leapt over buildings, I cringed, fearing them as they met my skin. The warmth was nominal, and it didn't shock me as my response may have indicated I thought it might. Instead, the only discomfort I felt was from the brightness of the beams themselves in my sensitive eyes. I squinted, hunching away from the prick of light that burned even when I wasn't looking at it. "Wow, it's so much brighter than I remember."

"Oh, yeah, here; I was prepared for this." Riftan pulled away and patted his pant's pockets before taking out a pair of sunglasses. "In all honesty, you'll never adjust to that. It's best to get friendly with a good pair of sunglasses before you start going out in the daylight." Flipping them open, Riftan set the sunglasses over my nose and tucked them behind my ears.

His fingers left a trail of goosebumps over my skin as they lingered on my cheek before finally dropping back down around my waist. When he returned his gaze to the color-changing sky, I did the same, able to appreciate it for its beauty without pain pinching at my retinas.

So close to Riftan, I was aware of every little movement he made, from his hand clasping tighter on my waist, to the hastening beat of his heart thrumming away in my ears. So, I took notice when he shifted to raise his hand over his eyes and shielded them from the glare of the rising sun. Turning away from the scenery, I found Riftan's squinting eyes already trained on me. I reached up, holding my hand against his to help shield the sun, hoping that would make up for taking his only protection from the harsh rays. His face relaxed, relief lacing a throaty chuckle.

"Sorry I took your sunglasses," I added.

"It's okay. I brought them for you." He took a step, pressing our bodies together until we shared the same space. With no room between us, my free hand landed on his chest, prudent for the time being.

His roving eyes dropped down my lifted arm and followed my outline up to my neck. Not far behind, the hand he'd been shielding with followed that same path. Like always, his touch didn't hold back. Soft but demanding, it was perpetually like a plea for more—or maybe it was my senses doing the pleading.

Though Riftan's eyes didn't waver from mine, locking me in a heady staring contest that never seemed to end, he made no move to close the distance between us. For someone so touchy, he was being awfully timid.

Maybe making the first move is my job. And why *not* make that move? I could find no reason not to fall head over heels for Riftan. He was chivalrous, more handsome than anyone I thought could exist, and he'd never been anything but kind to me—except when he bit me and left me for dead, something he had long since made up for. So, without a reason not to, I was going to kiss him.

Pulling my hand that'd been blocking the sun against his cheek, I leaned into him. Slowly, I diminished the gap that'd existed between our mouths. The idea of his sharp fangs against my lips tantalized every bit of my being to the point I was nearly yanked from consciousness when our lips never did meet. Instead, the hand Riftan had gently set on the nape of my neck was pulling me back, away from him. Tone nonchalant, he asked, "What are you doing?"

I'd never been much for timidity when it came to romance, so I answered truthfully, "I was going to kiss you."

"Well, don't." His lips moved simply, like what they said was a given. "The manner of our relationship can't be romantic, so don't make it that way."

Didn't he hold me whenever the hell he wanted to and touch me like my skin was practically his own? How was I the one acting romantic? *What about our relationship up until now has been anything but romantic?* "And why can't it be romantic?" I asked, not to push it on him, but out of genuine inquisition.

"Many reasons. First and foremost, we are going to be together for the next couple of years, and I don't want trivial relationship issues to make things harder. Plus, I'm over seven hundred years older than you are and I am also your teacher for the time being. I must hold power over you as your mentor, and I can't in my right mind court a lady whom I don't treat as my equal."

His words and his actions seemed to disagree as he held his arm around my waist and his hand on my neck. Not to mention, leading up to this, he'd hinted that this kind of fun was what he had in mind for us. "When you turned me, you said it was going to be fun. You made me think that this was what you had in mind."

A playful smile spread over his lips, and Riftan suppressed a giggle. "You'd only think I meant it that way, my dear, because you were once a dirty-minded hooker."

I tapped his chest with an irritated finger. I probably snarled, too. "I told you. I'm *not*, and never *was*, a hooker!"

He ignored me, smirking at the fiery response that'd gotten him, only to go on and say, "Besides, you'll learn soon enough that things are different now that you're immortal. The biggest change will be that of your relationships—be they romantic or platonic. Love is an emotion that is only meant to last a human lifetime at most. Immortal relationships always end in heartbreak, and then you're left with an ex who never dies. I assure you, I don't need to be that for you. You'll have plenty of time to collect broken hearts with other immortals. I don't need to be your first."

Still determined to have him, I asked, "And what if it really is just for fun and not a relationship?"

A dirty smile crept over his fangs. "Do you honestly think that the both of us could keep emotions completely uninvolved? Because if you do, I can assure you that you're lying to yourself. Especially not with the heightened emotions that you have yet to experience—much less control—as a vampire."

"So, you think *I'd* be the one to catch feelings?" Obviously, he didn't know me well enough yet. I was the queen of one-night stands—before Johnny, of course.

"I'm saying that *any* immortal with overly sensitive emotions makes for bad friends with benefits."

"So, you really aren't going to let me kiss you?"

"Mm…" he thought for a moment before settling with confidence, "No."

"Ugh." I pried myself from his arms and strolled inside, plucking the wings off of every last butterfly that'd been fluttering in my stomach for him.

"Don't be mad, love," he called after me, his voice a sickening sweet lull from his accented tone.

"Don't call me that!" I shouted, leaving the budding sunlight in exchange for my dark bedroom, where I slammed the door shut.

It was one thing to nix the romance, but I wouldn't stand for his lovey-dovey attitude if it was only leading me on.

Riftan had somehow, miraculously, inexplicably, unattainably, terribly, and *successfully*, gotten under my skin. If I was being entirely honest, I had *never* been turned down like he'd done to me. After years of boys throwing themselves at my feet, my ego had grown large, and maybe that's why Riftan's rejection had my entire body gripped with this foreign, unsettling angst. If it wasn't that, then it meant there was a much more regrettable reason for how his refusal irritated me—and that was that I had already fallen for him.

In any case, Riftan had a point. We were stuck together for the foreseeable future, and I simply had to find my own way to make that time together bearable. Even if it meant acclimating myself to the way he treated me without falling any harder for him.

Speaking of the devil—a knock on the door cued his inevitable arrival. "Can't I be alone for *five minutes?*" I draped the question in sarcasm, since it'd been much longer than minutes. I'd actually been sulking in my room for several hours. It wasn't like I was avoiding Riftan, since that was usually when I would have been going to bed anyway. But I *had* been hiding in my room despite my mind being too busy to fall asleep. Instead, I'd looked for a different way to distract myself. Since I couldn't talk to any of my old friends anymore, I'd settled onto my bed and started painting my fingernails with a dark green polish I'd brought from home. The sun had long since risen and I'd been basking in its glory from my bedroom window, even if the view wasn't as good as from the balcony where I'd left Riftan. So yes, in a way, I was partially avoiding him for the sake of some time to myself—something I hadn't had in *weeks* with him around. Unphased by the subtle suggestion I'd given him to leave me alone, Riftan barged into my room.

Hardly sparing a glance, I asked, "Did I say you could come in?"

"Did I ask for permission?" He closed the distance between the two of us and extended an offering of a steaming hot mug.

"What's that?" I would have taken it, but I didn't see a reason to stop what I was doing for him without knowing what for.

"It's coffee. Something you haven't gotten to try yet with new tastebuds."

"Will I like it?"

"Undoubtedly. It's black and slightly burnt, which might sound gross to you, but you'll understand once you try it."

"I'm going to bed soon; I don't need coffee." I refuted his offer, focusing on my nails once again as I moved to my toes.

Riftan got on his knees in front of where I sat on my bed. "You won't feel any effects from the caffeine anymore—it's simply for the taste. I promise it's good." He pushed the cup within the boundary of my personal space, and I nearly took it given the plea in his voice. He continued. "I'll trade you and paint your toenails for you. *Please?*"

When my eyes flicked back to his, I found the most hopeful, sparkling puppy dog eyes, wide as blue saucers, imploring me to agree with his proposition. His brows flinched under my gaze, cheeks teasing at a smile his lips didn't convey.

"Why?" I probed.

"To make up for being an ass earlier. You were mad at me,

and rightly so. I may have been leading you on a little, and if it's what you please, I'll try and be better about that."

Did that mean that he was going to keep his hands to himself going forward? And if so, was that truly what I wanted? My heart responded before my brain could catch up, trading him the polish for the mug of steamy coffee.

He lit up. "Does that mean you forgive me?"

"We'll see how well you can do with my nails, then I'll decide."

"Psh," he scoffed. "The nineties were practically yesterday for me. I'm undeniably great at painting nails." He reached a gentle hand over my ankle and slid it toward the edge of my bed. From there, he focused on each of my toenails with precision, ticking his head to the side as he worked.

I let him do as he wished, though I didn't think having his hands all over my delicate feet was necessarily the best way to *not* lead me on. However, he did seem content with it, and I was content when he had his hands on me. So maybe it'd be fine if nothing changed between us. Riftan and I could stay the way we were—no more and no less. Though it'd be strange, and I'd never quite get used to the yearning he summoned deep in my bones, I'd take this relationship we had over no relationship at all with Riftan.

Or so I hoped I could tell myself.

HOMEWRECKER COULD DEFINITELY HIT THE SPOT

WEEKS PASSED as I settled into my new life in Prague. Before I knew it, it'd been a month, and then two. We were deep into August, with the promise of longer nights trailing behind the earlier sunsets.

Riftan told me not to get comfortable in the city because we'd be traveling again soon, but I couldn't shake the feeling that the condo in Prague had already become our little home. I loved everything about the space we shared together. I loved the dining table where we laughed over evening coffees, the balcony where we admired every sunrise, and the study where we had Thursday crafts. For that reason, I argued that Prague should remain our hub—the place we came back to between trips—and Riftan wasn't hard to get onboard with the idea.

While we were in Prague, my training remained the foremost priority. Riftan had taught me some basics. First, it was feeding from a human, and then it progressed to *control* while feeding from a human. I'd nearly lost control that first time, but—per usual—Riftan had been right when he said that it gets exponentially easier after the first feed. Blood lust was real, and he had to teach me to recognize it, as well as stave it off. At one point, that included starving me for three weeks, simply so I would know what it felt like. He then proceeded to tell me he should have had me fast for several more weeks. That's what he did in the past with other apprentices, but he "couldn't cope with how miserable I looked." As much as I wanted him to treat me equally to those he had trained in the past—because I'm a strong, determined woman who doesn't need special treatment—I was indeed too miserable to say anything like that to Riftan.

In the end, I was glad for those three weeks of starvation. Thanks to them, I had gained a relatively strong control over my blood lust and a robust understanding of why such control was important. I'd also picked up on some of the history of vampires, such as what stereotypes stemmed from truth, and what was complete hooey.

I hated the pungent smell of garlic, but it wouldn't kill me. Silver jewelry had become unwearable—even briefly touching genuine silver elicited an itchy, burning reaction that was mild at first, but grew more aggressive if the jewelry wasn't removed. I could always see my reflection in the mirror unless it was an old-fashioned one backed in real silver—then I was nowhere to be found. I could definitely enter a church, but Riftan noticeably strayed from where they kept the holy water. When I asked, he said that holy water was rarely dangerous to us, but that it could be if it was blessed by a priest and collected from a spring as they did in the old ways. Regardless, he said it was best not to test it.

As for some of my immortal abilities, I'd begun learning the extent of my speed and strength. Both of which were hard to test, given their near limitlessness. But with that limitlessness, there was still a proper and improper way of using them. Using them properly could make you unstoppable and using them improperly could make them practically useless. After all, what is speed without dexterity, or strength without restraint? As Riftan had explained it, "it's like being great at singing but not knowing a single popular genre of music." What I think he meant by that is that it's one thing to throw a rock as far as the eye can see, and another to throw a rock and successfully hit a specific target a hundred feet away. As well as it's one thing to run faster than a trolly car, than to trip on your own two feet in the process. Both of which were things I'd done—but that's not important.

Of Riftan's lessons, my favorite was using my heightened senses to cheat at poker. That ended as one very long and *very* entertaining night out. There was one glaring lesson, however, Riftan had yet to teach me, and it happened to be the one I'd been begging for: I wanted to learn how to use hypnotization. I would need plenty of practice to be as good as Riftan was at it—so I wanted to get started as soon as possible. Even knowing how eager I was, Riftan changed the subject every time I brought it up.

It felt like longer, but it was only another month and a half before he *finally* told me what I wanted to hear: "If you'd like, I'll start teaching you to thrall mortals tonight."

I nearly dumped the contents of the coffee table onto the floor as I jumped up in excitement. "Seriously? You will? You're not teasing me?"

His ivory cheeks pulled into a demoralized frown. "Why would I tease you about something like that?"

I ignored his hypothetical, too thrilled to focus. "Thank you!" I squealed, wrapping my arms around his neck and tackling him onto the couch where he'd been lounging with a book.

The embrace of his fingers tantalized my waistline. "Well, I figured that I'd made you wait long enough, so it's only fair."

Still holding tight, I suffocated myself in the soft skin of his neck. I could have stayed wrapped up in him for the rest of forever, but I knew I'd have to separate myself eventually—or else we'd indeed lose the entire day to that embrace. One of the many things I'd learned about Riftan in our time together was that he was unable or unwilling to push me away, no matter how long I held him. But heaven forbid I try to kiss him. That was just heinous.

"I'd like to go out before sunset. The park will be a calm place to teach you something as intricate as hypnosis, and sunset will be a good time to find people walking alone." I nodded, finally gaining the composure to pull away and observe him. He showed his teeth in a squinty-eyed grin and patted me on the cheek. "Go rest before we go out. Okay?"

"Okay."

Waiting patiently for the evening to arrive, I got very little of anything that could be considered rest. Once the sun had finally started to darken to a deep orange, casting golden-hour light over the cathedral-esque city, Riftan and I made our way to the grand park a quick jaunt from our condo.

We'd been to the park a couple of times before, but it seemed forever-changing. The leaves of the once rich green trees and bushes now twirled to the ground, creating a bright amber and scarlet carpet underfoot. Pigeons cooed in the distance, ruffling their feathers as they fluttered atop the oaks. Once upon a time, I may have noticed my cheeks flushing from the chill in the air, but I no longer paid much mind to temperature. I could feel it and recognize its shift, but it wasn't of much significance to my temperate body.

Riftan linked his arm through mine, leading me around the park at a mellow pace as the shadows of the waning sun tightened their grasp on the scenery. We passed by a few people—some walking their dogs, some with a partner, and one with a baby stroller. Riftan didn't deem any of them worthy for me to try things out on, so we continued down the asphalt path.

When we were alone on the trail, Riftan mentored me on how to use my powers of hypnosis. I did, after all, already have those powers residing inside of me. I just didn't know how to bring them out. "Remember that what you think and what you feel is what you'll be sharing with the victim. If your thoughts aren't in order, theirs won't be either. So, if you need to say your intentions out loud, or scream it inside your own head so that it's all you think about, then so be it. Do what feels right. Also, that goes for you and your victim alike. It's a two-way street, and their confusion or other emotions will try and take control of you once you open your mind to them."

He stopped us only when a young girl jogged by, her blonde ponytail swinging with each bouncy step. She was cute and supple. Her high cheeks were red from the cold and her breath left her over plumped lips in continuous puffs of fog. She looked young, maybe still a teenager, but obviously trying to meet some societal beauty standard—much like I had been when I was her age. "Her." Riftan turned to watch the girl pass and then pointed when her back was to us. "Go try it on her."

"But she's so young," I argued.

"You won't hurt her, so don't worry about her age."

Nodding, I jogged up to the girl and tapped her on the shoulder.

Her long ponytail whipped around with a start from my sudden appearance. She pulled earbuds out of her ears and muttered with an eastern accent resonating from deep in her throat, "You scared the sh*it* out of me."

"I'm sorry." My heart thrummed fast, but I smiled cordially to make up for it. *What do I say next?*

The girl raised her brows at me as though she were thinking the same thing.

"Um…" I hesitated, contemplating the best approach. With a sigh, I opted to forgo the formalities and cut to the chase. "Will you bark like a dog... please?"

"Excuse me?" She stepped away, furling her eyebrows at the bizarre question.

Looking her directly in the eyes, I focused hard on the small black orbs that were her pupils. "Bark like a dog," I commanded, this time with intention, the way Riftan had instructed me to.

The girl's smile fell, her expression becoming flat. She obeyed, making the smallest dog bark I'd ever heard. "*Arf, arf.*"

Maybe I was thinking about a chihuahua, or maybe that was the version of a dog the girl was thinking of. "Now, sit?" I was stuck on the dog commands.

The girl did as told, dropping to the ground and putting her butt on asphalt. She sat with her knees up and her hands between them, much like she was mimicking a dog. I could only imagine that was, again, because I'd been thinking of how a dog would sit.

Riftan busted into laughter from the spot where I'd left him. "You made her sit like a dog! That's my girl!" He slapped his leg and continued to chuckle to himself.

I muttered to the innocent girl at my feet, "I'm sorry I had to embarrass you like that," and hurried back to Riftan.

The girl I'd thralled staggered to her feet and cocked her head at the ground before looking around with a bitter, confused expression staining her made-up face. Sparing us only a passing glance, she hurried on her way with her figurative tail between her legs.

Riftan asked me, "How was it?"

"It was fine. I understand making demands. You'll have to help me some more with the altering memories part, though. She definitely remembered that whole interaction."

"That's okay for now. It's why we are practicing." Riftan's lips turned up in a way that denoted something mischievous to come. "How about you find me a meal and practice it on them for real this time?"

"Here in the park? It seems like a strange place to find women worthy of murder." We usually found those women at clubs—be it social clubs, night clubs, or even country clubs. I'd originally been surprised at how many terrible people could be found at country clubs and other places where rich people gathered for no better reason than to flaunt their wealth. But the park wasn't that kind of place.

Riftan shrugged. "I'll leave it up to your discretion. Just find me someone. Unless you don't think you can do it?"

"Is that a challenge?"

In lieu of a better response, his shoulders simply gave another bob.

But that was all I needed. I was already on the hunt. Riftan had an obvious type and finding him a meal was never difficult. In fact, I usually found Riftan's mortal meals for him. Since I didn't really care about the gender of those I fed on, my pool of options was large, and on the occasions when I picked out a woman, Riftan wasn't sneaky about stealing her from me. I'd discovered early on that it worked out best that way. He needed to feed on living flesh every once in a while, just like I did.

At first, it wasn't weird; he'd find a woman from a club like

I would and take her out back or into a private area. But at some point, it made him act dodgy, looking my way too many times before actually settling on a human. When I chose them, however, he didn't get like that. Instead, he seemed more at ease settling his fangs into someone I'd deemed worthy as my own meal.

While I didn't find that the park was a great place to find a woman worthy of Riftan's taste, there *was* a small private dock along the riverside, not far from the end of the park. Usually, I wouldn't think twice about somewhere like that, except that I could hear voices in that direction speaking in hushed tones— the kinds that were laced with lust and signified undoubtable depravity. While I could have been wrong, it wouldn't hurt to check.

With Riftan in tow, I made my way through the woods on the outskirts of the park. Over a fence and down the embankment waited the small dock housing several large yachts. The gates were closed, and the docks were silent save for the squeaks and groans of metal on wood as they swayed on the water... and something else—a woman's muted voice carried from one of the boats.

"My husband thinks I'm out of town for work tonight. There won't be any interruptions, I promise. Just meet me on the docks in twenty, okay?" The woman spoke in a hushed tone, the only response being a distorted and staticky voice that garbled through a phone speaker.

While I'd thought I'd heard the chatter of two distinct voices before, only the woman's was present in person now.

Chalking that up to a mistake on my part, I moved closer.

In the shadows of the embankment before the entrance to the docks, I asked Riftan, "You in the mood for a homewrecker?"

"Homewrecker could definitely hit the spot," he agreed, right on my heels. Before I could make my way down the docks, Riftan stopped me long enough to add, "Make sure you don't let her scream. I'll help with her memories, but you need to remedy her emotions, okay?"

With a nod and a zip at nearly the speed of light, I made my way down the dock and to the boat where the woman's voice had carelessly led me. She was startled to see me, reasonably so, as I leapt over the tall gold railings and into her boujee-ass boat without a second thought. I didn't give her a moment to panic, closing the distance and locking my eyes with hers. She went silent as I calmed her to near sedation before things could get hectic. With an assertive hypnosis, I commanded her to "hush and wait quietly."

Behind me, Riftan hopped over the side of the boat. "Are you positive this is the one you want to pick?" he asked.

Completely thralled and leaning against the table in front of me was a blonde woman in her late thirties. She wore a sweater with a short pencil skirt and jewelry that racked up price tags into the tens of thousands. Though she may have been average-looking, she obviously had the money to make herself up, with plump lips and cheeks higher than was normal at any age. The exterior was up to par with Riftan's taste, but I did need to ensure that she'd be an appropriate match for murder.

"I suppose I'll check, just to make sure." Staring into the depths of her soul, I asked for reassurance, "What's the worst thing you've ever done in your pitiful life?" Using my thrall, I implored her to be honest.

She answered in the same monotone voice I'd become accustomed to hearing from hypnotized mortals. "I've been stealing money from my disabled son's charity to pay off my debts."

A chuckle bubbled from my lips. *This is too easy.* "She's all yours." I motioned to Riftan, and he nodded his approval.

Not waiting another moment, he seized the girl by her neck and dug in his fangs, feeding off her sweet, aromatic blood. The smell of her tickled my nostrils, making me salivate though I'd already fed that week. Her scent completely overwhelmed the muddy aroma of the river we floated on.

In the few months that I'd been doing the whole vampire thing, I'd become entirely desensitized to blood and feeding from human flesh. It helped exponentially that feeding came with such a euphoric high. It made watching Riftan feed feel like something enticing for me. It didn't make me hungry, like watching someone else eat cake; if anything, it made me kind of horny, like watching someone else make out... with a cake. But in this case, cake was a delicious, blood-filled human being.

Riftan always insisted that I shouldn't make feeding sexual, but I struggled not to. The feeling of feeding from a human was probably most akin to some *really* good—be it short-lived—sex. But Riftan would blow a fuse if I ever made that connection out loud.

Taking a seat with a good view on the couch nearby, I watched with roving eyes as Riftan devoured the girl. I expected that he would suckle at her neck until she became too weak to stand and then he'd probably stop. Swinging my legs up onto the coffee table, I settled in to enjoy the second hand high until then.

The girl leaned against Riftan, her weight in his capable hands as he held her close. His fingers splayed over her waist, careful not to pull her sweater but firm enough that she'd feel it. That was enough to have my butterflies, butter*flying*, but in a way that breached my normal longing. These butterflies felt chaotic and angry... maybe a little jealous? Not that I envied this woman's situation—a situation I so gravely knew for myself.

"That hurts," the woman whispered, barely breaking out of my hypnosis enough to voice a single thought.

An ache in my fingers sparked the realization that I was *clutching* the couch beside my knees.

Riftan pulled away and grabbed the woman's chin with his fingertips. He looked into her eyes and assured her, "It doesn't hurt."

Goosebumps covered my skin—Rifan's sentiment seeped into my bones like he'd said the words directly to me.

I had the vivid memory of myself in this woman's shoes. Riftan's breath hot against my neck, firm hands tight around my waist, and tender words numbing my brain into a confused bliss. But that's where the similarities end, because in my memory he pulled away and looked me in the eyes to say,

"Actually, that's no fun. This'll hurt you a little bit, how's that sound?"
Once again, I caught myself gripping the couch, this time tearing through the fabric with my thumbnail.

My heart hung on his words in the here and now. I'd heard his routine dozens of other times: always, "This won't hurt you." But never the cruel extension that I'd received on the night he bit me. That brought my jealousy full circle. "Riftan! What the hell?" I yelled as he was going back in for more of the woman.

"What?" he whipped around to face me, a red hue brightening his lips.

"When you bit me, you told me it was going to hurt! You wanted me to suffer! Why are you concerned if it hurts *her* now?" I pointed to the woman who slouched in his arms like a zombie.

He hesitated, his lips curving into a sheepish smile. "The circumstance was different. We were in the middle of nowhere and nobody could hear you scream. I'm sorry, it wasn't personal; I was having some fun with you."

"Jerk." I reached for a couch pillow and threw it at him.

Batting it away, Riftan lit up, his eyes playfully locking onto mine. "Hey, I'll come over there and bite you again if you don't watch it."

"I dare you to try!" was my eager response.

I would have happily taken a bite from him if it meant getting to feel his lips on my skin again. I'd been too distracted with my demise to properly appreciate what it'd felt like before—and that haunted me *daily*. All I wanted was to appreciate what he felt like in the meager moments I'd gotten to have his lips on my neck—even if it meant having his teeth buried in my skin. And luckily, there was no ill response from a vampire biting another vampire, which was a question I'd cleared up long ago—definitely no reason for asking.

Looking like he might oblige, Riftan dropped the woman he'd been feeding from to the ground, where she fell in a heap. The fact that she was no longer conscious told me that Riftan needed to stop anyway.

He maneuvered the coffee table, only feet away from granting the secret wish I'd been pleading for, when another elevated heart rate and erratic breath joined us. Riftan noticed it too and stopped dead in his tracks, gaze following the sound over the edge of the yacht.

Below, on the dock, a woman stood shivering in the shadows, one hand clasped around her mouth. Her wide eyes glued to the unconscious body on the floor, and her heart rate spiked, a telltale sign she would attempt to flee. I should have heard that woman coming, but I'd been so distracted by Riftan's every little nuance, my mind so focused on the fantasy of having his teeth in me again, that I hadn't heard the girl coming up the dock. *My bad.* I failed my job as lookout.

As I'd suspected, the woman fled. Running up the dock, she attempted her escape, but I would make up for my blunder and stop her myself.

"Leanne, wait!" Riftan demanded, but I was already gone.

The woman hadn't made it up the dock in the milliseconds it took me to reach her. I was in the woman's space as she stumbled away, her face contorting with fear and dripping in tears of dread. Pulling her close so she wouldn't stagger back into the water, I locked eyes with hers. My thoughts were clear, and they resembled the words, "Calm down, everything is okay. Go home and forget all of this." But immediately, this thrall felt different.

I'd been clear in my judgment and feelings of peace when we locked eyes, but I hadn't finished the thought before an unrealistic terror conquered my thoughts, gripping my throat like a shadowy entity. Drowning in the emotion, I gasped for air, my heart racing like it wished to jump right out and escape the feeling.

I released the girl and scrambled to get away from her. The dock under my feet was only so wide, and I was teetering off the edge like I'd feared the girl would do moments earlier. Before I could tumble in, strong arms were righting me back onto the dock and wrapping around my shoulders.

My skin prickled from Riftan's touch—but not the way it usually did. This time it prickled in repulsion, like my cells themselves *feared* his embrace. "Don't touch me," I commanded instinctively as my body and mind screamed.

Riftan held me tighter despite my verbal wishes. "Calm down, everything is okay. There's nothing to be afraid of."

Am I really afraid of him?

That was what it felt like. Or maybe it was more of a general feeling of fear.

What am I *afraid of?*

The emotion was so chaotic and confusing, it felt as if

there was an itch in my throat that could only be scratched if I screamed at the top of my lungs. "What just happened?" I asked, tucking my head into Riftan's chest, letting my mind take back an ounce of control and resist the urge to cry out.

His breath fanned softly over my hair. "You opened your mind to that girl, and she was frightened. Don't you remember what I told you? It's a two-way street. That's why I yelled for you to wait. When are you going to learn to listen to me?"

"I didn't think it'd be like that."

"Of course not, because you have a lot to learn." He sighed and the atmosphere shifted around me as he lifted me off the ground. "The way you're feeling will wear off in a little while. I'll take you home and we will practice this more tomorrow."

Just like that, the night was over, and I'd failed my first full lesson in hypnosis.

*H O W   D I D   Y O U   T A M E   M Y   G R U M P Y
L O N E   W O L F*

LEARNING HYPNOSIS turned out to be more about learning what *not* to do. By the time I'd done it wrong in every possible way, I'd become rather good at it.

Though I was sure I wasn't nearly on par with Riftan, I could handle almost any thralling situation at the drop of a hat. Curious onlookers in the alley, check. A proper Sunday meal, you know it. A Karen yelling on the sidewalk, bye, bitch. I liked to think I was as competent as most other immortals would be.

In the next six months following my initial thralling failure, it felt like I'd learned every lesson there was to learn in vampirism, but Riftan insisted there was much more work to do before completing my training. By April, he confirmed that I'd accomplished all the basics, which meant it was time to start employing those tactics in unison and without fail.

When I asked if there was anything he could have forgotten to teach me, he'd poke an introspective finger to his chin and then confidently say, "nope!" Which I knew was a lie, because I still couldn't disappear and reappear somewhere else like he often did in a puff of black smoke. I'd tried running so fast that I thought I might disappear in a zip of motion, but it wasn't the same as his little vanishing act. What he did was more like teleportation—a mystical entrance I'd had no such luck in getting Riftan to talk about. It wasn't like how it'd been with hypnotism and him wanting me to be patient. Instead, he had an actual aversion to the topic, telling me an outright "no" whenever I asked about it.

Luckily, I wasn't feeling pushy over it. I trusted Riftan to teach me everything that I needed to know in due time. It wouldn't hurt to go with the flow. Not like I was in any kind of hurry. I didn't have anywhere else I wanted to be. I would happily let Riftan take his sweet time teaching me. After all, our time together technically had a deadline, and my heart had taken to dropping whenever I thought about reaching said deadline.

I was immersed in the little life we'd created together, and our relationship surpassed the point of an easy goodbye a long time ago. Riftan and I had lived together in Prague for a long time. Hell, we'd be creeping up on a year in a couple months.

Leaving Riftan would be like going back to the real world after almost a year wrapped up in a fantasy. I didn't think that anything—or anyone—could compare to this world that consisted of just Riftan and me. I was so absorbed in our private life together that it was by some means unsettling when Riftan proposed the idea of meeting new people. More precisely, that he wanted *me* to meet someone new.

"Someone new? Like, who?" I asked, lacing my words with a cautious undertone.

"Some of my friends."

Something sounded fishy, so I joked—though it was hardly a joke, "You have friends?"

"Well, to be fair, I have *one* friend, and he's bringing some of his friends. I simply thought it would be good for you to get out and meet other immortals for once. It's about time you started getting acquainted with a bit of the underworld community."

"Hmm." I was already fiddling with my hair, nervous tension creeping its way into my stomach at the mere thought of meeting new people. Did I know how to talk to other people anymore?

"Scratch that." Riftan butted in before I could answer. "I have two friends: you are my friend as well."

"Gee, thanks. I'd hope we were friends," I noted. "But seriously, who's the friend we are meeting?" If Riftan had only one friend, then I would have heard him talk about them.

"Jameson. He said he wanted to meet you, and I thought this was a good opportunity for you as well."

"Jameson, like the Jameson you turned in the late 1800s?"

"So, you *do* listen to me sometimes?" he teased.

"It's selective listening, I assure you."

That night, I dressed to impress because Riftan had gone on to make it sound like he and Jameson were talking about me in their personal time. Moreover, it seemed that a select group of Jameson's friends had traveled to Prague with the sole intention of meeting me. And though that was completely ludicrous in my opinion, Riftan said it was no big deal—as though traveling across the world to meet a friend for one night was common and nonchalant.

The nerves piled on as we stood in the elevator of one of the fanciest hotels in the center of the city. Riftan had failed to mention that we were going to a private party in someone's hotel room rather than meeting at a bar.

The elevator walls around us gleamed like golden mirrors, meticulously polished, not a fingerprint in sight. The foyer we'd come through before the concierge had been equally as grand: gold accents and lush green foliage highlighted every corner in a sophisticated but opulent style. The place was regal, to say the least. We'd needed a key to access the elevator that would take us to the penthouse.

"Jeesh," I sighed, hating how unaccustomed I'd become to the idea of social interaction. "Don't tease me, but I'm really nervous." My stomach tied into knots while I fiddled with the hem of my dress. I'd never been so nervous to meet new people. I used to love it.

"There's no reason to be nervous," Riftan cooed as he

adjusted the hair over my shoulder so some of it draped down the front. "Here, would it make you feel better if I held your hand?"

With wary eyes, I looked between him and his outstretched fingers. "Well, since you offered." I accepted his hand and held it tight, feeling immediate relief to my restless nerves. He gave my trembling fingers a squeeze, pulling me snugly against his side. Between us, a shared warmth blossomed—a feeling I'd familiarized with a comfort only Riftan could provide me— calming what remained of my heart palpitations.

Accompanying the ring of a bell, the golden mirrored doors before us slid open, and Riftan whispered, "Don't worry. I'll be right here with you," before tugging me out of the elevator.

We entered directly into a hotel room, no hallway to traverse or door to knock on. The room, though dimly lit, sparkled like a polished diamond. In stark contrast to the gold theme of the lobby below, this space featured dark metal fixtures and black furniture. A lively group of people gathered around the heart of the room: an expansive black marble countertop, which cascaded onto the floor in a robust modern design. It was centered in the kitchen, lit by bright hanging pendants which spotlighted the area in an otherwise dark space. This bar, an island of laughter and camaraderie, attracted the majority of the room's dozen occupants. Elsewhere in the shadows, a few individuals were sprinkled across the suite; some drawn to the large windows, where they stood silhouetted against the city's sprawling view, while a couple canoodled on the large L-shaped couch that took over the rest of the hotel room, sunken below the kitchen bar. A stair-step up to the kitchen gave the living room a conversation pit sort of look—though it was the kitchen that had been elevated instead of the room sunken.

"Riftan!" An enthusiastic but deep-toned voice stuck out from the crowd, and a man with ebony skin separated himself from the others, meeting us before we'd reached the group. A giddy smile plastered over his high cheeks as he closed the distance and grasped Riftan's free hand in a firm handshake. The man was tall and thin, his chiseled jaw and pearly white smile—fangs and all—making him appear young and carefree. The button-up shirt he wore messily pushed up on the sleeves made him look younger than he'd probably been when he was human. Dropping his attention to me with a quick glance toward Riftan's and my conjoined hands, the man took my free hand and kissed it cordially. He then added, "It's nice to meet you, Miss Leanne. My name is Jameson and I welcome you."

Riftan's fingers squeezed around mine. I bolstered up, putting effort toward my confidence. "Thank you. It's nice to meet you as well."

Giving Riftan his full attention, Jameson asked him about the last seven years since they'd seen each other. Riftan's opening line was accompanied by a hearty laugh, a sight I had never witnessed in public before. Instantly, their connection resembled old friends. Observing Riftan interact like that with someone other than myself was heartening. His joy enveloped me, creating a warm and cozy feeling that melted my taut nerves back into place. His infectious smile contaminated my own, spreading over my lips.

When the two of them had sufficiently caught up, Jameson took my hand again and offered to introduce me to the crowd of others who still chatted around the bar. With a quick squeeze, Riftan released his hold on me, permitting Jameson to take his place as my safety net. I smiled at Riftan, feeling my cheeks pull into something reassuring, and he nodded in accord.

Taking me up the step and into the kitchen, Jameson interrupted the playful group at the bar's banter to introduce us one by one. Since I'd never been great with names, they all went in one ear and out the other, but I had a feeling the only important thing was that I remembered Jameson. The others would simply have to remind me half a dozen more times.

Even if I couldn't remember their names, I would remember their faces. Each individual possessed a distinct look that set them apart. The taller girl had shoulder-length blonde hair with perfect ringlets, the guy in a glitter front, black button-up lacked eyebrows and had striking grey eyes, and the dark-skinned girl on her tiptoes wore intricate pink braids that entwined with her naturally black locs. The only similarity the group shared was that they were all awe-inspiringly gorgeous. If I had encountered this group in a public setting, I would have sensed that something was unusual, even without knowledge of some mythical underworld community. Their collective presence was simply too striking to go unnoticed. The women exuded beauty; the men radiated charm. Although I had experienced a similar transformation in my own appearance after turning, it still seemed improbable for so many extraordinary individuals to congregate in one place.

That alone would have been intimidating enough to have me turning tail if I'd predicted it back in the elevator. But with Jameson's radiant confidence wrapped at my side, I could feel the bold and poised Leanne begging to be set free again. She'd been hiding for so long that I worried she no longer existed. *I should have known better. She is me.*

Taking up an offered martini, I found easy conversation with this new set of individuals. Among the group, there wasn't a trace of malice, and from the beginning, each person treated me with the warmth and sincerity of a true friend. They nearly fumbled over each other to talk to me, poised with a million and five different questions to ask about my past, my future, my opinion on life as we knew it, and a myriad of other crazy hypothetical inquiries.

As I should have expected, Riftan saved his attention predominantly for my interactions, keeping a close vigil on everything I did as a constant presence by my side. Despite his quiet demeanor, he didn't appear out of place in a room filled with extroverts. Everyone approached him at least once or twice, and he responded each time with a soft smile and genuine conversation. However, beyond these brief exchanges, he didn't actively seek out interactions with the others. Instead, he seemed content observing as people mingled around him, pursuing their own enjoyment and engaging in their own conversations.

Though he had expressed his concerns about acting out

any romantic antics between the two of us while we were staying together, his actions were contrary. What started as mere proximity slowly progressed into a level of touchiness I hadn't expected from him. At some point, his arms had found their way around my waist when I'd been leaning into him, inviting his warmth. Eventually, I didn't have to entice his touch to have him pulling me into his arms while my interest focused elsewhere.

His attention burned the butterflies in my chest into a fire that was only minimally kept under control by the many exchanges keeping me busy chatting with the room. I was used to Riftan touching me as he pleased at home, but this was, in so many ways, different. His intimate behavior in a room full of individuals he knew personally was significant. Riftan was openingly welcoming others to make their own judgments about us. He was making a public announcement that we were indeed as close as I liked to think we were. Among a group of *his* peers, I assumed Riftan would want us to appear as platonic as he was constantly trying to say we were. Instead, his hands roamed freely, holding tighter than when in the privacy of our home.

With his arms yet again draped around my waist and holding my back captive against his chest, I waited for the lull in conversation. When Jameson stepped away to get us more drinks, I whispered, "What do you think you're doing?"

Riftan angled his head between the space over my shoulder, breath too hot in my ear to be more than inches from it. "I don't know what you're talking about."

My heart dropped a little. He knew what he was doing. He knew the way it would affect me, and he knew the way it already had. He could hear my heart race when our bodies got too close. How it leapt when he drew his fingers over my stomach and down my waist. Everyone in that damn room could hear it. They all knew, so the least he could do was admit to it. Maybe my disappointment came through in my voice, because it was soft, negligible in volume, and dripping in dejection. "Yes, you do."

Something about that response made its way through Riftan's thick skull because his hands dropped away from me as Jameson was returning with a glass in hand.

Taking the glass, I glanced back at Riftan. His look had soured, lips donning a bitter purse. Knowing him, he wasn't mad at me for telling him to retract, but more so that I'd been right and that he'd let himself get carried away, as he sometimes did.

Giving him my most doe-eyed smile, I saw him correct his features before turning his attention elsewhere.

I'd like to say that lasted more than minutes, but it wasn't much later that one of the other partygoers had meandered into our conversation, laughing it up and leaning into me with a roguish grin. His blond hair was pulled back to show the strength of his wide jaw and the thick muscles that traced his neck. The guy was super hot, but then again, everyone there was. He'd only just mentioned meeting up outside of that party, when Riftan's fingers were gripping my dress, tugging me back into his bubble, where he could wrap his arms around my shoulders and hover over me. That action, paired with whatever look he was flashing from behind me, was answer enough for the guy who'd taken up flirting with me. He didn't retract from our conversation, but straightened up and made his banter much more modest in nature, never mentioning the possibility of meeting again.

That wasn't the last time Riftan put on that possessive front either. The few times I'd been far enough from him to elicit overly friendly conversation from other men, Riftan slowly meandered to my side, trying to look ever so casual as he intervened. Men seemed to be the only thing that concerned him, though I knew he knew my sexual preferences—or lack thereof. Which made me wonder if this was about me, or more about him. Was he jealous, or merely feeling some strange need to mark me as his property in some male ego contest?

While I ached for the satisfaction that came from thinking he wanted me for himself, I didn't entirely appreciate the implications of ownership that would entail. I wasn't his to claim for his own—leastwise, not if he wouldn't claim me in the privacy of our home. But the ache of *wanting* to be his and *wanting* to think this relationship was more than forced and inconsequential was confusing against that conviction, especially to my already puzzled heart.

Luckily, the one guy Riftan was not prickly around was Jameson, which meant we spent a lot of the night side by side, bonding over way too many drinks. Getting to know him was like meeting a best friend for the first time. He was authentic and playful, hooting and hollering one minute and sharing profound philosophicals the next. His humor was witty, and his smile could cure depression, fangs and all.

He and Riftan were a strange pair. The two of them got along like two peas in a pod, but the acts they put on were far from parallel. Jameson flaunted as the life of the party, and Riftan was like a fly on the wall. It made me wonder how they might get along in private, since I knew my Riftan was a little different than the Riftan who silently lurked at my side. In a different setting, the two of them might show more similarities than one would think from the outside looking in. But I was no longer an outsider, and I knew Riftan well enough to see they were one in the same: they laughed at the same jokes, celebrated each other's accomplishments like they were their own, and I could swear they'd finished each other's sentences at least once or twice. If I could get the two of them out of this crowd, I thought I might see Riftan climb right out of his shell.

About half-past five in the morning, things started to settle down. Several guests had already said their goodbyes. As it turned out, not all vampires had access to spells or items that permitted them to go out in the sunlight, and they had to be back in their respective hotels before sunrise. As they'd made it seem, many of them were accustomed to living their lives that way. It wasn't a nuisance to them, merely a way of life.

The dwindling number of party members hadn't affected Jameson's and my banter. Rather, the two of us had started prattling on about past lives and long-lost loves. Things were getting personal, juicy, collusive—Jameson was spilling *all* the tea. I hadn't had this kind of ginger platonic gossip since talking with Jayleen back in Creswell. I'd missed it... more than I'd realized.

I leaned in, hanging on Jameson's every word like I might fall off the edge of his story when Riftan squeezed my waist from where he sat on the counter behind me. In a whisper, he gently urged, "We should go soon. You two are the only ones still carousing."

My heart dropped off the ledge, and Jameson's story came up short when he focused his attention back on Riftan's stoic form at my back.

Jameson pulled away, glancing around the room with high brows like reality had only presently begun to exist for him. I followed his gaze to see that the room was mostly empty. A couple chatted quietly on the couch, and someone admired the few remaining stars in the morning sky out on the balcony. The two whom I'd met as the owners of the hotel room were nowhere to be seen, assumingly having retired for the day. Jameson agreed with Riftan's notion. "Yeah, it's probably time to get out of here."

"You can come back to our condo," I offered, before looking up at Riftan for confirmation.

His grumble vibrated against my back before he could express his complaint. "It's early. Can't we go home and go to bed?"

It had been a while since the last time we'd had a full day's rest. I'd noticed I didn't need as much sleep as a vampire, but I did eventually get rather tired if I wasn't resting long enough. "Please?" I begged, blinking rapidly at him.

Jameson imitated me, pleading, "Please," in the same tone.

Riftan rolled his perfect eyes at Jameson before looking back at me. "Fine. But you both owe me. I wanted to go to bed."

"Thank you!" I twirled around, taking him by the hand and pulling him off the counter and toward the exit elevator.

Back at the condo, the three of us played two rounds of blackjack, in which Jameson was the resounding winner. It was much harder to win the game when everyone else had the same abilities to cheat as I did.

Taking his victory lap, Jameson got up from the table to refill our drinks. With merely a step toward the kitchen, he disappeared in a flash of smoke and reappeared once more behind the counter.

I cocked my head at him, stopping mid-sentence with my mouth agape. My prior subject forgotten, I asked, "Hey, how do you do that?"

"What, this?" He disappeared and reappeared in front of me again with a mischievous grin smattered over his lips.

He wasn't moving at some indiscernible pace, he was actually *teleporting* the same way Riftan did.

"Yes! How?"

"Magic, I suppose, is the best answer."

"Did Riftan teach you that?" According to Jameson, Riftan had taught him almost everything he knew, like he was now doing for me.

"Hell no. That's the one thing he said he wouldn't teach me. I had to figure it out on my own." Jameson snickered and shot a teasing glance at Riftan.

If he'd refused to teach Jameson, then he probably wouldn't teach me either. So, I went out on a limb and asked, "Will you teach me how to do that, Jameson?"

He looked at Riftan, who was already arguing against it. "Magic is complicated," Riftan said, "especially for beings like us who weren't born to handle it. Shadow fading is a simple spell meant for vampires, but it opens you up to other, more dangerous, options. That's why I didn't want to teach it to either of you."

Is Riftan seriously describing it as a gateway drug—gateway magic?

Jameson nodded in agreement. "I know. But what if I promise you that I'll only teach her this one thing? She's going to figure it out eventually, and wouldn't you prefer it was from someone trustworthy?"

Again, with the strange, illicit substance innuendo. "You guys are only making me more curious," I chimed in from behind their conversation.

"Fine," Riftan finally conceded. "I trust your judgment, Jameson. Don't let her get into any trouble, okay?"

Straightening up and plastering a smooth grin over his lips, Jameson bowed toward Riftan respectfully. "I wouldn't dream of it!" With that, Jameson was pulling on my elbow, coaxing me out of my chair.

"Right now? Where are we going?"

"For a walk. You need more space for me to teach you this." He linked his arm with mine and ushered me toward the front door.

Behind us, Riftan watched closely, his gaze flickering between the two of us. Our eyes met and his softened, lips curving tenderly until the ends of his fangs showed. He raised his glass to me in farewell, never dropping my gaze.

"Are you not coming?" I asked.

Without looking back, Jameson added, "He needs to stay here. He'll only be a distraction."

Riftan didn't budge from his spot at the table. "You two can go have fun, I'm going to bed. Just remember what I said about staying out of trouble. It's mid-day, after all."

"Oh, okay. Bye." Before crossing the threshold of the door, I waved goodbye, my heart sinking as if I wasn't going to ever see him again. This was, after all, the first time since we'd met that I'd gone anywhere without him.

Unconcerned by the way I dragged behind, Jameson led us down the stairwell and out onto the streets below with a bounce in his step.

The cobblestone sidewalks were relatively barren of humans, the weather that day was too crisp and cold for their liking. Out there, Jameson and I were solitary, not a soul in sight.

"Sorry to steal you away." Jameson squeezed my arm in his. "But now we can talk without Riftan over your shoulder."

Something in my chest strained thinking of how attentive

Riftan had been, practically loitering everywhere I went that night.

"I'm simply curious," Jameson continued, "how did you tame my grumpy lone wolf?"

A puff of fog followed the laughter from my lips. "What do you mean?" Against the cold air, heat still stained my cheeks.

"I mean, Riftan is completely different with you than I've ever seen him before. Unless it's work-related, I've never seen him show an interest in someone the way he does you. You know he only befriended me because we were working together, right?"

"Well, yeah. But even now, he still likes having you around."

"For short periods, maybe. He's always been that way. As long as I've known him, he's been solitary. He's never liked keeping *any* company… except for you."

My laughter turned to a nervous babble. "I think you're mistaken. He's simply training me. Like he did you and everyone else he's turned. That's all."

"You've already been with him longer than I'd have expected him to keep anyone around. He only trained me for about a year, and I know that was longer than normal. You're running up on a year now, aren't you?"

Bile singed my throat, the thought of completing my training with Riftan being too icky to manifest. My life was aligned with his. I couldn't imagine living without him again. "I suppose you're right." I simply had to admit the facts. "But do you really think he'll send me on my way soon? I don't feel ready for that."

Jameson looked me over, his dark eyes thick with sympathy for an emotion that must have been oozing out of me. In response, his look softened. "It's hard to tell with him. He seems so smitten with you, it's hard to imagine that he would."

"Honestly, I don't want to go anywhere that isn't with him."

"I know. I can tell." Silence lingered for a moment before Jameson chippered up, bringing his voice back to its normal cheery octave. "Don't worry about it too much. He's hard to read, but I think it's all going to end up fine. You both care about each other, and he's not going to do something that'd hurt you. I know that for sure."

"Right, of course..." I wished I could convince myself of that beyond my lingering doubt.

With the sunlight barely making its way through the clouds, Jameson brought us to the park only blocks from the condo. There were so few people out, it was easy to find a wide-open space away from onlookers. Jameson insisted that it didn't *really* matter if any mortals saw us, because they wouldn't believe what they were seeing anyway.

For the next thirty to forty-five minutes, Jameson educated me on the basics of magic and how that pertained to shadow leaping, or as some called it: shadow-fading. "At first, you'll have to recite an incantation. As you become more accustomed to using it, it'll become second nature to recite it to yourself. Eventually, you won't think about the words, you'll simply be doing the action—much like it can be with hypnosis."

His teachings were simple, and he spent as much time on the many rules as he did the actual lesson. But, in due time, I was doing it. I was *actually* using magic to teleport! More specifically, I could leap between shadows that were in sight. So, it wasn't as profound as the mainstream concept of teleportation, and I couldn't jump to Spain, but it was still really cool.

As the day waned, Jameson brought me back to the condo and said his goodbyes at the door.

"Can't you stay longer?" I complained like a lonely child.

"I'll stick around town for a little while so I can get to catch up with Riftan some more, but I've got work to attend to tonight. How about we all get drinks a couple of nights from now?"

"Okay, sounds good!" I gave him a warm hug and a goodbye.

Jameson was the first real immortal friend I'd made, and in that short time, he'd become my *best* friend.

In the end, I was grateful Riftan had made me go to that trivial party. I'd made connections and had valuable experiences with other immortals that taught me a lot about this new world I'd gotten myself ensnared in.

Those bonds may prove to come to my aid sometime in my eternal future. Maybe earlier than predicted if Riftan decided to dump me off on my own soon.

14

HOW DID I GET STUCK WITH A CHEEKY LITTLE MINX LIKE YOU

THE BLINDS in the condo were drawn, leaving the room as dark as I would imagine the interior of a casket was while six feet underground. That didn't stop me from throwing my shoes off and hopping through the dark, cheer radiating from my every exaggerated movement.

"How was it?" Riftan's deep voice carried from the couch, though it was rough and groggy, like I'd woken him.

Not having seen him and too distracted in my joyous celebration to locate his heartbeat, I jumped. "You scared me. I thought you went to bed."

"I didn't want to until you got back, but I fell asleep."

"You didn't have to wait up."

"It's okay, I wanted to hear how it went." He patted a spot

on the couch and beckoned me over.

Already chipper and thrilled to get cozy with Riftan, I leapt up and settled in next to him. Laying my legs over his lap, I pressed into his warmth, letting it melt away the outside world until we were all that existed. In the short time I'd been out with Jameson, reality felt heavier; I'd missed the dreamy weightlessness Riftan added to my existence.

Gentle fingers caressed the bare skin on my legs as he traced the line of my veins that traveled under my knee and up my thigh. I knew he'd indulge me with his touch if I presented him with my bare skin, and it was undeniably the response I'd desired.

"Well, how'd it go?" he asked, his breath close enough to brush against the tip of my shallow nose.

"It went great! I can do the thing now, and I got to practice it quite a bit. Jameson said I'd picked up on it well. And before you complain—he told me to promise you I wouldn't learn or ask to learn any more magic. And I promise, okay?"

"I wasn't going to complain. I'm glad you had fun." One fang slipped past his lips in the slightest little grin he gave me.

"I did have fun! I really like Jameson, and the shadow fade is pretty cool, too. Bare minimum, it's a great parlor trick. I could certainly entertain parties or impress my grandchildren with it someday." I spoke figuratively as though I'd plan on having children—though I didn't and never had.

Riftan's smile fell, and his hand halted its traverse over my leg, pausing on the outside of my thigh.

"What's wrong?" I asked, unphased and unaware of what

I could have said to bother him.

"You're not going to have grandchildren, Leanne."

"What do you mean? Like, I can't?"

"No, immortals can't have children. I should have told you that before. I simply didn't think about it."

I knew that. Even if it hadn't been brought up in conversation, I knew that if I no longer menstruated that I would no longer be capable of having children. Though I didn't care much, I still mused, "Hmph, I suppose that could definitely be a hang-up for some people."

"I'm really sorry," he continued, his tone softening and brows furrowing. "I should have told you before letting you decide to be turned. I wish I would have had the forethought to remember—"

"Riftan, really, it's fine," I assured him, nodding distinctly to convey how certain of that I was. "I'm not one of those people. I honestly never wanted to have children, anyway. It wouldn't have changed my decision; I was dying, after all. It's totally not a big deal."

"Right." His gaze lingered on my legs in his lap. "I'm still sorry, though. I should have at least told you." His voice was low and drawn out, almost... remorseful?

"Does it... bother you?" I questioned his sudden change in emotion with a raised brow. "That you can't have children, I mean."

He looked up without a trace of the remorse I'd suspected I'd heard. "No, not at all. I've been this way for so long and I've never been in the kind of relationship that would warrant that kind of desire. So, I never have cared. But you're still young and I can't assume it'll be the same way for you."

"I can assure you, you don't need to worry about that. But…" I drew out the word, veering the conversation back down a path I wasn't going to let pass me by. "What do you mean you've never been in that kind of relationship? You mean like the kind that'd make you wish you could have kids?"

"No. Nothing like that."

"Even in eight hundred years? You never met someone who made you wish—even for a moment—that you could have a family with them?"

"No. I've never been in a relationship that serious." He was forthcoming but avoided looking me directly in the eyes.

"Not in *eight hundred years*?" My high pitch did very little to veil my disbelief. I'd always been open with him about my relationships, and Riftan knew every little detail about Johnny and me. But Riftan had never talked about past relationships of the romantic variety with me.

"Nothing serious. Maybe one, if you could count it. That's never been something my lifestyle catered to." He looked me over before letting his dark eyes plead with me. "I can see that you want to start, but can you please not make such a fuss about it?"

With a deep breath, I calmed my enthusiasm. "Well, you never talk about past relationships, and you know *everything* about mine. So, will you tell me about them? The serious and the not-so-serious alike? I want to understand what you mean when you say that you've never—*in eight hundred years*—been in a serious relationship."

"Fine, but it's not exciting. The first woman I ever turned was a mistake, and we'd been in a relationship of sorts before that. I was still really young; I'd only been a vampire for a few years—less than a decade—and I still thought like a human. As you know, when I turned her, I panicked and left her to fend for herself, which in turn was what caused her end. For the most part, after that, I wasn't interested in anything but mortal wars for the first couple hundred years of my life. I never had time or interest in relationships. Women—obviously—but kinship, not so much. After I was sick of the battlefield, and after I'd killed Meridith, I was extremely desensitized and what I could best describe as murderous and more than a little messed up." He paused and touched a finger to his brow. "During that time, I met an immortal named Rosaline. She made me feel justified and sane, even when I absolutely wasn't. She took care of me during a very fragile part of my life, and in return, I sincerely thought I was in love with her. In a way, loving her was quite helpful to my healing, so I suppose I can't regret everything about being with her. But as my emotions started to re-evolve and I started coming back to my senses, I realized Rosaline was a leech feeding from my misery. She didn't want me to get better, but instead found ways to drag me down into what I'd suffered from before. She genuinely got off on my agony and it destroyed her to think that I may recover—that she'd lose her little miserable toy. It took me twenty-four years, but eventually, I had the presence of mind to get the hell away from her."

"Woah, woah, woah. You were with her for twenty-four

years? And this is the first time I'm hearing of it?" I didn't think
I needed to point out to him that the time he'd spent with that
woman was the entirety of my living lifetime—and thus seemed
excessive to me.

"Yes." His chest rose and fell in monotonous succession,
his delivery lacking in emotional emphasis. "It was a vast
amount of time for me to spend with another person, but I
don't find that I need to reminisce about it much anymore. It
was conclusively inconsequential to any bit of my life outside of
those twenty-four years."

"So, it was a long time for you as well, then? I'm not the
only one who considers that to be inordinate? I mean, did you
never consider in that amount of time getting married or
anything?" I asked, knowing it was not a groundless question.
That night, I'd met two married immortal couples and heard of
others—it certainly wasn't culturally unheard of.

Riftan maintained his impartial façade, never breaking the
posture he held around my legs. "Inordinate, maybe, but neither
of us had any concern for marriage of any sort. It may seem less
profound to you, being that you were born in a time in which
marriage is something that is acceptably and commonly
reversed in a divorce. But I was born, and turned, and lived a
majority of my long life, in a time that took marriage vows a
little more seriously. And unfortunately, 'until death do you
part' holds a bit more value when you do not die. So, I suppose
that as enchanted as I was with Rosaline for a greater part of
that time, there was still a part of me that knew I wouldn't
survive an eternity with her. Which is not to say she would have

agreed if I'd asked her to marry me; Rosaline always needed to have the upper hand, and I think that marriage would have made her feel belittled to stand on the same ground as me. She also always favored keeping her options open." Finally, a glimmer of anguish crossed his lips in a remorseful grimace that instantly abated when he added, "I suppose she wasn't as inconsequential as I like to think. Ultimately, she made it a little harder for me to trust other immortals—or more like, she made me more cognizant of the way they can be. Many of them are as cunning and deceptive as her. Eternity will simply do that to some people, I guess." He shrugged as though that was it—the story was over.

"Is she the reason you don't open up to others?" I'd have trust issues too if someone did that to me for twenty-plus years.

"No. That was over two hundred years ago. The strife I may have had from her is long gone by now."

"Then why do you insist on always being alone? Jameson told me you've always preferred isolation. How come?"

Riftan wrapped his arms around my legs and pulled my knees into his chest. With a simple shrug of his shoulders, he responded, "I suppose that's more the result of getting old. I got tired of dealing with everyone else. People—immortals alike—are draining. I no longer feel obliged to be around them simply because I feel as though I have to put on a friendly front. I care about very few people, and they're the only ones I see myself needing to be concerned with. Everyone else is just a hassle."

I teased, "Wow. You *do* sound like an old man."

"I know. I'm not going to deny that, either." He winked at me, eyes glimmering in the darkness of our living room. "It's okay. You've always had a thing for older guys." That was most certainly a jab at Johnny, since Johnny was the only *older* man I'd ever been with. But Johnny was much too easy of a target.

"If you're referring to Johnny, he wasn't that old," I argued. "He seemed older than he was because he had premature grey from being a dick all the time."

Riftan scoffed. "Obviously your judgment of age is off since you've been hanging around me, but Johnny was old enough to be your grandfather, love."

Usually, I'd suggest he not call me that, but this time I'd let it slide since we were having an intimate conversation. "Riftan, I think you're probably old enough to be my great, great, great, great, grandfather… to like the tenth power. So, what does it matter?" I pushed into him, butting my nose against his with a playful giggle.

"It matters that I—much like he was—am too old for you, dear." He grabbed ahold of my chin and pushed me away.

Disdain weighed heavy on my features, eyes narrowing and lips dropping into a sour scowl. "You're *seriously* still sticking with that?" Even after he'd been all over me hours earlier in front of Jameson's friends? *He's so confusing. Does he even know what he wants?*

In a rational tone, he responded, "Of course I'm sticking with that. Because it's true."

"So, you're going to tell me *honestly* that you've never once thought about what it would be like for the two of us to be intimate?"

He eyed me before answering. "Obviously I've thought about it. How could I not when we are so close? But that doesn't mean I've ever actually thought to act on it."

"If that's the case, then why are you constantly touching me the way you do?" I gave an unambiguous look toward where he held my legs firmly against his chest. "If I were to ever do the same, you'd consider it perverse, you know?"

"Yes, I would. It's okay when I do it. Because I, in fact, can control myself. While you, my dear, cannot." As he contested with me, his voice was still so sympathetic. "If I let you do whatever you please, you'll push things too far and get hurt in the process. I don't need to be the first immortal to break your heart. Regardless, I would never want to risk the possibility of tainting your exquisite, pure virtue."

I scoffed at his statement, reeling only a moment before retorting, "Did you say that *you* are concerned you'd taint *me*? You know I was sleeping with Johnny for his *money*, right? That's not exactly *virtuous*."

"Yes," Riftan agreed. "But that's the first time I've ever gotten you to admit it outright."

My cheeks burned, flustered by how precisely that made me sound like a hooker—though I'd never been! And I'd take that fact to my grave—or in this case, my eternity. *Smug bastard.* Continuing my argument, I acted as though I'd ignored his comment. "I don't know why you'd think I was any sort of pure, regardless, we share the same blood. How could you expect to taint me any further?"

The glint of his teeth signaled a mischievous smirk. "Oh, love, there are *plenty* of ways I could think of."

That made me weak. Butterflies rumbled in my core, and I knew Riftan could hear my heartbeat grow louder. *What I wouldn't give to have him follow through with that threat.* "All I'm hearing is empty promises, Riftan."

He pushed his forehead against mine with sudden force, speaking low and hot over my lips. "How exactly did I get stuck with such a cheeky little minx like you?"

"Well, I don't know what a minx is, but I think you mean: how did you get *blessed* with one?"

"Hah." His breath lingered in the tiny void between us. Both perfect sapphires of his eyes flickered between mine, filling the space with palpable adoration.

I'd be content if eternity consisted of an endless moment of this. Sharing his breath, watching the glimmering blue that shielded the windows to his soul as it remained uninterpretable, even for me. Still, I could have stared for hours. The only thing that could pull me away—the only thing more powerful than his gaze—was the potent tingle of his fingers over my skin. As the tingle forced its way up my arm and his fingers settled under my jaw, I couldn't help but give into the feeling, my eyes rolling back from something so meager as his touch. An eternity would not be long enough to revel in the ecstasy I felt when he put his hands on me. Heaven, transcension, divinity; none of it was equal to the feeling of his skin on mine.

I wasn't so naïve to believe anything would come of this or that Riftan would follow through on whatever was going on between us. So, it was in no way a surprise when he pulled away from me, leaving the place where his skin had been on mine a cold and lonely shadow of what could have been.

Before I'd opened my eyes, a flick stung my nose and Riftan simply added, "Don't tease me like that. It drives me nuts."

Me, tease *him? Why that little—*

He pushed my legs off his lap in a rough motion that was contradicted by how carefully he set them down on the couch. "You should go to bed," he said. "You could use some rest after learning to use magic."

I made to argue, pausing with my mouth agape. My contention was that I didn't want to go to bed. I wanted to stay with him. I wanted to tell him how I felt. I wanted to live some naïve happily ever after where we could be together... but he wouldn't want to hear that. When my dispute got lodged in my throat, unable to make itself heard, Riftan rose, leaving the spot beside me empty.

He started to retreat, and my chest ached more with each distancing step. The place he'd occupied next to me was suddenly too cold to bear. Just for the night, I didn't want him to leave me. I wanted the warmth of his presence to swaddle me until the sun came up—until I was no longer tired and lonely. It didn't have to be intimate. We would never *have* to be intimate or romantic if that's what it took to stay with him. Friends. Lovers. It didn't matter. All I wanted was to never leave his side.

"Riftan," I called, my voice shallow, "wait."

He stopped only feet away. "What is it?"

"Are you going to make me leave soon?" The thought surfaced again for the first time since Jameson had put it at the forefront of my mind.

"No. Whatever would make you think that?"

"You don't ever keep anyone around this long. Even Jameson, you trained him for less than a year before setting him out on his own."

"Well, he was done with his training then. You are not and won't be anytime foreseeably soon."

"Am I... a slow learner? Is it because I don't catch onto things—"

"No," he interrupted. "You pick up on everything very well, I assure you. I've simply been soft on you because I like keeping you around. That's all."

Even if it meant staying platonic, my aching heart was soothed by his words.

"Will you keep it that way?" I asked, trying my damndest not to make it sound like I was begging.

"Yes. Don't worry about that. I have no intention of letting you go anytime soon."

With that, he left for his bedroom, and I was alone in the darkness of our living room.

If I could stay with him in our little world pretending like our time together would last an eternity, then I would do so for as long as I could.

I'd stay naïve for as long as Riftan would let me.

Two Years Later

15

MUCH LIKE MY MORTAL LIFE, I'LL KEEP THIS BRIEF

HAVING TOLD my story this far already, I suppose I'm obligated to provide a little context to it. Don't worry, much like my mortal life, I'll keep it short.

My name is Leanne Cowitz—though I don't hold much reverence for my family name. I was raised by a selfish mother, who never married the man whose name she gave me. It has always seemed strange that I'd keep the name of a man I'd never met when the person who raised me went by another—and yet, I am still the only Cowitz I've ever known. My father died before the realm of my memories—a victim of organized crime, so my mother claimed. She spoke of both his life and his death with dissidence, though she herself was guilty of all the things she hated about him. She despised the man, and yet she'd given me his name. She'd always been a hypocrite.

I couldn't blame her for her actions. Everyone in the city of Creswell was guilty of wrongdoings and lapses in character. It was a city filled with crime and misfortune, and if you didn't learn to roll with the punches… well, you might get knocked out. That was mostly the fault of the overwhelming mafia influence there. With the Roufe's chokehold on Creswell's crime system, and the many greedy factions clawing for their position—including the Fedoravs one town over and the Grioris lurking in Creswell's gutters—it was impossible to live any sort of life in the city or the surrounding areas without entangling yourself in organized mischief.

I'd always thought it was because of that nobody had ever heard of our flourishing city despite its growing stance in the tech industry and other notable characteristics that otherwise made it a viable hotspot for fame and status in this generation. But, as it turns out, in contrast to what I'd believed my whole life, the mafia wasn't solely at fault for that. I'd only recently found out there'd always been a heavy concentration of vampires in the tri-city area of Creswell, and it's thanks to them and their manipulation Creswell has continued to fly under the radar.

Other cities around the world existed with a similar dynamic: places where vampires have convened throughout the ages, some hidden from the outside world like Creswell, and others well-entwined in it like Prague. Vampires thrived through this "underworld" community—sometimes referred to as the underground—where they shared information, resources, and much more. Simply being a part of this community was enough to obtain the kind of knowledge most mortals would think to be unobtainable. However, the cities run by the underground weren't the only places where you could find immortal communities. Vampires are everywhere— sometimes focused in groups, and sometimes wandering out on their own.

Among this secret society of vampires was a social hierarchy, as well as established governments—referred to as councils. But this is something I still have limited knowledge of. Unfortunately, before a few years ago, I knew nothing of this underworld filled with vampires and fairytale creatures. Back then, I would have never believed if you'd told me that such things were far from mythical. Maybe if I'd known the truth, I'd have seen how big the world truly was and realized the many options mortality offered. Possibly, I never would have dropped out of college to date Johnny Roufe, the current head of the Roufe family. Alas, I was once young and naïve and could only think small.

At one point in time, before Johnny, I wanted to be a nurse, and despite my upbringing by a sole drug addict who'd overdosed when I was sixteen, I was determined to get an education that could lead me out of that dreadful city. I suppose, somewhere along the way, I lost sight of that dream in the pursuit of the many shiny things that Creswell could offer, and Johnny Roufe did *indeed* offer me many shiny things in return for my company.

At the time, a relationship with him seemed ideal—like a

celebrity picking me out of a crowd and choosing to love me over any of his other devoted fans. Johnny got every woman imaginable, and he could do with her as he pleased. That usually meant he slept with a lot of women, all the while keeping the prettiest one officially on his arm. But I was different, and that made me prideful. Johnny didn't sleep with other women when he was with me—at least not outright. I was his one and only, which was something he hadn't shown an interest in having since his first wife many years before me. I was proud, like I'd tamed the untamable, like being Johnny's one and only was something I could put on my resume—something that could overrule a college degree.

I'd once sought to marry Johnny Roufe.

Looking back on it, that thought is painful in its own right. But at the time, I'd thought I loved him—in a strange, unexplainable kind of way. Yes, Johnny was so much older than I was, and he didn't have the best looks, even for someone his age. He didn't have the ability to make my heart race, or the butterflies in my stomach stir, but what he did have was money and power, enough of it to make the idea of sharing it with him a very addicting and alluring prospect. It was enough to make me decide that I could fall in love with a piece of shit like Johnny.

I almost married Johnny Roufe, and that, in hindsight, makes my blood boil.

Though I now can admit I hated Johnny more than I ever loved him—and I absolutely did not regret leaving his ass—there were still times I thought about my old life. I wondered what Jayleen was up to, if she was still working that same shitty job. When I thought about her, it was reflective, but not melancholy. She always was proficient at overcoming the odds; I imagined she was doing just fine.

I often speculated how easily Johnny may have forgotten about me, a consideration I brushed from my mind as soon as it surfaced. More ruminatively, I pondered if his boys ever missed me. Each time, I clung on to the image of them longer than I should. Closing my eyes, I could see all three boys' happy little faces at the dinner table. I could feel the warmth of their hugs and smell the spiced pinecones that filled the air when they'd gather around me on Christmas morning—the Christmas mornings when they weren't with their mother, at least.

The reminiscence from those thoughts didn't sting because I didn't feel somber as if I missed them, but I still felt *something* from it, my heart murmuring a little when I thought of them. I couldn't say I'd *cared* about those boys, but I couldn't really say I *hadn't* either. My feelings for them were confusing. They were probably the closest thing I'd ever have to sons, and someday I'd probably cherish the three years I'd spent as their makeshift mother. Maybe I was starting to—maybe that's what the feeling I felt for them was.

Other than those moments, few and far between, I had no reservations left over from leaving my old life behind. In fact, I had nothing but certitude that I'd made the right decision. *Nothing* could hinder my love for my new life.

Not only had I escaped from a hell I'd made for myself,

but I'd been *rescued* by my very own devilishly handsome knight. Riftan was the hero in my fairytale story, though he adorned sharp fangs instead of the typical weapons of a knight in shining armor.

It'd been almost three years since the day I decided to become a vampire by his hand. Since then, not a moment has passed when I wasn't thankful to him for giving me this new life. Riftan would always be special to me, and not only for the blood in my veins that we shared, but because of the bond we'd created.

Though he refused to admit that we could ever be anything but companions, Riftan was loving to a fault. He'd always had trouble disconnecting affection from romanticism, which only made me fall head over heels for him—over and over again. Though I shouldn't have let him lead me on the way he did, I couldn't help it. His touch was addicting, like it was the only thing I needed to survive, and I didn't care if it never became more.

Every day provided a new opportunity to get my fix. Out in public, or in the privacy of our condo, Riftan would hold my hand so nonchalantly, interlacing our fingers the way lovers might. Sometimes, he'd cuddle up on the couch with me and play with my hair, twirling it in his fingers before he'd plop his head down on mine. He'd look for any excuse to hold me as close as he possibly could, not caring if it caused both our heartbeats to stir.

We were more than physically affectionate; we were close in so many other ways, too. There wasn't a part of our lives we didn't share anymore. We laughed and cried together, even if I was usually the one crying and he was the one laughing about something that was supposed to make me feel better. We ate, traveled, joked, lounged, and lived *together.*

We were inseparable, and we were both content that way.

In Riftan, I'd found more love and acceptance than I'd ever attained in another relationship, even if we weren't entwined in a *relationship.* Not only had I grown to love him, but I'd grown to love myself in new ways, embracing my identity beyond simply enjoying my vampire existence. For the first time in maybe ever, I got to be my most natural self—a refreshing and profound change.

Growing up, I'd strived to fit in, dying my hair, wearing all the jewelry, dressing in fancy clothes, and putting on the confident act that I'd gotten used to adorning—efforts I didn't regret but recognized weren't true to me.

While I was adapting to my senses as a newborn vampire, all of my energy was focused on surviving, and any facades of a fancy Creswell girl became the last thing on my mind. Because of that, Riftan had seen me at my worst from the start, which made acting my normal feel like a vast improvement. He'd been the first person to see the real me, and his acceptance of that made it feel like it was okay to shed my self-imposed facade. For the first time, I could breathe freely without the weight of some fake role on my shoulders. Steadily, that act—that girl— was becoming a thing of the past. And back there is exactly where I wanted to leave her.

Even my bleached blonde hair had grown back to its

natural gingery red, which I hadn't sported since before college. Though I'd once despised the red, it now fit my vampiric glow. Luckily, immortality really seemed to speed up hair growth— Riftan's constantly grew past his ears despite monthly cuts, turning me into a skilled stylist over the last few years. The rapid growth made ditching my blonde easy, avoiding what would have been tedious and frequent bleaching. Riftan's persistent compliments on my natural color only sealed the deal, and always made my heart ache in the best way.

While our relationship wasn't traditional, I was thankful to share the little life we'd formed together. I'd take all the aches and beatings Riftan put my heart through. Our time together was priceless, and I wasn't going to let some unrequited love between us stifle it. I never would truly *need* more from him, even if sometimes I wanted it. I was happy with him the way we were.

If our time didn't last forever—if it was given a deadline— I still loved Riftan. I didn't care if that meant someday suffering a broken heart at his hand—even if it was one that lasted an eternity.

WHY ARE YOU IN MY BED

AS THE SUN shone through the few lingering cloud tufts on a bright spring day, I found myself partaking in the most human of routines: making a cup of coffee.

Since becoming a vampire, I quite enjoyed the taste of black coffee, though the caffeine had no effect on me. But today, the coffee wasn't for me. For the first time in weeks, I was the first one to wake in the condo, and I was determined to bring Riftan a morning beverage in bed like he often did for me.

It was strange how much a little ritual like that could bring back some remnant of my human life. It was always pleasant to partake in the little things that could make us feel normal on occasion. Especially when many may consider a habit such as murdering people and drinking their blood very abnormal.

Taking the steaming cup of coffee in my hand, I strode toward Riftan's open door. We no longer seemed to close doors in the condo—it was like an unsaid pact between us. There was something about shutting doors that made things seem private, and neither of us required any privacy from the other.

Inside the open doorway, where warmth still enveloped the smaller space, Riftan was already standing by the gold mirror, fiddling with the sleeve of his unbuttoned shirt. He greeted me with a smile that lingered over his shoulder for only a moment before he returned his attention to his shirt cuffs.

The room was still dark, but that didn't make it any harder to see. With my heightened senses, it was no different from a well-lit space. On my way to Riftan, I meandered past a wood dresser where he kept a small assortment of belongings. His leather-bound journal was collecting dust, save for the spot where he always tossed his watch on top of it, and beside it was a photo of us in a frame older than my entire family lineage. Feeling the familiar stack of things draw my attention, I stopped, tracing the pile with a curious gaze. The glint of the gold frame shone in the dim light, but it wasn't what had caught my eye. The photo housed within wasn't as familiar as it should have been, given how many times I'd passed it in the last three years.

Originally, the photo had been a picture of us when we'd first come to Czech. My hair was still blonde, and I'd been blushing like a tomato from Riftan's proximity to my cheek. He was smiling, but not enough to see his teeth, and I seemed too distracted to so much as match his meager look. The sky in the background was as grey as a Prague fall morning, and the moment it'd been taken was inconsequential—I didn't remember the circumstances.

That was far from what was in the frame now. It'd been replaced by a picture I recalled from our trip to Curacao months earlier. Riftan had the camera in one hand and my bare waist in the other. We were both in swimsuits, standing in front of the most beautiful, clear turquoise water. Riftan's cheek was squished up against mine with a giant, childish smile spread over his whole face. I was laughing at him so hard that my eyes weren't open for the photo, and my baby fangs weren't so little anymore—in fact, they were about as obvious as Riftan's. My red hair had grown past my shoulders and was soaking wet from the tropical waters. Riftan was just as drenched, droplets of water dripping from his hair and flattening it like a wet dog's.

It wasn't the best photo of either of us—not by a long shot—but the memory it evoked was matchless, bringing a smile to my face.

"When did you replace our photo?" I asked.

"I don't know." Riftan hardly spared a fleeting shrug. "A couple of weeks ago, I guess."

"Why this one?" I couldn't help but scoff. The photo wasn't great, and we probably had many that were better from that trip, let alone one of the many other trips we'd taken together.

"Because of how happy you look in it. I love it. It's my favorite of all the ones we have together."

I *did* look overly thrilled, but with that said, so did Riftan.

It was hard to believe he could look as authentically cheerful as he did in that photo. It was hard to believe *anyone* could look as jovial as the two of us did there. While it was sloppy, that photo was a proper snapshot of our happiness together.

"I suppose you're right. Here, this is for you." I offered him a mug, closing the distance between us.

He took it from me, careful not to spill the hot contents. In return, I took his free hand and straightened out the sleeve he'd been fussing with. Twice, I rolled the cuff like I knew he wanted but hadn't quite achieved yet.

Crossing his coffee-bearing arm over my head, Riftan traded the mug to his other hand before taking a sip and holding out his second unrolled cuff for me. Matching it to the other, I moved on to his open shirt. Wiggling my way in front of him, I hopped up onto the dresser that he'd been leaning against and grabbed his shirt placket, tugging until he took a step closer, permitting me to reach all the buttons.

In all truth, buttoning his shirt for him was merely an excuse to stare at his bare, inhumanly toned chest. But I couldn't make that too obvious or else I wouldn't get away with it. There was always a line with Riftan, and he'd let anything happen as long as it didn't cross that very thin line.

Hell—I wasn't sure if what I was doing counted. I only got to know what was and wasn't acceptable through trial and error. Or, as some might say, fuck around and find out.

With that in mind, I slipped each button through its partnering cotton hole in his shirt with due prudence. All the while, I could feel Riftan's watchful gaze boring a hole right through my forehead. My cheeks flushed from his stare, and my heart pounded more rampantly. If he didn't notice the former, he'd surely notice the latter. Unfortunately, he probably wouldn't understand it was his roving eyes that did it to me, and not the firm, rippling velvet of his abdomen under my hands.

Sinking the last few buttons much quicker than I'd intended to, I finished up by patting him on the chest and sharing my most harmless smile.

Riftan's lips did not match. Instead, they were devoid of any expression. Adding to the obscure look, his deep eyes appeared empty as they scattered over me like he was lost in some recessed thought. The only thing hinting through his vacancy was the flare of his jaw as he gritted his teeth at me.

"Is everything okay?" I asked, masking my tone in a chipper façade. "Did I do something wrong?"

He slackened, adjusting to an admirable smile, his eyes lighting up to a vibrant blue once more. "No, of course not. Thank you, love."

He'd started calling me that again. Though I'd once chastised him for doing so when we aren't lovers, I'd long since stopped correcting him. Now, I simply let it roll off my shoulders, only lightly tugging on my tender heartstrings on the way by.

Patting my cheek, Riftan tucked an arm around my waist and pulled me down off the dresser. Using my shadow fade— as I did from time to time to get used to it—I teleported to my side of the bed several steps away. Jumping into the covers, I crossed my legs and watched as Riftan went about his morning.

And no, I'm not merely going to skim over the fact that I said *my side* of the bed when referencing the bed in Riftan's room.

I had been sleeping in the same bed as Riftan for a while—maybe years by this point. At first, it'd been completely against his will, and warming him up to the idea had taken a while. Now, it was simply routine. And as much as I'd love to claim the reason we'd first shared a bed was some passionate quandary of loneliness, it hadn't been anything near that romantic or even quixotic.

We'd already slept with the doors open, and we'd often find ourselves sleeping on the couch at times, when loneliness was a potential threat. There wasn't anything deviant about the idea of sleeping together, but the act of doing so in the *bed* was something that crossed one of Riftan's invisible thin lines. I'd never wanted to push that, because it was understandable and easily avoided.

Except for one little hitch.

For as long as I'd been with him, Riftan suffered from the worst night terrors. I knew this because—like I'd said—we weren't ever shy about sleeping near each other as long as it wasn't in his bed. Since sometimes his nightmares manifested with him tossing and turning, or murmuring and whining in his sleep, it was obvious enough when he was dreaming, and the longer they persisted, the worse it got.

He could be skilled at hiding his emotions while he was conscious, but while asleep, he did no such thing. The pain he felt from the trials of his subconscious was painted all over his face and evident in the shallowness of his breath. At first, I'd merely woken him up every time the terrors didn't subside on their own. He'd appeared grateful for that, even when I'd have to wake him up several times during the day. Eventually, I no longer had to wake him—simply sliding my hand up over his chest until he recognized my presence was enough to soothe him in his sleep. Some of the times he'd pull me close and continue to snooze like a pacified baby, while others, he'd lay his hand over the spot where our warmth conjoined on his chest. Either way, he was usually mollified after that, and the both of us could sleep without trouble the rest of the night.

After a while, I'd become hypersensitive to the little sounds of his anguish that started when he was suffering from a day terror. The moment he'd begin to stir, I'd awake like I were the one having a bad dream.

It was like that when we'd slept apart.

I'd dreaded the sound of his subliminal agony like it was my own. That was the only time I felt helpless against it, unable to climb into his bed and save him from the unknown horrors of his subconscious. My acute senses made even tuning him out impossible.

So, at some point, I'd finally reached my wit's end and found myself outside of his doorway, pacing the entrance, unable to decide if going against his wishes and climbing into bed with him would be something I'd get away with. When I heard him murmuring a meager little plea with the same lips that spoke so strapping and unflappable while awake, my feet moved toward him on their own.

I would never get any sleep with the rate at which he had

those dreams. The suffering he felt, even when he was asleep, was practically manifesting as my own. It couldn't always be about him; I needed to get some sleep too—and I wouldn't ever at that rate. If he'd complained about my actions, that'd simply have been my argument—I just wanted to get some sound sleep.

As I'd gently crawled into his bed, Riftan was restless, sweat beading over his scrunched brows. My heart pounded, induced by the helpless look on his otherwise masculine face. The idea that anything could torture him that way would haunt me for eternity. Slipping my hand under his soft cotton sheets, I paused a moment before laying it over his bare chest.

"Don't," he'd murmured, the tone hard and commanding as my fingers contacted his skin. I froze dead in my tracks, only a moment passing before I'd realized he was talking in his sleep. With my palm flat over his chest, his brows still knit in anguish. He was so deep into his subconscious; I'd regretted I might have to wake him to get it to stop.

Gently, I'd shaken him, tapping my fingers against his smooth cheeks in an attempt to rouse him as tenderly as possible. A little groan escaped his lips before he went completely still. Then, in an instant, he was on top of me, pinning me to his bed.

I wasn't all that surprised by his reaction. It'd happened once before when I'd tried to wake him from those nightmares. His response to being awoken was only ever so bad if the dreams had progressed too far.

His lips snarled and a droplet of sweat dripped from the

dark hair that danced by his cheek.

Helplessly fastened between Riftan's grip and the sheets, I'd waited for him to come back to his senses like I knew from experience he would. The methodic rise and fall of my chest was my only movement, quelling his breathing to steady like mine.

"It's okay. It's just me. Leanne." I'd reached up to touch his cheek with the hand not pinned under his. As his brilliant dark eyes began to signal some recognition, his grip on me loosened, but his expression didn't seem any more pleased.

"Leanne, why are you in my bed?" he'd asked in a low but ireful tone.

I'd twirled my fingers in a piece of his sweat-slicked hair. The action lightening the grimace in his brow. "You were having one of those nightmares again. I've told you I hate listening to it. There's no way I can sleep soundly while you're suffering like that."

"They're just dreams." He'd pushed off me and laid back down on his pillow. "Stop worrying about me and go back to your room."

Silence filled the space between us, and Riftan put his back to me.

Shimmying under the covers, I'd tucked myself into the open space Riftan had left in his oversized bed.

He'd groaned without sparing a glance. "What do you think you're doing?"

"Shut up and go to sleep," I'd snapped back at him. "I'll stay on my side. Pretend like I'm not here."

"Fine. But don't try anything, okay?" he'd warned, scooting away and pulling up the sheets.

"I would never," I'd lied.

From that day forward, I hadn't slept in my own bed a single time. It was easier to stay by Riftan's side, especially when we were away from our condo. Traveling was worlds easier when we only had to get one bed in a hotel or share a small space in a jet or train. As we got used to that arrangement and it became second nature to sleep together, things grew more relaxed between us. There were fewer awkward interactions, fewer moments when the sexual tension seemed to drive us apart, and a strange blur developed between the lines Riftan had set for us. It was like the closer we got, the more it became impossible to sense what was and wasn't abnormal for a platonic couple to carry out.

We did nearly everything most conventional romantic couples did. Most recently, it seemed like the only thing we *didn't* do was kiss and make love. For a couple who weren't dating, we especially went on a lot of dates. The kind where we held hands and made small talk as though we were a real couple. Dates much like the one I'd been so excited for today.

Sitting there on *my* side of the bed, I looked over at Riftan as he thumbed through the closet. "Hey, do you remember what today is?" I hummed, my tone light as though I were impartial to the answer.

Riftan glanced at me with the flattest expression, one that nearly looked like a glare over his eyes. "Of course I know what today is. Who do you take me for? Besides, why else would I be getting ready so early in the day?"

A couple weeks earlier, I'd heard of a big farmers' market in one of the countryside towns. It was being held during their spring festival and promised a myriad of spring festivities. While I may not have been much of a farmers' market kind of girl when I was with Johnny, growing up in Creswell the county fair was one of my fondest memories. I imagined a spring festival in the countryside of beautiful Czech would trounce a county fair in Creswell any day of the week.

Riftan was certainly less interested than I was, as he'd protested that I wouldn't like the taste or smell of anything we could buy at a farmers' market. I also knew that he didn't love going out during the day. Not that it bothered him, but more that it didn't appeal to him. Over his many years, Riftan had conformed to his vampiric veneer on all fronts, but he'd quickly conceded to indulge me, regardless of his personal restraints.

Though his get-up wasn't quite farmers' market attire, Riftan *had* gotten dressed despite the sun's trajectory being not quite overhead yet. It was much earlier than he'd usually decide to go out, and in jeans and a button-up dress shirt, he was dressed about as casually as I'd seen him get for leaving the condo.

"You, however," Riftan pointed in my direction, "are not dressed yet. I thought you were so excited about this silly festival; you've been talking about it for weeks. Now, go get dressed before we miss it."

Sticking out my tongue at him, I agreed with a hop and a skip into my room, where I, too, threw on some jeans and a cute black knit sweater. I'd adopted a lot of black in my closet, which seemed ironic given the obvious gothic stereotype for my kind. But, as my hair grew more ginger each month and I no longer had to dress to please a rich mob family, it was out with the reds and patterns, and in with the easy-to-style black. It went with everything, and I'd found some amusement in leaning into the vampiric cliché.

After I was dressed, I pranced my way right back out into the living room, since I hardly wore any makeup anymore, and my hair kind of did what it did. My red mane was shinier than it'd ever been when I was human, and I no longer had to style it for it to look flawless. *Oh, how I* love *being immortal.*

Once we were both ready, Riftan and I took the car up through the countryside until rolling fields of green dotted the landscape between small, dilapidated buildings and quaint cottages. The sizable farmers' market took up a couple blocks in a small town, where once-colorful buildings were stacked up on both sides of the street. Vendors filled the area with makeshift stalls and filtered music into the air where I could frolic amid the mortals to my heart's content.

Riftan, of course, had been right; I didn't necessarily like any of the overwhelming smells that may have once roused my olfactory senses with nostalgia. But that didn't make the sights and sounds any different from how I'd remembered them being when I was human. Yes, I was akin to more of them, but they were all still the same as I recalled.

After taking it all in for a better half of the day with Riftan in tow as my stoic tag along, I decided to offer something a bit more his speed. "I'm hungry. Can we go out tonight?" It wasn't a lie. I hadn't had a living meal in nearly a month and, as Riftan had once warned me, pre-packaged blood couldn't sustain a vampire for long. I could go longer without fresh blood now than I could a year ago, and Riftan could go *much* longer, but eventually, the time would come between living meals when packaged blood did nothing but make me hungrier.

He squeezed my hand from where our fingers laced together. "Yeah, I'd like to go out tonight if that's what you want."

"The Old Eagle is having a karaoke night. There will probably be lots of people there."

"Yeah, a lot of hipster tourists. You won't find a proper meal there."

"True, but it sounds like fun."

Riftan offered a chipper laugh. "Are you hungry, or do you want to go to karaoke?"

"Hmm." I thought hard about his question before settling. "I suppose I'm hungrier than anything."

"Okay, then we can go to Sanctum tonight. They are hosting a VIP event sure to pull in a crowd: the kind of crowd you can choose from." He pulled me to a stop in front of a booth full of greenery and exchanged a few coins for a couple of pink and white cylindrical-petaled flowers. They were the least pungent of the assortment and flourished in large, bushy blossoms. Riftan offered the stunning flora over to me with a smile that lit up his expression even through his dark sunglasses.

"Thanks," I offered, my gaze finding purchase on the

sidewalk ahead of us as my cheeks surely blushed outright.

Riftan went on. "But we can karaoke next time we go out, how's that sound?"

"Sounds like a deal," I agreed with a chuckle at the mere idea of Riftan among a karaoke crowd.

T H E   C L U B we frequented was certainly more packed with people than I'd ever seen it in the past. Each attendee at the VIP event was decked from head to toe in gaudy accessories that glimmered in the many lights like coins in the eyes of the greedy. They had only shown up to flaunt their wealth and status, but I suppose it was hypocritical of me to judge all of them equally. I had, after all, once been one of those who would love to attend such an event wearing as many diamonds as possible with the city's most revered man on my arm. Then again, maybe I would choose to kill me, too, if my previous self was put before me now.

"Well, you were right," I told Riftan as we entered the club, taking my seat that he'd thralled to be open at the bar. "There's certainly plenty to pick from tonight."

"If I'm being honest, there's more than I expected. It's going to be more difficult to go unnoticed. As I warned previously, I'm not going to lend you any aid tonight. Not like last time."

He was referring to a specific scenario in which I was supposed to be feeding on my own and successfully cleaning up after myself, but had encountered a bit of a hang-up. A passerby witnessed it, and I hadn't detected them. Riftan thralled the man and sent him on his way, but I'd gotten a stern talking to over it. Now I knew better, and I could handle the cleanup on my own. I was certain of it. I *was*, after all, supposed to be self-sustaining after so many years with Riftan as a guide. "Last time was a fluke. I've got this. I've done it on my own multitudes of other times."

He continued to press with an air of unyielding concern. "I'm serious. If something like last time happens, I'm going to let it go. I won't always be here to back you up for the rest of your eternity, and if someone like that slips through the cracks, you'll probably have to answer to the Council. Though that'd be a minor reprimand, it's best to stay off their radar, okay?"

The Council to the underworld was an entity that I was only recently becoming acquainted with. They were the "government" that oversaw vampire relations and drove to keep our inner workings a secret from the mortal world. I'd met a member once, a nice girl named Suzua. They were merely normal vampires appointed to their positions to keep order; nothing sinister or malevolent. Though there were many vampires within the underworld who did have vindictive minds, many of them were older and more revered, which put them in high positions in the council. So, it was still a rather humorless place that I did wish to avoid.

"Yes, I know, I know," I repeated, touching my hand to Riftan's, where it sat at the counter of the bar.

Ordering us a round of drinks, Riftan made a point to pull my seat closer to his so that our legs were together before I turned toward him.

I was in no hurry to find a meal, though I *was* rather hungry that night. As usual, I would simply be content to spend my time out with Riftan. We could talk some, then maybe dance a little—or a lot. *Then* maybe I'd look for my meal.

With a mere glance around the room, I could see any number of potential victims, and they wouldn't be leaving anytime soon either. I had plenty of time.

A holler from the large group of guests toward the back caught my attention as my gaze scanned past them. Several blonde women with low-cut dresses entertained the group of mostly men who hooted and clamored as if they were the only ones in the joint. A man at the table grabbed one of the blondes by the skirt and she protested, futilely pushing against him. He complained, but one of the other women at the table bickered at him and he unhanded the girl. Another man at what seemed to be the head of the table stood to his full height, looming over the others and reprimanding the group in a gruff European language. He threatened them with a hard stare until they settled into a mediocre hush that matched that of the clubgoers around them. The man, with a short, blond head of hair and alarming broad features, then sat and continued to talk with his closest guests as though nothing had transpired.

While I was nearly certain that I'd never met the man, my brain tingled with recognition so strong I could nearly taste it. It was as if I'd seen him in a photograph. Something in passing like... a news article. But not just any news article, one I'd committed to memory.

The article was about a man who owned a large construction firm that'd built many of the newer buildings in the cities east of Czech. He was someone who would hardly be of interest to me, except that there was a rumor I'd heard floating around the underworld about him. Immortals had warned he was using his company to front a large human trafficking operation. While I didn't like to feed into rumors in my past life, I'd found that rumors from the underworld were always based on some sort of fact and always held an abundant weight of importance. We knew of things many mortals wouldn't find out about for years. Sometimes that meant being witness to atrocities that could have been stopped.

When I'd heard about this man, and some of the graphic things he'd done to innocent people, I'd promised myself then and there that if I ever saw him for myself, I'd kill him on the spot. And this was him.

No longer was I in that club to have a jolly time with Riftan. I was fixed on a target.

"That guy over there." I patted Riftan and pointed at the man. "He's Iosif Sokolov, I saw him online the other day. He runs Sokolov Inc. I heard he's responsible for orchestrating all those human trafficking scandals," I recounted, lost in thought, and then adding casually, "I'm going to kill him tonight. I don't care about anybody else here. He's going to die."

"No way." Riftan was firm. "He's way too high profile. We are not getting into that tonight."

"Riftan, I'm not asking you. I'm telling you. Tonight, he dies."

"Seriously?" Riftan questioned, though his lax expression noted that he was not completely surprised. "What about his entourage? I told you I won't be helping you tonight, and that's a lot of curious onlookers. You're making me nervous." His tone lacked the fervor it might have if he intended to stop me but was instead thick with something like worry.

My eyes remained fixed on Sokolov, determined not to miss out on this opportunity to devour a *real* plague to society. "Yeah, I can handle this on my own. Just you sit back and watch." With that, I got up and wandered to the roisterous table of men in the back.

"Hi," I offered to the burly man who headed the group. "Do you mind if I join you?"

Iosif looked up at me with wide green eyes. He quickly nodded. "It'd be my pleasure, lovely." His accent was thicker than most, and he was obviously native to the area, which only helped me to solidify his identity.

Scooting in close, I made some flirty small talk with him and his guests. It was easy to tell what he liked from the girls he kept at his table, and it wasn't hard for me to copy. Before long,

I had him eating out of the palm of my hand, both figuratively *and* literally, as I fed him the cherry from my drink. Iosif only had eyes for me, and I knew I'd struck gold. He was *mine* now. I would be able to do whatever I wanted with him, and I hadn't even thralled him yet.

Taking a peek over my shoulder, I spied Riftan at the bar where I'd left him. He wasn't watching me intently like I'd expected from his anxious manner before I'd left. Instead, he was nearly nose-to-nose with some other girl. She was cute and blonde and sliding her delicate fingers up his arm like she was trying her damndest to seduce him.

My skin crawled, my blood instantly boiling over the way she touched him and the way he watched her do it so complaisantly. I'd touched lots of other men while I was with Riftan, and I'd seen him feed from other women, too, but there was something about this interaction that made my skin burn hot and my heart ache like it was gripped in a vise.

I was biting my own tongue, nearly drawing blood as I fought against the urge to stand right up and walk over there when I saw Riftan lean over to whisper in that woman's ear.

Iosof's voice distracted me long enough to miss what Riftan had told the girl. "Hey cutie, what's caught your eye over there?"

I looked at the fair-haired man whose lap I'd occupied before whipping back around to watch Riftan. The girl was already walking away from him, though he had the smuggest look on his face as he watched her leave. It pushed me over my boiling point. Riftan would never give me that look, and I *loathed* that he'd given it to a girl he didn't know instead.

"Sorry, I was distracted for a moment." I masked an innocent grin toward Iosif.

My heart was in my stomach, manifesting into a knot. The feeling was unpleasant, burdensome, and it felt like the only thing that would ease it was retribution. While I wasn't naïve enough to believe copying Riftan's offense would phase him, I still needed that fair level of payback.

Gently, I slid my hand over Iosif's thigh, anchoring my nails into the expensive fabric of his slacks. "Hey, do you want to go somewhere more private?" I asked, fluttering my long eyelashes like the skanks I knew he liked.

He smiled like he might give in, but then sighed. "I can't, dear. I have a whole table of guests here with me."

I insisted, *"Let's go somewhere private."* All the while sprinkling it with a little more sex appeal and a dash of thrall.

"Yes. Of course." His expression fell blank.

"And don't forget to tell your guests you'll be right back," I added with a wink.

He turned to his dinner guests. "I'll be back in a few minutes. Order another round on me."

"Good boy," I murmured, pulling him by the hand toward the back exit.

Outside, the air was beginning to crisp, and not a soul was in sight. Whipping around to meet Iosif as he slipped out the door, I pushed until he was flush with the wall, laying my body against his large frame. He smirked, taking my face in his palm with surprising gentility for someone so gruff and big.

He was no Riftan, but he was certainly attractive in his own right. His blond hair shimmered in the light from the closest streetlamp, and I could confirm the chiseled features he was so well-known for. I would have fun with him for a little while to make myself forget about the way Riftan had looked at that girl.

Bringing my lips to his, I let Iosif set a pace. He was remarkably tender for such a notorious asshole, which almost had my heart dancing over the intimacy of our embrace. His lips painted mine with the kind of attention I hadn't gotten in *ages*. It was divine and sorely missed.

Exploring his mouth, focused on nothing more than the taste and feel of him, my imagination could wander. His hands touched me so freely, light but curious—the way Riftan's often were. I could pretend—no matter how unrealistic it may have been—that Iosof was Riftan, and that the warm, whiskey-tinted tongue that grazed over my teeth was Riftan's. My heart skipped beats and I grabbed onto him, begging him to hasten his placid pace.

After wandering down my back, his hand grabbed under my thigh, pulling my leg up around his hips. In a split second, he flipped us around, pinning me to the wall and giving me his weight.

If I kept my eyes pinched tight, I could stay in my fantasy world as he kissed my cheek and my neck, down to my bare shoulder. His lips were soft and warm on my skin. They didn't give me butterflies the way Riftan's fingers could, no matter how much I pretended they were his, but I was still feeling *something*.

I knew that I could—and would—kill Iosof whenever I desired, which made the feeling of his warmth on me that much more enticing. He wasn't my Riftan, but he was a toy I could break whenever I wanted. A disposable tool that was doing exactly what I needed it to.

This is fun. I haven't had this much fun in—

"That's enough of that." Sharp displeasure edged Riftan's voice and cut through my pounding heart. He grabbed Iosof by the cowl, pulling him off me and tossing him to the ground. Riftan's lips snarled over sharp fangs, red highlighting his otherwise pale cheeks.

Some raw hope in me wanted to think Riftan's look was in any way an admission that I'd gotten under his skin. That feeling bubbled up, lacing my voice with humor and a staved-off giggle when I asked, "What're you doing?"

Iosif shuffled on the ground and Riftan grabbed him by the face, pulling him beside me and pinning him to the brick before he could make for any escape. Naturally, Iosof attempted to scream, but Riftan had his hand properly gripped over Iosif's mouth, muffling the sound to near oblivion.

Still scrunching his dark brows at me, Riftan replied, "Shouldn't I ask you the same question? I thought you were going to kill him?"

Iosif squirmed and Riftan knocked his skull against the wall until he stilled. His muffles, however, were getting more rattled by the second.

"I am going to kill him. I was having some fun with him first, Riftan."

"What have I told you about—"

"About sexualizing my meals? Yeah, yeah, yeah. I'm pretty sure it goes something like 'I'm a grumpy old man, don't kiss your food more than you need to in order to lure them to their death.' Blah, blah, blah." I rolled my eyes at him for added effect.

"What's this about?" Riftan looked me over, his tone heightened to something akin to authentic curiosity.

"I don't understand why you get to have all the fun," I complained. "I saw you with that girl. You certainly didn't have any qualms about having some fun with *her.*"

He raised a brow at me. "What girl? Are you talking about the girl at the bar?"

I shrugged, feeling my cheeks weighing down into an irritated frown.

"Leanne." His voice was suddenly soft again. "I thralled that girl to go out on the dance floor and bock like a chicken for two hours straight because she was bothering me."

"What? Why would you do that?" She was cute. Didn't he want her? That look had certainly said he did.

"Okay, look." He turned his attention away from me and towards Iosif, who continued to wriggle. Clearing his throat, Riftan demanded, "Stand still, don't move, don't think." He then dropped Iosif's face, and his feet fell to the ground, where he obediently did what he'd been told: staring off into the other wall daftly without moving a muscle.

His hands now free, Riftan reached up and took my cheek. With a single step, he put the two of us eye to eye before continuing. "I have never been interested in any other women while you've been around, and I promise I never will be. You have my undivided attention as long as we are staying together. I swear it. Okay? Will you trust me on this?" His fingers trailed off my cheek and his eyes watched them as they followed the curve of my neck.

His touch both quelled and engaged my want. It was his touch I longed for in every waking moment. I needed it constantly, but what I *wanted* was more. I wanted him to kiss me the way Iosif had. I would do any number of horrible things for it.

"Leanne?" His eyes came back to mine, awaiting a response.

Swallowing my pride, I nodded. "Yeah. I trust you."

Stepping away, his fingers left my skin, leaving the tepid night air in their place. An uncontrollable shiver came over me despite the atmosphere, and I did my best to shake it off before Riftan noticed.

"Well?" He straightened up and nodded toward Iosif. "He's all yours. Hurry up, I want to go home now. I'm over this."

Without further contention, I took a bite of Iosif and nearly sucked him dry. I wanted to make him suffer as much as possible, so I took at least enough of his blood to leave him unconscious, lying there by the dumpster looking like a drunken asshole. Before he'd fallen wholly unconscious, I thralled him to do multiple things when he woke up. First, he needed to go back inside and end his party. He would then donate his entire operation's wealth to a charity that'd been started by a family affected by his human trafficking ring. And finally, at 3 p.m. the next day, he'd cut off his legs and kill himself.

All of that was unnecessary, as he was going to die from my venom in twenty-four hours anyway, but I wanted him to go out with a bang for all the innocent souls that'd suffered at his hands—and I assure you, I'd heard of a few. His punishment wouldn't be nearly enough for his crimes, but I did my best to make it near equivalent.

Riftan didn't step in anymore. Instead, he waited patiently until we walked side by side down the sidewalk and away from Iosif's unconscious body.

Riftan didn't reach for my hand like he usually would have, and the air between us was thick with silence. I should have noticed how out of place that silence was from him, but I couldn't be bothered after feeding from Iosif, thanks to the blood euphoria still pumping through my veins. The sensation would fizzle through my insides, massaging my brain and tingling under my skin. Until it started to fade away, everything would roll right off my shoulders.

It wasn't until we were in the kitchen of our condo that the world began lacking its heavenly buzz and reality regained its normal level of dense once again.

Standing across from me at the counter, Riftan stared into a murky dark drink without making a sound. His glass grated along our marble countertop in repetitive circles, spinning its contents in a way that seemed absorbing to his interest. I knew that little tick, and I knew the look that paired with it.

Once his behavior caught my eye, I stared and waited until he noticed me. But he never looked up, choosing rather to ogle at that glass as though it held the answers to the universe.

"What's wrong, Riftan?"

He looked up and quickly shook his head in denial. "Nothing."

"Seriously?" I asked with piercing indignation.

He shrugged, taking a drink and dropping his gaze.

My heart dropped, the first thing coming from my lips being an aggrieved, "Hell no," before I was hopping onto the counter and crawling toward him. The ice-cold granite countertop prickled my hands and knees for only a second before I was face to face with Riftan, taking the glass from his hand and sitting my butt down on the cold slab in front of him. I demanded, "Tell me what's wrong. Right now," from a position where he couldn't deny me his attention.

He blinked, empty eyes shielded with dark lashes, and didn't give an answer. When the muscles in his cheeks flared, denoting how hard he was clenching his jaw to hold his tongue, I feared he might make an escape rather than tell me the truth.

The breath in my lungs halted, but I grabbed onto the tie at his neck, spinning it until I had it wrapped several times around my fist. With his eyes held only inches from mine, he looked between me and the fistful I'd gripped at his neck. The only thing that changed in his demeanor was the beat of his heart, thrumming like it'd started taking lessons from mine. When I thought he officially wasn't going to talk to me, he gave in, gaze settling on my wrist. "Leanne, did you ever stop to think how I might feel seeing Iosof all over you earlier?"

"What?" I froze.

His hands found my knees dangling on either side of him, but they sat idle, not caressing my skin like they usually would. "You said that you were jealous that I was flirting with that other girl. But what about me? How do you think I felt about you and Iosof?"

My heart might have stopped beating all together. "You were... jealous?"

His head dipped, feigning an answer.

"Riftan, tell me. Were you jealous?"

Clenching his jaw, he raised his gaze back to mine, lips parting to answer, but falling short with only, "I..."

Tightening my grip, I pulled him in until we were flesh to flesh, nose to nose, our breath uniting in an amorous dance. "Don't you dare lie to yourself, Riftan," I demanded, hardening my tone. "You know that I only have eyes for you. If you're jealous, I can promise you I will never look at another man again if that's what you want. But you have to tell me that it's what you want."

Finally, his eyes embraced me, darting back and forth, drowning me in the ocean that lived below his brows.

I pleaded, "Tell me it's what you want."

Light as air, more meager than I'd ever heard from his lips, Riftan replied, "It's what I want. I hate it when you look at other men the way you look at me."

My heart danced, making a ruckus in response to his remark. Before I knew it, his was doing the same so close to mine.

"What does that mean for us?" I asked, holding out hope for the kind of exclusivity he could be suggesting.

He shook his head, delicate enough to not disconnect from mine. "It means nothing." So he claims as he begs for me to love him and only him. *Nothing my ass.*

Wiggling past him, I jumped off the counter, letting his tie slide through my grip until I had a fistful of the end. His eyes grew heavy as I departed, lips twitching downward. He reached out a hand to grasp at my wrist. My poor boy seemed to think I would merely walk away after an admission like that. If he did, he was sorely mistaken.

Pulling on his tie, I beckoned him. "Take me to bed, and you'll never have to worry about another man ever again." In a surprising stint of obedience, he followed like a lost puppy on a leash as I backed toward his bedroom.

Never breaking eye contact, he slinked along with me, slow but steady. His newfound docility expiring all at once, he closed the distance between us, grabbing me up and tossing me over his shoulder.

"*Eek,*" I squealed but didn't protest. There was only a moment to appreciate that his hand was gripping my ass before I was dropped onto his bed.

A breath lodged in my chest as his shadow encompassed me, pinning me against the sheets. I reached for him, craving his warmth in my hands, but he was quicker, snatching my wrists and pushing them both to the mattress. Interlacing our fingers, he supplied the kind of heat my hands had longed for.

As he stretched both hands over my head, that heat traveled up my limbs and throughout my core, mingling a conflicting shiver with the overwhelming warmth seeping into my bones. Since becoming a vampire, I hardly noticed temperature changes, and very rarely felt too warm, so this was a foreign experience—the consuming feeling of broiling alive.

Riftan's marvelous eyes held me fast in their grasp, unwavering and burning me with every second they stared down at me. His eyelids sunk into a ribald, haughty look, a snarl lifting over his perfect lips, searing me over the edge. The sensation was dizzying, disorientating, and adrenaline-inducing in a way I'd long forgotten.

Riftan had done exactly what I asked for, and yet the actuality that he'd indulge after all these years of continence had me completely flustered. Unfortunately, the fire rushing through my body pacified the longer he held me motionless. His look gradually fell to a newly forlorn expression, dark brows scrunching over his eyes. With a somber sigh, his forehead dropped to mine, our noses meeting.

Between us, the air was stagnant, hardly another breath escaping from either of our lips.

He didn't retract but didn't go any further. The stillness should have been unsettling under the circumstances, maybe even causing some saudade emotion, but I was in no way dazed by his behavior. This was the Riftan I knew. He could so easily make my blood rush but as easily run it cold. At some point, I came to expect this, and I could hardly hold animosity for it anymore.

As they say, fool me once, shame on you—and everybody knows the rest.

So, I was indeed the only one at fault for getting my hopes up.

Though, this wasn't entirely the Riftan I knew, who astutely nipped my advances in the bud. He'd let me get this far and waited obediently for me to order onward. I *could* order him onward. I could ask him to give me more like I'd asked him to take me to bed. The passive look in his eyes told me he'd do what I asked, even if it went against his principles. And his twisted scowl told me it so clearly *did* go against his principles.

I wanted him. I wanted to be wrapped in his embrace until the end of eternity. I wanted more than that. But was it worth getting exactly what I wanted if he didn't want it, too? Even if I played the devil's advocate and believed his body wanted this, and he was merely holding himself back for some foolish ethics in his head, I couldn't push him to do something he'd regret. His eyes squeezed shut under the v of his brows.

I could tell he would regret going further with me. As much as I hated denying myself a taste of him, I couldn't put my longing above his. "Riftan, just hold me," I whispered, letting go of any pent-up sexual tension with a hefty sigh. "I don't expect anything else from you. Just hold me tonight. Please."

Relieved of his painstaking duty as my dog, Riftan released a crushing breath, falling beside me on the bed. Wrapping me up, his arms pulled me in until I was practically melded into his being. Fiercely, he implemented my request, holding me tight against his racing heartbeat.

The thought that I may have missed my only moment to be intimate with him didn't elude my mind. I'd denied myself the moment I'd always dreamed of, but the pain was marginal, vastly diminished by the comfort of his embrace. His arms were the greatest comfort I could ask for, even if they were the origination of my strife.

As close as we'd become over the years, moments like this shouldn't have felt so cataclysmic. We shouldn't be on the verge of some unbridled incident every time we got too touchy, and we shouldn't be hiding our feelings from each other. Because, regardless of what he said, Riftan did have his own intricate set of feelings for me. The signs of it were too bright and too blaring to ignore. But his unsaid feelings didn't mean I could rip them out of him due to my own impatience. If Riftan needed time, then I'd give him time.

Every day we shared together was a day closer to him giving up this chaste charade.

*EVERYTHING GETS BETTER FOR
THOSE WHO CAN WAIT*

THOUGH I'D BECOME decidedly hell-bent on charming the pants off Riftan, he was stubbornly not coming around.

It'd been weeks and our relationship had shifted no further than it had on the night he'd confessed his desire to have me all to himself. If anything, things were worse, which I blamed entirely on the sexual tension that now ran rampant between us.

After spending many nights in each other's arms, there were some things that neither of us had the heart to admit to the other. We were a balloon, its air getting filled past capacity. The more we touched, the more we cuddled, and the less we talked about it, the fuller our balloon got. Eventually, we'd pop, and everything would be out in the open. Unfortunately, I couldn't predict the outcome of such an event. In fact, the more we stretched our figurative balloon beyond its means, the flightier I felt about the situation. Explosions harm, and I couldn't stand to think one of us was going to get hurt by this.

The only way to stop it would be to relieve the tension, meaning one of us needed to bring it up and try to talk about it—before it was too late. A sinking feeling told me I was that person, since Riftan was the most obdurate man I'd ever met.

On a typical night in our serene little condo—with the world around us hushed and rain gently pattering against the windows in an unexpected whisper in the spring evening—Riftan had made himself at home behind me at the counter, encircling my waist in a familiar embrace. He loved doing anything that'd make my heart race, and this was undoubtedly one of those things. It was as though he thrived on the stress he created between us, his own heart mimicking mine where it pressed against my back. Adding to the chaos inside my chest, he laid his head on my shoulder and clasped his hands over my stomach to show he wasn't going anywhere anytime soon.

Dropping the knife in my hand onto the counter, I waited for my heart to compose itself, but no such change happened. I couldn't think with it making a fuss like that, much less focus on chopping up the little bits of dark chocolate on the cutting board in front of me. Fed up with this haywire feeling, I squirmed in Riftan's arms, wiggling until he let me turn and face him.

Where I usually could have expected to find a chipper, fangy smile on his face, all that stared down at me was an enigmatic downturn of his features. That look clutched the air in my chest, tightening into a heavy ache as though I was mourning his absent smile.

"Riftan..." I wanted to say something—needed to—but when I began, his attentive eyes settled on mine, unwavering and ready to listen to anything I had to say.

As his look diverted my thought process, he waited patiently for me to continue. But I didn't know where to start, so we stared at each other, the silence amplifying every little gesture between us.

I lost the courage to say anything, the feeling of betrayal to my own convictions a foreign sting. "Never mind."

My mind raced with possible outcomes to the conversation I needed to have with Riftan, and they all had their own intimidating consequences. But that wasn't a good enough reason for me to surrender.

The image of us out on the balcony when he'd first given me my necklace came to mind, as if my brain was reminding me exactly why we don't confess our feelings toward Riftan. Though, admittedly, things were different now. We openly talked about our other feelings, and we shared our lives together. Communication should have been the last thing I feared with him. Yet, my voice had dried up.

Clenching my fists tight, I turned away from Riftan's roving blue eyes and back to my task on the counter. Of course, that didn't stop him, only put him back to distracting me with his body pressed against mine.

A chill ran up my spine when he leaned in, breath tickling

my ear. "I have a surprise for you."

My ears perked up. and I threw a look over my shoulder. "You do?"

"Yes. It should be here in…" He stole a fleeting glance at his watch. "Oh, I lost track of time. It'll be here any minute."

"Really?" Excitement clouded all other surface emotions. "What is it?"

"Well, I can't tell you, it's a surprise." I pursed my lips, an expression he brushed off, continuing without hesitation, "Do you know what the significance of today is?"

"No?" I didn't have to think twice to know it wasn't a holiday.

"Right, well, I didn't think to celebrate it the last couple of years, but I was more prepared this time around. So, tell me, do you know what happened exactly today, three years ago?"

"I guess this is right about when we started living together… so was that when I was turned into a vampire?"

He graced me with that radiant smile I had so dearly missed, effortlessly gliding to my side against the counter. "Well yes, you could say that. But more specifically, what we are celebrating is the birth of your new life. I told you that we wouldn't celebrate your birthday, merely because it served no purpose as you'd no longer age. Instead, we can celebrate the day that you became something new. In a way, it is akin to both a birthday and a funeral. You can mourn what has gone but rejoice in the endless opportunities the future holds. One day you might come to hate what I made you…" His gaze faltered, his wandering palms brushing over my bare arm before he returned his eyes to mine. "Until then, we can celebrate it for what it's worth."

"I could never foresee myself hating what I am now."

A smile cradled his cheeks again, and he leaned in, setting his head on mine. It was impossible to do anything except drop everything and welcome him into my arms. I cherished that embrace like I cherished his smile. Time went by, sharing his warmth, before footsteps echoed up the typically silent stairway out front.

"Your surprise is here," Riftan said, but it fell on deaf ears.

I was trained on the door, listening to the very distinct click-clack of feet getting closer. Without hesitation, I ran for them, throwing open the door to greet my best friend before he'd made it down the hall. "Jameson!" I squealed, leaping into his arms.

He caught me effortlessly, responding with a joyful laugh as he spun us in circles, and our shared exuberance echoed through the narrow hallway. I hadn't seen Jameson since his last visit nearly half a year ago, a memory associated with the laughter and late-night conversations that had filled the condo for weeks on end.

"What are you doing here?" I asked.

For months, I'd been begging Jameson to visit again. My messages were often met with his apologies about the relentless demands of life. Unlike Riftan, who seemed to drift effortlessly through his days, Jameson was deeply entrenched in the immortal community's politics, aspiring to join its council—a pursuit as time-consuming as it was prestigious. And that was just a fraction of his world, with his multitude of business ventures demanding equal attention.

"I'm here to see you, of course!" he answered, his words accompanied by his familiar, playful grin. "Besides, I was told we'd be having a celebration of rebirth, and I would never miss an opportunity to celebrate my best friend."

"Celebration of rebirth?" I repeated. "You actually celebrate that?"

"Well, the more optimistic of us do." Jameson beamed.

Riftan peeked through the doorway. "What, you didn't believe it when I said it?"

"I didn't know you were saying it was actually a customary celebration."

Jameson hooted, "Of course. What's not to celebrate? It's both the death of an old life and the birth of a new one!"

Ushering us inside, Riftan added, "Well, now you know. Come inside and we can all catch up together."

Jameson nodded, then bent to pick up his grocery bags from the ground—bags I hadn't noticed he'd dropped in his haste to catch me moments earlier. I snagged one, offering a smile as I led him inside.

Jameson's presence was a breath of fresh air in the stuffy, tense atmosphere Riftan and I had created. His sudden arrival had me giddy; thrill-filled jitters exited my body through the little hops I made all the way to the counter.

The three of us were quick to catch on like the three musketeers, as we always were. After Jameson started pouring drinks, it was like life had gone back to normal and Riftan was another platonic best friend again. That was a steady vibe for the night. Jameson never ran out of conversation starters and life updates. With his busy schedule, he had lots to tell us about every time he visited. From the sounds of it, this time around, he was struggling with council chores and prerequisites to being appointed.

In my opinion, he worked too hard, and the last thing he should be concerned about was adding more to his workload. But that was how Jameson preferred his life—demanding. Very much unlike Riftan—or at least the Riftan I knew.

Jameson went on, recounting the trials of his ventures with an infectious cheerfulness. "I went above and beyond with some of the acquisitions I made on behalf of the council—way better than anything they've done in the last couple of decades. But even with all the efforts, I seem to be going backward. I've worked way harder than any of the other members have to get their positions. There's always one thing holding me back: a little lady with a big grudge." He waited, twirling his glass of whiskey while Riftan rolled his eyes, as if knowing Jameson's plight.

"Rosaline is killing me," Jameson confirmed. "She's going out of her way to act like the gatekeeper to the council, barring entry with a maze of bureaucratic obstacles nobody's ever heard of before."

My interest piqued. "Rosaline? Are you talking about Riftan's ex-girlfriend?"

Riftan's brow flinched nominally at the mention.

Jameson paused, huffing a laugh before saying, "Yeah,

same one. That bitch—pardon the derogatory term—is awfully bitter. I wasn't alive during her and Riftan's little escapade, yet she still holds animosity toward me simply because I share blood with Riftan. I've been doing nothing for the past two years except kissing her ass, but she only gets fouler. Making a name for yourself in the underground community is impossible without going through Rosaline first. Unfortunately, the second she catches wind of my name, she makes sure to shut my advances down on the spot—regardless of what it is I'm trying to accomplish."

"Oof," was my best response, not envying Jameson's situation.

"Sorry mate," Riftan groaned, a lopsided smile gracing his face. "I'd help you if I could, but I can't quite undo anything that's already happened, and anything less would only make matters worse, I'm sure."

Teetering on the edge of tipsiness, where words were flowing more freely, I found myself blurting out a thought that, in any other circumstance, I might have deliberated twice on. "Could she really be so bad? I mean, nobody is as bad as you guys make Rosaline out to be."

Riftan's lips parted to respond, but Jameson beat him to the chase, leaning in and bracing against the table as he protested, "She is all that bad and more. Knowing Rosaline is a torture I suggest you not experience for yourself. Actually," his eyes widened, his stature straightening, "for you, it could be deadly." He combed a hand over his clean-shaven chin. "Given your and Riftan's questionable relationship and how it may look to others," he pointed between us and Riftan glared in response, "I think it's best if you stay away from her for as long as possible. If there's anything more potent than her grudges, it's her jealousy. You are, after all, the only living female with Riftan's blood, on top of the way the two of you already look to the few who know you in the community; I don't want to think about what Rosaline would do to you if she ever got you alone. There's no guaranteeing she wouldn't try to kill you on the spot."

"Seriously?" It was hard to believe anyone would be so illogical, but I felt my eyes widening regardless of its likelihood.

"Don't scare her like that," Riftan hissed at Jameson before patting his hand over mine. "Yes, it would probably be advisable that you don't go out of your way to come face to face with Rosaline, but I don't want you to think she'll be coming after you either. She may be powerful in the underground, but that also makes her a busy woman. She has plenty of other things to keep her above and beyond occupied. The last thing on her mind would be seeking you out."

Jameson added, "Right. Obviously. And I'll be keeping her occupied as well. I've still got a place on that council with my name on it, and I'll be damned if I let her debar my efforts. I'm not giving up. I can play her game of chicken for another millennium if that's what she wishes." His fangs tucked over his lips in a smile brimming with pride. That familiar sentiment was so uniquely Jameson; it filled my heart with nostalgic bliss. He went on, sharing with us exactly all the ways he planned to succeed.

Basking in the glow of his enthusiasm, I nodded along, savoring the rich, full feeling I got from listening to his aspirations unfold layer by layer. He looked to me for gratification and advice, which made me feel significant even with such little life experience compared to him.

By the time the cards were out and Jameson was threatening a poker game, I'd forgotten completely about the tense, stuffy feeling that'd clouded my thoughts the last couple of days. The usually dizzying image of Riftan's lips so close to mine nights before had become a distant dream. After all, Jameson was the king of poker and beating him would take all of my brain power.

Luckily, I'd been practicing for this moment. Riftan, however, was not as thrilled since he hated forever losing to Jameson, and now, he'd be losing to me as well. He knew that better than anyone since he'd been my practice dummy this past year.

"If you're getting out the cards, then we need more drinks," Riftan grumbled, leaving the table to scrounge through the cabinetry for something stronger than what we'd been drinking—which was a strange mixture of blood, vodka, and grapefruit Jameson had thrown together. "We have bourbon, a couple different kinds of tequila, sake, and a little of the vodka Jameson brought. Lee, what do you want?"

"*Hmm*," I hummed, thinking over my options. Finally, I answered, more to Jameson than Riftan. "I kind of want an extra dry, kind of dirty, martini. Is that weird?"

Jameson lit up. "Oo, with extra bitters. That does sound

good."

Riftan's tone was curt as he rained on our parade. "We don't have any of that. Not gin, vermouth, or bitters."

"Awe," I complained. "But now I really want it."

Jameson nudged my elbow and then hinted with his eyebrows as he nodded in Riftan's direction and whispered an incomprehensible jumble of words.

"Huh?"

"Ask him to go get us the stuff." This time, he said it clearer, but covered it up with a cough like that'd make it a secret between the two of us.

I turned my attention to Riftan, who frowned behind the kitchen counter. "Would you go pick us up the stuff to make martinis?"

"No. I don't want to do that," he responded flatly, looking between Jameson and me with a scowl that said we were scheming against him.

Jameson tapped me again. "Bat your eyelashes at him," he demanded, hardly holding back a giggle.

I wouldn't do that. Instead, I looked at Riftan and gave my best submissive smile. "Please?"

Riftan looked at Jameson, who'd engrossed himself in pretending to shuffle the deck. "Fine. But not because you made Leanne ask me like that."

He made his way to the door in a fizz of smoke and Jameson called after him as he gathered his coat and glasses from the rack. "Don't forget the bitters!"

"Whatever," was his only response before sliding out the

door.

I should have pinched myself because I could hardly believe that'd worked.

Jameson read my mind. "I know he's an idiot for you, but damn, I didn't actually expect that to succeed. That charm of yours is as effective as hypnotism." He laughed, throwing a pointed finger in my direction.

The idea of Riftan being "an idiot for me" kindled my heart. If it were true, then it made no sense why he'd keep the distance he did between us, even if it was as thin as it was.

"Well, since it's just the two of us, you want to play something simple until he gets back?" Jameson asked before offering, "Go fish?"

I laughed. "Sure thing. Go-fish it is."

After silently dealing out the cards, Jameson stared at his hand with an introspective look casting a shadow over his usually sparkling smile. It persisted through several go fishes later, darkening as his hand of cards consumed his interest. Finally, he set down his hand and sighed. "Truthfully, I wanted to ask you something while Riftan wasn't around. That was the idea behind having him leave."

The timid version of him, devoid of his usual boisterous nature, sent blood rushing behind my ears. Seeing my shaken appearance, he mustered a feigned laugh, as if that'd help lighten the heavy air between us. He asked, "Would you consider leaving Riftan and coming home to New Orleans with me?"

"What?" The question came so out of the blue that I barely

understood it.

"Only to get you on your feet and starting your own life. Somewhere you can do so without Riftan in the picture."

My heart dropped. "What do you mean? Why would I?"

"Well, the two of you have been together for so long. You've only ever lived your immortal life with him. Have you considered what you'll do when you part ways? When Riftan is done teaching you how to live among immortals?"

"I..." Truthfully, I told him, "I don't like to think about it. Where is this coming from?"

Jameson's voice carried defeat as it reflected off the wooden table. "There's a lot of life out there for you to experience on your own without Riftan's influence. I think you should consider leaving. I think it'll be... better for you if you leave before he has to ask you to. You'll feel better about it, anyway."

It was so absurd to hear those words coming out of his mouth. Jameson was the one rooting for Riftan and me to be together. He was always pushing me practically into Riftan's lap, begging us to dance together, goading Riftan into complementing me, and telling me that he saw a future where the two of us were exactly what I wanted us to be. He had always been my wingman. This wasn't like him.

Wiping my sweaty palms on my jeans, I asked, "Did Riftan put you up to this?"

Jameson's dark eyes shot up, his acknowledgment enough to confirm what I feared.

I demanded, "Tell me exactly what he said to you."

Jameson shook his head, defeat storming his downcast eyes. I knew he couldn't hide this from me; he never could. His penchant for sharing every little secret with me, always so open, so unguarded, had never changed.

"It's not a big deal. His exact words were, 'feel her out.' He wants to know if you're truly happy like this. I know he won't admit it, but he's scared he won't be doing right by you if he keeps you here with him. Not to mention, he's obviously uncomfortable with how close the two of you have gotten." He followed the statement with a grimace and a shrug. "I don't think he'd ever try and hurt you, but sometimes it scares me that he won't know what hurts you the most."

I nodded. My heart ached at the idea of leaving Riftan. Not mentally, but a physical constriction that clutched my chest and forced the air from my lungs. The pain was obstinate until it was wrenching tears from my eyelids, forcing me to hide my face on the table to avoid a flush of embarrassment at my own over-emotion trailing down my cheeks.

"Oh no, Leanne." Jameson rushed to my side, pulling me into an embrace meant to soothe away the aching of my heart. "Please don't cry. I hate tears more than anything on the planet."

"I'm sorry." I took several deep breaths to fight the tightness in my lungs, but that didn't stop the waterworks. Frustration rushed in my veins, heating my cheeks on top of the embarrassment of my outburst. Leanne Cowitz doesn't cry— least of all, about men—and it killed me to feel how far I'd fallen. That helpless emotion came out through clenched teeth.

"I thought Riftan was over this. He said we were exclusive. Doesn't that mean something? We both promised to be each other's..."

"Don't apologize—wait, did you say he said you were exclusive? Like, you can't see other people romantically or...?" Jameson's tone piqued, turning into something akin to a schoolgirl's curiosity. "And you're saying that he said that verbally? Not, like, implied?"

"Yes. He said that he gets jealous of other men and he doesn't want me flirting with anybody else but him. And vice versa."

Jameson's jaw was slow to drop to the floor. It took him several moments to pick it back up and respond, "Well, that makes the conversation he had with me a little bit more unwieldy. What a foolish idiot."

The faintest smile tugged on my lips, curiously lightening the grip on my heart. "Finally, a sentiment I can agree with."

The smile that spread over Jameson's face was almost enough to dry my tears. "You know," he started, mood eased, "no matter what happens, I'll always be here for you. We will always share blood—even if it is Riftan's. And beyond that, I'll always be your best friend. I'll always come rushing if you need me. Besides, no matter how wishy-washy he may be, I know Riftan loves you to pieces, even if the way he does so is confusing. Everything will work out in the end, and I will bet you money on that. Be patient with what life throws at you."

I laughed some more, squeaking out the remainder of my tears. "How much money will you bet?"

"I'd bet you more than you could ever get at one time. That's how certain I am that everything gets better for those who can wait out the turmoil. And you know I'm always right on this kind of thing."

I nodded, letting him wipe away my tears with tender fingertips.

The pummeling of Riftan's footsteps up the stairs had both Jameson and I flinching a glance at the door.

Tears dotted my eyelids. I was so not ready to face Riftan. Sensing the same, Jameson clapped me on the shoulder. "Go to your room and get a hold of yourself. I'll stall him for a bit."

Nodding, I jumped up, fading into my darkened room at the other end of the condo. Riftan barged through the front door moments later and Jameson attempted nobly to distract him. No matter his excuse for my absence, Riftan was more insistent on checking on me the longer I hid in my room.

With very few arguments left, Jameson squabbled his last-ditch effort to hold Riftan off. "She's fine. She said she'd be right back. Can't the woman have five minutes to herself?"

Ignoring him, Riftan pushed open the door to my room and slinked his way inside.

Listening to Riftan and Jameson bicker had helped to distract my teary emotions, but that didn't make my current place sitting alone in the dark of my room look any more natural. Attempting to rectify the scene, I grabbed my phone charger off the nightstand and met Riftan at the foot of the bed, feigning as much normalcy as I could without looking him in the eyes.

He looped his hand under my arm as I tried to walk by, bringing me to a stop. "Is everything okay?" Such genuine concern laced his voice that it stuck to my heart like a knife.

"Yeah," I snapped. "Just needed my phone charger." I pulled against his grip.

His fingers tightened, tugging my arm until I faced him. His sapphire eyes roved over me, the dim light shadowing his features and carving them into a more perfect visage than in the light of day. The fingers from his free hand caressed the heated apples of my cheeks where I must have been red from the leftover tears. He whispered to me in that same achingly tender concern. "Promise you'll tell me what's wrong later, okay? You don't have to do it now if you don't want to."

Wrapping my fingers in his shirt, I clung to him, silently begging for his eyes to not waver from mine. If I could wade through their ocean a little longer, the aching from Jameson's and my conversation might drown in those waters.

Denying it, Riftan dropped his nose to my forehead, hot breath lingering over my skin when he whispered again. "Come now. You need to beat Jameson at least once before the night is over."

That was true, and I nodded in agreement.

After that, I couldn't shake Riftan from my side. His attention, gaze, and touch were all concentrated on me. He was the first to lose every game of poker we played, and hardly conversed with Jameson, his closest friend, who sat right next to him. He was too busy watching what I was doing and caressing circles over my jean-clad leg where he'd perched his hand. After we'd shuffled to the bar, and I was no longer in arm's reach, he used his long legs to make contact, tapping his toes over mine and playing footsy with me like we were a couple of school kids.

Finally, after four games of poker, I did beat Jameson once. That was my sign to stop while I was ahead—or as ahead as I'd ever get against Jameson.

The last thing I wanted was for Jameson to leave and forsake Riftan and me to our bursting stress bubble, but I knew I couldn't keep him forever. He had businesses and council duties to get back to. This had merely been a last-minute vacation he'd taken to join in our celebration of rebirth.

Though I dreaded the silence that would weigh heavy in his absence, I knew it was necessary to see Jameson out. He had brought up a conversation Riftan and I needed to have in private, and it was due time we hung the subject out to dry— along with the laundry list of things that had gone unsaid for too long between us.

19

IN IMMORTAL RELATIONSHIPS,
THERE IS ALWAYS SUFFERING

RIFTAN HEAVED a sigh and plunked onto the couch, beckoning me over with, "I'm not very tired. Would you like to watch a movie with me, love?"

Jameson had only recently left, but my body already felt like lead. Though my weary bones disagreed with Riftan's sentiment, I joined him on the couch.

His gaze followed as I plopped down into the open seat next to him, brows arching when I only offered silence. The blue stare didn't falter, lingering in the corners of my vision after I looked away. Close behind was the stroke of his fingers, prodding me in all the places his eyes had trailed. First over my hair, and then under my chin, where he tugged until I faced him. The softness in his look matched the longing in his touch. Both that and his eager hands pulled me in until I sat side saddle in his lap.

Eyeing my bare shoulder, he padded his fingers along my chest where my shirt met my skin. "I like this sweater, it's cute," he offered.

"Oh, thanks." I looked down to remind myself that I'd dressed in my trusty black knit sweater that night.

"You should wear it more often." Riftan followed the statement by tracing back over the line that it made across my chest until the loose neckline dropped off my shoulder.

His contact had my eyes rolling back in my head, provoking the feverish tingly feeling only his touch could.

His voice was low, but closer now. "You have the most beautiful..." The warmth of his breath invigorated the skin on my neck and I flinched, surprise snapping me from my stupor. "Delicate..." His head tucked into my neck, the plush sensation of his lips on my collarbone freezing me stiff. "Shoulders," he finished quietly, pecking a kiss on my neck and trailing it down my shoulder. At my arm, he pulled down on my sweater, exposing more skin and planting another kiss where it was once concealed. His lips paused there, his only movement the shallow breaths he huffed over my sensitive flesh.

In his grasp, breath eluded my lungs and thoughts slipped my mind; my heart was the only functioning part of me as it raced at an ungodly speed inside my ribcage. A startling pinch under Riftan's lips kickstarted my functional processes. I gasped, following the outburst with an aggrieved, "Owe!" while pulling away from his bloody fangs.

He criticized through clenched teeth, "Why do you have to do this to me?"

"Me? You!" I barked, throwing a leg over his lap so I could straddle him in a position that would assert dominance. "Seriously, for one, you bit me. And more importantly, you keep doing things like this, and acting like it's my fault! You're the instigator, but you refuse the idea that we can be any sort of romantic, or intimate, or anything. You don't make any sense. I don't think you know what you want!"

His response was mellow. "You're right. I don't know what I want. But truthfully, that doesn't matter. What I want is of no consequence when it comes to what is right."

"And you think it's so wrong for us to be together intimately? We are already so close, in so many different ways. What does it hurt to be physical, when emotionally we are already intimate? Can't you open your heart to me the rest of the way? I promise I won't get hurt regardless of what happens." My chest constricted, a bodily reminder of how severely that was a lie.

I'd lie a thousand times more if it meant convincing him to give me a chance. I'd pretend he couldn't break my fragile heart, though that was already an inescapable fate, regardless of what he decided. Admitting that hurt, but not as bad as it would to experience it firsthand. That's why Jameson wanted me to take control and leave while I still had some remnant of an unbroken heart that didn't completely belong to Riftan. But was that what Riftan wanted of me, too?

When he was silent, I let that thought weasel its way out of my pathetic lips. "Do you truly wish that I'd leave you?"

Instantly, his eyes flickered up to regard mine. "Of course not. Why would you think that?"

I tried not to let my voice drag into dejection. "Jameson told me the two of you talked about it. He tried to convince me to go home with him. He thought it's what you'd prefer."

Riftan winced. "No, no, love. Is that why you looked upset earlier?" A harrowed whine cut through his tone. "I swear I didn't say anything of the sort. Admittedly, I did talk to Jameson, but I merely asked him to feel you out. I wanted him to ask you questions about how you were doing, not tell you that I wanted you to leave. And yes, repentantly, I wanted him to ask you how you'd feel if I wasn't around, but it's because I want to make sure that I'm doing what's right for you, and not because I don't want you here with me. I want you to live out all the lives I have given you the opportunity to live—even the ones that don't involve me."

His recollection was definitely closer to what Jameson had truly said, but in my mind, it meant the same thing. Heat flared in my veins, anger at his implication hot on my nerves. I hadn't solidified my scowl when his hand was icing the feeling, clasping onto my cheek and bringing with it the comfort and affection I recognized in his touch.

I softened around him in a way I was afraid I couldn't reharden again. Dominance and control, whether I'd meant to use them as leverage to finally communicate with him, were beginning to elude me as I sank into Riftan's embrace. My voice escaped too soft to sound eminent, "And what if I don't want any of those lives that don't involve you?"

His solace vanished, hand slipping down by our side. "I think you should at least try it out before you make that kind of decision. You still think like a mortal. There is no point in being stuck with me from the very start of your long eternity."

"That's not fair Riftan, you can't tell me to try something before I decide when you aren't willing to do the same with me."

"There's a reason for it. You know that. I'm not willing to be someone who hurts you. In a strange sort of ironic twist, I care about you too much to see you suffer on my account. And in immortal relationships, there is always suffering. That is something you'll simply have to take my word on."

I had no response if I wanted to keep things civil. The welling emotions were hot under my skin and they wanted release—which would be unacceptable.

There was a long moment of silence between us, where I held his gaze, anchored to mine. I could imagine all kinds of things going on behind the opalescent pools of his eyes, but I had a feeling I never would guess exactly which one was accurate to what he was thinking. As it usually did, staring into those eyes only added to my bound-up frustrations—or in this case, maybe a combination of frustration with some sort of protracted grief.

As if he was seeing my emotions written upon my face, Riftan's shoulders fell. His hands met my cheek once again, this time pulling me in until my forehead rested in the crook of his neck. There, with the distinct impression of his body against mine, the comforting and familiar smell of him could envelop me.

When he spoke again, the vibration of his vocal cords drummed against my ear, offering the contentedness his words tried—and failed—to duplicate. "I'm never going to stop insisting you harness your new life to its fullest, but don't ever get that confused with me not wanting you around. You're the greatest companion I've ever had, and I'll never let you go, not fully. Like Jameson and I are good friends, you and I will always be close as well."

Jameson's visits weren't nearly often enough to make that sentiment meaningful.

"You're the worst." I let the words slip past my lips, small and feeble enough that a mortal may not have heard me even as close as I was to his ear. But Riftan could hear me plain as day. I knew it for a fact. That made my heart ache harder. I didn't mean it, but I wanted him to know how much I hated what he was putting me through.

His arms only tightened their embrace, holding our bodies together in unfathomable closeness. In a shallow breath that fluttered over my scalp, he finished, "I turned you so you would be free of men like Johnny, not so you'd be constrained to a new one like me."

My heart was too weak to reply. Arguments with Riftan were a whole new level of draining. There was never a winner, only two sad saps who hated hurting each other's feelings.

*CALL IT YOUR FINAL LESSON IN
IMMORTALITY*

THE NEXT DAY was slow to start. Neither of us
wanted to get out of bed, which we would claim was because
we didn't need to, but I had a feeling it was more the result of
a minor case of depression dampening the mood.

I made the best of it, considering doing absolutely nothing
was a newfound hobby of mine. Whenever I felt less than
chipper, it was easy to fall back on the laziness living with Riftan
had cultivated within me.

Being an immortal, there was no downside to chronic
lethargy—except maybe the occasional boredom if I'd been by
myself. Because I no longer ate, I didn't need to get up and
make food. My body type would never change, so I didn't have
to worry about getting any sort of exercise to stay healthy or in
shape. Plus, I was immortal; I didn't have to worry about aches

or pains from sitting in bed all day.

Though the slothfulness had come from Riftan himself, he reminded me from time to time that it wasn't good to get used to the profound idleness we often succumbed to. But his argument remained that this was his down decade and all he wanted to do was rest until the decade was over—which from my calculations was still several years away.

Regardless of his reasoning, I'd always enjoyed it when we didn't bother getting out of bed. Even with our budding situation, it was easy enough to pretend we weren't passing any of Riftan's thin lines by accepting the comfort of each other's arms under his sheets. To any normal person, that may have been crossing a lot of lines in terms of platonic-ness, but we'd been doing it for so long it seemed stranger to stop doing it.

That meant lazy days were spent in a circulation of drifting in and out of sleep while cuddled in Riftan's arms or reading raunchy romance novels—my newfound obsession.

In the past, I'd always thought reading to be for the intellectual types—something I never saw myself as. Since procuring endless amounts of time, I'd dabbled in reading romance, only to find out how perfectly it suited me. I was easily enchanted with the many stories of love and passion—the *spicy* kind I wasn't allowed to have myself—and found myself tantalized by the vivid and lustful pictures an author could paint in the minds of their readers. The kind that could make my heart race while sitting still. Maybe that was an externalization of my own sexual tension. Regardless, I could officially admit that it'd made me a book girl.

Shoulder to shoulder on our bed, Riftan always noticed how my heart would stir, though rarely looked over, knowing well what the cause was. For whatever reason, this time, he'd been bolder, peeking over my shoulder.

No matter the contents on the page or how well they pulled me in, I'd always notice when Riftan got close, his gaze like electricity sending a gentle zap whenever he looked my way. Unlucky for him, I wasn't shy about what I was reading. I let him skim the page, waiting patiently for him to get an eyeful of more than he'd bargained for. I knew he'd seen enough once he pulled away, muttering something about "raunchy smut."

I giggled. "What? You don't like it?"

"It's rather gruesome," was his answer.

Setting my Kindle in my lap, I cocked a look at him. "I don't think gruesome is really the right word for a romance novel. Obscene, maybe, but it's not really the same thing."

Riftan shrugged and gestured to the Kindle. "You know nobody actually does that, right?"

"What? The thing she did in the novel?" I asked, recounting the steamy specifics that had been so brilliantly interpreted by the filthy mind of whatever pervert had written it.

"Yes, that. It was embellished to the point of inaccuracy."

"That's not true. I can do that," I quipped.

Riftan blinked at me, the muscles in his jaw jumping under the skin but not displaying any further emotion. A glimmer of pink on his nose was the only indication of the cause of his expression—or lack of.

Jumping onto my hands and knees, I maneuvered the sheets so I wouldn't be tangled and crawled toward Riftan. With a teasing and sensual bat of my eyelashes, I asked, "Would you like me to show you?" It was a joke—I knew he'd refuse—but it still made my heart run like a racehorse.

His eyes widened and I reached out, trying and failing to catch him before he skillfully slipped off the bed and ran from me. He murmured something about a "flippant minx," which surely was me, and rushed off toward the bathroom. Thankfully, he didn't sound upset; more dumbfounded than anything.

"Hey, wait." I laughed, flopping down onto the bed where his heat still resided. "I was kidding, Riftan, come back."

He didn't respond but shut the bathroom door behind himself, clicking the lock into place.

I sighed. The unfamiliar sound of a lock being used in the condo was a small grievance that weighed heavier on me than it should have.

After listening to the water run for a couple of minutes, a short stint of silence, and a sigh, Riftan unlocked and peeked his head out of the bathroom door. "Do you want to go dancing tonight?" he asked, his tone as ordinary as ever.

"Yeah, sure. What for?"

"Because I want to," he scoffed. "But if you really must make it out to be some sort of lesson or something, then the reason will be to teach you that you can do whatever you want, for whatever reason you want. Call it your final lesson in immortality. You don't answer to anyone but you anymore, so do whatever you wish."

He hadn't meant anything negative by that, as I could see plain as day by his relaxed appearance, but I couldn't help feeling put down by his justification, especially the "final lesson" part. It made me feel like our time together was coming to an end—that this was our last hurrah. Sensing my apprehension, he added, "I promise it will be fun. Please, love? I want to get out tonight."

I wondered if he genuinely believed the lack of possible fun was what soiled my mood toward the idea. Regardless, the irony of his pleading with me didn't go unnoticed. He had, after all, insisted an immortal should answer only to themselves. I supposed that argument was slightly different when they had a partner to please.

A partner. The idea of sharing a mutual partnership with Riftan made me weak in my bones.

If positivity was the goal, then I'd tell myself that after my final lesson I'd have gained enough mutual respect for Riftan to consider me a partner. Though, that wouldn't solve the issue of him being afraid to break my heart.

"Whatever, I'm fine with going out," I responded, my mind wandering on to so many variable opportunities with him.

Uncaring to read into my vacancy, Riftan re-shut the bathroom door and I listened as he started the shower. Once he'd stepped inside, the pitter-patter of water against his skin drummed restlessly through my ears thanks to their formidable hearing.

The noise painted a picture of him, completely bare and

standing under the cascading water. He probably had to duck to wet his hair, but it was long right now, and I could imagine how he'd brush it out of his face, flexing the muscles in his arms as he raised them up over his head. Water would fall over his chest, cascading along the many ridges on his abdomen and dripping from his... My breath halted, my heart pounding with such a sickening ferocity that I had to clutch my chest to know it wasn't going to beat right out.

Seeking distraction, I picked up my Kindle, only to get one line in and remember what I was reading and know that it would only make my condition worse. My core was already throbbing, and reading as little as I had sent a hot spasm flooding from it.

Tossing the Kindle onto the bed, I didn't watch as it bounced onto the floor. I was already face down on my pillow, whining because I knew Riftan would come running if I screamed. Though screaming into my pillow was what I'd have preferred.

I slipped a hand between me and the sheets, clamping it tight between my legs. The pressure only marginally relieved the ache, which I knew wouldn't subside from my own hand—not when it was Riftan it wanted.

Once upon a time, I knew a version of me that would obey my natural instincts to abate this feeling and jump right into the shower with Riftan, regardless of his presumed arguments. Unfortunately, I no longer knew her, and Riftan had been completely wrong about my ability to control myself.

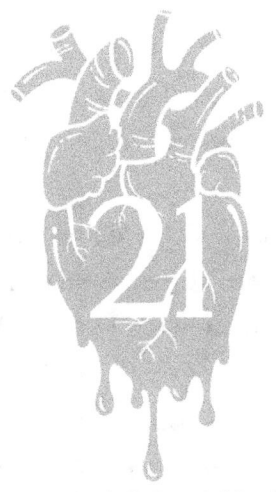

21

A   LITTLE   WAGER   IN   LOVE   AND   WAR

DANCE CLUBS were a testament to how far I'd come since becoming immortal.

The music was loud, voices chaotic. Smells were pungent, from bodily to artificial, like a brothel inside of a perfume factory. And I won't even start on the lights. But with Riftan pressed against my form, swaying to the music in a heap of mortal bodies, I almost felt at home. What was once an assault on my senses had become a numbing embrace of the madness.

It helped that Riftan always started the night by ordering us a round of drinks. I'd learned to follow his routine, throwing back his drink of choice for the night even if I felt content being sober. Most of the time, it was Riftan who needed that inebriety to let loose, since he tended to tense up in thickly mortal-populated places, but after a couple of drinks, maybe a few shots, he was the most jovial person in the room. Then, we could dance until the sun came up as if we were the only two people in the world.

We had spent many nights doing exactly that. I was no stranger to dancing with Riftan. Somewhere along the way, clubbing became the only real tension release we got. It was the only time we could get away with *anything*. On a dance floor, Riftan would allow any form of perverse behavior, and the once self-renowned club skank in my blood fed off that. Riftan never complained. If anything, he instigated it. At the end of the night, it didn't mean anything. Even *I* understood it was fun and nothing more. There were no sentimental or romantic attachments to the act of dirty dancing whatsoever—not to either of us.

Not usually.

However, I couldn't say the same for this night. Maybe it was that ticking time bomb, our over-blown balloon, whatever you wanted to call the stupid tension between us, but I couldn't dance with Riftan the way I usually did. Every movement his hips made, riding my ass with startling force, shot a shockwave of heat throughout my being. Working in circles, he attempted to coerce my body to follow like it'd done thousands of times in the past, but I couldn't match his intensity for fear that I might overheat—maybe turn into a puddle right there on the dance floor.

Like it'd persuade my movements, Riftan slid his hands down over my smooth, silver dress, taking his time to cover every curve.

Oh, how that isn't helping.

His breath prickled at my neck as he reached down past my hips, his long arms assisting in easily closing the distance separating his fingers from my bare thighs below the high hem of my skirt. The contact was tantalizing, and it snatched the air from my lungs when he dug his fingers into my legs. My tiny little skirt hiked, hardly shy of flashing the other clubgoers as Riftan skimmed his hands back up in the direction they'd come.

The glitzy little silver dress I wore fit me in all the right places and shined like it'd been made from the guts of a real disco ball—but God was it short. While I loved showing off my legs, this risque number wasn't leaving enough to the imagination in the situation between Riftan and I. *God, why do I have to be such a slut?*

I shouldn't have asked, because I knew the answer: the dress was a showstopper, and I'd *really* wanted to get Riftan's attention. Oh, how I needed to be careful what I wished for.

Looking to catch my breath, I shimmied away from Riftan, the idea to make it look intentional, like it was part of the dance. But he pulled me right back; his strong grip pressed my metallic dress into the skin around my waist, and his words were hot in my ear. "Is everything alright, love? Do you need another drink?"

God, his lips are touching my ear.

He knew I was stiff, but he didn't understand the cause of it. I *had* gone through a phase before when I couldn't loosen up without a few drinks. That was right when I'd been getting used to my overwhelming senses and settling back into society. But that was long ago, and social anxiety wasn't the issue anymore.

I shook my head, deciding to toughen up rather than make a big deal out of it. Riftan was the one who'd wanted to go dancing, and I didn't need to ruin it for him. If all else failed, I could fake it till I made it. I'd always been good at faking it—I did date Johnny, after all—and usually, if I faked it well enough, I could start to feel it, too. Preparing myself for a little mind over matter, I took a deep breath and did what I knew—regardless of how much it stoked the blazing inferno inside me. Steady and sure, I swayed with Riftan, letting him dictate our pace. My hands grazed his at my waist before pressing into my unrestrained breasts, brushing over my hair, and landing on his cheek, where it hovered above my head. He leaned into my touch, letting me reach through his hair and settle against his neck. With my hold on him, I could leverage our bodies together and keep tempo with him without having to think about it.

Pressed into him, I emptied my mind—or I tried to. But what I wished to be numbness was instead a deafening static that transcended tolerable limits once I focused on how much of him I could feel against my back. His hands dug into the fabric that very much still clung to my stomach, a meek reminder of the flimsy dress that was doing nothing to muffle the desire between us. Every protruding muscle pressed against me, and an unambiguous bulge wedged against my ass. Molded together, I theorized I could paint a picture of his naked body as though there were no clothes between us.

Finding that my mind was too weak to outweigh this matter, I spun in his grip until we were face to face. He smiled at my change of pace and pulled me in, breathing the air that expelled from my lips when our bodies met once more. His eyes clutched my gaze, only inches away, begging me to get lost in them the way I often did. But I'd already fixated on the much more distracting lump pressed between my thighs and grinding against my most sensitive spot.

The fast-paced electronic beat pounding from the overhead speakers wasn't conducive to any other kind of dancing, and we weren't doing anything different from every other attendee in the club. But not even that knowledge helped me fight the chaotic internal combustion Riftan's body evoked. My gaze wavered, finding purchase on his grey button-up shirt. My nerves screamed to get away from Riftan, or to have more of him; I didn't know which was worse.

His breath tickled my scalp as he nuzzled into my hair and trailed slowly toward my neck, where his lips settled against my skin.

Like his lips had zapped me with electricity, I jolted away from Riftan, putting an arm's length between us fast enough he couldn't stop my retreat. "I'll be right back," I yelled over the commotion of the dance floor.

Riftan nodded, but his smile lessened. It knew I wasn't my normal self. That smile knew so much more than it would let on. Turning away from him, I breathed in the offensive scents of the mortal crowd and cleared my mind while I made my way off the dance floor. I wasn't taking that moment merely to run from Riftan, I actually had an idea to turn our night around, and it involved a necessary tempo change.

Tucked away at the front of the club, there was a doorway that led onto the DJ's tiny stage. It was flanked with bouncers who were simple enough to thrall—though even before becoming immortal, I probably could have still persuaded my way past them. I charmed the young man on the soundboard without the use of any immortal hypnotization. I then requested a change of pace and gave him an idea of what I wanted—something jazzier. He winked at me, nodding a response that told me I wouldn't have to thrall him. Apparently, Jameson had been right, and my charm alone was as good as any hypnotism.

Satisfied, I returned to the mass of people filling the dance floor. As I sunk into the writhing crowd, the music softened, hardly a lull between tracks as it seamlessly blended into a new song. A smooth woman's vocals set the mood, silence behind it coating the room as club goers adjusted to the change. Carried by the gentle synth and upbeat tempo, the singer's voice started to take a familiar shape, resembling the lyrics of a popular Nine Inch Nails song. A peppy violin added to the mix as I reached the center of the mass where I'd left Riftan.

I swayed to the music, finding the funky rhythm easy to follow and definitely suited to what I'd asked for.

Riftan's wavy black head of hair stood above the others in the crowd. Sneaking past the horde of other vacillating mortals, my view opened up to show another much smaller being standing toe to toe with him. Though everyone was mashed close to one another in the crowd, this little blonde creature had perched her petite made-up face practically against Riftan's chest. She batted her eyelashes at him, shimmying in an ugly orange cocktail dress.

Riftan's brows formed a harsh V before he scanned the crowd over the blonde head. When our eyes met, he relaxed, a smile creeping up his cheeks. He took a quick glance at the woman and back at me before raising both his hands to show that he didn't have his hands on the girl. Without another look her way, he slipped away and met me where I stood on the dance floor.

"I like the music." He took my hand and spun me in a circle. "Do you have something to do with that?"

"Nope. Coincidence I guess." I winked.

Without letting go of my hand, Riftan stepped into me, putting us chest to chest. Instead of grinding his hips on mine, he swayed with me, swinging us to the disco style beat with none of the unchaste undertones from before. I giggled with every spin, my cheeks becoming sore from an overbearing grin that was merely mimicking Riftan's.

We could have danced like that until the world stopped.

When the vocals faded out and all that remained was a dwindling trumpet solo, my heart dropped to think it was coming to an end. But the tempo didn't change, even as the song did, fusing into another upbeat dance tune.

Thank god, I really charmed the pants off that DJ.

The throng around us cheered, a merry vibe coating the atmosphere for what felt like *hours* of dancing. After a certain point, the dance floor usually began to filter out, but not this crowd. The lot of us were caught up in a contagious aura that had formed one comprehensive body moving to the music.

I'd never tire of that, but I hit pause on my fun to offer Riftan a drink. He agreed, as I expected, and I made my way to the bar. Without my superhuman abilities, it still would have been easy to spot that I had a shadow following me there. The shadow was small and blonde, not tall and handsome like one I'd left in the throng of people.

Ordering my drink, I eyed the small girl who took the seat next to me at the bar. Her gaze glued to me, penetrating my personal space with only a look.

"That boyfriend of yours is pretty hot," she bit out, the words rolling off her tongue that lingered against her parted lips.

"Boyfriend? Oh, right. Riftan." I was so accustomed to our situationship that our appearance slipped my mind. No fucking duh we looked like a couple from the outside.

Beside me, the petite blonde smacked her lips, shaking out a head full of fake hair. She was the same girl who had pressed herself against Riftan earlier; I'd recognize a gaudy orange dress like hers anywhere—it'd probably haunt my nightmares. She carried herself with a high horse kind of air that said she thought she was the hottest skank in that club. To be fair, she was pretty, even if her caked on makeup and fake tits weren't really my style.

"Oh, Riftan. Damn, even his name is hot." She nearly drooled over the bar, looking in his direction and then back at me with a mocking arched brow.

The bitch was bold, I'd give her that. Even if she wasn't my type, I was starting to like her—in the, I want to murder you and drink your blood, kind of way.

"How about this," she continued in my silence. "I'll offer you a little wager in love and war."

I looked her over.

"How much do you believe in his loyalty to you?"

"Excuse me?" I narrowed my eyes at her.

"Your boyfriend. If I can get him to kiss me, then I win. And in return, I keep him. That's the wager."

Skank. I didn't know if Riftan was necessarily *loyal.* We had no relationship for him to be loyal to. But that hadn't stopped him from making a promise to me—one he had blatantly been adhering to.

"Fine. He's faithful to me, so you can do your worst. I don't give a shit." I feigned nonchalance, rolling my eyes and signaling for the bartender.

"Suit yourself," the girl hissed, her face contorting in wicked delight. With that, she bobbed her little blonde head through the crowd until she reached Riftan, who swayed haphazardly while he waited for me.

The second that girl opened her mouth, Riftan looked at me, his expression flat.

I shrugged, gesturing at the girl by his feet. It wasn't until I nodded at him that he looked at the girl, like he'd been permitted to talk to her.

Their interaction wasn't as nerve wracking as it should have been. Riftan had already stoked my confidence by not giving that chick the time of day without looking to me for permission. Though we weren't romantic, at least I could depend on him to be loyal—if that combination of sentiments made any sense.

Only moments into their conversation, Riftan glanced at me, then back at the girl. In feigned obedience, he nodded and the girl took his hand, leading him off the dance floor.

My heart skipped a beat, but my faith was restored when Riftan tipped his head for me to follow them. I did so, leaving the drinks I'd ordered behind and stalking the pair as they made their way toward the back rooms that hid behind velvet curtains and ropes.

The girl slipped into one and pulled Riftan in behind her.

I lingered for a moment, giving them some time before thralling the bouncer to let me follow.

Behind the thick velvet curtain, it was dark, the loud music muted. Against the back wall, a candle illuminated a round cushioned booth matching the plush velvet of the entryway. Riftan and the woman both glowed in the warm light, side by side, cuddled up in the booth. He still had that bored look on his face, but it wasn't an abnormal expression for him. Contrarily, the girl showed her teeth in the most uncontrollably smug way, already leaning into him, all too rushed to win her bet.

Riftan held up his hand between them, covering her entire face with his palm, never flinching in his expression. Instead of thralling her to stop, he pushed the girl away by her face, making her teeter backwards.

She scoffed, her neck flushing red as she patted down her

nose to adjust the smudged makeup.

Unable to contain myself, I let out a laugh and closed the distance in the room.

The girl whipped her head around to meet me, her thinly plucked brows furling. "What are you doing here? We had a bet," she complained.

"We did." I leaned over the table, crossing my arms against it in a way that heaved my cleavage taut across the neckline of my dress. "And I think you've lost, honey."

Riftan's eyes darted to my chest before he cleared his throat and accused, "So, this exchange is *your* fault?"

"No." I leaned in further, craving the attention he'd so swiftly lent to my body. "I merely went along with this hussy's idea of a fun wager."

The girl spoke up, her voice whiny like a spoiled teen. "And I would have won, too, if you hadn't stepped in so early. Are you really so insecure that you couldn't see it through till the end?"

"Ha," I offered her a patronizing laugh. "I simply know when I've won. Riftan, make this simple. Tell the girl she's not cute and that she can fuck off."

"Well, I wouldn't say that she *isn't* cute."

I eyed him with what may have come across as a death stare.

"Darling, I think what you want me to tell you is that she's not as cute as you are." He stood from his spot across the table and leaned into me, his nose inches from mine. Swift hands caressed my cheek, bringing me closer. He continued, low and sultry, his words meant for me, and only me. "In which, I can assure you, nobody is. But she *definitely* does not deserve the privilege to be compared to your beauty."

The girl groaned in disgust, her noise like an afterthought in the precipice of my mind.

Riftan nipped his fangs at my nose before retreating, dropping back into his seat with a satisfied smirk.

When I stared at him, completely dissociated from anything else that had been happening before, Riftan broke eye contact, smacking his hands on the table and shimmying out of his spot. Leaning against the table next to me, he twirled a piece of my hair but still avoided my stare that'd followed him to my side. "Well, do let me in on the surprise. What'd you win in this little bet?" He flicked a look at me, then back on my hair.

Letting out a breath, I looked to the girl who very much still sat in the booth, regardless of how insignificant her presence had become to me. "I don't know. The slut was too full of herself to consider the possibility that I'd win. She didn't ask what I wanted in return."

"Yeah, yeah," she played along, at least a good sport. "So, what is it you want for winning? I'll give it to you."

I had a feeling she'd cough up almost anything I asked for, just to show she could. But unfortunately for her, I didn't want money, and I could get my own things.

Without hesitation, I made my request. "How about your life?"

IS THAT... KINKY

A FANGY SMILE infested my cheeks as I looked down on that girl. Turning toward Riftan, it morphed into a sneer. "I just found you a meal. How's that sound, *babe*?" I asked him, getting a little too entrenched in the boyfriend-girlfriend act.

His lips mimicked mine, grinning as sultry eyes snaked their way over my face. Exchanging my hair in his hand for my face, he tapped his forefinger against my cheek. "Are you sure about that? I mean, I know she's gotten under your skin, but is it worth killing her over?"

The girl snorted a laugh. "Excuse me?" She raised her eyebrows, waiting for the joke's punchline.

Ignoring her, I convinced Riftan, "I'm okay with killing her. Does it bother you?"

"No." He shrugged. "But have you asked if she has a family? I don't want it weighing on your conscience, that's all, my love."

Glancing back at the girl, I found her out of the booth and trying to slip past me. She may have thought my offer was a joke at first, but she clearly wasn't sticking around any longer to find out. Once our eyes met and she'd been caught in the act, the girl stopped in her tracks.

"I don't care," I answered Riftan, my gaze never leaving the girl. "I want to watch you feed off the skanky mortal regardless. And I *promise* you it won't weigh on my conscience one bit."

The girl started to fiddle with her hair. "This is weird. Look, you won, I'll give you some money. I have lots with me. That should square us up, right?" She offered a phony grin that failed to cover her growing anxiety.

Pulling me back, Riftan's finger dug into my cheek, not hard enough to hurt, but enough to guarantee I wouldn't look away. He spoke gentle words over my lips, "Thrall her to follow us home, and we will feed on her there."

The girl's heart rate spiked, and she made to bolt. I grabbed her by the arm, the force almost pulling it out of the socket, but not phasing Riftan and me. "Why not here?" I asked. "We've got this nice little VIP suite all to ourselves."

"Because…" He traced down my chin, watching the trail of goosebumps he made in his wake. "We are both going to feed on her and if she can't handle it, she'll die. That's not something I want to have to deal with here in public. It's better if we do it at home."

"Both of us?" I repeated, the connotation sinking in. "Like, together, at the same time?"

"Yes."

"Oh." The idea was provocative, like an untried taboo. Something we'd never done before. "Is that... kinky?"

"Maybe a little." That same sultry little grin passed his lips again before his hands left my chin and he backed toward the exit. "But I'd say it's more romantic than anything." He didn't wait to watch me melt before turning away and ducking through the velvet exit.

Feeling light as air from the possibilities that admission could hold, I almost forgot that I had a mortal tugging against my grip.

"Hurry up, love," Riftan called, peeking through the curtain to ensure I was following.

"Coming!" I jumped, the opportunity to share a romantic meal with Riftan filling my veins with excitement. Turning to the girl, I caught her by the eyes and thralled, "Follow us home, but not too close. I don't want you to look suspicious." I shadowed the request with a little wink and nipped at her nose playfully. The girl lifted her lips in an exuberant smile. I hadn't hypnotized her into a vegetable, but enough to make her unafraid and obedient.

Fading to the curtain, I found Riftan not far ahead as he made for the door. I hopped up next to him and we left the club together, then we meandered hand-in-hand back to the condo. All the while, our little tag-along did the same, following behind at a reasonable distance.

At our condo, she entered through the back of the building where nobody could see her, which was quick thinking for a daft, thralled mortal. Not that it mattered, nobody was watching us and there weren't any cameras around our place, but staying under the radar was always a good practice if we wanted to keep on the council's good side or stay out of the sights of potential vampire hunters. From what I'd been told, those were both concerns to keep at the forefront of immortal decision-making.

Once we were all inside, I pulled the girl by the hand until we were both sitting on the living room couch. I brushed my fingers through her long blonde locks, twirling a few of the loose curls. She was indeed cute, even with the smudged makeup and gaudy dress. But Riftan was right, she wasn't as cute as me. Her plump lips were too fake, eyes lackluster, and skin kind of dull, even after all the makeup. That made me more comfortable with the idea of Riftan feeding on her. She wasn't as cute as *me*, she was just food.

Lagging behind, Riftan stopped in the kitchen. "I'll get you a glass of wine, love. Do you want that cabernet I got you last month?"

"Sure," I offered, sparing him only a glance before my attention was back on the girl.

She looked around curiously, musing under her breath, but unable to make out a communicable sentence through my thrall. Every calm little breath she took lifted her chest, heaving her firm-looking breasts in cadence. More than a little intrigued, I reached for one of them, wondering if they felt how they looked. The girl wasn't too scrambled to sink into my touch, uttering a little moan through her teeth.

I swallowed a lump forming in my throat from how badly I wanted to explore her more. She wasn't my type, sure. But it hadn't always been that way. There was almost certainly a version of Leanne from the past that would have gone for a girl like her.

"You can think freely," I whispered to the girl, releasing my thrall and only adding, "but don't move, and no sounds any louder than my voice."

The moment she was released, trepidation invaded her face. She had so many questions and they all came out at once. She begged for her life, offering loved ones and strangers in her place. A tear even trickled down her paltry little cheek.

The more she groveled, the more that desire in my throat grew, heating my core in the most perverse way. It was awful how much her misery turned me on. I knew it was, but it didn't stop the feeling. *When did I get this way?* I hadn't been a vampire that long, in the grand scheme of things, so maybe I'd always been this way.

"Shh," I whispered, licking my lips as I nuzzled against her neck where the veins rushed with blood. "Keep babbling and I'll make you shut up again."

The smell of her was more vibrant the closer I got, a faint floral perfume hardly masking her natural mortal scent. I rubbed my lips against her velvety skin; my tongue ached to taste her blood. It was surely more intoxicating than her scent.

I licked her—just a taste of what was to come.

"Hey!" Riftan's voice was sharp from the kitchen. "Do not start without me."

A groan ripped from my lungs, and I pulled away. "Hurry up, then!" I could hardly wait to sink my teeth into this girl.

She whimpered under my touch, her painted voluptuous lips trembling. If I couldn't take a bite of her, I might as well have tasted her in a different way.

Careful not to smudge her lipstick on my own skin, I took her quivering lips on mine. Though she couldn't pull away, because she was thralled not to move, she didn't protest. When I stopped to gauge her response, I found her with her eyes closed, shaking ceased. In her meek, shallow voice, she said, "You are so sexy and so terrifying at the same time."

"Well, I suppose that's why you lost our little bet, now isn't it?" I winked.

She parted her lips, pursing slightly, welcoming me to kiss her again. I did, this time laying in, less gentle with her.

The sound of Riftan's footfalls pulled me away, embarrassment creeping into my cheeks.

He was right over us. "Don't play with your food, my little minx." Reaching down, he grabbed ahold of the girl's chin and demanded, "Everything is fine. Shut up and be a good girl."

She silenced and stared ahead mindlessly.

"That's no fun," I complained, taking the glass of wine Riftan offered me. "Don't you want to hear her plead for her life a little more?"

He answered, "I don't want to hear or think about anything but you tonight."

My heart flew into my throat.

"Come now." He motioned to the girl. "You wanted her, right? Ladies first."

Swallowing the lump that could have very well been the entirety of my immortal heart, I obeyed, leaning into the girl and kissing at the base of her neck. The veins throbbed under her skin, and I indulged, digging into her, wary not to drip any of her succulent blood onto my grey couch.

Usually, I'd close my eyes to enjoy the euphoric blood lust that came rushing at the first bite. But this time, I stayed attentive, watching Riftan bite in and experience his own ecstasy. He was slow, careful, dropping his eyelids as the first wave of pleasure from her blood settled over him. Seeing that feeling written over his face and feeling it for myself at the same time was a new kind of rapture that shattered the world around me.

Nothing would ever be better than this moment, when all that existed was our mutual bliss.

Riftan's lips grazed skillfully over the girl's skin like a tender kiss, not the violent bite I knew he was digging into her. Underneath the torment of her demise, how did it feel to have Riftan's lips on her? Sans the familiar pinch of his teeth, I could almost feel his lips grazing my own flesh, tickling my neck, fluttering over my lips.

I needed that more than I needed to get my fill of this girl's blood. I hadn't taken more than a few drinks before I was only suckling at her veins, too distracted by my fixation on Riftan.

As if through magnetic pull, his eyes flicked open, gaze

fusing to mine. He didn't move, but drank the mortal's blood with long pulls that were much more effective than mine. Quicker than I was used to, the woman's heartbeat slowed, and my instinct was to pull away, regardless of Riftan's prior approval to drain her dry. Knowing that, I thought to go back for more, but Riftan's hooded gaze held me captive.

He plucked his fangs out of the girl but didn't falter his stare.

My desire to have him clouded my brain to near inanity, only amplified by the blood intoxication. It manifested in a quivering heat between my legs.

Riftan's eyes smoldered, radiating the kind of desire I felt for him. He reached over, swiping a thumb against my lips, the sensation warm and wet. Pulling away, I saw his finger coated in a crimson red smear of leftover blood. Before he could completely withdraw from me, I took his thumb in my mouth, sucking off the succulent substance he'd stolen.

Riftan's expression changed in an instant, a snarl curling on his lips but a fire burning in his eyes. It was nothing I'd ever seen on him—something red hot and seething with lust.

I only got to savor it for a moment before he plucked his thumb from my mouth and grabbed me by the throat, pulling our lips together in an insatiable kiss.

Softly, Riftan moved his lips over mine, offering the taste I'd been craving. It was exhilarating, the taste of him so warm and sweet on my tongue. A numbing relief rushed through my body—it's constant coveting finally consummated. It felt like static being silenced—that old TV finally turned off.

Not letting up, Riftan pulled me closer, gripping my neck and blanketing my lips in endless, profound kisses. He kissed me like there were thousands of lost kisses to make up for, his warmth enveloping me for only a moment before it turned to *fire*. The heat that'd built between us erupted, and I was taking every smoldering kiss he gave me and returning it tenfold.

Without stopping, I pushed past the mortal girl and jumped into Riftan's lap, where he welcomed me greedily, clamping his hands over the bare skin of my thighs as I straddled him.

Our passion was quenchless. Barring the end of the world, there would be *nothing* that could stop us from finally seeing this explosion of sexual tension through to the end.

I just hoped this ending would be the happy kind.

23

I WANT TO BE CLOSE TO YOU

PARTING MY LIPS, I welcomed Riftan's roaming tongue into my mouth. It grazed over my fangs, erotic in a way that sent shivers down my spine. Loving the sensation, I returned the favor, flicking the endless nerves of my tongue against his sharp incisors for the first time.

I'd never kissed another immortal, so I didn't have any basis on what to expect when it came to the fangs. In all honesty, it hurt when I'd get too excited and bump my lips into his teeth, and that initial passionate collision had done just that. Fortunately, our kiss was deepening as I settled in with my knees over each side of Riftan, and there were no more jarring collisions to bump our fangs together.

As we slowed, the kiss remained insatiable, lacking the hectic movements, but not missing the desire that burned between us. Riftan's lips were demanding, exigent, ravenous even. They gripped me in existential heat that blurred my mind. There was no more thinking—I was running off autopilot and bliss.

Wrapping my arms around his neck, I ran my hands through his hair. He nipped at my lips, and I grabbed a handful and bit him back. A guttural groan bubbled from him, lingering in the area where our lips entwined and pinching at my already very swollen heartstrings.

His hands drifted toward my skirt. Pushing under the fabric, they settled on the very cusp of my ass. I'd say he was being shy by stopping there, except that he didn't have to go any farther to cup the entire mass of my cheeks in his copious hands. Completely void of any leftover inhibitions, I gently rocked my hips over his lap. He responded by grabbing me tighter, forcing my hips down to grind on him in a much more outrightly obscene motion.

The tighter he squeezed, the more of my backside his fingers encompassed. The tips of them tickled at the underside of the flimsy thong I was wearing. A little bit farther, and he could have slipped right under.

Be it purposeful or by accident, Riftan flicked one of his fingers out, grazing the threshold of my delicately covered core, and I practically jumped out of his hands. The sensation of him anywhere near the bundle of nerves between my legs, even as chaste as his brush had been, was almost enough to fling me into a random onset orgasm right then and there.

Like he loved that reaction, he did it again, all the while

nipping at my lips, suckling on them in a vivacious attempt to swallow every bit of my heart and soul that didn't already belong to him. He continued to tease a finger over my underwear, hardly having to move it as I gyrated over his lap, doing the motion for him. Against my movements, a rigid bump was pressing through his pants and growing past the point of disregardable.

While I was no stranger to the male anatomy, it was difficult not to salivate at the thought of his—much less his being so turned on by me. I may have drooled all over him if he wasn't all over my lips the way he was.

It wasn't the first time I'd witnessed him get a hard-on. He was a guy and random boners happened. But this was different; it wasn't random, and it was most definitely persistent and poking me in the thigh, very close to my lady bits that were already screaming for him. I rode against the growing bulge hardly contained in his pants and let the animal instincts that idled in my DNA take over a little more.

His lips withdrew only long enough to utter a husky plea. "I want you so bad right now."

I could tell—erections don't lie—but that didn't make the admission any less incredible.

His lips begged for reconnection, but it was my turn to pull away, thoughts shadowing my lust for a split moment.

He watched me, arching his brows over pleading eyes. He leaned in again, but I didn't let him connect, making his jaw tic in frustration. I had to tell him though. I needed him to hear it from my lips. "Then have me. I'm yours and only yours."

He growled, the noise gurgling from within like some wild animal, and we collided again.

I muttered his name through mouthfuls of his lips and his hands drifted over me, brushing past my hair and pulling at the strings that held up my dress. One of the straps toppled off my shoulder and he exchanged my lips for the vulnerable skin at my neck, suckling and tracing it down my shoulder.

With my cognizance unclouded enough by the exodus of his lips against mine, I had the presence of mind to pull at the buttons on his shirt. I kissed his ear until my hands could freely traverse his bare chest.

Riftan had the hottest chest known to mankind—or any kind. Maybe men were built differently in his time, or maybe it had something to do with being a knight when he was mortal. Either way, his body was amazing and an opportunity to truly appreciate it shouldn't have gone unexploited. I could have traced every muscular line on his stomach, kissed the scars on his chest from before he'd been turned, and truly taken my time to appreciate his perfection, but I was greedy, and the more of him I got, the more of him I wanted.

Tracing his chest all the way down to his belt, I touched the fabric that strained to conceal his not so furtive arousal.

He groaned, "Leanne…"

"Riftan," I replied, fiddling with his belt.

His trail of kisses stopped above my breast, where he sunk his teeth into my skin, halting while I toyed with his buckle. Not even his breath graced my flesh until I'd gotten the belt undone and moved on to his button.

"Wait, Leanne." He extracted his teeth from me and grabbed at my feverish hands.

"No," I murmured, swatting his hands away.

He pulled me in by the back of my neck, connecting our lips again, letting me taste what it felt like to evanesce into him. The incorporeal feeling had me reeling momentarily before I was fiddling with his pants all over again.

"Wait... Leanne," he repeated in between our kisses.

My heart pounded with the familiar panic of his impending cessation. "Please, don't you dare stop me," I begged between panted breaths.

I was so used to him getting in the way. Almost as though his goal was to drive me completely mad, he insisted on keeping me on the verge of this unrelenting necessity for more of him.

"I'm sorry." He replaced our positions in the blink of an eye, pinning me to the couch, my hands seized in his. One last numbing kiss was all I got before he pulled away, quietly interjecting, "This is a mistake. I shouldn't have done any of that."

With restraint, I didn't let my jaw drop the way my heart did. "You said that you wanted it. How could it be a mistake?" When my words did little but push him further away, I begged, "Please don't leave. Don't do this to me. Don't do what you always do. Don't push us apart because we got too close. I want to be close to you. *Please.*"

What a degrading plea.

Riftan stared at the floor, shadows shielding me from his gaze. "I need some time alone. Please let me think about this on my own."

My hand fell through the space he'd occupied, his form dissipating into a grey vapor cloud that parted from my intrusion.

Silence followed, his feet not even padding over the hardwood before our door slammed shut, the lock clicking into place with a heart wrenching *click*. The sloppily crafted plea he hadn't waited to hear still hung on my parted lips, leaving me crumpled on our couch, half undressed and gawking into the emptiness.

The comedown was quick as reality set in—or more accurately, came crashing down. Feeling like I was prying at dream ridden eyes, I dreaded the idea of waking up. As acceptance of my awakening became unavoidable, I was left with the realization that I'd be sleeping alone in my old bed. If all my circling emotions weren't enough, I'd have to deal with an empty bed—and my favorite pillow was locked in the bedroom with Riftan.

Racking my head against the back of the couch, I looked over at the girl slumped unconscious on the armrest. Her heart rate was faint, but her back still rose and fell with monotonous breaths.

Everything from the last five to ten minutes was a little hazy and frantic, but I could recall that neither Riftan nor I had taken enough to hurt the girl immediately.

Reaching over, I shook her awake. She shot up in the mannequin-esque way that mimicked her prior vacancy.

The wounds on her neck had dried up, but I could still

smell the blood that'd crusted over her wounds and dripped down her chest. I eyed the source of her luring scent, contemplating finishing her off to satiate my hunger—even if that's all that got satiated that night. Or, I could let her live and take her to my room—not for promiscuous reasons, but merely to warm my otherwise uninviting bed. Unfortunately, she wasn't the one I wanted lying next to me, and she wouldn't suffice as a replacement, either.

"Ugh, go home." I thralled her and sent her away.

Then it was just me, alone in the deserted expanse of our living room. Eventually, I would have to muster the courage to get off the couch and make my way to the cold, solitary confines of my bed, but the idea was daunting. For some reason, it felt as though if I did, it was like admitting my own defeat.

24

ONCE YOU MAY HAVE BEEN A HERO, BUT NOW YOU'RE JUST A COWARD

MY BIGGEST FEAR was that Riftan would act as though that night never happened. Naively, I believed that would be the worst-case scenario.

I should have known better. Because, while I wanted more than anything to talk to Riftan about what was happening between us, he'd decided the solution was contrary. He wasn't pretending it'd never happened; the man was *ignoring* me. Two days in a row, he'd locked himself in our bedroom, sharing with me nominal moments in passing where he'd say, "I'm not ready to talk about it," and then withdraw to his hidey-hole.

He'd atoned the second night, pleading for my forgiveness before locking me out of our room again. But no apology could warm my vacant sheets, and I hated the situation he was putting us in.

Just my luck, Riftan was determined to prove to me *exactly* what "worst-case" was.

At our kitchen counter, late into the morning when I'd almost given up waiting for him, Riftan settled onto the bar stool next to me. He narrowed a cold gaze at the granite but hadn't said a single word past "good morning" since emerging from our bedroom. The weight of his look said he was saving his words for something more important than small talk. Then, he detonated the bomb I'd been trying to pretend hadn't been ticking away in the peripherals of our relationship.

"Leanne, I want you to leave."

"Pardon?" It seemed like a derisory joke, and certainly not the proper conversation starter I expected over our first shared cup of coffee in nearly forty-eight hours.

His gaze fixed on mine, the sea in his eyes painting a clear but unbreakable resolve. "I've taught you above and beyond everything you'd need to know to safely live on your own. I have faith that now is a good time to part ways."

Clutching my mug, it took several moments to catch my breath, the action of filling my lungs taking conscious thought. In my stead, Riftan offered little more than an unchanging, tight-lipped expression and a thick silence.

My retort was forced through my teeth. "No, I'm not going anywhere."

"I wasn't asking, Leanne."

"Is this about the other night?" I griped. "If it is, then I will pretend that it never happened." I'd do anything to stay with him, no matter how much I hated it.

"It's not necessarily about the other night. You need to go out and start your own life. Letting you do anything else would be irresponsible on my part." Still no change in his guise. "The other night was merely what made me realize that now is the time to insist on your departure. I know now that my restraint is declining, and I can't resist you like I thought I could anymore. That's why you can't continue to stay with me."

What a roller coaster of emotions that confession was.

He went on when I was too shaken to spit out my own words. "Please don't be angry with me. I want you to go out and live all those lives that you get to live now. Immortals are the only people who get this kind of chance. I changed you so you could get it, too. I want that for you, and I think you should want it too. There are so many new things for you to experience on your own—an endless number of new opportunities with each life you explore."

"But a life with you? That's not one I'm allowed to have or explore?"

"No. I don't want you to continue blindly following my existence. I want you to create your own."

My voice raised in pitch, no matter how hard I tried not to yell at Riftan. "That isn't fair to me, Riftan. You must know that I don't want to leave you. The thought of leaving you hurts more than anything I can imagine. Aside from the feelings I have for you, you're my best friend. I don't want to lose my best friend."

His resolution cracked, if only slightly, his brows crouching over dark eyes. "I'll still always be your friend. I'll always be here for you, never more than a phone call away. Losing friends in this day and age is nearly impossible, right?"

A heaviness in my throat ached with a welling emotion that begged for release. It boded tears—the kind that only piled on with the idea that I couldn't let them loose. Not here—not now—in the face of his strength. Planting my hands on the counter, I feigned courage. "What am I supposed to do without you? Without your positivity or someone to share my dreams with?" My voice cracked before I could finish my sentence—so much for feigning that courage.

Remarkably, I wasn't the only one stirred by that. Dropping his face into his hands, Riftan's demeanor crumbled into smithereens. "Leanne, please don't make this harder than it needs to be," he begged, pain punctuating every word.

I laid it on, hoping to pull on his heart a little more—almost like I wanted to see if it was possible. "What am I supposed to do every night if you aren't there to hold me, or to dance with me, or to tell me that I'm yours..." Heaviness turned to a shooting pain in my throat and the reality was that I couldn't stop the tears, whether I wanted to or not. "I thought I was yours and you were mine."

"Stop," Riftan snapped, his head shooting upright, heavy eyes settling over me. Any further response was only the harsh shake of his head, the muscles in his jaw flaring to show how violently he fought to hold back his contention.

"Riftan, please don't make me leave. I can't—I don't want to live without you... I love you." A handful of tears dribbled off my cheeks, warm and wet. They were errant, and I had to force the forte to stop before they got out of hand.

Riftan's eyes flinched, the only evidence of emotion escaping the windows to his soul before he obscured his face from view, this time rubbing a finger over his brows. Muffled through his hands, he grumbled, "Why can't you appreciate this for what it is? It's better for both of us this way."

For both of us? Did he want me out of his hair? He'd never acted like that was the case. Separation was supposed to be for my good. This whole time, we'd been feigning some thin lines because he didn't want me getting hurt by him. Our lack of romanticism was so I wouldn't end up brokenhearted. Or so he'd said.

And yet, those lines were never there to stop him, they were there to stop me. We could touch on his terms, cuddle on his terms, *love* on *his* terms, because that's how he was in control. Riftan could control when feelings were felt, but only for himself. I was along for the ride—a casualty of *his terms*. Words fell like icicles from my lips. "Was it really ever my heart that you were concerned about being broken, or was it yours?"

He didn't answer—which was answer enough with him.

My chest felt cold, whipped by some internal frostbitten breeze when I realized how little control I truly had in this situation. Any semblance of equality between Riftan and me had only ever been a well-established ruse, and I'd always known that.

The delusive cold left my remaining argument sounding numb. "You already have my heart. Making me leave will break it. But you're willing to let that happen as long as it's not you getting hurt, right? As long as you're in control of the situation like you always are. Is that all you care about? Are you truly that stubborn and *scared*?"

His face emptied, devoid of any emotion, even the anger that hinted on his tongue. "I'm giving you the control of getting to leave on your own accord. If you refuse, then I will leave you, and I assure you that'll hurt you a lot more." He blinked, sipping from his mug with a nonchalance that belonged at a Sunday brunch. Any passion in his eyes had subdued, no longer giving me the satisfaction to see inside.

For some reason, that hurt me less. Sometimes Riftan exhibited the most emotion by shutting himself off to those feelings. It was somewhere I'd only seen him a few times before, but it always looked the same. I could recognize his version of empathy in letting me push him to that point. Regardless, the conversation was over. Emotionally, he had nothing left to give me, and any argument I voiced would be spoken to a brick wall.

Careful not to share any of my own precious emotions with him, I offered my closing statement. "Once upon a time, you may have been a hero. But now you are just a coward."

He gave me little more than a flinch and deflected his gaze onto the countertop.

That seemed like a shitty way to end things, so I added, "Thanks for your honesty, Riftan. I'll be out of your hair by midnight, but I hope you have a wonderful eternity." Then I left him.

I'd have to pack a few things from my room, but it

wouldn't take long, and I wouldn't drag it out. Though I wanted to hang my emotions out to dry right then and there, it didn't feel right to let Riftan hear me cry over this. He didn't deserve to witness the proof of how much this hurt me.

At my bedroom door, I made the mistake of taking one last look over my shoulder to where Riftan had his head on the counter. He combed a hand through his hair, brushing the dark strands away from his neck. A shaky sigh flattened his back, feeling like it'd emanated from my own lungs. No matter how pissed I was at him, feeling that shared moment reminded me he'd hurt from this, too. He was stubborn and selfish, but he had the same feelings for me that I'd grown for him. Sharing them wasn't pleasant. There was no justice in knowing his pain.

It took all my willpower to tear my eyes from him and dip into my room.

Since I had very little to my name that wasn't *ours*, packing was short. A couple of clothing items, my electronics, and some shoes were all I owned. Looking at my entire life—so insignificant that it fit into a carry on—broke me.

If I could have things my way, I'd pack that entire condo in a suitcase and bring it everywhere with me. I wanted to bundle up every memory, every little emotion I'd felt there, and put it in my bag. Reliving the last three years on repeat seemed like the only thing that could fix what was breaking. My biggest fear was that those memories were now tainted, and nothing would repair this feeling I had.

Unfortunately, I had more pressing fears I needed to face first, and at the top of that list was: *where the hell do I go now?*

I'd never been *alone*. After my mom died, I had Jayleen's family, and after that, I had Johnny. I'd always depended on someone for something, or at least had people around me who understood my situation. Now, who would I lean on? I was more isolated than when I'd been an orphan, or the plaything for a fucking mob boss. The only kinship I'd find these days was other immortals, and even then, most of them were hundreds of years older than me. What did we have in common besides an interest in blood? We weren't peers—certainly not friends. Riftan and Jameson were the only immortals I ever had any real connection with… maybe I needed to give others the same kind of chance I'd given them.

Dredging away my fears, I took my suitcase in hand and made for the front door.

It was all happening so fast, but that's how it needed to be. The longer I stayed, the harder leaving would be. But Riftan was always right: if he'd left first, it'd hurt so much more. Even if he was forcing it, this way I would still be walking out of this condo with my dignity. And dignity was the only thread left holding back my tears.

Riftan waited at the door for me. Seeing him through my teeming tear ducts was gut wrenching, but thinking that was the last time I could ever see him was heart shattering.

Under all of my superficial disdain for what he was putting me through, I still loved him, and this wasn't how I wanted to remember him. I didn't want my last image of him to be marred by blurry tears or distinguished by the defeated hunch that put him nearly the same height as me.

No matter how much saying goodbye would hurt, I wanted him to do it with his head held high. I wanted him to remind me how tall he could stand, show me how bright the flame behind his eyes could burn, and smile—just one last smile. But he didn't. He kept his hands in his jean pockets and his chin tied to the floor. Opening the door for me, he didn't make eye contact until I was at the threshold.

"Lee…" He didn't reach for me like that statement usually foreshadowed. "I…" He straightened up, only nominally closer to the image of him I wanted to see. Clearing his throat, Riftan asked, "Can you promise me one thing before you go?"

"What is it?" I forced composure by way of counted breaths.

"Please promise that you will reach out to me if you ever need help. No matter what it is, I will come running."

"Alright. Don't change your phone number then, because that's the only way I know to get ahold of you." I managed a smile.

He attempted the same, but it fell, dragging mine with it.

Leaving it on that, I broke away, passing him without another look.

"Be good," he told me, like one might say to their dog before letting them out to potty or a child before dropping them off at daycare.

"I never am." I was no obedient dog, and certainly not a virtuous child.

I left him, and this time I wouldn't make the mistake of looking back. It didn't matter what look he had while watching me go. It didn't matter what emotions he wore or which ones he shrouded. He was behind me—everything we had was behind me—and I couldn't allow myself to look back. Not on any of it. Not now that I was so boldly going forward.

*I WAS NOTHING BUT A GLIMMER
IN HIS BRIGHT ETERNITY*

I FELT LIGHTER after crying out half my body weight on the way to the airport.

There was no shame in it, and I thralled the driver to forget about it while I additionally thralled him to give me the free ride. Hypnotization was how I'd be getting everything I needed for the foreseeable future—since I certainly didn't have any money.

While it never seemed like Riftan was working real hard at being a mentor—and more like he was showing off every once in a while—he *had* taught me a lot. At the top of that list of things was how to get anything when you have nothing. *That* was a fundamental lesson I'd utilize the shit out of for the next couple of months. I was certain of that. Unfortunately, being able to thrall myself any array of transportation was of no use if I didn't know where I was going.

That's where a map of Europe and a short game of blind darts with my finger came in handy. The first country I landed on was a small one I'd never heard of, and my guess was that the language barrier would make matters tougher than I was willing to deal with in my condition. Without Riftan's multilingual qualities, travel would definitely be more difficult than it'd been when we were together. The second location I'd blindly picked was one Riftan and I had already been to together, and it wasn't somewhere I wanted to return without him. The third time I dropped my finger on the map, I may have been half peeking and aiming in the France direction. In the proximity of where my finger landed, I settled on Paris, where it'd hopefully be touristy enough that my language barrier wouldn't matter. It hadn't mattered much in a big city like Prague, after all.

After that, it was only a hop and skip over a few countries, with the help of hypnotizing myself some aerial and land transportation, before I was in one of the most famous cities in the world.

The heart of Paris hummed with the constant whisper of music on the wind. Buildings lined both sides of every street, stacked close on the cobbled sidewalks, but here they were much more uniform; the symmetry of the geometric brick buildings lacked the many tall spires and medieval architecture that broke up the roofline in Prague. The most notable difference was that of the Eiffel tower, which jutted above everything, taller than any of Prague's many crenelations.

Breathing in the smell of freshly baked breads from my balcony, I vowed to make the best of my situation. If anything could keep me out of a beckoning depressive state, this would be it—my *real* eat, pray, love journey.

It was three years late, but Riftan had forecasted this moment before we ever left Creswell. Now, I just needed to read the book, so I could know what the hell an *Eat, Pray, Love* journey really consisted of.

Update: the book sucked.

Two hundred pages in and nobody had sex. I'd like to say I toughed it out and finished it anyway... but I didn't. And while the ideas I got from it were somewhat relevant to my situation, finding myself through food and spiritual meditation wasn't so profound when I couldn't eat normal meals and my kind was shunned by literally all religions.

Only eight days into my little adventure, I was staring up at a glass chandelier with half a bottle of wine propped under my arm. Thankfully, the floor of my expensive hotel was plush, and I wasn't uncomfortable laying on it. In fact, between my velvet blanket and the short bristles of the carpet, I'd found some comfort in running my hands over the surfaces—a tick I thought I'd kicked back when I'd adapted to my senses.

The movie I'd left playing on the flat screen had ended a

while ago, but I was too drunk to want to get up and put on another. That left me in a half-lit room, void of noise save for the occasional honk from outside. In eight days, I'd learned how adverse isolation could be for my disposition. I recognized that, but acknowledging it didn't make it any easier to fix.

I went out often, fed more than was necessary, and tried to talk to new people. But at the end of the day, I still slept in an empty bed, ate my meals by myself, and had nobody to laugh with. So, when I was alone in my room, I preferred noise—any kind that could distract from my solitude. But when the movies came to an end or the playlist ran out of songs, I couldn't stop my asinine mind from wandering into the silence.

It always stumbled upon the stupidest questions, begging to know: How long does this feeling last? Is it an eternity? Can I really bear it that long?

Doubting my eternity always summoned thoughts of Riftan. He'd warned me about all of this: how much more heartbreak hurts as an immortal, that I'd hate feeling it for eternity, that I'd see it as a curse. He was right about all of it, which made me wonder if he'd felt it all himself. I wondered if he was feeling it all right now, like I was.

Tears sprung to my eyes when I imagined him on the floor of our condo, mimicking the sorrowful position I found myself in now. But the thought was fleeting because I knew deep down that he'd lived too long to let this bother him—he'd definitely moved on already.

Sitting up, I took a swig of wine from my bottle, attempting to drown the feelings like Riftan probably would—if he had any.

I was sure he had plenty of ways of forgetting about me, and I liked to think he'd utilize them—or I liked the idea of him *needing* to utilize them, but when I actually thought of him doing so, all I could imagine was that it involved other women in our bed, soothing his nightmares and giving him all the things I never got to.

The bottle in my hand shattered under my grip, splintering into a thousand tiny shards and spilling what little was left of my specialty cabernet onto the carpet.

"Damn it," I whined, shaking off the blood from cuts that had already healed. "That was my last bottle."

Stumbling off the ground, I grabbed my phone by the bedside with the intention of checking the local liquor store hours. When the screen flashed, I squinted, blurrily making out a new message.

Jameson's contact name, *JJ*, sobered me up quick.

Three missed calls and two texts.

> Can we talk??

> PLEASE call me

My heart pounded, but I couldn't tell what for.

I should have called Jameson a week ago, when this all happened, but every time my finger lingered over his contact name, I trembled. I had nothing to fear from J, but I was still scared to call him.

He was my best friend, but he was Riftan's, too. Though I knew he'd choose me over Riftan any day, calling J would mean having to talk about what had happened. No doubt Jameson would be ready to help me, prepared to wipe every tear and stitch up every broken piece of my heart however he could. Maybe that's what actually scared me most—knowing how easily J could make this sadness disappear. He could snap his fingers and every emotion I felt over losing Riftan would be invalidated.

I couldn't let that happen because these were emotions I was meant to feel. All of the misery and heartbreak were proof of Riftan and my time together. They left a sickening ache in my chest that felt like my organs were simply giving up and crumbling out of my body, only a hollow void left in their place. The pain was a physical manifestation of how real everything we had was, and I wasn't willing to give that up, no matter how awful it felt.

My phone vibrated.

> Your read receipts are on

"Fuck."

This was another one of those moments when I hovered over the *JJ* badge on my phone, too shaky to return a simple text. My heart pushed and pulled, begging for the welcoming sound of Jameson's voice but fearing its effects.

> Fine. Call me when your ready to talk. I'll be here.

His message blurred under my teary lids. I needed to talk to someone, and I knew it should have been him—or a therapist—but like the brutal masochist it was, my heart wanted to hurt. It seemed to be calling the shots yet again, taking control like it'd done for so many years with Riftan.

Frantically clicking the back button out of Jameson's texts, I landed an errant finger on the contacts icon on my home screen. It was in the J's—probably because the last person I'd called was Jameson a couple weeks back. Below him was Jayleen.

We hadn't talked since Creswell, and I'd be lying if I said I didn't miss her. She was the only person I loved who had nothing to do with Riftan. Her memories weren't associated with him in any way, and she didn't have the power to make me forget about him altogether.

I stared at the phone a long time before hitting call.

The line rang.

My heart thumped in my chest, fingers tingly from more than the wine. The feeling heightened for several monotonous rings, a bodily indication that I might be making the wrong decision.

I bit my lip, eyeing the red circle on my phone screen.

Calling Jayleen was a bad idea. She's mortal, after all. Someone I left back in a past life I wasn't supposed to return to.

Her voice was on the other end, her chipper tone clenching my stomach into knots. "You've reached Jayleen, leave me a message!" *Beep.*

"Umm, hey, Jay… It's Leanne. I know it's been a while, but give me a call, I guess… Whenever you're available. Or don't, it's not a big deal." I hung up the phone. Hardly catching my breath before it was ringing in my hands.

I connected the call but hadn't gotten it to my ear when

Jayleen was already speaking through the line. "Leanne? Is that really you? I recognized your voice in the message. I know it's you! Where are you? Where have you been? Are you alright? Tell me you're safe."

"It's me. I'm safe." The statement was awkward as it left my mouth.

"And? Where have you been!"

"Well, that's a little bit longer of a story." I laughed, but it was uneasy.

"Well, holy shit. I'll cancel my plans, start talking!"

I did, a weight lifting from my shoulders as I shared with her the last three years of my life. I had so much to share, and she stayed on the phone to listen to all of it. Riftan, Prague, our condo, I weaved a truth about all of it without ever telling her what I'd become. Topping the honesty sandwich, I told Jayleen the profound truth I'd never actually admitted to myself. "I was an idiot for thinking I'd be anything but a meager glimmer in the face of his long and bright eternity."

"Well, I don't know what this poetic eternity thing you're going on about is. While it sounds very romantic—I don't know that it quite suits the Leanne I know." She took on the mom tone I was versed to hearing from her after I suffered a bad breakup. "I'm going to be honest, and don't take this the wrong way, but *none* of this sounds anything like you. I mean, staying with some guy you aren't *fucking* for *how many* years? Letting him push you around for nothing? Not even a little finger action? If it weren't for your voice on the phone, I wouldn't believe it was really you talking to me right now. Not to mention, I've *never* met a man who wasn't putty in the hand of Leanne Cowitz."

I offered a measly breath of laughter through the phone. "Ha, I used to think the same thing. My confidence has kind of crumbled after this whole situation, though."

"Well, that doesn't suit you either. I don't like hearing these kinds of things, Leanne. I don't like hearing you sound so depressed, and I don't like hearing you doubt yourself. If you tell me where you are, I swear I'd be on the first flight to you. I don't care if it takes every penny from my house fund." She sounded like she'd really do it, too.

"Actually, you wouldn't believe it, but I'm in the heart of Paris right now."

"Oh," her determination faltered. "Well, I don't think I can afford a plane ticket to Paris. It's super expensive and crazy far away."

She pulled a real giggle out of me this time. "That's quite alright, Jayleen. You don't need to fly to Paris to make me feel better."

"I would if I could. *Seriously,* Leanne. I really miss you." Her saddened tone grabbed my heart.

"I miss you, too. More than I can tell you."

"Do you think there's any possible way you could come back to visit me sometime? Even if for a moment so I could see your face again? I know you have things to worry about here, like Johnny, but what if you just stopped through town?"

I shouldn't have considered her request. The answer needed to be downright "no." If I went back to Creswell, it'd be a mistake. There were a lot of immortals there, which could be good for me, but there were a lot of people I didn't want to see, too. Yet, home called, and if I couldn't go back to that condo in Prague, then Creswell was all I had left of a home.

"Jayleen…" The thought was escaping me before I had the foresight to stop myself. "If I did come back, would you let me stay with you for a while?" I didn't need her charity. I could easily get my own place that was much nicer than hers, but I was sick and tired of being alone.

"I'd love for you to stay with me, but is it a good idea for you to stay for long? What if Johnny finds out you're back?"

"Don't you worry about Johnny. That's my problem to deal with."

"Are you sure?"

"Yes, I promise I won't be putting myself in any kind of trouble, seriously." I tried to assure her with the confident tone of my voice since I couldn't outright say, *"It's Johnny who should be scared of me."* That wouldn't make any sense to Jayleen—more than as a comical joke.

"Then my door is open to you, girl. I'll be here to pick you up, waiting desperately for your arrival."

She wouldn't be waiting long, because I was already throwing on my shoes and zipping up my suitcase. There was no doubt in my mind that it was wrong to return to Creswell after I'd gone to such great lengths to separate myself from it. But at this point, why should I care? If deciding to become immortal was wrong, and everything Riftan and I had was wrong, then did I want to be right?

Screw right. I was going to go home to learn my lessons the hard way.

I'D FORGOTTEN how different the States *smelled* during my travels.

The sentiment was strange, but everywhere seemed to smell different, and America had its own odd, familiar scent. The air in Creswell was a specifically delightful, fresh breeze after living in old cities for so many years. While ancient architecture was beautiful beyond description, Prague, Paris, and many of the other European cities I'd been to over the years possessed a stale scent—human odors having seeped into their very existence for centuries.

Creswell was different. While our downtown area was highly populated with many skyscrapers painted against the fabric of the sky, we also had a lot of trees. Numerous luscious parks dotted the city's blocks, and the nearly fifteen square urban miles were completely surrounded by forested areas, with only two highways in and out on both sides of town. Thanks to the help of those oxygen producing pals, and the many environmentally conscious immortals who controlled our community, Creswell's air lacked smoke or pollution, and instead smelled crisp and invigorating.

Taking in a big huff at the airport doors, I was hit by more. Nostalgia smacked me across the face, the pang of something sharp like defeat settling between my ribs.

A squeal rang out, and Jayleen knocked the bitter feeling away, replacing it with a crushing hug—well, maybe crushing to a normal person, but she'd hardly staggered me. I returned her embrace, hugging her little body too tight to be normal, even while holding back. What can I say? I got excited.

Squirming out of my grip, Jayleen rubbed her arms and complained, "*Jesus* Christ, you've gotten strong."

"Oh, yeah, I'm sorry. I've been…" I thought up a quick and dumb excuse. "Pumping a lot of iron, you know?"

Jayleen pinched at my thin arms. "Really? Because you're as skinny as ever."

"Right. It's all strength, no muscle." I saved my second sorry excuse with a positive, cheek-burning smile.

That only made her more suspicious as she narrowed her eyes on my lips. I realized I'd made a major oversight. I had fucking *fangs*, and they weren't small like they used to be. Closing my mouth, I did my best to conceal my outrageous vampire fangs under a closed smile.

A gruff voice yelled from the lane of traffic meandering through the pickup area, "Don't leave your vehicle unattended! Let's keep it moving!"

Jumping into action, Jayleen tugged me toward her old ass Honda Accord—the same one she'd had before I'd left—and we hopped in. Excitedly, she listened to me recount my adventures on the drive to her apartment, all the while updating me on hers.

She'd started going to school again and volunteered at an animal hospital in her off time. She was finally doing all the things she'd wanted to do with her life, and it sounded like she'd started as soon as I'd left Creswell. All she'd needed was for me to stop holding her back.

Hopefully, I wouldn't ruin that by staying with her again.

Throughout our relatively short drive, Jayleen also took to staring at me rather than the road, which I strongly urged her to stop doing. At least some things hadn't changed—she was still a shitty driver.

Once we were safely inside her little two-bedroom abode, Jayleen was hot on my heels, hardly a footfall away. From right over my shoulder, she mentioned, "I cleaned out the guest bedroom so that you'd have it all to yourself."

Ignoring her lingering proximity, I took my time to admire the emotions displayed within her apartment. Green plants flourished in every nook and cranny, a testament to how nurturing Jayleen could be. The small couch still had a stain from the time she'd brought home a blind foster cat that we had a hell of a time potty training, and incense permeated the walls themselves, its smell nostalgic to Jayleen's place, but a bit pungent for my olfactory now. Even if I had to plug my nose until I adjusted to the smell, I'd definitely be happy in her home. No doubt being there would at least help me get back on my feet—emotionally, that is.

"Hey, Leanne." Jayleen was in my face and nearly poking me in the cheek. "Can I ask you, what's with your teeth?"

I touched a finger to my fangs and then came up with one of my now constant stupid excuses. "It's cosplay. Haven't you ever heard of cosplay, where people dress up as fictional characters?"

Before I could retreat from her curious fingers, Jayleen was jamming one into my mouth and pushing on a fang—*hard*. I jumped, my surprise only forcing her finger harder against my tooth.

"Owe!" we both screeched and recoiled at the same time.

The succulent taste of her blood dripped onto my tongue, evoking the realization that I wasn't the only one hurt by her intrusion.

Her taste, as faint as it was, sent delightful shivers down my spine, making me absolutely loathe how good she tasted. That was my best friend, and I was already imagining the heady feeling I could get from drinking that sweet blood of hers. Physically shaking the thought loose from my head, I took Jayleen's bleeding finger in my hand and pressed on it until it stopped bleeding.

"Cosplay my ass," she bickered, a suspicious brow darkening her already brown eyes. "Those things are cemented in there. *Besides*, no Leanne I know would ever do something as geeky as cosplay!"

I let her go. The bleeding from her tiny wound ceased, but now her blood was on my hand, and I could smell it. The smell was *pervasive*, even for such a tiny dribble.

While I wasn't concerned about biting into Jayleen—because I wasn't a wild animal with no control over myself—it was still abhorrent how tempting her blood was to me. It'd be so harmless to lick it off. It wouldn't send me into some spiral or anything like that; it'd just be a nice treat.

Before I could give in, I rinsed her blood off into the metal kitchen sink. Focusing on the stream of water before me, I mentioned, "Let it go. It's a new hobby, not something you should tease me about."

Her heart rate elevated, the sound of it and her movements right by my side again. Instincts setting in, I whipped around to her, fearing whatever kind of reckless behavior her abrupt pulse spike may have been indicative of. Her eyes went wide, my arm stinging as the knife in her hands dropped to the ground with a metallic *clang*.

"I'm sorry! That's not what I meant to do!" she gasped.

Blood pooled at the cut on my arm, but it'd healed so fast that it didn't drip.

Jayleen's dread morphed to curiosity in an instant, her hand swiping at my nonexistent cut to reveal a woundless arm. Her jaw dropped.

Snatching her hand, I thrust in under the running water—hoping and praying she hadn't gotten my blood in her cut.

"Don't you *ever* do that again," I disciplined her like a *very* angry parent who'd witnessed their child do something *exceedingly* dangerous.

"Wha-What—Why?"

"My blood is very dangerous. Do *not* touch it under any circumstance, understood?" I huffed, emotions surfacing through my very brittle shell.

Jayleen's hand was washed clean, and I couldn't find any sign of envenomation in her skin where she'd hit my tooth. I heaved a sigh of relief, the knowledge Jayleen had been *that* close to being poisoned heavy on my chest.

When I dropped her hand, Jayleen retracted against the countertop, sliding down the cabinets until she was seated at my feet. Pulling her knees against her chest, Jayleen's wide eyes stared across the empty kitchen. I sat beside her and tucked my head into my hands, feeling the need to hide from her.

Bewilderment clouded Jayleen's tone. "What did I just see? Did you heal in the blink of an eye? And the fangs, and the strength. And that illness before you left. The bite on your neck. Is this real? Are you serious?"

"Jayleen"—I decided to speak candidly; whether or not that'd be a mistake was yet to be foreseen—"I may have left out a couple bits of my story."

"The guy you were with. Was he like this, too?"

"He is the same guy who bit me that night I was kidnapped. It might have been a joke back then, but that whole vampire thing ended up being real. Riftan turned me into an immortal after you and I spoke that day when I was sick. If he hadn't, I would have died from the bite."

"Are you *fucking* kidding me?" Jayleen shouted, her tone a stark difference from how quiet she'd began. "*He* was that bastard you talked about biting you and leaving you on the park bench? And you *fell* for him? You were in *love* with that son of a bitch? After everything he put you through, he still wouldn't give you his heart? And then *still* you fell for him? Who even are you? What kind of stupid, romantic, love-struck fool have you turned into?"

My cheeks hurt because I couldn't contain my smile, even if I wanted to hide my fangs from her. "I love how you care about that more than the fact that I'm a real-life monster."

She reached out and touched my cheek, a loving gesture that turned my insides with reminiscence. "Nothing could ever make me think you were a monster. That *man,* however, is the monster."

I wished I could sympathize with her, but Riftan could hardly qualify as my story's villain. After everything, he was still my hero.

Wrapping her arms around me, Jayleen pulled me in until I could tuck my head into her chest and listen to her slow, mortal heart pound away. It wasn't like Riftan's but its effects were similar, soothing my ache. Being in her arms reminded me of the days when one of us would go through a traumatic break up or school exam and hold each other until things felt better. We may have both changed since those days—in *so,* so many ways—but that feeling, wrapped up in each other's empathy, would never change.

Living with Jayleen was an adjustment for both of us.

I hadn't lived with a mortal since turning, and obviously, Jayleen had never lived with an immortal. There were several times when she made me breakfast, and I had to remind her I didn't eat the same stuff anymore. Not only that, but I had to hide in my room with the window open until the smell of cooking food was gone because I *hated* it—especially in her tiny apartment that so easily soaked up smells. There was also the strange agreement we'd had to make, in which I needed to store blood bags in the fridge—which was clearly an odd concept for Jayleen. As far as my living meals went though, they *never* came home with me.

Jayleen knew full well the necessity of my feeding, and she knew that it meant killing a human being. At first, she was wary, asking me, "You seriously take someone's life like that?"

"Well, yes." I'd promised to be truthful with her since she'd found out about my condition. "But to be fair, I only ever kill very bad people…"

"Are there really so many readily accessible bad people?"

"Definitely. I was also skeptical at first, but I promise you I've never killed anyone who didn't deserve it. And I have to feed to stay under control. It's the lesser of the two evils. Especially while living with you, I want to make sure I'm well fed. I'm not going to potentially risk your safety."

She was satisfied with that, almost flattered, like I was

doing something heroic by merely keeping myself full on the blood of other living mortals. Still, I kept my feeding habits outside of her apartment. But more than just my eating behavior affected our situation.

I had to tell Jayleen multiple times that I could hear every little detail of what she was doing in her bedroom across the hall, including when she brought guys home after a night out. She had to learn to not light candles or incense when I was home, and she had to be careful of my blood—or any of my fluids, really—as well as her own.

After a few weeks, life with Jayleen smoothed out. We found our balance, living two separate lives under the same roof, and got along like we used to. With her help, I was slowly stitching up my broken heart.

Some days, the thread I used to stitch wasn't strong enough, and even Jayleen couldn't stop the hurting. Those days made me feel like hunkering down in my bed with a bottle of merlot and crying myself back to sleep. Rather than wallow, I'd seek distraction from those moments in Creswell's vibrant immortal underground, a haven of clubs, cafes, and bars catering exclusively to immortals, away from mortal nuisances. Some were blatantly closed to the "public," while others had mortal fronts and served vampires in the back.

Despite my aversion to befriending other immortals, I'd found these establishments were essential places to acquire underground information and pre-packaged blood. I also understood the importance of networking, so on the nights when I needed to stay busy, I put on my friendly face and played buddy-buddy with the immortals in Creswell. My hope was that one day, in a time of need, the underground connections I'd made would prove beneficial.

That meant I often found myself playing human with Jayleen during the day and frolicking among the immortals at night, carefully avoiding the cold confines of my lonely bed. The sacrifice was sleep, but that was okay; I could subsist without sleep for as long as I needed to if it meant finding a place where I belonged. I had nothing but time to search—an eternity, in fact—and I wasn't sure if that was a blessing or a curse.

In a plush velvet booth that looped around toward the center of Lilith Night Club, I found myself tailoring my personality to please the small gathering of immortals who sat with me. Over both shoulders, I had a man bragging about his last decade, talking up the accomplishments like he was the most important immortal who'd ever lived. At the end of the booth, a girl stirred her drink, bored of their egocentrism and probably wanting to go on about her own ventures.

Turk and Isaiah, the two men talking *at* me, were relatively young—for immortals—but they spoke as if they'd been around for millennia. I'd come to the observation that vampires got more narcissistic the older they got, but these two men were proving me wrong.

Riftan had defied that statistic, too, but in the other

direction. Sure, he didn't care about many people outside of his circle, but he cared hard for those within it. Rarely did Riftan talk about himself—only sometimes he did gloat—but narcissism was not something I associated with his character. Maybe I was simply pandering to an egotistical crowd. After all, I most commonly found them alone in clubs and bars.

Turk, the man to my right, had been going on about his company's development in neurological technologies; the conversation nearly became white noise as I zoned out. My gaze raked through the crowd, searching for any escape from the monotony. I probably could have spotted a mouse scurrying between the dozens of club goers—at least that would offer some form of excitement. As if that very thought had come true, the crowd on the dance floor parted, a thin walkway forming between moving bodies. What emerged was, however, *not* a little mouse. Alternatively, a very striking feminine form, gilded in a black velvet dress and draped in long brunette waves, appeared. Despite her petite stature, she did not have to push through the crowd. In fact, neither did the two bodyguards at her sides. This woman's aura demanded its space from every immortal it graced.

The split on the dancefloor opened straight to our booth, carving an obvious path for the woman. I tensed, feeling her aura bear down on me and unfamiliar with what it meant. The immortals at my table, however, did seem familiar with it. They exchanged weighted glances with each other, their boasts suddenly silenced.

Before she'd come to a stop in front of us, the woman

addressed both the men beside me with a haughty, clipped remark. "Turk, Isaiah, it's nice to see the both of you again."

Turk scooted away, the spot where he'd cozied up to me now open, and my skin relished the cold of his absence.

The girl at the end dismissed her attentiveness to her drink and leaned over the table, posturing toward the brunette before us. Not waiting for her own introduction from the woman, the girl spoke through a playful tone, "Hey Rosy. We missed you the other night. I thought you said you were going to join us this time?"

Rosy completely ignored the girl at my table, keeping a steady look on me. "You must be Leanne. It's nice to finally meet you."

Turk dismissed himself, slightly bowing toward the brunette and offering her a generous farewell. After that, he was basically running from her.

The woman motioned with a gold-decked hand at the remaining two immortals who sat with me. She pointed her chin toward the exit, demanding them to get lost, only offering the girl at the table, "I'll call you about getting together later, Carla." Taking the hint, they both fled like Turk had done.

My stomach dropped, puzzle pieces falling into place. *Shit, I am in so much trouble.*

As she slid into Isaiah's place next to me, I cringed away, tensely offering my first words to this woman with the foreboding aura. "What do you want with me, Rosaline?"

R O S A L I N E   W A S   nothing short of a goddess.

Her hair snaked in bountiful chocolate waves around her shoulders. Green eyes shone from the inside out, but somehow still looked a dark green, like the deepest depths of the forest. Her ivory skin glistened like a delicate doll, yet her posture demanded subservience like a drill sergeant—or more familiar to me, a mob boss. Her presence needed no introduction. I'd never seen anything so beautiful and yet so terrifying.

"Oh, come now, don't be so standoffish. I'm merely here to officially introduce myself." Her sharp tone hid a playful cadence, each syllable dripping with arrogant amusement.

"I have nothing to do with Riftan anymore, so please leave me be." My voice was timid, but my words could have been more cautious.

"Why are you acting so afraid, darling?" She reached out one of her slender fingers, decked in gold, and twirled it in my hair. "I'm here to offer you company, not hurt you. After all, we have something in common. We've both had our hearts broken by you know who. Don't you want to gossip about him, write it in our burn book, or put a curse on him with the use of black magic? You know, whatever it is you girls do these days after a breakup?"

"It wasn't a breakup," I mumbled, mostly to myself.

"Regardless of what you call it, a broken heart is a broken heart, and I know what it feels like to be crushed by Riftan. I was in love with him once, and he knew what kind of misery I'd feel to be discarded so deftly. Once I could see past my feelings for him, I realized how much of a selfish prick he was. A real pansy ass twat." She colored each of her insults like they were meant specifically for my ears.

She stared at me with a raised brow as if waiting for me to agree. But she'd be waiting forever. Yes, I was broken hearted and it was completely Riftan's fault, but I didn't harbor ill feelings for him for it. Riftan had never treated me poorly. In fact, he'd only ever taken care of me like I was his princess. He was foolish and maybe a little bit self-inspired, but that was about the extent of his downfall. A prick or a twat? Absolutely not.

When I had nothing to say in agreement with Rosaline, she tilted her head at me and added, "Don't tell me that you still care about that pompous bastard."

I scowled, my lips failing to hold back my tongue when I

snapped, "Please stop talking about him like that. It's not that I have any sort of feelings for him anymore, it's that I do not like the level of disrespect you are regarding him with."

"Pardon me?"

For some ridiculous reason, I went on, "I've heard the story about your relationship with him from enough perspectives to know that Riftan was not at fault for the way it ended. He did what was best for himself—which was get away from the manipulating, parasitical leech you'd become. You are the villain in this love story, so don't you dare try to soil his name with duplicitous statements." By the end of my rant, my breaths came is short, harsh huffs.

A dumfounded look crossed Rosaline's perfectly manicured face. As quickly as it'd come, she wiped the look away, snapping her hanging jaw closed and refuting, "I assure you that the stories you've heard have been exaggerated. Regardless, I'm not here to talk about me. I sought you out for the purpose of offering you my consolation—a shoulder to cry on, or what have you. I want to help you through this time that I know so personally can be very hard to recover from."

I sighed, breathing out the remnants of my frustration, knowing the emotion wouldn't get me anywhere except six feet under. "No. I'm doing fine. I don't need any help. Thank you, though, for the offer."

"Are you doing fine, darling?" Rosaline's fingers tickled at my chin, tugging until I looked her dead in the eyes. "Because it seems like you are merely existing through the days. You can't lie to me. I am the woman who sees all. It's why every immortal comes to me when they need information nobody else can get them. There's nothing I don't know about you, and I've seen the way you battle with your own instincts to stay within some bounds of morality that permit you to live in two different worlds. Believe it or not, you are not human anymore, and it's not becoming of you to act as one."

She poked at one of the fangs in my mouth and continued, "I mean, look at you! You are a *vampire*, dearest. You drink blood to survive. But merely surviving is not the same as living. To live, you must embrace what you are. Yes, you must murder to survive, drink to survive, but you should do so for *fun* as well. You are the predator, and these little peons are your prey. Even basic *mortal* instincts tell you to eat when you're hungry, kill when you're threatened, and fornicate when you're horny. Now you're of immortal blood, and those instincts in your DNA are even more important to listen to. Feed, prey, fuck—giving in to those raw urges is the only thing that will make eternity bearable. You are free of the mortal restraints they trained you to refrain from. I can teach you to embrace this way of life—how to *thrive* the way an immortal should. You don't merely have to *face* eternity, revel in it. Don't you think that'd be superior to the life you're living now?"

Feed, prey, fuck... that certainly sounded more titillating than *eat, pray, love.*

While my heart ached at her candid insinuations of my life, the truth was, "No. As I said, I'm doing perfectly fine." *But I won't be for an eternity.*

I *was* subsisting—not living. I had an eternity, but I didn't know how to live it. I wasn't happy living this life. At least I was healing—maybe—but it wasn't *enjoyable* merely biding my days. Foolish optimism could only get me so far and last so long. I had nothing to look forward to. Eternity looked bleak.

"So, you are fine now, but I can offer you more than fine. I can offer you *fun*." Rosaline sunk in beside me, batting her long, thick eyelashes. She was stunning, her looks almost making up for her aura that still drove shivers down my spine. She bit a little fang over her voluptuous lips, making my heart pound. I couldn't tell if it beat out of jealousy or desire from her beauty. Hell, maybe Riftan and I actually had the same type, because I was getting closer to the possibility of accepting her offer with each little inch she pushed closer to me.

My chest ached when she snaked her hand over my showing leg, the change in my heart rate so obviously noticeable to her a little snicker flicked over her lips in response. She went on, hooding her gaze as she looked me over. "Let me help you over this little hurdle in your eternity. I can promise you that I will love you better than Riftan ever did—better than any man can."

Her sharp tongue almost had me. She'd seen my weakness and played off my momentary lapse in judgment—but *momentary* it had been. Shaking it off, I responded, "Knowing the things I do of you, I'd be crazy to accept your offer."

She retorted, "Knowing what you do, you'd be crazy *not* to accept my offer."

She was right on that account, too. I knew that denying her could be bad for me. She could make life hard for any immortal.

Being *the* Rosaline, she could kill me if she so pleased—though even she'd struggle to get away with it right then and there. I'd have to look over my shoulder every day for the rest of my life, but I still had to tell her, "The answer is no, Rosaline. I'm no fool, and I know you have a game you plan to play with me if I give in to you." I stood and shimmied out of the booth.

Both Rosaline's large bodyguards held their hands out to stop me. Her superficially frail-looking fingers grabbed onto my arm with startling force. "There's plenty of fun I could have with your pathetic little heart. You'd make it easy for me to torture you, but at this rate, you're going to do it to *yourself.* I don't need you as my toy. You're too pitiful to last long enough to be worth keeping around. The only thing you have left to offer me is the anguish that it'd bring Riftan if I had you for my own. This is my last offer. I won't keep you as my pet like I so very much wish to, but in return, let me wear you like a sexy little badge of honor. Some arm candy, that's all I'm asking of you, then I'll let you go back to your useless existence."

Her words cut through the shield I'd attempted to erect against her, slicing into me with a tender ache. So that was the game she was playing at.

I wished she couldn't get to me the way she so obviously wanted to, but everything she said was too close to factual. My existence was *useless*, and my heart was probably too pitiful to withstand anything she threw at it.

Avoiding eye contact, for fear of giving in to her, I pulled out of Rosaline's grip and pushed past her bodyguards. To my surprise, they let me through, but Rosaline still yelled after me,

"Watch your back, Cowitz. I own the underground, and it encompasses this whole fucking city. You make one wrong move here, and I'll seize the opportunity to have your head."

Her voice faded into the suddenly silent crowd as I retreated. Everyone's eyes were on me, but Rosaline and her guards didn't follow.

They'd let me go, but that almost felt worse than if they'd stopped me. Rosaline knew she'd already said everything she needed to say. She'd cut my wound, and attempted to sew in the seed that she could heal it. Unfortunately, her weapon didn't need to be very sharp, as my wounds were far from healed up. But if she thought I'd come running back to her after everything she'd said had time to settle in, she was wrong. I didn't need her to fix me, or to save me; I could fix *myself*.

To be fair, Rosaline had been right about a lot of things, and the sickening feeling her words gave me was proof of that. My existence was sub-par, living off my human friend and tiptoeing around the underground. I needed to take control, live like a vampire—because I was one. Not this lowly, homeless, dependent burden on society—immortal and human alike. I'd chosen to become immortal so I could make more of a legacy for myself than merely being a name on Johnny Roufe's list of bodies.

I was tired of letting people do whatever they wanted to me. No longer was I going to be a pawn. Only I would tell myself what to feel and how to act. Fuck anybody else who tried, starting with Riftan and ending with Rosaline.

This is my story, and I didn't need anyone's help to write

it.

I had a legacy to create.

Feed, prey, fuck. Those were the fundaments Rosaline called the basics of immortal living. I had a strong feeling that strictly following that list would mean forgoing my humanity, so I decided to use it more as a guide than a rulebook.

First things first, I wanted a clear roster—no debts—which meant I needed to repay Jayleen for everything she'd done for me. I could get anything I wanted from the hands of foolish mortals, and I should have been taking from them all along. I could have been swimming in riches like the rest of the immortals I knew.

After getting some cash, I would need a meal—because I *wanted* the thrill of a kill. That was the feed and prey part of Rosaline's little lecture. She'd also said something about fornication.

I'd never had any trouble hooking up with guys before Riftan, but since leaving him, things weren't so simple. It was admittedly pitiful, but even feigning romance with other men hurt to an extent I wasn't yet able to overcome. But I was a vampire, and Rosaline was right—I needed to *fornicate* if I was really going to enjoy my infinite years on this miserable planet.

A man would never let emotions get in the way of him getting laid, so I shouldn't either. Riftan probably wasn't...

No! I can't think about that right now!

I'd have to find the proper victim. If I did, I could accomplish all three of my tasks at once.

A rich guy who I was willing to sleep with in Creswell wasn't hard to find. The city was full of hot young go getters fresh into their positions as VP at one of our many large tech firms. There were even more daddy money boys riding off their families' trust funds or organized crime rings.

I made quick work of convincing one of these promising young men to get me a large sum of cash. That was something I'd been able to do before becoming immortal, but now it was a piece of cake with the help of hypnotism. The last two parts were a little harder. I still struggled to bed the guy, getting far enough into our encounter to know that I didn't enjoy kissing him because all it did was remind me of Riftan. And after that, it was like the image had soiled my meal.

I suppose becoming a powerful and autonomous immortal woman didn't require an immediate fuck. So, I'd continue to work on that aspect and not let it weigh down my ultimate motive.

Back at the apartment, I dropped several rolls of cash onto the kitchen table and watched as Jayleen's jaw dropped.

"Rent, for letting me stay here these past couple weeks despite the obvious challenges," I declared, chin held high—where it was going to stay.

"Rent?" She poked at the rolls curiously, but with unwarranted caution. "But this is, like, thousands of dollars…"

"Would you like more? I can get you more."

"Leanne… What's gotten into you? How'd you come by

this? You didn't steal it, did you?" Her tone wasn't helpful in cluing me in on whether she was mad, concerned, or curious.

"Is it stealing if the owner hands it to you willingly? And nothing's gotten into me. This is what I should have been doing this whole time. I'm *immortal* Jayleen. I can get *anything* I want. I can get anything *we* want!" I merely hoped she'd want in on the fun. Everything was more fun with an accomplice—and I had that position to fill.

"Is the person you took this from still alive?"

"Don't ask questions you don't want to know the answers to."

Jayleen nodded, the thoughts behind her eyes distant while she sorted through the information I'd given her.

Looking up, eyes certain and unclouded, she told me, "I want in on this charade. What kind of stupid shit can we get into?"

And with that, I'd found my new partner in crime— literally.

28

I WILL ALWAYS LOVE YOU, NO MATTER WHAT YOU CHOOSE IN LIFE

I HAD MANY answers to the question: "What kind of stupid shit can we get into?"

To start things out simply, I acquired us a little extra glitz here and there. That meant getting the both of us an exorbitant collection of some of the things we'd always wanted but could never get ourselves, be it price or accessibility that had stopped us. Jayleen and I could dress however we wanted, decorate the apartment in any array of excellence we desired, and get into any social splendor we wished to.

Be it the hottest clubs or VIP events, none of it was new to me anymore. But to Jayleen, it was foreign and remarkable. Getting to share those experiences with her was like getting to experience them myself for the first time all over again. It was almost like reliving everything Riftan had introduced me to, but through Jayleen.

I bought her the car she'd always wanted, the shoes she couldn't afford, and every little sparkly thing that caught her eye. Together, we found every trivial object to keep us on cloud nine, and when we started to come down, we'd find something new. It was a more exciting way of life than how I'd been living before, but I knew it wouldn't last forever.

I had my best friend with me, and I wanted to spoil her while I could—all the while having more fun of my own thanks to her company. But Jayleen was mortal, and while she still had many years left to live, she did have her own mortal life to experience. She'd age out of this behavior sooner than later, which meant this wasn't sustainable debauchery, only temporary amusement.

Given the nature of our activities, I was very careful to keep our ventures on the down low. Riftan had drilled the importance of keeping a low profile into my head, and I knew how to do things without raising the notice of the Council *or* vampire hunters.

The group I was *not* versed in avoiding was a much more mortal annoyance—the Roufes. That was evident when I noticed Johnny's goons lingering in the shadows, thinking they were unseen. Such a sighting could mean only one thing, and it was that Jayleen and I had been ostentatious enough to get Johnny's attention. He knew I was back, and he surely wanted to "talk." The outcome of such a conversation would either be to make me disappear or force me to take him back—or so he thought—because Johnny Roufe couldn't let his favorite piece of ass make a mockery of him by returning after all these years without a single word.

Misfortunate for Johnny, there's no conversation between us that wouldn't go my way—not anymore. He couldn't push me around, and no amount of mortal money or power could scare me.

So, I'd made quick work of disappearing from the sight of his goons whenever they thought they'd pinned me down. If I wanted to, I could have run and hid every time I saw a Roufe member. The game would never get old, and it was easy as a vampire to disappear from plain sight. That was my plan going forward—or it had been before Jayleen planted a seed of doubt in my head.

On a Saturday morning, Jayleen skimmed through the news on her tablet, a common morning routine before she went off to class. Out of the blue, she slammed it onto the kitchen table, looking straight at me like I was the cause of her outburst. "Why do you think the immortals in this city let the Roufes get away with whatever they want? If this 'underground' is the way you say it is, then shouldn't they do something about them? The mafia influence has practically burned this city to the ground."

I nodded to her sentiment, taking a small sip from the coffee I'd recently poured and leaning against the table opposite of Jayleen. "I believe the underground wants the Roufes and their competitors to have a large influence here. It keeps the heat off them and lets them work and live under the very large shadow the criminal activity casts here."

"Still, wouldn't it be nice if they used some of their power to at least take control of something? Can't they pull the Roufes strings from those

shadows you speak of?"

*"And do what with them?" I was genuinely curious to hear what she
had in mind.*

*"I don't know." She threw her hands up in exasperation before
slumping into her seat and continuing, "Couldn't they use some of that
influence and money to fix this city up? If everyone wants to rule this city
for themselves, then why not make it something worth ruling? Any
successful business would know they need to keep their product shiny and
new to make any real money or power. Then, maybe they could win the
hearts of the people here, too; helping their influence and all the while
making life for those who live here a little more bearable at the same time."*

*Eying the somber look on her face, I asked, "So who are you saying
that's the responsibility of? The Roufes or the immortals?"*

*"Well, I haven't known about immortals for that long, and I always
thought that about the Roufes. Now, I don't know."*

"So, you've been thinking about this for a while, huh?"

*"There's never a moment I'm not thinking about this. You remember
what it was like to live here as a human, right? We've all suffered somehow
at the hands of organized crime in this town. Children grow up homeless
and on the streets because of the Roufes. Children like you, Leanne."*

I shrugged.

The truth was, I didn't really remember what it was like
living as a mortal. I'd completely forgotten the way it felt to fear
for my life if I walked down the wrong street at the wrong time.
I'd lost the feeling of mourning every time I heard about
another child caught in the crosshair. I wasn't human anymore,
and the same things didn't concern me like they used to. I
wasn't privy to the influence of any mafia because it didn't

affect me in the underground. I'd lost sight of what ailed my human companions, merely because I was too selfish to see past my own nose.

While I'd changed in many ways, I didn't want to believe that I'd lost the entirety of my capability for altruism. Being one of those immortals Jayleen suggested should do something about the city's Roufe problem, I did feel, in some way, accountable for only ever watching from the sidelines. I had so much limitless potential, much like the other immortals who stood by and did nothing, so why not use it in a setting I was familiar with? I knew the Roufes and their inner workings, and with Johnny, I may even have access.

I thought I wanted nothing to do with Johnny, but he'd only live what, forty more years tops? With an infinite number of years left in my own life, it wouldn't hurt to spend a few pulling some strings. And if that was all it took, then wouldn't the sacrifice be worth it?

Days after Jayleen's comment, I'd dropped the idea. It was silly to think for a moment that I wanted to get involved with the Roufes again. Instead, I'd keep my eyes peeled for other opportunities to help make Creswell a better place.

After a coffee date with Jayleen at midday on a Friday, opportunity hit me like a truck. Unfortunately, it was the former opportunity—the Roufe variety.

At the corner of Fifth Street and April Avenue, I was cornered by Roufe goons one and two—of whom I recognized as Carl and Freddy, Johnny's right-hand guys. Opposed to shadow fading right off the sidewalk in the brightness of day, I decided to see this opportunity through. It'd probably be more interesting than running, and I was curious what could come from the interaction. I lacked the fear this scenario should cause, and without the deterrent of natural selection, it felt more like a game. There was no harm in seeing the next play. Putting my hands up, I feigned an exorbitant naivety. "Hey there, guys, long time no see."

With a professional level of gruffness, Carl said, "Our boss would like a word with you. Do you mind coming with us, Ms. Cowitz?"

Though saying no was exactly what I *should* have done, I said, "Don't be so formal; it's only me," with a casualness in my voice that I hadn't expected. "How could I say no to such a warm welcome party? Lead the way."

I followed the two large men into their tinted black SUV, and the following familiar ride to the Roufe mansion was quiet. Both Carl and Freddy refused to engage in my small talk. With nothing to do but twiddle my thumbs in the back seat, it was harder to ignore the emotions surfacing as we passed through the tall green forest shrouding the compound.

Crossing the wrought-iron gate made my stomach drop, only because it'd done so, so many times before.

When the car jerked to a stop in front of the white marble water fountain out front, Carl was at my door, ushering me out, and I had to remind myself who I was, and what I could do.

They have no power over you.

Glaring at the two chauffeurs who refused to humor me in conversation, I tipped my head up so high it might have poked the sky. Not waiting for them to lead the way, I strutted toward the mansion's double doors. Two armed men in expensive grey suits held open the doors for me. Another inside waited to lead me in the right direction.

Tapping through the marble corridor, footsteps sounded in the void, outlining the many suited men I'd adopted as an entourage. Carl and Freddy were close on my heels, and one of the men from the door had joined them. I wasn't sure if this was the VIP welcome, or the convict's farewell. Given the stares of everyone we passed, ranging from frightened to curious, nobody else knew what kind of parade this was, either.

As I'd remembered, the walk to Johnny's office was long and arduous down the main corridor, but it *was* a straight shot from the front door. Every footfall of my entourage and me rebounded off the rounded roof and marbled floors. Each echo carried an intensity that was both hollow in sound, but dense in significance. I used to think that resonance was the sharp, derisive taunt of my own footsteps laughing at me. Maybe it still was, but I planned to laugh with them this time.

Real laughter came to life in the distance like a manifestation of my heeled boot clicks. Another bubbly laugh—the sound of children's play—echoed through the halls, losing its volume by the time it'd reached my ears.

I stopped in my tracks, almost obeying the pull on my heart from those little giggles. They were so much more inviting than the situation I was walking into, and there were likely familiar faces behind the laughter. Seeing Johnny's boys was another pro on the board for agreeing to this interaction.

The thought of going to them was short-lived, destroyed by a grating voice that spoke the words, "My girl."

My stomach turned, my heart dropping into the acids. Stiffening, I tore my gaze from the hallway where I'd heard laughter and found the one and only rushing toward me from his open office.

One of the men at my back poked me to continue, but I didn't need to go anywhere. Johnny was already crossing the threshold of his grand double doors, meeting me head on. Ambling forward, he wore the wear of three years on the surface, looking older than the last time I'd seen him. Skinnier, greyer, scruffier. If anything, he may have looked better now that he'd lost some weight, but it'd certainly aged him. He scrunched a tentative brow over the pair of brown, worried eyes that sat recessed in his wrinkled olive skin. "It's been so long. Where have you been? We were all worried sick when you left without warning." He was being nauseatingly sweet, reaching up to hold my cheek as though he had an inherent right to touch me as he pleased.

In my heeled boots, I looked down on him, several inches shorter than me. That was why I hadn't been allowed to wear heels when I was with him. Even in flats, we were about the same height. Even now, in my obvious physical eminence over him, confidence was eluding me, my lungs no longer intaking the necessary air.

He continued in my silence, "Well, it doesn't matter now. You are back, and that's what matters. Do you need my help with anything? Do you need money? A place to stay?" He cocked a genuine smile in my direction, his eyes weighed with a concern beyond the kind I knew he had the capacity to fake. It was like he'd forgotten I'd ever left him high and dry in the first place.

I shook my head. "I don't need anything." My voice was meager once it finally did leave my trembling lips. "Are you really not mad at me for leaving?"

"Mad? At you? Of course not. I could never be mad at you, *my love.*"

Time stopped. It was like the birds outside stopped chirping, the clock in his office stopped ticking. My chest ached; those two simple words, *my love*, pulled the thread from my heart and let it fall back into two pieces. No matter how painful, I loved the beating, and my masochistic heart longed for another. Even if it was from someone as deplorable as Johnny, I wanted to hear him say those two words one more time. Pitiful as ever was the tear that rolled down my cheek.

"Don't cry, dear." Johnny's calloused hand wiped at the moisture that'd fought its way out of my eyes. "I will always love you, no matter what you choose to do in life. If it's what you wish, I will take care of you now that you are back. I promise you won't have to worry about anything ever again, *my love.*"

His words iced my wounds. Their promises kneaded my nervous muscles and restarted my halted lungs. Breathing once again, I nodded, a slave to the comfort provided through his tender delusions. It was a strong enough feeling to think I could put up with anything he put me through, as long as it meant having the opportunity to feel love again. Unlike how it was with Riftan, Johnny would love me back. And I craved to *be* loved, even if it meant feigning my own love in the process.

Johnny closed his arms around my back, embracing me in a gentle hug before pulling away to pat my cheek. "You can stay here in the house with me whenever you'd like to. I'll make sure the help has your every need met and the guards know you will be coming and going as you please. Tonight, we will have dinner to celebrate your return."

I would regret this interaction. Not for its outcome, but for how it happened. Like a pitiful, useless creature, I'd lost my footing, unable to stand up against a pathetic, mortal Johnny Roufe. My heart and my emotions had done all the talking—or lack thereof—and I'd been pushed around, like I'd sworn not to be. He'd hooked me like the guppy I was the moment he said the word love. And whether or not it was weak of me to give in to such a prospect as true—albeit one sided—love, I couldn't find it in myself to hate the outcome. I was exactly where I needed to be in a game that had only just begun. All I needed was to remember my strength and not let it get buried in emotions.

It wouldn't hurt to have Johnny giving me the affection I deserved in the meantime. Especially when his form of nostalgic love was what my heart wanted. While he was distracted serving *me*, I could check his balances and keep an eye on his little business. Don't get me wrong, I certainly was no crime boss, but a mafia wife could have some pull of her own. And being that I could have Johnny's mortal mind doing

whatever I wanted of him: who better to pull some strings than
I, in the shadow of his right hand.

BEING WITH JOHNNY again didn't mean I'd change the way I chose to live my opportunity at a second life in Creswell. He'd given me another place to stay and a little extra attention, but I still lived with Jayleen and spent a large majority of my time with her or among the underworld.

What did change was my attentiveness to how I kept my two worlds separate. After all, Johnny was supposedly aware of the existence of vampires and the underworld, so how I participated in my normal immortal activities had to be altered. That most notably meant I went home immediately after our agreement and ground down my fangs until they looked like normal teeth. My sharp incisors would be the first giveaway something had changed about me. Next, managing any strange nightly behavior, which I could hopefully keep to a minimum or thrall out of his memories.

Things would be different than when I was with Johnny before, but these changes were for the better. Slowly but surely, I *was* warming up to the idea of being with Johnny again.

After finding such intense happiness with Riftan, I'd almost forgotten I wasn't necessarily *unhappy* in my old life. The most painful part of it had been my inability to escape—like a bird with clipped wings—but now, my wings were back and bigger than ever, and I was staying because I *wanted* to, not because I had to. I didn't love Johnny, but I loved everything I got from our life together.

I'd always been susceptible to the language of money and power, and this was no different. I loved the money, the jewelry, and all the fancy things that were showered over me simply for existing for Johnny. I loved the supremacy I felt when people on the street would part ways or stray from their path simply so I could walk unhindered. And I loved the strange feeling of *family* I got by being an unofficial Roufe. Not only did Johnny's kin treat me like their own, but his kids treated me like the mother I'd never get to be.

The two youngers were still children—neither had crested high school. The oldest of the three, however, had somehow grown beyond recognizability. In three years, the little boy I remembered had morphed into a young man in his last year of high school, making me feel horribly old, despite my un-aging body. The once small and chubby boy now towered over his father with a broad and sturdy build, much like Johnny had appeared at his age. Unfortunately, his build wasn't the only thing he'd picked up from his shitty father. Alex had adopted the disposition he was the hottest shit in the room, and rarely did he listen to anyone for anything—except his father. Luckily, he still had enough sense to fear the wrath of ignoring Johnny Roufe.

Whether the guiding factor for that was indeed fear or actually some level of respect wasn't clear. Strangely enough, Alex had taken to regarding me with that same level of posterity upon my return. I could only guess his interactions with me were more based on respect, since he had nothing to fear from me, and he knew that.

It wasn't long into my stay before Alex made a point to confront me. Calling my name, he rushed down the stairs to meet me as I made my way out of the mansion one night. His smile painted a layer of confidence that almost covered up the way his heart beat rapidly in his chest.

"Hey, I don't mean to interrupt you if you're busy. We just haven't gotten to talk much since you've been back. The boys would probably appreciate it if you took them to lunch sometime soon, the way you used to. I'd like to go with so that we could all hang out like before you left." His smile turned painstakingly genuine, showing the straight white teeth I remembered strapped in braces.

The tingly warmth his words elicited caught me off guard. In response, I shrugged. "Yeah, I'd love to. Do the boys really want that? Do *you* really want that?" Something in me thought they'd be angry with me for disappearing for years.

"Of course. Here, the boys made these for you, but they

were too shy to give them to you themselves." He extended two sheets of paper, both folded into handmade cards. The outside of each had a unique version of "welcome home." One with a picture of what looked to be an arrangement of different flowers, and one with a very bright red-headed cube lady holding the hand of another, smaller cubey boy. The art was drawn in colored pencil, and the lines were smooth, unlike the old messy crayon drawings the boys used to give me. They'd even colored inside all the lines.

Alex went on while I admired my gifts. "They missed you a lot. We all missed you a lot. Nobody admitted it, but everyone knew there was something missing when you weren't around."

His words meant more to me than he'd ever know. They almost brought a tear to my eye, tugging on a part of my heart that was unfamiliar to me. His and his brothers' love was unconditional, something I got merely for being me. There was absolutely nothing I'd done to deserve it. Maybe that's what it felt like to be a maternal figure. If so, then I wanted to cherish this opportunity to experience something I may never experience again. I had the chance to be a mom. Not just any mom—but a *good* mom. One who didn't selfishly want their love. One who wanted to give them a better future outside of their father's plans for them. Righting the Roufes' wrongs may have started with the intention of protecting the city of Creswell, but it would end as a scheme to protect those boys.

"Thank you," I told Alex. "I needed to hear that more than you know."

His cheeks blazed red in the waning light of dusk. Pursing

his lips to hide a smile, Alex shuffled his feet. Impishly, he added, "By the way, I like the hair, and the new style." He gestured from my head to my black leather boots. "It's kind of edgy compared to before, but I think it suits you better. You seem more confident this way."

"Thanks kid, I suppose I am." I laughed a little, but Alex wasn't laughing.

Instead, he looked down at me, a few stairs below him, with a heavy gaze that oozed admiration against his blushing skin. I liked to think his admiration was like that of a son for his mother, but I knew this look better. I was acquainted with it because it wasn't familial, it was closer to infatuation. Thanks to that, I wasn't surprised by his next statement. "I didn't think it was possible for you to get even prettier."

I should have known. He was so much like his father; he wouldn't be able to help himself from flirting with me at this age. It's not like I was much of a motherly figure to him, so obviously his version of admiration toward me would be different than his brothers'. After all, I wasn't technically old enough to be the mother of someone his age.

A little crush from Alex wasn't anything to worry about. He'd never infringe on his father, so I wasn't worried about him doing anything that might make me uncomfortable. Instead, he'd probably showcase his feelings as an overabundance of affection. And if I made it obvious that the kind of affection I wanted was of the motherly variety, he'd probably be more than willing to oblige that.

"Thank you so much, buddy." I ruffled his hair like I used

to do when he was a little younger and a lot more self-conscious. "I missed you and the boys tons. I know I made a mistake by leaving, but I'll make it up to you guys. I'm not going anywhere this time, and I'm going to mother the shit out of you until you're absolutely sick of my motherly love."

"I don't think moms talk like that. They certainly don't curse." He couldn't hold in a coquettish laugh when he pulled away from my teasing palm.

"Shit is hardly a curse… but you're right, don't say that word. And if you do, you didn't hear it from me."

"Okay, *mom*." He exaggerated the honorific in the most joking way possible, but it still kind of pinched my heart strings.

After that, Alex wasn't ever far away—kind of like a teenage shadow. It'd been common to run into the kids in the house back in the day, but now it was a lot more as though Alex was dedicated to finding me whenever I was home.

Honestly, I liked having him around like that. I wished he'd treat me a little more like his mother than the schoolgirl he had a crush on, but at least he did still feign the respect he should have for a motherly figure. Fortunately, his brothers—who usually acted as *his* shadows—*did* treat me like a mother. So, having Alex around more meant Danny and Anthony were around more, too, and they were slowly accumulating the same level of interest that Alex had in me.

The lot of them probably liked me more than Johnny did, and I *certainly* liked them more than I did Johnny. I probably loved those kids, and loving those kids was about as close to healing up my broken heart as I was going to get. Being their makeshift mother let me experience both love and being loved like never before. Unfortunately, it wasn't always pretend to be mommy time when I was with the Roufes—as much as I'd have liked it to be—I did still have work to get done.

Johnny still needed to be pleased, and though I no longer had the stomach to please Johnny the way he wished me to, I *could* thrall him into thinking I'd pleasured him in any way he could possibly dream of. And dream of it, he would—because of all the things I was willing to do, I absolutely wasn't willing to break my dry spell on Johnny, of all people.

So, while I sent him off to dream of the many indecent things I could do with him, I took my time versing myself in his business. There were paperwork, records, and people to research in order to get up to date on his dealings. Once I'd caught up, I could start taking control.

I thralled Johnny into telling me everything he'd been up to every day when he wasn't with me, and other times I'd convince him to let me be involved myself. Eventually, I had a grasp on every little crevice of his operation. It was all too easy for me as an immortal. The hardest part was making sure no mortals slipped through the cracks. Every one of them who had communication with the other needed to have a cohesive story. That meant if one was thralled, then their thoughts needed to make sense to anyone else they came in contact with.

Unfortunately, that meant I couldn't thrall Johnny whenever I wanted for whatever reason I wanted to. It had to be calculated, or things would fall apart.

And yet, day by day, they never did. Instead, I placed

myself more and more in his shadow as the unseen benefactor who called the shots.

I came to love my place by his side. I had a goal in mind— the objective to check the power that the Roufes' held over the city of Creswell. But I quickly came to the realization that I needed to become a Roufe to truly control the Roufes, and I no longer feared the repercussions of taking that plunge. I eagerly wrapped myself up in their world at the top of the food chain, welcoming the throne that waited for me. I didn't need to destroy them up there, but become them—not crush, but control. Once I had a tight grasp on their empire, I could ensure it'd flourish, and be sure that Creswell didn't suffer in its wake.

I'd be a more efficient leader than Johnny could ever be.

Leading such an empire all while feigning innocent housewife took *hard* work and *careful* calculation. I'd grown a hardened spine and a wicked poker face, and it felt natural to me. I was confident in my place, and I no longer dreaded the emotions I felt thinking back on Prague because I'd replaced them with more current and pressing affairs. I'd officially become too preoccupied to grieve.

Instead, my saddened memories remained, not as something to avoid, but as a reminder of who I didn't want to become again—the love-struck girl who was pushed around by another man. The more I came to terms with that, the more I thought I might be able to view my time with Riftan for what it was—a gift. I learned more about myself during our time together than I could have in a millennia alone, and I was grateful to him for that. Though it was fleeting, I appreciated the love Riftan gave me while I learned those lessons. Maybe one day I'd get up the nerve to call and thank him.

I wouldn't hate hearing his voice again, though I knew it might be painful. There were still those meager hours of silence when my mind could drift to thoughts of him and I'd wondered what his life looked like now. More so, I worried about him, as silly as it might seem to *worry* about a very competent *eight-hundred-year-old* adult. There was an awful ache in my chest every time I imagined him suffering from the nightmares he used to get. I couldn't tell if it hurt worse to think there was no one there to soothe them, or to think my job of comforting him had already been taken over by another.

Truly healing meant I needed to settle on the acceptance that Riftan deserved to heal as much as I did, and it would start with letting someone else in. My anger always flared at the thought of another woman in his bed, which told me that I wasn't ready to fully let go yet, but the finish line was in sight, and that was a start. In the meantime, I would busy myself with Johnny's business and focus on making my own legacy.

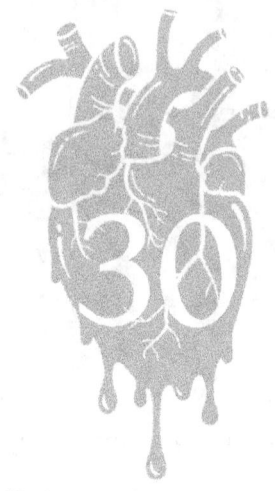

30

I KNOW HOW YOU TOIL IN THE SHADOWS

"I THOUGHT I told you to have the Fedoravs push out that shipment." I lightly badgered Johnny, who stood close by my side at the railing overlooking the pool. When I say *lightly*, I do mean *lightly*. When he wasn't being thralled, I still had to act the gentle housewife I was supposed to be.

Johnny's brown eyes narrowed at me for only a moment before peering back at the blue water below, where his boys splashed about. He spoke in a hardened whisper. "Pavel is no longer in charge of the trade."

Gentility eluded me and I wailed, "Then who is? You know what this could do to us if they steal the market out from under us with this shipment, right?" I'd reached my wit's end with the conversation that'd already gone on too long and happened too many times.

Johnny didn't break composure, though I could see him turning red. "Ksava is in charge of it. We already agreed to offer our assistance, so drop it already."

I calmed, reflecting on the newfound info. "Ksava? His wife? This could work out well, actually. I'll handle this the way it should have been handled from the get-go."

"The hell you will!" Johnny screamed, grabbing ahold of my wrist and pulling me in close. He seethed, finally forfeiting any and all of his strained poise. "I know you've been running around here acting as if you own this place and call the shots, but I've had it up to here with your shit. You are *my* piece of ass, and that's all you need to be. If you know what's good for you, you'll step off that fucking high horse and get back on your pretty little knees. Do you understand me?"

With his thick fingers almost doubling around my wrist, I was in a position most human girls wouldn't have been able to escape. Thus, I was probably supposed to cower and fear incurring any more of his wrath. But I could snap him in two like a twig. I could drink his blood and eat his heart as a snack. He had nothing over me. He was a peon—he was mortal. I would *never* fear him again.

Locking eyes with me, he immediately let go, my thrall having hit him before I ever opened my mouth to say, "Hey, Johnny, fuck you." It wasn't the first time I'd thralled him and then told him those exact words, but it was still justifying to say to his face.

His dead eyes steady on mine, I whispered for his ears only, "I'll never kneel to a piece of shit like you. And in truth, I *do* call the shots, so it's you who needs to get on your fat little knees and ask me for forgiveness."

As my obedient dog, he knelt on both knees and gave the most convincing of apologies, calling me "his beautiful" in the process.

I continued, "I'll be going to teatime on Tuesday with Ksava's group of ass kissers, and you are perfectly content on letting me go. You've even asked me to attend the event in order to brown nose the Fedoravs before next month's shipment."

He nodded vehemently, pawing at my hand until I let him take it, only to pour kisses over it.

Johnny's behavior once he was thralled was always a little peculiar to me. Though I was melding his mind to my will, he still seemed coherent enough to pander at me—sometimes reaching for my hand or kissing at me innocently. Maybe that was the way I wanted him to be, and it came through my thrall. Maybe it was something else—I really wasn't sure. Curious, I added a question, "Do you love me, Johnny? I demand that you tell me the whole truth." I laced my thrall with the clearest intention of wanting a factual answer.

Johnny nodded, his eyes widening. "With all my heart. You are my everything, Leanne."

I wished those words gave me the heartening, joyful response I wanted them to, but they couldn't. I wanted them to be true because I *needed* his love, but it still wasn't enough to fill the void in my heart.

It was, however, enough to keep my sanity—at the very

least.

Teatime with Ksava Fedorav was a pitiful excuse for "quality time with the girls." And yet, many of the wives of other rich men joined the group every Tuesday for golf and drinks. They were really only ever showing off their money or attempting to bolster their husband's images, which was a pitiful display of dependency I loathed to see from other women. *But* I wasn't one to talk. I was, after all, playing that exact same part—putting on the exact same facade. Unfortunately for them, underneath that facade I was the kind of monster they could never dream of becoming.

At the head of this game of charades they called a tea party was Ksava, the mafia queen herself. Ever since taking over Johnny's affairs, it seemed like Ksava had her grimy mitts all over everything I had my eyes on. Even operating outside of Creswell's border, Ksava was single-handedly pushing the Roufes off the top spot in the Creswell area with the hold she had around her husband Pavel's balls.

I did have to hand it to her though, she was doing what I'd been doing, all without the help of supernatural vampiric abilities. The woman was a true testament to female power, and I revered that in her, but it meant she was a continuously pesky thorn in my side. She was the kind of trouble I couldn't put up with any longer. She was mortal, and mortals deserved to do my bidding or suffer the consequences.

Politely, I took Ksava off to the side, her bodyguard obediently following us to a private corner of the country club's deck. "I'm so sorry to interrupt, Ksava, I just wanted to ask you a couple questions about that shipment next month." Tenting my hands meekly, I played my part the way I was versed to do.

"Right." Her voice dripped with sarcasm, obverse to the polite smile plastered over her face. "I don't wish to talk shop, darling. Let's let the boys soil their hands with such matters."

My innocent mask crumbled enough to squeak out a smirk and respond, "And what? Let them have all the fun?"

"It's not a wife's place to meddle in their business."

"Oh, come *on*." I exaggerated an eye roll for her. "I know you meddle plenty, Ksava. I know your secrets; I've seen your activities in the shadows."

Ksava pointed her chin up and down at me, making it obvious how she looked me over despite cat-eye sunglasses concealing her gaze. Through thin pursed lips, she countered, "That's a glass house you throw your stones from, Leanne. I know the kind of secrets you keep and how *you* toil in the *shadows*."

"You don't know shit, Ksava."

"I know enough to know I'm not afraid of you. Your weakness is when Johnny finds out his little trophy bitch is exactly the kind of immortal monster he loathes."

My heart dropped quick, but not as quick as my hand snagged the sunglasses off her face. Before I could thrall her, she snapped her eyes shut and her bodyguard pushed me away from her with a grunt. As if he had the ability to actually stop me, the large, suited man kept a tight grip on my shoulder, keeping me separate from Ksava.

She laughed, the natural fear she should have felt for me eluding her. "I don't fall for the dirty tricks of blood suckers."

That made my blood boil—not only her laugh or her statement, but that she was *justified* in it. She knew I couldn't rip her to shreds right here and now like I wanted to, because it was too obvious of a kill. Somehow, she knew my secret, which meant she could blackmail me into submission, despite my power over her.

If Ksava knew I was immortal, then others could know, too. She'd use that against me, making me fear using my abilities in the open. She thought she could neuter my immortal eminence. Blinded by her own arrogance, Ksava thought she could corner me without my vampiric abilities.

What she didn't account for was how much I'd learned at Johnny's side. Though the Roufes had been known to employ the assistance of immortals in recent years, their merciless perseverance built their supremacy long before they had the prominence to invite immortal aid. They'd built an empire among an otherwise immortal dominated city, and they did so with their own bare hands. As would I.

Thinking like a Roufe, I eyed the gun in the bodyguard's hip holster. "Fine," I snapped. "Then I'll kill two birds with one stone—thrown from my glass castle." In the blink of an eye, I grabbed it and cocked the weapon in Ksava's direction. With a silencer screwed onto the barrel, the weapon was long, and it closed the distance between us, the metal only inches from

Ksava's forehead.

Her brows twitched, eyes shooting open but never looking into mine—only staring cross-eyed at the barrel above her brow.

Before her bodyguard could stop me, I'd caught his gaze, hypnotizing him into stalling his advances.

Ksava's bold disguise wavered, her voice breaching alarm. "Wait, Leanne—"

Maybe she planned to plead for her life, but I would never know, because I'd already pulled the trigger. The silencer did very little to deaden the sound in such close quarters, and I had to refrain from doubling over in pain. Her bodyguard still stood motionless, now smattered in Ksava's blood.

Looking into his eyes and reaching for his soul, I asked him, "Why'd you do that? Were you threatened by her power? Did you wish it to belong to Pavel like old times?" Playfully, I leaned into him. "Or was it some fucked up love affair? The two of you, barred in a forbidden relationship. After a falling out, Ksava threatened to tell Pavel about your affair. He'd certainly kill you with such knowledge, so to get away with it, you'd have to kill her yourself. A true crime of passion... How *spicy*." I gave him a wink, handing over the weapon into his readily thralled hands. "Here, take this," I insisted. "You pulled the trigger, after all."

Dropping my smile, I screamed, feigning fear as I ran from the bodyguard. Other women noticed the commotion and ran themselves, familiar with this kind of situation. The other women had bodyguards of their own, and they were ushering us toward safety. As one of those innocent bystanders, I cried fake tears to the wives of killers who weren't afraid to clean Ksava's blood from my face. Nobody suspected I'd killed Ksava myself. Thus, I'd gotten away with murder—not that I didn't do that on the regular.

IT'D BEEN LESS than twenty-four hours since Ksava's murder, and word had yet to get out. It was possible they weren't going to release the information. Ksava would die quietly and the Fedoravs would peaceably go back to taking orders from their less-than-competent leader, Pavel.

Killing Ksava didn't bother me—at first. After all, I killed all the time, and Ksava was the type I went for. What bothered me was the heat I'd get if anyone found out it was me. Dwelling on our interaction sparked anxiety. Hearing her call out my immortality rang loud in my head in the silence of every waking moment.

Ksava wasn't a resident of Creswell, but instead ran her arms business from the smaller town of Pleasant Valley to the

North. That didn't mean she was naïve to the ongoings of Creswell, and I was sure she was as familiar with vampires as the high ups were here. But the fact she'd put together that I was one of them, even though she was an outsider, was concerning. I'd been cautious, but not cautious enough. Johnny couldn't find out.

With that heavy on my mind, I was wary of every little change in his tone, and uneasy when he called me into his bedroom.

"What's wrong?" I asked with a slew of innocence and a demeanor ready for anything.

He seethed at the foot of the cavernous bed, face red and tone vicious. "Did you really think I wouldn't put two and two together?"

"What do you mean?" I held my breath, meeting him head on and holding eye contact, prepared to thrall him once necessary. I'd unfortunately also have to thrall Harry—the guard who waited at the door, watching us—if I wanted to get away with it.

Johnny went on, his tone the same. "You *know* what. Did you really think I would assume with the way you've been that you had nothing to do with Ksava's death yesterday?"

A breath left me in the most errant wave of relief.

Raising his hand above my face, he continued, "Tell me the truth. What do you have to do with her death?"

With Harry right at the door, I decided not to thrall Johnny. Instead, I admitted, "I killed her. Can you really say you'd have done anything different? She was threatening your entire livelihood. With her gone, the Fedoravs have no hope of regaining their position. She was the head of the snake, I just cut it—"

I'd almost finished my argument, but Johnny's hand was quick. He struck across my face hard enough to send me to the floor. As fast as I was, I should have seen it coming, and maybe I had. Though he couldn't do any real damage to my immortal body, my overactive nerves *screamed* at his assault. The sting faded quickly, but the rancid feeling that his actions left in my guts didn't.

"Johnny, I—" My argument was again short-lived, split by Johnny's interruption.

"Have I been so soft on you that you really cannot see your place?" He knelt, grabbing onto my shirt and hauling me within an inch of his face. "If I have, then I can fix that. I will teach you your place under my foot, right here and now."

Johnny laced his fingers around my throat, squeezing until there was no hope for oxygen to pass through. The air thickened, viscous as I tried to suck it down through my narrowed windpipe. My ears rang and vision blurred with a frantic panic, not from unconsciousness, but from lack of. I wouldn't die like that; my body would regenerate before the lack of oxygen could do any damage. Even knowing that, I tried not to fight back, letting the roar of blood pound against my ears as I gasped for what little breath I could gain in Johnny's grasp. My heart hammered in my chest until it was like my entire body vibrated from it. When it felt like I might actually burst from the beating, the natural urge to abate the feeling took over, and

I shoved Johnny away. I welcomed oxygen with forceful gulps and let myself reprieve despite the looming threat of a momentarily staggered Johnny.

Wide eyed, he grabbed a fistful of my hair and tugged, pulling until I was falling onto the bed. Despite my screaming follicles, I let him toss me around, still not sure at what point I would get away with fighting back.

I need to thrall both him and Harry.

He let go only long enough to reach into his pocket and close the distance on my form strewn out over the foot of his bed. I jumped to meet him halfway, leaving me awkwardly half sat on the mattress when he pressed the sharp metal of a blade against my neck.

Our eyes met, but not before the sting of his knife grazed my skin, sitting nimbly against the surface.

Shock pounding in my chest, I questioned him without the influence of a thrall, "What are you doing? You wouldn't hurt me."

He spit out his words. "And why not? You are useless and replaceable, just like the rest."

I faltered, his words punching me in the guts. The metaphoric strike was closely followed by the searing incursion of his blade as he took it from my throat and sunk it into my midsection. The tear in my flesh sent me reeling. Pain blinded everything. The white noise of panic buzzed in my ears.

Johnny's smug, vindicated snarl focused on my face, but I was staring at the pool of blood that seeped from my bleeding stomach in agonizing waves. His marble handled switchblade sat in the wound, holding it open to bleed out my suffering. It wouldn't subside until I got the weapon out of me, and that was all I could think about. Wrapping my fingers around the stone handle slicked with blood only made the feeling fester, pulsating in blinding, painful swells that nearly took my consciousness.

All at once, I ripped the obstruction from my body, relief instantly washed over me, and I took a deep breath of fresh, unhindered air.

Looking down on me, Johhny's face fell, disappointment heavy in his cheeks as he watched my misery absolve. His response filled my heart with a burning hatred—an enflamed, rabid indignation that could only be cured by retribution. With zero thoughts in my head except vengeance, I took the knife that'd previously been buried in my guts and jammed it into Johnny's.

"I knew it." The revelation struck Johnny too late. "You *are* one of them."

The smell of his blood filled my olfactory senses with delight as it poured over my hand. He coughed some up, bringing it closer to my nose. The culmination of revenge—the smell of his blood, and the fury that'd plagued my mind to near blindness—filled me with a palpable bliss near numb nirvana.

I twisted the knife and Johnny fell to his knees with a weak cry that sounded like music to my ears.

Licking his blood from my hand, I enjoyed the quiet peace it gave my senses in the chaos.

On sky high, my mind blurred all reasonable consequences, and I easily overlooked the elephant in the room. I wasn't privy—or just completely indifferent—to the cocking of Harry's gun in the doorway. It wasn't until his bullet actually penetrated my rib cage, following the ring of his shot, that I cared to look at him.

Pain like fire blossomed from the spot where the bullet penetrated my flesh, but the worst part was that it didn't stop there. The blast was followed by one, two, then three more shots.

The room spun, the sight of Harry going blurry as he stood on the ceiling. My body begged for the end of this horrible feeling. I faded to the door, my hands taking ahold of Harry and ripping his head from his body—all before I'd told my muscles to react. His blood splattered over my face, coating my lips and darkening my vision. The smell of him was everywhere, and I loved it. I licked my lips, bit into his headless body, and smiled. His taste made my heart dance, gravity no longer affecting the way I flew around the room. Everything was red—a blurry, bloody, but glorious color of unfettered death.

I didn't care when more bullets hit me. It meant fresh blood, and I killed the culprits of those attacks, too. The hallway rang with gunshots mingled with screams. Each bullet added to my rage, but every kill blinded me from the consequences. In a feat of bloody self-preservation, I killed as many men as came to attack me, taking a bite of each of them as I tore their limbs from their bodies.

From head to toe, I tingled with pleasant delight that shrouded all of my intellectual properties. Without them, I was a slave to my instincts, letting the vicious nature of my immortality take over—whether I wanted it to or not. Sitting back in the theater of my mind, I had no choice but to watch as the scene played through the blurry window of my optic nerves.

Coating the hallway in viscera, I bulldozed through the Roufe mansion like a bull in a China closet. Around every corner, a new enemy came and a new enemy fell. Somewhere in the middle, the memory of it became hazy, too much happening at once to really understand it all, or to see it through my blood-soaked eyes.

Too many people fell by my hand. When I thought the slaughter was over, I found another victim. At some point, they were running from me, and I killed the harmless in my frenzy. The guilty, the innocent—I murdered them all the same.

Time had become a construct, only slowing back to normal as the blood euphoria waned and I found myself staring up at the domed coffer ceiling in the foyer. My mind was reassigning where it dictated control, the feeling in my limbs returning first as I slicked my fingers through the pools of fluid at my sides. The smell of blood still plagued my senses, but I was so full I didn't crave it.

Once my intellect snapped back into place, I shot up, looking around the room with unclouded vision. Disfigured bodies littered the foyer, scattered blood stains followed the carnage up the stairs and down the hallway. Silence filled every gap in that giant house, nothing shifting except the birds outside.

The reality of that silence weighed heavy. It was evidence that I'd killed the Roufes. Not only Johnny and a few others,

I'd murdered *all* of them—with my bare hands. Bile singed my throat, the room narrowing as everything fell into place. The only Roufes who got away from this massacre with their lives were the ones who weren't present, which would be very few mid-day on a Wednesday.

The only consolation that kept me from spewing my emotions right out onto the floor of bloody bodies was knowing the boys hadn't been home. They'd been saved from my onslaught by the simple fact that they were still in school.

Scrambling to my feet, I slipped in blood, catching myself on a decapitated body that wore a maid's uniform and held no weapons. "Oh god…" I groaned, but God's judgment was not what I feared. Immortals didn't answer to God, they took these kinds of transgressions up with the Council. And in my case, offenses with the Council certainly meant the end for me. Their lead bitch, Rosaline, was already looking for a reason to off me.

"Fuck, fuck, fuck." I scooped my sopping hair away from my face and assessed my options for getting away with this. No one runs or hides from the Council, not with the all-seeing Rosaline there, and I knew flight wasn't an option. Fight, however, would almost certainly mean an even quicker death.

Solving this on my own wasn't possible, but my contacts list was still small, and the list of immortals I knew with enough pull to help me out of a situation like this was even smaller. In fact, it was compiled of exactly *two*: Riftan and Jameson.

They'd both know how *foolish* I had to be to get myself into this situation, and I didn't want to have to admit to either of them what I'd done. Regardless of how stupid it was, they'd both be willing and ready to help.

Pulling my phone from my pocket, I skipped to one of the many missed calls I had from Jameson. Taking a breath, I steadied a shaky finger on the screen and hit call. The phone rang. And it rang. I went over my excuses in my head—both for not calling him all this time and for the blood bath I was standing in. When his voice carried through the line, it was only his voicemail. My pulse skyrocketed. The tonal beep queuing me to leave a message nearly toppled my wobbly knees.

"Hey... Jameson, I've really messed up. I'm so sorry for not calling you all this time. I just—it doesn't matter. I need help. Like, immediately. I know I don't deserve it after giving you the cold shoulder the last few months, but this is kind of life or death. *Please*, just call me back as soon as you get this."

I hung up, instantly wishing I'd given him a better goodbye—especially if it was going to end up being my *last* goodbye.

Tears stung in my eyes, the thought of never getting to apologize correctly stabbing me in my delicate heart. I waited in the silence for multiple heavy moments with my phone in hand like it was going to miraculously ring. It didn't, and I shouldn't have expected anything different. Jameson was a busy guy, even for an immortal. He likely wouldn't see my message for a few hours, minimum. Thus, I was forced to go with option B.

Opening my phone again, I ignored my pounding heart but couldn't avoid the weakness in my legs, so I crouched in the pool of bodies. Riftan was one call away, and he had nothing better to do during his down decade than answer my call. He'd be disappointed in me for getting carried away by blind rage like this, but I would be more disappointed in myself for having to grovel at his feet for help. But this wasn't the hill I wished to die on, and I'd rather grovel to Riftan than accept Rosaline's victory when she took my head.

Scrolling to his contact through my blood-smeared screen brought an awful spark of excitement to my skin. It tingled like it still craved his touch, crawled like he had already gotten under it—and I hadn't even called him yet.

A *creak* sounded in the silence, light joining the room through the growing crack between the double front doors. My soul left my body, only to find the wind blowing through the open door. Forgoing my lamentation, I hit call on Riftan's number, deciding to act before somebody actually did walk through that front door to see this massacre.

The wait while it rang was agonizing. My heart went through every stage of grief all over again, in a matter of seconds. All the healing it'd done in the past nine months was instantly null—completely broken again and *excited* for the beating it would get by hearing Riftan's voice over the line. It was a glutton for the kind of punishment only he could give to it.

"Leanne?" Riftan's voice was as tormenting as I'd expected it to be, tantalizing every cell in my body, shaking my very being on a molecular level.

Frazzled, my mind and my emotions fought for dominion in the chaos, and I blurted out, "I killed him. I killed all of them," completely forgoing a proper introduction.

Riftan was calm, but his concerned tone seeped through the phone, pummeling my heart. "You killed *who*, Leanne? Are you alright?"

"The Roufes—as in *all* of the Roufes. I don't know what happened. One minute I was in control and the next they were all dead." I tried to remember the extent of my carnage. Too many faces came to mind. "Oh god, I think I killed Nonna."

"Where are you?" He was immediately airing toward stringency.

"At the Roufe's main house, past Hall Street."

"Okay, don't move. I'm minutes away."

Acknowledgments

Thank you so much for reading my debut novel.

Like many authors, I've always dreamed of publishing. After getting lost in agent query after agent query for many books and even more years, I took the leap into self-publishing. And holy *hell*, I am glad I finally did it. Not only do I get to be artsy fartsy, but learning to publish has been the most fun—and most daunting—experience I've ever had the pleasure of working through (and I've competed in professional snowboard competitions). That being said, I was far from doing it on my own. Through this process, I've met more helpful individuals than I can name here, from Reddit and Discord groups to my family members and my partner who totally didn't understand my desire to write romance novels but were still wildly supportive of my eccentric dream. Every single one of you has impacted my experience for the better, whether you realize it or not.

I'd like to give the HUGEST thanks possible to my editor, Sage, who put up with my raw manuscript and deleted every single "that" and "even" without complaining more than twice. This would be a very different book without the polishing and praise Sage gave it; for that, she will forever be considered the true MVP. She also helped me with about a million other things along the way that I won't even get into.

Secondly, I'd like to thank my critique partner, Hannah Levin, who might not be expecting this callout. Until recently, I was quite bashful about my writing, and Hannah was the first person ever to read my manuscript for HTFE, making her the first person to read anything I'd ever officially written. Sharing my writing with Hannah not only improved my confidence in my work but also, watching her succeed in publishing her debut novel while I was working on my own was the most inspiring experience to be a part of. So, the next book you'll have to read while waiting for part two is "The Treasured One" by Hannah Levin. And Hannah, when you read this, don't make it weird— I'm just really appreciative of my first author friend, okay?

Finally, as said in the wise words of Snoop Dogg, "Last but not least, I wanna thank me. I wanna thank me for believing in me. I wanna thank me for doing all this hard work. I wanna thank me for having no days off. I wanna thank me for never quitin." Because the truth is this process wasn't easy in the slightest. Seriously, it blew my mind the amount of time and effort that went into merely *formatting* this novel, not to mention *all* of the other things I had to wrap my brain around to orchestrate a polished debut *cries in author*. But we made it, I'm overjoyed to be here, and I'm beyond thrilled to have this book—my baby—in the hands of readers like you. YOU make it all worth it. So, thank *you* above all else. I can't wait to share more stories with you all.

Love you to eternity and back.

PART II
IN THE FACE OF ETERNITY

If you enjoyed this book, you will hate me right now. I know, I know, but one does not simply release an eight-hundred-page debut novel.

Thanks to all of you amazing supporters, ITFOE was released April 4th, 2026, despite many setbacks and mental breakdowns<3

You can find Part 2 at SHClasen.com, Amazon, Kindle Unlimited, or B&N.com.

If you'd like to see HTFE or ITFOE at your local bookstore, please request to have it stocked. There's nothing an indie author appreciates more than being requested by local readers and seeing their baby on shelves.

The Lover of Many Things

A life-long resident of the Pacific Northwest, Sierra either loves to be immersed in nature or lost in a fantasy world. If she's not out snowboarding, surfing, or skating, Sierra can be found at her desk writing fantastical romances or cosplaying like she belongs in one. Though the local high school students know her as snowboard coach, her friends know her as an anime-loving, metal music-listening, role-playing busybody who's always got something new to obsess over.

Since you're here, it means you know her as the author, SH Clasen. As a self-proclaimed romance enthusiast, Sierra's novels revolve around romance of all varieties, particularly fantasy, sci-fi, and paranormal. In her opinion, if it fights or bites, it's probably sexy.

Above all, Sierra's favorite thing in the world is talking about the many things she loves with like-minded people, so don't be shy to hit up her socials and start up a conversation about something cool!

@SHClasenAuthor (Tiktok, Instagram, Threads, & More)

SHClasen.com

Or scan the QR Below: